A VERY PRIVATE AFFAIR

*When she got married at the age of twenty-two,
Margaret took the past and buried it deep, the way
you hear of nuclear waste being buried in layers and
layers of concrete, in bunkers of steel, deep down in
the ocean. Deep down deep. Locked and padlocked.
Out of sight and out of mind. Buried it deep.
And threw away the key.
Until one day, someone found that key...*

First published in 2000 by
Marino Books
An imprint of Mercier Press
16 Hume Street Dublin 2
Tel: (01) 661 5299; Fax: (01) 661 8583;
e.mail: books@marino.ie

Trade enquiries to CMD Distribution
55A Spruce Avenue
Stillorgan Industrial Park Blackrock
County Dublin
Tel: (01) 294 2556; Fax: (01) 294 2564
e-mail: cmd@columba.ie

© Dee Cunningham 2000
ISBN 1 86023 109 8
10 9 8 7 6 5 4 3 2 1

A CIP record for this title is available
from the British Library
Cover design by SPACE
Printed by Cox & Wyman Reading
Berks

A VERY PRIVATE AFFAIR

DEE CUNNINGHAM

To my children,
with thanks for their unfailing encouragement

PROLOGUE

Mick rinsed his hands under the hot tap and watched the soapy water empty out of the cracked washbasin. He frowned over a flake of white paint embedded under his thumbnail.

'Got any turps, Fran?'

She was watching him from the doorway. 'You'd swear it was a girl you were meeting.'

'In a way it is.'

He eyed his reflectio n doubtfully. Maybe the suit was a mistake. Something less formal? But what? He shrugged quickly. Forget it. No time to change. It would have to do. He caught Fran's eye in the glass. There was a pleading look on her face.

'It's not too late to change your mind. You don't have to go.'

He said nothing. Went past her into the bedroom of the flat. Sean was asleep in his cot, his rump stuck up in the air, one little fist clutching the edge of the sheet under him. The serviceman's crew cut he'd been born with had grown into a confusion of blond curls which clung damply to the curve of his head. Mick reached in and touched them gently.

'Will you listen to me.' Fran's voice was urgent behind him. He turned, surprised to see tears in her eyes. 'Don't go, Mick.'

Despite the knot of excitement in his stomach he tried to

summon up patience. Put his arms around her, gazed down into her anxious face.

'It's going to be okay, love. Nothing's going to change.'

'That's what you think. I've got a bad feeling about this. Don't ask me why, but I have.'

'You and your feelings.' He grinned down at her. 'Look Fran, this is what I've been waiting for since the day I was born.'

He grinned at her again and the knot of excitement grew.

'Are *you* going out?' Vincent looked up in surprise as he pulled his golf stuff out of the cloakroom and piled it up on the floor.

Margaret's fingers plucked nervously at a bowl of dahlias on the hall table, picked a petal off the polished mahogany.

'Thought I'd go into town. Do a bit of shopping. Browse among the bookshops.' A mistake to give too many explanations, she told herself, afraid that Vincent would spot her uneasiness.

'Grafton Street's a slum on Saturday mornings. Can't think why you'd want to go near the place. You're not thinking of bringing the Merc in?'

'No, no. I'll take my own; it'll be easier to park.'

He gave a half-mollified grunt. 'Don't forget to put the alarm on.'

'As if I would.'

'Wouldn't surprise me if you did. Half the time you go around with your head in the clouds.' He nodded towards the staircase. 'Why don't you bring Caroline with you?' His face softened momentarily. 'She'd enjoy a shopping trip.'

Margaret kept her voice casual. 'Caroline? She won't surface till lunchtime. She probably wouldn't want to come anyway. You know what they're like at that age.'

He looked unconvinced. 'All the more reason to make the effort. It's not easy on her being an only child.'

She sighed inwardly. *Not that again.*

'She has her friends. Talking of which – ' she tried to keep anxiety from her voice as she glanced at her watch. 'Shouldn't your – ?'

A car horn sounded outside.

'That'll be them now,' Vincent said.

Opening the front door Margaret saw three men sitting in a large car half-blocking the entrance to the driveway. The driver waved to her as he got out and went around to lift the lid of the boot.

'See you.' Vincent hefted the golf bag on to his shoulder, grabbed up the wheels of his caddie car. Aiming a kiss in the general direction of her left ear he crunched away across the gravel to throw his gear into the open boot. As she closed the front door she saw the two men slap each other on the back before getting into the car.

Now that there was nothing to delay her she no longer felt impatient to leave. Although she knew she'd need to hurry she went into the kitchen and sat down. Staring down at the gleaming pine of the table she tried to still her trembling fingers, calm the beating of her heart. *You fool,* she told herself. *You stupid fool!*

The light was dim in the coffee shop. It took a few moments for her eyes to adjust to it after the brightness of the street outside. A young man sat at a table reading a newspaper. He looked up as she approached. Although she had never made his acquaintance until that moment she felt she had always known him. He had the build and colouring of a man she had known briefly many years before. Yet when their eyes met she felt for a moment she was gazing at her own face. She looked away confused. When she turned back again she found herself looking at a familiar stranger.

Mick stared as the girl in the trench coat came in. Nice looking, with fair hair to her shoulders and a blue cowl neck showing under the coat. She headed straight for his table. Must be some mistake, he thought. She looked too well-dressed, too respectable to be a pick-up. And it wasn't that kind of place anyway. Besides she seemed to know him. When she got closer he realised that she was a bit older than he had taken her for at first. But still much too young to be the woman he had come to meet. Disappointment knotted his stomach. 'She couldn't make it, could she?'

The woman's smile faded. She looked taken aback, unsure. Then her face cleared. 'No, no, you've got it wrong.' She glanced around quickly. The only other customer was an old woman ordering a pot of tea; neither she nor the waitress was paying any attention to them.

She turned back to him.

'I'm Margaret,' she said quietly. 'I'm your mother.'

PART ONE

He didn't find out he was adopted until he was eight. A boy called Danno told him. He wanted to hit him but Danno was the class bully and Mick was the smaller of the two. He ran home to the little terrace house in which he lived with his parents and interrogated his mother instead.

'Why didn't you tell me, Ma?'

'That young pup!' Nan Cleary looked up from her ironing board and frowned. 'How well he'd have to get in first with it.'

He felt a stab of alarm. 'Ma! He said you weren't my real mother.'

She sighed, straightened her shoulders and seemed to come to a decision. 'What do you want to know, Mick?'

'Everything,' he said firmly.

There wasn't a lot to tell. Unable to have children of their own, Ma and Da had applied to adopt one. They had to wait ages before a suitable baby turned up. It wasn't the same as buying a puppy in a pet shop. They went in a taxi to collect him from a convent a few days before Christmas. He was just three weeks old.

'I loved you the minute I seen you.' There were tears in Ma's eyes.

'Did you meet her?' His voice was eager.

'Your mother?' She shook her head. 'Just this nun. She told us all about feeds, that kind of thing. God, I'll never forget the first time I gave you a bottle.'

'But my mother? Who was she?'

Ma shook her head again. 'As to that I don't know. They never tell people. It's a rule they have.'

'But – ' He didn't want to leave it there.

'Look Mick, I don't know.' There was a note of finality in her voice. 'It's only natural to be curious but it won't get you anywhere.' She put her arms around him and gave him a quick hug. 'I'm your Mammy now and that should be good enough for you.'

'But you're not my real mother, are you?'

And Da wasn't his real father.

'And Uncle Thomas? And Auntie Carmel? What about them?'

'Well, of course they are.' But Ma sounded unconvincing. 'Look love – '

'They're Clearys, aren't they,' Da said in that dogmatic way he had when pressed to give an opinion, which was seldom. Ma was the one with opinions. 'And you're a Cleary, son.'

Son?

He'd always had this picture of 'his father and *his* father before him'. It was in some prayer Ma said when reciting the Rosary. It was like a long string of fathers stretching back to Adam and Eve – 'our first parents'.

And now it was gone. The picture. Like a slate wiped clean.

And then there was Granny O'Neill, a sharp-faced old woman with cold hands and a drop at the end of her nose.

He didn't mind too much about Granny O'Neill. She smelled of cigarettes and wore black like a witch. Only she wasn't a witch because she was always saying prayers.

'But the cousins. What about the – ?'

'For God's sake will you give over, Mick.'

'But I want to know, Ma.'

'That cur! That Danno! Some people have an awful sin to answer for the way they rear their children. I've a good mind to – '

'Go easy, Nan.' Da hated falling out with the neighbours. 'No call to be upsetting yourself like that.'

'I wanted to tell him years ago. But *you* said – '

'No use crying over spilt milk. What's done is done.'

'Oh you!' Ma sniffed. 'If the roof fell in you'd say there was nothing to worry about.'

'The roof hasn't fallen in. There's worse things. And the lad will get over it.' He smiled at Mick. 'Won't you, son?'

There was something solid and comforting about Da. Mick wanted to believe him.

'I suppose so,' Mick said reluctantly.

There was a puppy in the pet shop window, his head slumped down on his paws. A fly crawled up his muzzle but he didn't seem to notice.

'Why does he look so sad, Ma?'

'He thinks nobody wants to buy him.'

'Couldn't we buy him?'

'You must be joking,' Ma said.

He dreamed about the puppy that night. He *was* the puppy. In a box, some rough material brushing his face. He felt stifled in the darkness. Screamed but no sound came. Then up. Clawing his way up. Up to light and safety and Ma's face gazing down on him in alarm.

Sometimes he looked back and there was nothing. It was as if he had come into the world newly minted, owing nothing to anyone who had come before him. Unique. Not like the other children in the street.

'Who does he take after?'
'She's the spittin' image of her daddy.'
'Put a skirt on Johnny and it's his big sister.'
'You didn't pick it up off the floor.'

As he grew older he learned about the Virgin Birth. He thought a lot about that. But it didn't fit.

Sometimes nothing fitted. Why would anyone want to give their kid away? It didn't make sense.

Ma wouldn't talk about it any more. He hoarded the few crumbs she had given him, took them out and examined them every now and then.

'Maybe they were too poor.'
'He might have been married already.'
'Some young one probably just up from the country. There's blackguards everywhere.'

It wasn't her fault anyway. And he *knew*, he just *knew* that some day she'd come looking for him.

Some day.

One winter afternoon when he was ten he looked up at a

sky that was covered in thick clouds like old cotton wool that has lost its whiteness. There was no wind but the air was filled with expectancy. A wish trembled on his tongue. *Tomorrow*, he thought.

The next morning, his nose pressed against the back window, he watched thick white flakes whirling in the yard outside.

If not today, then some time.

You could live on hope for years.

There's two sides to everything. That's what Da was always saying. As he got older he realised that Da didn't know everything. But he was right about that.

Two sides to everything. Bad sides and good sides. That time Lizzie called after him in the street and the boys he was with asked: 'Is that *oul' wan* your aunt?' And he was able to say: 'No, she's not.' And not have to tell it in Confession, although he still felt a bit guilty about it. And one time Uncle Thomas cuffed his ear when he caught him and some other kids playing Knockers in the next street to his.

'Next time it won't be your bleedin' ear, know what I mean,' he warned. Although he felt shamed in front of the others, a part of Mick exulted in the knowledge that he wasn't really related to this balding man with the beer belly and ham-like hands. When I grow up, the boy promised himself, I won't even give him the time of day. That'll teach him.

One time Mick took a pound out of Ma's purse. Well, actually, it wasn't just the one time. He'd taken twenty pences and fifties before; it was the one time he was caught. He hadn't wanted to steal but he was desperate. Danno was running a protection racket with some other guys in the class and all Mick's pocket money was gone. Ma was angry when he wouldn't tell her why he had taken the money. He hid his embarrassment under a show of bravado.

'I don't have to do what you tell me. You're not my real mother.'

The look on her face cut through his heart like a knife. He wanted to take back what he had said but it was too late. She wouldn't talk to him. She told Da when he came home and Mick got a hiding. 'You're never to talk to your mother like that, d'ye hear me?' It was the first time his father had ever beaten him and the boy hated him for it. And he hated Ma for betraying him. He carried a knot of resentment around in him for days. When Danno tried to shake him down again Mick told him to go eff himself.

'You just made a bad mistake,' the other boy snarled. 'Wait till I tell my mates about this.'

'*They* can go eff themselves too.'

Danno looked baffled. 'I'm warning you, Cleary.' He went away muttering curses under his breath. At break time Mick saw him summoning his henchmen, watched the three of them conferring together. What tortures were they dreaming up? They had threatened to throw one boy into the canal if he didn't pay up. That time Mark Clancy came in with a black eye, people swore it was Danno but then other people said it was his own Da who gave it to him. You wouldn't know what to believe. But if half the stories were true Mick was in for a rough time. She'll be sorry then, he told himself bitterly. When his body was dredged up out of the canal, she'd be sorry.

And she'd understand why he took the money. But it would be too late then.

He skulked around for a few days waiting for the blow to fall, ready to take to his heels if Danno and his friends approached but, to his relief, the bullies didn't bother with him again. The word spread around the school that someone must have snitched because the head brother had found out about their activities and put a stop to them. No thanks to Ma and Da, he thought, reluctant to let them off the hook.

But then Ma got a bad bout of bronchitis and he forgot his grievance. She got a cough every winter – the doctor said it was the cigarettes – but this year was the worst yet. She was in bed for three weeks. A fire burned every day in the bedroom grate and Aunt Lizzie, Da's widowed sister, came to take care of her and look after the house. A thickset woman with short grey hair and a vigorous manner, she had a loud voice that grated on Mick's ears. 'If that woman doesn't eat, she'll fade away to nothing. I'm telling you no lie.'

Da looked at her uneasily. 'Not in front of the boy, Lizzie.' To Mick, he said: 'She'll be all right. All she needs is rest.'

Mick was not convinced. 'Please God, don't let her die,' he prayed every night, listening to the racking cough through the bedroom wall. Each day when he came home from school he rushed upstairs to see how she was, unable to hide his alarm at the sight of the wan-faced creature lying listlessly under the bedclothes.

'This fella's missing his Mammy something desperate.' Aunt Lizzie came heavy-footed up the stairs one evening and plonked the tea tray down on the bed. 'He's been moping around the house like a dog without a tail. Isn't that right, Mick?'

He reddened under her gaze and said nothing.

'You've no call to worry about me, love.' Although Ma looked frail in a pink bedjacket, a spot of colour glowing in each cheek, she smiled reassuringly at him. 'I'm feeling much better tonight.'

'Are you sure, Ma?'

'Course I'm sure.'

After Lizzie had bustled downstairs to get Da's meal, his mother put out a hand to him. 'Come here and sit by the bed, Mick.'

'Eat your eggs,' he said anxiously. 'Auntie Lizzie says – '

'Don't mind Lizzie. She's an awful big mouth.' She stroked his hair gently. 'Are you still my boy, Mick?'

He shifted his feet in embarrassment. That stuff was for babies. Yet it was oddly comforting too. A part of him wished he was a little kid again. 'Course I am.'

Ma sighed. The firelight cast shadows in the corners of the room, softened the angles of her face. 'Mick – '

'Ma, I – '

Both stopped and looked at each other.

'What is it, Mick?'

He struggled to find words to atone his guilt.

'The bedjacket. That colour suits you.'

He saw Ma smile.

He looked down at the floor. The words came out in a rush. 'I'll never steal money again, Ma. Honest.'

Aunt Lizzie had a loud laugh to match her voice. It made him cringe inside to hear it, especially if there were other people around. Sometimes when he'd go into the Mini Market at the corner of the street and hear her exchanging banter with one of the assistants he'd want to turn and run but the bell over the door would have alerted them and there was nothing for it but to go in. He'd keep his face blank and sidle over to the most remote corner of the shop, hoping she wouldn't see him, but she always did. And no matter how much time he spent reading the messages on the greetings cards or pretending to compare the nutritional advantages of one breakfast cereal over another there was no escape. With a sinking heart he'd feel a heavy hand on his arm and hear that laugh. 'Is that where you are, Mick? I thought it was you. I was just saying – '

Because she'd taken care of him when Ma was sick she seemed to think it gave her special rights. She'd touch his arm, pat his cheek, insist on buying him a bag of crisps or a blackjack, piling guilt on his embarrassment. When she came to the house she'd demand a kiss. It got to the stage that when he heard her voice at the front door he was out through the kitchen, haring across the yard, out the back gate into the laneway.

Ma said not to be too hard on Lizzie. She'd neither chick nor child of her own. And her husband had died several years before. They had been childhood sweethearts. 'Never looked at anyone else in their whole lives. Then he got cancer. Just wasted away. Poor Lizzie.'

Mick knew he should feel sorry for her too. In a way he did. He knew she meant well but he just couldn't warm to her. She was too loud, too overpowering. And he felt much the same way about Uncle Thomas, her brother, who liked to hold forth, when he came to tea, on the efficacy of using your fists, or the threat of them, to keep children in line.

'Ya hafta nowadays. God almighty! Kids these days'd walk all over you if you let them, know what I mean?' He would ease his belt across his large stomach and belch openly. 'Am I right, Carmel?'

'Ask me something I don't know.' His wife would look up from the knitting that was her constant companion. 'It's no joke rearing boys, Nan.'

'Boys!' Ma would scoff. 'Your crowd are over the worst.'

'That's what you think, Nan.' Carmel held up an oblong of shaggy wool against Mick's chest, measuring it for size. She never used a pattern. She had her own way of calculating. So many rows to the oxter; then cast off. So many stitches for the cuff. Her knitting bag was crammed with woolly pieces that eventually teamed up to make a baggy, shapeless garment, just recognisable as a sweater or a cardigan. 'It's when they think they're men, that's when your troubles really start.'

'I hope you're not making that for Mick,' Ma said sharply. 'He still has all those jumpers of Pete's to get through.'

'No, this is for Henno.' Carmel's fingers sketched in the extra rows needed.

Mick, dodging the hairy tendrils tickling his nostrils, hid his relief.

'*If* he'll wear it for me. He's got awful fussy since he took up with the girlfriend. You don't know how lucky you are, Nan. Your little fella's quiet. My Henno – '

'Mick, quiet?' Ma laughed derisively. 'That's all you know.'

'You don't know when you're well off,' Carmel sighed. 'I could never get any of mine to read books.'

Ma looked pleased. 'He's one of the best in his class, the teacher says.'

'Books are all very well.' Uncle Thomas was anxious to get back into the conversation. 'Wait till he starts looking for a job. It's not what you know. It's who you know. Am I right, Maurice?'

'Aren't you always.' Da took his eyes from the racing column and glanced over at the mantelpiece. 'Is that clock slow?'

'They'll be wondering what's keeping you down in Foley's,' Ma said tartly.

'Ah, Nan, will you give over.'

'Hold your horses. It's early yet.' Uncle Thomas didn't want to be sidetracked from making his point. 'I heard a man on the radio the other day with degrees and certificates to burn and *he* can't get a job.'

Ma's lips tightened but she held her peace.

'That clock *is* slow,' Da said.

When he was little, Mick had looked up to Henno and Pete, his cousins, had enjoyed their visits to the house. But this changed as he got older. Before he finished primary school they had become men, shaved, drank pints, went with women. They had loud voices and confident swaggers, especially Henno, the elder of the two.

'How's it going, professor? Swallowed any encyclopaedias lately?'

'Sounds painful, head.' Pete had an irritating laugh and pimples all over his face. He looked at his brother for approval.

'Fuckin' painful,' Henno said.

Pete laughed again. 'Bloody fuckin' painful. Am I right, Henno?'

Looking from one gleeful face to another Mick was tongue-tied, resentful.

As time went by, another thing that put a wedge between him and his relatives was his size. Although originally small for his age, Mick began to grow once he reached his teens. The Clearys were stocky people who ran to fat in later life, solid-looking but low-sized. Ma's family were thin and bird-like. He had never thought of his family as being small – they were in such perfect proportion to their surroundings – but, by the time he was sixteen, he was towering over them. And the house seemed to have shrunk. He began to feel hopelessly out of scale. He could never understand how other houses in the street had accommodated whole families of normal-sized people. As soon as he began to stretch out he felt the walls of the house closing in on him, ceilings mysteriously lowering. Chairs and tables developed minds of their own and put out legs to trip him up, ornaments did kamikaze dives from sideboards into his unsuspecting path. 'You're like a bull in a china shop,' Ma said.

It was easier at school. He wasn't the biggest fella in the class. He wasn't even the second-biggest. Somewhere in the thick of the bunch, unremarkable. True, he had passed Danno out and could have given him a hiding if he wanted to. But there was no need. With the advent of testosterone, Danno had abandoned his role as class bully. He was one of the crowd who hung around the back of the bicycle sheds smoking cigarette butts and discussing women. Outside school hours he could be seen hanging around street corners smoking and chatting up girls.

Mick wasn't interested in girls. Not yet.

'Why aren't you out enjoying yourself on a grand evening like this?' Da, ready to head off to the local for a pint, stuck his head around the bedroom door.

'I'm okay. I'm reading.'

'What's this?' He picked up a book. '*The Golden Treasury?*'

'It's poetry.'

'Poetry? What next?' His father sounded affronted. He began riffling through the pages. 'Where'd you get it?'

Wish he wouldn't do that.

'The teacher.'

'It's the Easter holidays, son.'

'I know.'

Da gave a baffled laugh. 'Can't make head nor tail of it.' He threw the book back on the desk. 'You ought to have more sense than to be stuffing your head with that kind of thing. At your age I was out playing football with the other lads.'

'I'm okay, Da.'

After his father had gone, he took the poetry book and smoothed its ruffled pages. Phrases darted up at him. *'What can ail thee ... alone and palely loitering?'*

He put the book back on the shelf, filled with a nameless longing.

The English teacher who lent him books was called Jimmy Joyce.

'No relation to the great man,' he'd grin. He came from a

small town in Mayo. His parents had been teachers before him, avid readers and devotees of the famous novelist. 'I was lucky not to be christened Ulysses.' A big, awkward bear of a man with a pasty face and auburn hair that curled down over the back of his coat collar, he lived in a small redbrick house in a cul-de-sac off the North Circular Road, with daffodils struggling up through the grass behind the front railings and a green plant in a terracotta pot in the window. The first time Mick called to the house the bell on the front door was broken and he had to hammer on the glass with his fist. The young woman who answered had straight brown hair down to her shoulders and a smile that reached up to her eyes.

'Sorry about the pong. Took my eye off the milk for a moment.' She had an accent he couldn't place immediately. An empty pram stood in the hallway. In an effort to avoid it he brushed his arm against hers and felt his face flame up with embarrassment.

She showed him into a room at the back. He had a confused impression of overstuffed bookcases, a comfortable-looking couch covered in faded chintz and a table with a typewriter on it in front of a narrow sash window. The teacher sat reading in an armchair in front of a blazing fire. Clad in sweater and jeans, his hair even more untidy than usual, he looked younger than he did in the classroom. His eyes lit up when he saw Mick. 'Get this man a cup of tea, Suzie.'

The boy shifted his feet awkwardly. 'I can't stop long, Mr Joyce.'

'Just a quick cuppa,' the woman suggested. Again that smile that reached her bright, brown eyes. Despite his embarrassment Mick found himself warming to her.

'No sugar, please, Mrs Joyce.'

'Suzie. We don't stand on ceremony here.'

'Suzie's from Yorkshire,' the teacher said when she had left the room. 'I worked over there for a couple of years after I finished college.'

The boy gazed around him in awe. 'I never saw so many books in my life, Mr Joyce,'

'Jimmy. You heard what Suzie said. But not at school. If some of those cowboys were to hear – '

'God, no!' Mick was aghast. Think of the mileage someone like Danno would get out of it. 'I'd never – '

'Okay now – ' He turned towards a bookcase, hand poised. 'You've a feel for poetry, Mick. That was a good answer you gave the other day.' The fingers grasped the spine of a book, eased it out from among its fellows. 'Let's see what you make of this now.'

As Mick glanced eagerly through the poems Suzie came back with a tray laden with blue pottery mugs and a plate of home-made shortbread. The tea was hot and strong, the chunky biscuits left a buttery taste in the mouth. He put the book down carefully, afraid that his fingers would leave smears on the pages. The girl left the room to return holding a baby with eyes just like her own and a head of reddish brown curls which glistened in the afternoon sunlight.

'This is Sam.'

'Hello Sam,' Mick said, suddenly awkward.

'Say hello to Mick, Sam.'

Equally unsure, the baby turned his face away and buried it in the front of her sweater, his chubby fingers pulling at the coarse wool.

'Poor love.' Suzie's brown eyes met Mick's over Sam's head. 'He's a bit confused after his nap.' With her free hand she fondled the bright curls. 'Take no notice of him and he'll be okay.'

They made an attractive picture, Mick thought. Her hair, falling straight to her shoulders, put him in mind of the gleam of hazelnuts at Hallowe'en. And the curve of the baby's head as he pressed his face against his mother's breast awoke a feeling of tenderness in Mick that took him by surprise. Bewildered, he picked the book up again and sought refuge among the poems.

'"*Man's mounting spirit in his bone house, mean house dwells* – "' There's imagery for you, Mick. Here, give me that child, alanna, and get a cup of tea for yourself.'

'Do you take milk, Mrs Joyce?' His arms felt too long for the sleeves of his sweater as he reached for the tea tray, dropping the poetry book in his eagerness.

'That's lovely, Mick.' Her eyes smiled at him. He felt his face redden with pleasure.

Later, as he left the house, his arms laden with books, he noticed that the smell of burnt milk had been replaced by a rich aroma that made all the glands in his mouth water.

'Spaghetti bolognese.' Suzie opened the front door and he felt the cold spring evening rush in to meet them. 'Next time stay for supper.'

Next time! His mind alive with images, he jumped on his bike, swung out into the North Circular past a line of cars, shot across the traffic, barely noticing the angry hooting, and made an illegal right turn to take a short cut home. Next time, his heart sang. Next time!

'He writes poetry himself. He's had stuff published in the newspaper.'

'Fancy that.' Ma was impressed.

Da looked doubtful, drinking his tea in short, deliberate gulps. 'Filling his head full of nonsense,' Mick heard him mutter later out in the tiny kitchen. 'Where will it all end? That's what I'd like to know.'

'Where's the harm in it, Maurice? It's nice to see him making friends.'

'What's wrong with the lads around here?'

'Them?' Ma sniffed. 'Crowd of cornerboys'

'They're his own age, Nan. It'd be more natural. Anyway, what do we know about this man? Some class of a culchie?'

'The wife is nice, Mick says. And they've a baby.'

'An Englishwoman.' He heard the note of dismissal in Da's voice. 'God knows what kind of –'

Resentment rose up in him like acid. Might have known he'd take it like that. How did she ever – ?

He got up abruptly and went out of the living room, slamming the door behind him.

He didn't understand Jimmy's poems. Spare, unadorned sentences, they didn't always rhyme. Though he knew enough to know they didn't have to.

'You prefer: "*Half a league, half a league, half a league onward*" or "*Don John of Austria is marching to the war.*" Good rousing stuff?'

'Yes.' It stirred the blood. 'Yours is –' He sought around for a word. 'Clever.'

'Clever?' There was a gleam in Jimmy's eye.

Mick reddened. 'No, maybe not clever – but – too intelligent.'

'For you? Don't underrate yourself, Mick.'

He floundered.

Jimmy took pity on him. 'Maybe "cerebral" is the word you're looking for? You wouldn't be the first person to say that, mind you. "Put more passion into it, boy." My old English professor. A Kerryman, of course. They know all about passion.'

'And you don't?' Suzie raised her eyebrows at him.

Jimmy whooped suddenly and made a grab for her. 'Come here my "nut-brown maiden". '

'Behave yourself.' She shook herself free. 'You're embarrassing Mick.'

'Who's embarrassed?' He tried to appear nonchalant. Her hair was all soft and shiny looking. He wanted to reach out and touch it, feel it slip through his fingers. Wonder what it would be like? He banished the thought hastily, tried to grin. 'But Sam shouldn't be listening to this.'

His face daubed with cereal, Sam surveyed them solemnly from his high feeding chair.

Suzie grinned at Mick. 'Stick to Keats or Tennyson. They're safer.'

That's what you think. *La Belle Dame sans Merci hath thee in thrall.*

'I'll remember that.'

He was glad she couldn't read minds.

The daffodils died down in the long grass. Then it was the summer term. 'A doss year, fifth year,' the slackers in the class said gleefully.

'Next year you're going to have to knuckle down to it,' Jimmy Joyce warned them. 'I'm expecting great things of you.' It was an honours class. 'Some of you are good for a "B". His eyes rested on Mick in the second row. 'Might even be an "A". But you just can't tell with English. If you don't get the finger out you'll be lucky to end up with "D"s.' He picked up a book. 'We'll do some work on the novel now.'

'Hardy's such a dry balls,' someone groaned.

Jimmy grinned. 'Nothing to stop you reading Edna O'Brien in your spare time.' Again his glance hovered over the second row. 'Some of you – mind you, only *some* – are beginning to discover the joys of literature for its own sake.'

Mick kept his face blank as he bent over his desk.

Suzie took the geranium from the front window and put it out in the porch, where it budded into flower. Rich salmon-coloured blooms that complemented the warm terracotta of its pot and the mellowed brick of the porchway.

'Front door needs painting. Of course poets don't paint. Not doors anyway.'

'I'll do it,' Mick offered. 'Soon as I get my holidays.'

The weather picked up. It grew warm enough for Sam to be outside in the back garden, where he sat in his playpen banging saucepan lids together, resisting all Mick's blandishments to get him to pull himself to a standing position by means of the bars.

'He'll do it in his own time,' Suzie said. 'He takes after my side of the family. They're a placid lot. Reminds me of my dad.' Her bright eyes rested affectionately on Mick. 'Who do you take after, your Mum or your Dad?'

He grimaced. 'Her – I hope.' He felt himself redden under Suzie's surprised gaze. 'Neither, actually. I'm a changeling.'

She looked at him blankly,

'A fairy left in exchange for a human child.' Jimmy, arriving out of the back room in search of coffee, was only too happy to enlighten her. 'It's part of our folklore – '

'That'll do to be going on with,' Suzie interrupted. She turned back to Mick, gave him a penetrating look. 'So the real Mick is somewhere else, then?

He was taken aback by her perceptiveness. 'No, I'm the real Mick. Somewhere else is where I was taken from.'

'And where's that, then?'

'God only knows.' Frustration gripped him suddenly. 'I wish *I* did.'

Aunt Lizzie heard they were taking on staff for the summer in the local supermarket. She put in a word for Mick with the manager. 'Just tell him I sent you.' He didn't want to go. 'I'll get my own job,' he muttered. But Ma said he'd be a fool to pass up the chance and Da said it was good money so he allowed himself to be persuaded. He spent most of his time opening cartons and stacking shelves, thinking wistfully of all the sunshine he was missing. Whenever there was an opportunity to escape outside the store, to run an errand or to push a customer's trolley out to the car park, he always took it. Thursdays and Fridays were late shopping nights but he had the other evenings free.

'Don't keep any dinner for me, Ma. I'll be home late.'

'We never see anything of you these days, Mick.'

'The job, Ma – '

'You're not working all the time, Mick. Those people will get tired of you. You don't want to wear your welcome out.'

'It's not like that. I'm a help. I promised to cut the grass for them. And Suzie wants me to give her a hand painting the kitchen.'

Ma's lips tightened. 'They're just using you, Mick.'

'No, they're not.' He was bewildered by her lack of logic. 'Look, I can't do anything to please you. First you say one thing and then – ' he turned away, filled with resentment. 'Oh, what's the use.'

'Mick!' Ma's face was stricken. 'I didn't mean any harm. I – '

'What's the use?' He hated the way she always made him feel guilty. 'Forget it, Ma.'

'Sam loves the goldfish, don't you, Sam?' Suzie held the baby out where he could watch the flashes of red gold darting among the water lilies. The air was heavy and languorous; the walkways in the hothouse lined with tropical plants gave off a steamy pungent odour that brought Mick back to childhood.

'I always liked them too.'

'Poor Jimmy.' She straddled Sam on her hip and they resumed their walk among the trailing plants, their footsteps echoing under the high, green-painted dome. 'Missing all this. Fancy spending your Sunday stuck indoors slaving over a hot stanza.'

'You have a way with words,' Mick said. 'Did you ever think of writing yourself?'

Suzie's eyes twinkled. 'My Dad had literary leanings. He wrote a play for the local drama group. It came to nothing though. They fell out over the parts.' She laughed robustly at the memory. 'He was so disgusted, he said: "Never again!" Probably just as well. I don't think it was very good.'

'But what about you?' he persisted, vaguely excited by his own daring.

She wrinkled her nose. 'One writer in the family is quite enough, thank you. When Sam gets a bit older, I'll look for a job. I might go back to teaching. Who knows?'

'You could do anything, Suzie.'

She smiled and said nothing. They came to a doorway which led into another hothouse. Mick stood back to let Suzie go through with the child in her arms.. A couple waited at the other side to let them pass. He noticed the way the man looked at her legs, felt proud and, at the same time, indignant. Put his hand protectively on her arm and guided her and Sam past the couple. Suzie gave him a thoughtful glance.

'What do you want to be, Mick?'

'When I leave school? I don't know. I hadn't – '

She smiled in sympathy. 'Exciting, isn't it. *You* could do anything, Mick. *Be* anything.'

Yes, it *was* exciting.

'Yes. I think I could.'

Mr Joyce thinks I should go to college.'

Ma's face went blank.

'He says I'm good enough.'

Usually so quick to comment, she said nothing.

'Course I don't have to decide till next January.'

'I think you should talk to your father first.'

'*Him?* You're the one who – '

'Talk to your father, Mick.'

'College? Nobody round here goes to college.'

'There has to be a first time, Mr Joyce says.'

'No,' Da shook his head. 'Forget it, son. I've been meaning to talk to you. Hennigan's are taking on painters. They'll train you.'

'But, Da, there are grants.'

'No buts, Mick. This is a great chance for you. You'll have a trade.'

'A trade?' He looked at his father in dawning comprehension. 'But what about my Leaving Cert?'

'The Leaving Cert's not worth a curse these days. Ask anyone. Getting a job's what matters.'

'But I'm going back to school next week.'

Silence for a moment. He glanced from one face to the other. Ma looked distressed, drew heavily on her cigarette, coughed, avoided Mick's eye. Da's face seemed to be carved out of stone.

'Forget it. I've put in a word with Tom Hennigan.'

'Da!' he pleaded. If only he could get through to him. But it was as if there was a glass wall between them. He felt his fists clenching, wanted to smash through that wall, wanted to grab Da and shake him. If only he could make him see.

'You'll thank me yet,' his father said.

'*Thank* you?' Mick stared at him in disbelief.

'You've heard your Uncle Thomas often enough. There's university graduates on the dole.' Da's voice brooked no contradiction. 'You're one of the lucky ones, Mick.'

'If we all had that attitude nobody would ever do anything.' Jimmy Joyce ran his hands through his hair until it stood up in wild curls around his head. 'Jesus, Mick! You're one of my best students. I can't believe this is happening.'

'How do you think I feel?' Mick put his head in his hands. As he slumped over the kitchen table he felt a light touch on his shoulder.

'Could Jimmy have a word with your Dad? Would it do any good?'

'No, it'd be no use. The only one he ever listens to is my Ma.'

'You could talk to him. He'd listen to *you*.'

'Leave it, Mick. It'd do no good.'

'But why?

Ma said earnestly, 'Me and your father, we never had much education. I left school at fourteen to work in the sweet factory. When I met him he was serving his time to be a carpenter – '

'Just because you never got your chance is no reason to – '

'Mick! Will you listen to me.'

'What's the use?' All at once the energy drained out of him, leaving him flat and dejected. 'You just don't understand.' He stared at his mother in despair.

Ma sighed. 'It's you that doesn't understand. People like us don't go to college.'

The men on the job were kindly enough.

'*Young fella, will you slip out and get us a packeta fags.*'

'*Put more tea bags in the pot, willya. That looks like it seen a ghost.*'

'*Somebody musta had a shock, all right,*' someone else guffawed. '*Looks like piss.*'

Paint under his fingernails. Paint in his hair. His hands

felt rubbed raw at night, fingertips tingling.

'Turps is your only man,' was the advice.

'White spirit is better.'

'It's all the wan,' said a third.

But nothing seemed able to take away the smell in his nostrils. One night he dreamed he was drowning in a vat of emulsion. He woke up in a panic, gagging and spitting and lay trembling in the darkness, waiting for the alarm clock to ring. The workday started earlier than school and the foreman was a stickler. 'You're only on probation, young fella. There's plenty'd be glad of –'

'Those overalls could stand up by themselves,' Ma would complain. But he sensed her pride. 'Mick's working for Hennigan's,' he heard her tell a neighbour.

'You don't have to keep washing them.' It was bad enough being a new boy without having to draw attention to himself. A new boy. A boy in a man's world. There was one joker called Benny who never lost an opportunity to remind him. 'That's a paintbrush you're holding, Mickser, not a cricket bat.'

He missed school, the company of boys his own age, the challenge of putting his thoughts on paper.

'You could study for the Leaving in your spare time,' Jimmy suggested, without much hope.

'Not this year,' Suzie said quickly. 'Just look at him, the poor love. Not ten o'clock and he can't keep his eyes open.'

His back ached. His neck. His shoulders. His arms.

'It'll pass off once you're used to it,' Ma consoled him. 'A good soak in the bath is what you want.'

'In the middle of the week?' Da looked askance. 'When I was a young fella – '

'When I was a young fella!' She gave a derisive snort. 'That's all you ever go on about. And the tin bath in the kitchen. Those days are gone, Maurice. Now that we have the immersion heater,' she smiled proudly, 'you can have a bath every night of the week if you want to.'

'But the cost, Nan.'

'Mick's bringing money into the house now,' she pointed out sharply.

'That's true,' Da conceded. 'But don't go buying all around you. His wages isn't *that* good.'

All the same, it was great to have a few quid in his pocket on a Friday night. He was seventeen in November and still under age but he was taller than his father, and the barman in Foley's made no objection when Da brought him in on his birthday to drink his first pint.

'What d'ye think of that, son? Eating and drinking in it.'

Mick grimaced. It looked so black and velvety. But it tasted thin. And sour.

'It's okay.'

'A man's drink.' Uncle Thomas said, blowing froth noisily from his lips. 'Am I right, Maurice?'

'Never said a truer word.' Da's glance rested benignly on Mick. In a rare display of emotion he tapped him on the arm. 'A man's drink, that's what it is.'

'Mick! It is Mick, isn't it? You've changed, filled out. It's been months since we – '

'Hello, Suzie.' He smiled awkwardly at her.

Her gaze fell on the carton of milk in his paint-stained hands. 'Are you – ?'

'Yes, I'm working. We're doing up the shopping centre. I'm on my break.' He hesitated, torn between his pleasure at seeing her and his embarrassment at being caught in his stained overalls.

'You never come to see us any more.' She was wearing her hair differently. It was shorter, curving around her face in a bell. It still had the nut-brown sheen.

'Yes – well – ' his eye was caught by the child clutching her hand. 'Sam? It can't be! You're not a baby any more.'

'You're not the only one who's grown,' Suzie agreed. 'He'll soon be two. This day week, the tenth of May.' She glanced down at her son. 'Remember Mick, Sam?'

Mick grinned hopefully at him but the little boy stared back at him blankly. Then he frowned and hid his face against the leg of his mother's jeans.

'*He* hasn't changed.' He tried to laugh off his disappointment. 'Still suspicious of strangers.'

'You don't have to be a stranger, Mick.' How could he have forgotten that smile, the way it lit up her eyes? 'Come and see us. Tonight?'

Conscious of his stained overalls, he was suddenly reluctant. 'I can't. Not tonight.'

'Some other night then. I know. Sam's birthday. Come to supper.'

Her smile warmed some forgotten corner of his heart. 'Okay Maybe I will. When did you say?'

'Next Friday, Mick. Don't forget.'

'Are you still on for tonight?' Donie asked when he got back with the milk.

'What?' He stirred his tea absently.

'Thought you might have got yourself fixed up there. Nice bit of stuff.'

'She's a friend.' He was stung. 'Besides – ' He reddened. 'She's a bit older than – '

'So?' Donie grinned. 'That never stopped a woman.' He rolled his eyes appreciatively. 'Great legs!'

'How would you know what her legs looked like?'

'Jesus! You don't have to bite the nose off me.'

'Back off, will you!'

He grinned again. 'Like that, is it?'

'Donie!'

'Okay, Okay.' He shrugged expressively. 'Now so. About tonight?'

'I don't know.' Mick said uneasily. 'I don't know these girls.'

'They're a great pair. From down home. I've told them all about you.' Black eyes glinted wickedly. 'You've nothing to worry about. They're mad for it, boy.' He made panting noises. 'Stone mad.'

'We-ell.'

'Come on, Mick.'

'Oh – okay.' It was Friday night, after all.

'Good man!' Donie gave a whoop. 'You can have the blonde.'

He was as good as his word. But the black-haired girl was the prettier of the two, with pouting red lips and creamy white thighs that revealed themselves to Mick's startled gaze when the other man pulled her into his lap and began to nuzzle her ear. As she made half-hearted attempts to deflect Donie's groping hand, Mick looked away in embarrassment.

'Have a beer.' The girl sitting beside him on the sofa pushed her face close to his and giggled. Tendrils of her hair tickled his cheek.

'I've enough, thanks.' He tried to remember how many pints he'd drunk earlier in the pub. Too many. 'I think I'd better be going.'

'Yerra, man, what's your hurry?' Donie's thin face was flushed and a lock of black hair fell over his forehead. 'The night's only a pup. Give that man a beer, Orla.'

'I –' Mick demurred but the girl just laughed and pushed a can into his hand. Closing her fingers around his, she smiled into his eyes. 'You're not going anywhere, are you, boy?'

He hesitated. 'Well – just the one. Then I'll really have to go.'

The blonde girl smiled in triumph and traced a wet finger down the length of his nose.

His stomach gave an answering leap of excitement.

'Will you take a hoult of that sheet. God, it's gone again.' She gave a shriek of merriment. 'What way were you reared? Have you never made a bed before?'

'I'm tired,' he mumbled. It had been a lot of work grappling with the mechanics of the sofa bed. Orla had been no help to him, firing out garbled instructions amid bursts of wild giggling. The room began to spin around him. His legs no longer wanted to hold him up. He sank down on the bed, which gave out a loud twang of protest.

'Watch it!' the girl hissed. 'You don't want to wake the nosy old wagon next door.'

'Sorry.' He clung desperately to the bed, which seemed to be travelling at about ninety miles an hour. The walls, covered in huge bilious splodges, whizzed by in the opposite direction.

'Are you okay?' She was beside him on the mattress, kneeling over him, her hair brushing his face.

'I'm fine,' Mick lied.

'Grand, so.' He felt the weight of her body on top of him, her tongue squirming into his mouth. He gagged. His stomach heaved.

'What's the matter now?' Her voice was aggrieved.

'I think I'm going to be sick.'

'Great. That's all we need.'

'Do you feel better now?'

'Not really.' His head ached and the muscles in his throat were stiff after his ignominious dash to the flat's tiny bathroom. The wallpaper had stopped spinning around him but it looked as hideous as ever in the harsh light of the ceiling bulb. He closed his eyes to blot out the bilious splodges.

Fingers touched his bare arm. 'Would you like to lie down for a bit?'

Yes, but not here. 'Thanks, but I – '

She had smudges of mascara under her eyes. Blue eyes set a little close together. What was that shade on the colour card? Azure? Iris haze? Not that it mattered. He glanced over at the door leading to the bedroom. 'Donie?'

The girl laughed. 'Yerra! That fella won't surface till

lunchtime.' She gave a meaning smile. 'You can stay the night if you want to.'

The smile didn't quite reach her eyes. Stupid of him to think it might. He felt cold and flat inside. Not drunk any more. 'Thanks, but – '

The smile vanished. The blue eyes narrowed. 'Suit yourself, boy.'

He felt himself reddening. 'My mother – ' he buttoned his shirt, glanced around for his jacket.

'Your *mother?*' She looked at him in disbelief.

He avoided her eye. 'She worries when I'm – if I – '

'*Jesus!*' She slapped the jacket into his hands. 'Your *mother?* How old are you anyway?'

'Another time,' he mumbled apologetically.

As she let him out the flat door, Orla hissed viciously: 'Next time send your big brother.'

It stood out from the other toys in the shop window. Chunky and red, with big black wheels and a helmeted fireman up in front.

'There are more figures in the box,' the shop assistant said. 'And a *real* siren.' She was a girl around his own age with red, curly hair and a scattering of golden freckles across her little snub nose. 'Listen to this.' Her eyes gleamed as the raucous wail sounded through the shop.

'It's brilliant.' He felt in his pocket for the envelope containing his week's wages. 'I'll take it.'

'He must be real special.' She handed him his change. 'Your own kid?'

'No.' He reddened. 'I'm not married.'

'That wouldn't make any difference.' The girl smiled wryly. 'Not around where I live, anyway.'

'Is that right?' He was only half listening, anxious to be off. His gaze fell on the fire engine in its box on the counter between them. 'Can you – ?'

'Yeh, no problem.' A thought struck her. 'Would you like me to gift-wrap it? No extra charge. You've paid enough.'

She used shiny blue paper with cuddly, red teddy bears on it, her small fingers working deftly, and inished it off with a gold satin bow. 'Isn't that lovely? You'll need a card. They're over there. Get one with a badge on it. Kids love badges. My nephew – '

'You've a nephew?' Although he wasn't really interested.

'My sister's kid. He's a real dote. That card'll cost you a pound. The other one's cheaper. It's just as nice.'

'Thanks.'

'We've other stuff besides toys.' Handing him his purchases, the girl winked at him. 'Remember now, if you've any more birthdays coming up.'

He couldn't help smiling at her pushiness. 'I'll remember.'

He was still smiling as he left the shop but by the time he reached the florist's on the corner he had forgotten her.

'You're home early, Mick.'

'Pay day.' He grinned at her. 'The foreman's out sick. The lads are in the pub since three.'

'Nice goings-on,' Ma sniffed. 'Still, it worked out handy enough for you. The water's grand and hot. I didn't forget to put on the immersion.'

He beamed at her. 'You're a star. Did I ever tell you?'

'I know. What would you do without me? Are you sure

you won't eat something? I've a nice bit of haddock. There's too much for the two of us.'

'Give mine to the cat.'

'What cat?'

'How do *I* know? The fella next door.'

'That brute. He's cheeky enough as he is.' Ma shook her head and laughed. 'God forgive you, Mick. And fish the price it is.'

Mick was laughing too. He felt absurdly happy as he took the narrow stairs two at a time.

'Heavy date?' Uncle Thomas was sitting at the table in the living room when he came downstairs.

'I gave him your fish.' Ma looked up from her own meal with a pleased smile. 'I didn't want it to go to waste.'

'Anything to help out, Nan,' his uncle said. 'I wouldn't mind but Carmel will expect me to have another feed when I get home.' He patted his belly with a resigned sigh. 'But you know me. I wouldn't see you stuck.'

'You're all heart,' Mick grinned. Even Uncle Thomas couldn't annoy him tonight. 'Have you seen my black shoes, Ma?'

'They're in the kitchen. I polished them for you.'

'What did I say? That's some heavy date.' Uncle Thomas put down his knife and belched pleasurably. 'Am I right, Maurice?'

Da looked blankly at him, said nothing and went on eating.

'It's not like that.' Ma seemed affronted by the suggestion. 'It's this family Mick knows.'

'*Oh, yeh?*' Thomas guffawed. He looked at his brother again.

'I'm keeping out of it,' Da said.

'It's a birthday party.' Mick's voice was stiff. 'For a two-year-old.'

'Oh, yeh?' Uncle Thomas gave another guffaw. 'Get a load of that aftershave! Who do you think you're coddin'?'

The geranium was still in its winter quarters in the front window. Although it was early May a sharp wind scraped old leaves and sweet wrappers underfoot and riffled through the tracery of green which was starting to fill out the branches on the few scrawny trees dotting the pavements of the cul-de-sac. Desultory birdsong murmured in the distance. As the house came into view he felt excitement grip his stomach, his heart beat a little faster. Shifting the bunch of flowers over to the arm carrying Sam's present, he was reaching out to the rusting gate when he realised that there was someone ahead of him standing in the porch. A boy about his own age. Thought he looked familiar. Bernard Murphy from school. What's he doing here?'

Bernard Murphy. Quiet. A bit of a nonentity really. It had been a surprise when he had come second to Mick's first in English at the end of last year. What's *he* doing here? Maybe he was just leaving in that parcel he had in his hand? Yes, that's what he's doing? Leaving a message. That's all it is. He thought of joining the other boy on the porch but decided against it. It was a bit awkward now that he was no longer at school. And Bernard had been heavy going at the best of times. Easier to scrape old paint off a wall than get a word out of Bernard. No, better wait till he's gone. It shouldn't take long. As soon as the coast was clear Mick would go in with *his* parcel. He couldn't wait to see Sam's face when he opened it. Couldn't wait to see Suzie's face.

Just then the front door opened and he saw her gleaming brown head, heard her voice raised in welcome. The sound of her laughter floated out to him on the evening breeze. As he waited impatiently for the other boy to finish his business and leave, he was surprised to see the front door open wider. In disbelief he watched Bernard step into the hallway and the door shut behind him,

Mick felt stunned. It had never occurred to him that anyone else might have been invited. 'Come to supper,' she had said, just like in the old days. It wouldn't have been so bad if it had been anyone else. But Bernard Murphy, of all people. That dummy! No, that wasn't fair. Bernard wasn't a dummy. But all the same, *Bernard Murphy,* for God's sake!

They're *my* friends. She's *my* –

Was, Mick, *was.* You shouldn't have stayed away so long.

But he'd no right. Who did he think he was? The resentment he felt towards Bernard grew. And then it was a huge pain that gripped his innards, making him want to cry out. He heard her voice again. The way she laughed as she shut the door. Bringing him in like an honoured guest! It hadn't been his first time to the house, that was obvious. But – how could she? How could she do this to him? And what about Jimmy? He had said Mick was the best student he'd had in years. And now look at him. Bernard Murphy! He couldn't believe it. Reading the same poems, taking Mick's place at the kitchen table, going for walks with Suzie and Sam. He just didn't believe it! He wanted to bang his head against the railings and howl.

A car pulled up to the kerb beside him and a man went whistling past him into the house next door. An old woman shuffling along the pavement with an ancient, wheezing dog in tow stopped and examined Mick suspiciously. Suddenly conscious of her eyes on him, he was brought back to a realisation of his surroundings. Can't hang around here all night. But what was he to do? All desire to enter the house had left him. There was no point now. The evening was ruined. He might as well go home. No, not home. Ma would ask too many questions. Where then? Anywhere but here, that's for sure.

He put the plastic bag with the brightly wrapped present in it down on the floor of the porch. Laid the bunch of flowers beside it. Changed his mind and took the flowers with him. At the end of the street he stuffed them into a litter bin, savagely crumpling the bright heads in their beribboned cellophane wrapper.

The shining brown hair curving past her ears in the shape of a bell was the first thing to catch his eye when he came into the pub. His heart gave a great leap and began hammering at his chest. Without stopping to think, he went up to where she was standing near the bar and put his hand on her arm. The woman turned enquiringly and his heart plummeted.

'Sorry,' he stammered. 'Thought you were someone I knew.'

'That's no harm.' Laughter lines appeared around her eyes and at the corners of her mouth. 'Sorry if I disappointed you.'

Her face was thinner and older than the one he had expected to see but there was something attractive about it. His heart steadied itself. He found himself smiling back. 'You didn't. What I mean is – ' he felt his face redden.

'Watch it now. You could say something you might regret later.' She had a quick, friendly manner, as if they already knew each other well.

'I – '

'Don't mind me. I'm only joking.' She looked at him more closely. 'You're new in here, aren't you? I've never seen – '

'Foley's is where I usually drink.'

She nodded. 'The craic's better here. You're right to come in early. It'll be packed later on. You won't be able to hear yourself think. Are you on your own?'

He hesitated. 'Well – yeh – actually I am.'

'Things are looking up,' she said to the barman.

He grinned back at her. 'This could be your lucky night, Bernie.'

Mick's face flamed. He glanced from one to the other, unsure of how to react.

'Watch your language, Jim,' Bernie said with mock severity. 'You're embarrassing the *crathur*. Come here.' She smiled at Mick. 'I'll have to buy you a drink after that. What're you having?'

He had the feeling that things were moving too fast for him.

'Just a drink,' the woman said quickly. She threw a glance at a table in the corner where a man and two women were sitting. 'I'm with friends. You don't have to join us if you don't want to.'

Well, why not? Better than sitting on his own. 'Thanks. I'll have a pint of Smithwicks.'

The middle-aged couple in the corner were called Mags

and Billy. They exchanged friendly nods with him before resuming their conversation with each other. The woman beside them had sharp features and short, straw-coloured hair. In some indefinable way she reminded him of his Aunt Carmel. Her thin, painted eyebrows nearly disappeared up under her blonde fringe when she saw Mick. 'Where did you find *him,* for God's sake?' She stared at him in disbelief. 'Does your mother know you're out?'

'Don't mind her.' Bernie patted him on the arm. 'Kay's bark is worse than her bite.'

Mick took a deep swallow of his beer, smacked his lips and tried to look cynical. 'I wouldn't want to get a bite from her, all the same.'

'The last one got blood poisoning.' She had a deep, throaty laugh. 'Isn't that right, Kay?'

The other woman sighed. 'You're incorrigible, Bernie. Do you know that?' She gave Mick another disbelieving look before turning away to talk to Mags and Billy.

'Don't mind her.' Bernie's deep laugh filled an awkward moment. 'What do you do with yourself, Mick? Are you at college?'

'No,' he said shortly. 'I'm working.'

She seemed surprised. 'If anyone had asked me, now, I'd have said – '

It was a sore point. To change the subject he asked quickly: 'You're not from around here, are you? I mean, not originally?'

'No, boy, I'm not. I'm from a small place in County Cork called – no matter – you'd never have heard of it.'

'What brought you to Dublin?'

'The train. What else?'

'Ah, come on,' he protested.

The smile left her eyes. 'It's a long story.' She patted his hand gently. 'You don't want to be listening to my troubles.'

Her touch sent a thrill of excitement through his body. He took another long swallow from his glass. 'That's okay. I've plenty of time.'

'What about that girl, the one you – ?'

'There's no girl. That was a mistake.' He was conscious of her hand still resting against his. 'Like I told you, I'm not going anywhere.'

A broken marriage was nothing new to him. 'I worked on a site last month and half the fellas on it were separated.' But it was usually the husbands who left home. Or were thrown out. 'What happened?'

Her face saddened briefly. 'I married too young. The babies came too fast.' She gave a quick shrug. 'What do any of us know at that age?'

He couldn't hide his dismay. 'But the children?'

'Their father has them. They're better off with him.'

'But – ' He was puzzled. 'Do you not miss them?'

'Ah, I do, I do. Sure I'm only human, amn't I? But you get used to it. God is good. They're well looked after, that's the main thing.' Her eyes slid past him and glanced quickly around the pub. The place was beginning to fill up. 'Friday night, Mick. Another half-hour and there won't be an empty seat.'

End of story? He wanted to ask more but thought better of it. 'Can I get you another drink?'

'Now you're talking.' Bernie beamed at him. 'Same again, please. Don't bother about Kay. She's all right. She can get her own.'

When he came back with the drinks, she pressed his hand. 'Do you know what? You're a great listener for your age. How old did you say you were?'

Greatly daring, he returned the pressure.

'I'm twenty,' he lied.

'Careful.' Bernie took the arm he was trying to clasp around her shoulders and gripped it firmly. 'The door's this way, big fella.'

The wind had dropped but the night air was cool. Although he heard car doors banging, engines starting up, snatches of conversation from people congregating at street corners, the scene had a dreamlike quality to it. The only realities were the sky overhead blazing with stars, the air cooling his hot face, her fingers pressing into the flesh above his elbow. They came to some railings beside a shuttered newsagents. Steps up to a front door with a row of bells beside it.

'This is my place. Want to come in for a cup of tea?'

The light was bright after the semi-darkness of the pub. He examined his surroundings with interest. The place looked clean and comfortable. Personal touches brightened the drabness of anonymous furnishings. A patchwork quilt was thrown over the divan, its gay colours echoed in the cotton window curtains; fleecy rugs took the monotony out of the carpet; photographs in brass frames crowded a shelf filled with ornaments. 'Those your kids?'

'Yes,' she said. 'Can I get you a cup of tea?'

'How old's the boy?'

'That was taken a couple of years ago.' Her voice was reluctant. 'He's nearly nineteen.'

A year older than me. For a moment he wondered what he was doing there. What would Ma say if she knew?

She shifted in her seat suddenly, crossing her legs. His eyes traced the curve of her stomach under the close-fitting jeans and then moved upwards to where the sweater clung to her breasts. He became aware of his own jeans beginning to tighten. Her eyes intercepted his. She smiled, and he felt his face grow hot.

'You don't look old enough,' he blurted out.

'Thanks.' She was unimpressed. 'That's what they all say, 'specially when they're looking for something. Like now.'

His face grew hotter. 'I'm not – '

'Oh, yes, you are.' It was said with such good humour it was difficult to take offence. 'And it's not a cup of tea you're after, is it?'

Despite his growing discomfort he met her eyes squarely, excitement building up in his stomach.

'No, it's not,' he admitted.

She had beautiful green eyes, sea-green with flecks of gold.

'It's your first time, isn't it?' Her hair was soft and fine; it slid through his fingertips.

'No, I – '

'That's no harm.' Her voice was low, barely above a whisper. 'There's a first time for everyone. Bernie will show you what to do.' He felt his collar being loosened. Then her hands against his bare chest. 'Isn't that better now?' Her lips found his gently, her tongue delicately probing.

A fire started up between his thighs. His hand sought her breast.

'Steady now, Mick. We've all the time in the world.'

She guided his hands around her back till they found the opening on her brassiere, until he felt the soft swell of her breasts, the nipples hardening under his fingers. A shudder of delight went through him. Then another.

'Wait.' She led him over to the bed, turned down the patchwork quilt, helped him out of his clothes. Then they were both lying naked under the quilt, close enough for him to feel the soft hairs on her body brushing against his stomach.

'Will I turn out the light?'

Suddenly and irrationally the thought of Ma came into his mind. What would she think? Supposing she found out? He banished her firmly. 'Yes, okay.'

Senses were heightened by the darkness. He tasted the inside of her mouth, his nostrils filled with the scent of her skin. The fire had turned into a furnace ready to burst into flame. Her hands seemed to be all over his body, gentle, insistent, unbearable, cupping him briefly, fingertips lighter than swansdown, then firm as they guided him gently but surely in between her thighs. As their bodies connected he heard himself moan, his breath coming in frantic gulps. Heard her breathing keep pace with his.

Oh God! Oh God! Oh God!

The furnace roared into life.

Oh God! Oh Jesus! Oh my Lord! It wasn't a furnace. It was a volcano! And it was ready to blow, taking both of them with it!

'I never knew it would be so noisy.'

'It always is when it's good.'

'Was it good?' He propped himself up on an elbow and gazed down eagerly, just making out the contours of her face in the darkness. 'For you, I mean?'

'It was, alanna. It was.' Her voice sounded sleepy. 'How about you?'

He laughed with a kind of disbelief. 'It was mind-blowing.'

'Good. That's good.'

He settled down again beside her, feeling the warmth of her body, her breath against his neck, a delightful drowsiness stealing over him. 'Can I stay?'

'What? You can. For a bit anyway. I've work in the – '

The pattern was beginning to be discernible on the window curtains when he opened his eyes. He could hear a bird singing in the distance, trilling the same long note over and over again. Must be a garden at the back of the flats. She was lying on her side, away from him, her head half-covered by the sheet. He reached out and touched her naked thigh. She twitched his hand away, groaned into her pillow.

'It'll be morning soon. You'd better go.'

'Do I have to?'

'Yes, dote, you have to.' She turned towards him and their bodies met. 'On second thoughts.' Her hand reached down, caressing him gently. 'Pity to waste this. Then you'll really have to go.'

The furnace started up again. 'Okay, I promise.'

'Can I see you again?'

'Was the shower all right? It can be tricky sometimes.'

'*Bernie?*'

'I heard you.' She gave a sigh, sat up in bed, pulled the sheet over her breasts, her hair falling into her eyes. 'Don't be tempting me, alanna.'

'But Bernie – ' He was crestfallen. 'Didn't you – ?'

'Of course I did. That's not it.' Her face was pasty in the morning light, dark smudges of fatigue under her beautiful eyes. 'Will you look at me. I'm old enough to be your – '

'But you got married young, you said so yourself.'

'Not *that* young.' Her voice was rueful.

'But – '

'Will you go away with yourself before you make me late,' she said fiercely. 'Some people have to work on a Saturday morning, you know. Come here and kiss me goodbye.'

As he bent down he saw a tear glisten on her cheek.

'You're a lovely boy, Mick. It'll be a lucky girl that gets you.'

'I'm telling you, boy, she was – ' Donie's hands sketched expressively ' – *powerful.*' His black eyes danced. 'What a night! Had you a good weekend yourself, Mick?'

He smiled slightly. 'Not bad.'

'*Not bad?*' Donie raised his eyebrows, pursed his lips. 'Now that could mean anything – or nothing?' He probed delicately. 'Did you – ?'

Mick's smile broadened. 'Mind your own business.'

Beside him, slurping tea out of a cracked mug, Benny gave a loud guffaw. 'A bagga chips in front of the telly and the mammy makin' a cuppa cocoa. That's *his* idea of a good night. Am I right, Mickser, wha – ?' He bared a mouth full of yellowing teeth as he looked around the group of men, inviting their laughter.

'Pay no heed,' Donie said when the chorus of guffaws had died down. 'Some people's brains are in their backside.'

'And his is big enough.' Mick put down his mug amid appreciative roars from the others. 'Isn't that right, Benny?' He couldn't keep a slight swagger out of his step as he moved away.

'Up yours!' the older man called after him, a baffled look on his unshaven face.

Yours too, Benny. Yours too. The swagger grew more pronounced. As if any woman would look at *him*, poor sod!

'How's the job going, Mick?'

'A piece of cake, Auntie Lizzie. Nothing to it.'

'He got a rise last week.' Ma couldn't conceal her pride.

'Go on?' Lizzie's voice boomed in his ear. 'Sure you're not a wet week in the place.'

'A year next month.' He felt a jolt of surprise.

Was it really a year? Where had it gone to?

'They think a lot of him in Hennigans, Lizzie. Mrs Hennigan told me her husband says Mick's one of his best workers.'

'Come on, Ma. It doesn't take an Einstein – '

'Maybe not.' His father had been following the conversation with one eye on the newspaper. 'But it's not everyone can learn a trade. And some never get the chance. Remember that, son. It takes more than brains. You've got to stick at it, be dependable.' He frowned suddenly. 'Do you hear what I'm saying?'

'Yes, Da.' He grimaced at Ma behind his father's back. 'I hear.'

'The Leaving Cert?' Donie mused. 'Much good it did me.'

'Yeh?' Mick bit into a sandwich morosely as he gazed into the nearby schoolyard. The air was loud with shrieks as teenage girls in bright, summer clothes stood around in groups, excitedly comparing exam results. Donie studied the long legs of one mini-skirted student and sighed.

'You won't believe this, boy, but I did a year of college.'

'I don't.' His class would all be out celebrating tonight. He would have been with them if things had been different. 'Pull the other leg, Donie.'

'It's the honest to God's truth I'm telling you. No, listen. I got Arts in Galway.' His black eyes lit up his thin face. 'Man, we had a ball! An absolute ball!'

'Arts?' Mick's interest was stirred. 'What was it like? The lectures – ?'

'Lectures?' Donie punched the air between them and grinned. 'Who said anything about lectures? The craic, Mick, the craic. And the women.' He laughed, reminiscing. 'I must have fucked my brains out.'

'That's all you ever think about.'

'Not true, Mick, not true. You're forgetting the drink. But seriously now, what else is there for the likes of us?'

His heart sank. Where had he heard that before? 'The likes of us?'

'Yes, boy, the likes of us. Don't pretend now. My dad's a labourer for the county council. And yours is what – a carpenter? The dice is loaded against us, boy. We just don't stand a chance.'

'But you got a place in university.'

Donie laughed. 'That was the easy bit. But there are no second chances when you're on a grant.' He drew his finger across his throat. 'Fail your exams and you're out.'

'I never knew that.'

'There's a lot you don't know, boy.' He drained the last of his Coke and threw the empty can down beside him on the pavement. 'Like I was saying, if my old man had money I could have repeated the year.'

'Maybe I don't know a lot.' Mick was nettled. 'But I know one thing – '

'And what's that, now?' Amusement lurked in Donie's black eyes.

He felt his face redden. If it was me I wouldn't have blown my chance, he thought. But there was no point in taking it out on Donie. It wasn't his fault, after all. 'It doesn't matter,' he muttered. 'Forget it.'

'Would you ever get sense, Mick.' He put his hand on Mick's arm, looked earnestly into his face. 'We're better off working. I wouldn't care if I never opened a book again.'

'But – '

'But nothing.' Donie's eyes travelled pityingly over the groups of chattering schoolgirls streaming across the nearby car park. 'Look at them. They think they're in heaven if they've made the points for college. But their troubles are just starting. All that hassle over studying and trying to scrape through the exams. For what? To end up, if they're lucky, with some job that gives ulcers or heart attacks. And look at us. Not a bother on us. We've avoided the rat race; the job's easy. We've money in our pockets and – '

'When you put it like that –' Mick couldn't help laughing, in spite of his misgivings.

'You'd better believe it, boy. And don't forget, there's a world out there full of beautiful women just waiting to be –'

He was right about one thing. The job *was* easy. As he had told Aunt Lizzie, there was nothing to it. Piece of cake.

Prepare the surface. Slap on primer, then the undercoat, then gloss, or emulsion, depending on whether it was walls or woodwork. His hands had toughened up, his shoulders had filled out, were stronger. His neck no longer ached all the time. His nostrils had become accustomed to the smell. Nothing to it, Auntie. But basically it was a boring job, slapping paint on walls. Ceilings were trickier but he was no Michelangelo decorating the Sistine Chapel. Sometimes when he was up on a scaffolding he pretended he was, picturing himself lying on his back, the ceiling a few inches from his nose, while cherubs and seraphim sprang into life above his moving brush. But that soon palled. Who was he trying to fool? Nobody would ever come and gaze in awe at his work. Who ever looked skywards in a shopping centre, for God's sake? Or at the classroom ceiling? And even if they did, what would they see? Nothing, that's what. Da would have said that there was the satisfaction of a job well done. But what did Da know about anything?

'Coming down for a pint, Mick?

He looked uncomfortable. 'Some other time. I've made plans.'

Da showed his disappointment. 'They were saying in

Foley's they never see you any more.'

'The crowd in Foley's is a bit – ' His mind sorted and discarded, then picked the word that seemed least offensive. ' – settled.' Wished he had chosen better when he saw his father's mouth tighten.

'Foley's is good enough for young Henno here.'

Mick looked at Henno, who sat at the table working his way through Ma's home-made fruitcake. Hair already starting to thin, his shirt creasing into folds over a spreading waistline.

'Come on, Da. He might look young to you – ' Henno was a married man, for God's sake, with a child on the way!

His father bridled. 'That's no way to talk to your – I don't know what things are coming to, Nan.'

Mick sighed to himself. He couldn't put a foot right these days.

'Leave him alone, Maurice.' Ma laid down the evening paper, glanced up over her reading glasses. 'You won't put an old head on young shoulders.' Her eyes softened as they encountered Mick's half-defiant face. 'What's keeping *you*? If you're going into town you'd better get a move on.'

'That place you're going to is full of *culchies*.' Henno finished the last slice of cake on the plate, licked a crumb off his finger. Glanced meaningly at his uncle. 'A mixed bunch, know what I mean?'

'The music is good on Friday nights.' When he saw their blank faces, Mick gave a shrug of defeat. Why did he have to explain himself to them?

'The *music*?' Henno guffawed. 'You have your head screwed on, all right.' He winked broadly. 'All those young ones with their own flats. No Daddies with shotguns to watch out for, heh, heh, heh!'

'Watch your language!' Ma was scandalised. 'The very idea! As if Mick would – !'

'That table over there, next to the pillar. The two girls.'

He saw a pair of tawny eyes studying him. 'The redhead?'

'Not that table. Jesus, where's your taste? She's okay. But the friend! No, a bit further to the left.'

'Blonde girl with the big – ?'

'They are, aren't they?' Donie said appreciatively. 'No, wait!' His face fell in disappointment as two men joined the girls he was watching. 'That's torn the arse out of it. Pity.'

'That one with the red hair seems to know me.'

'Forget it! The other one's a dog.'

'She might have a nice personality.'

'You have her, then.'

'No,' Mick said. He knew if he moved his head he would catch her looking at him. Where did I – ? Tawny eyes, snub nose, cheeky grin. I'm sure I've – but where? He risked a quick glance but she turned away quickly to talk to her friend, laughing, absorbed in the conversation, pretending to be unaware of his scrutiny.

'You're wasting your time, boy.'

'No, I'm not. The redhead's definitely interested.'

'The night's young yet, Mick. We can do better.'

'Come on, Donie. Humour me.'

'Have it your own way.' His friend's shrug eloquently abdicated all responsibility. 'But I'm telling you, they're a waste of time.'

'What makes you so sure?'

'God bless your eyesight, Mick. Do you not know a couple of virgins when you see them?'

'I'll have a glass of orange.'

'Mine's a diet Coke.'

'Could be worse, I suppose. Could be vodkas.' As Donie got up from the table he glanced at Mick. 'Let's be thankful for small mercies.'

Embarrassed, Mick said, 'Don't mind him, he's always joking.'

The friend, a dumpy girl called Freda, eyed Donie's departing back with disapproval. 'He has a funny way of talking.'

He felt put on the defensive. 'What's that supposed to mean?'

'He's not from Dublin, is he?' She made it sound like an accusation.

'No. Does it make any difference?'

'I was only *saying* – Anyone can make a remark.' She retired into an offended silence.

'It's just her way.' The red-haired girl grinned at Mick. 'She's all heart, really.'

'Aren't we all?' He found himself warming to her smile. 'Fran? What's that short for?'

'Frances, but no one ever – '

'Have we met before?'

Her eyes sparkled suddenly. 'Thought you'd never ask. I used to work in the Kabin.'

For a moment he was puzzled. 'That place near us? Sells cards.'

'*And* toys.' She grinned at him. 'Now do you remember?'

He shook his head. 'God knows when I was in there last.'

'Must be about a year and a half ago. The summer before last. I used to work there after school. Let's see, what's this you bought – ?'

She pretended to consider, head cocked to one side like a cheeky robin. He had a feeling she knew already. 'A red fire engine. Did he like it, your nephew?'

He felt flattered that she had remembered. 'I haven't got a nephew. I'm an only child.'

She grimaced. 'Wish I was, sometimes. No, no, I don't mean that. Only joking. Did he like it, the little boy?'

'I – suppose so. Yes, I'm sure he did.'

She looked puzzled. 'You're a funny one, do you know that?'

'I – it's a long story.'

'Tell me about it.' Her voice was eager.

He shrugged. 'It's history. Are you still working there?'

'No – the hot-bread shop across the street.'

'You didn't move far. But then, I suppose it's handy. You can walk to work.'

She grinned. 'It'd be a long walk.'

'You mean you don't live in the neighbourhood?' He was surprised to feel a pang of disappointment.

'No, I get the bus in every morning.' She threw him a quick glance. 'Does it make any difference?'

'Why should it?' It wasn't as if he was interested in her, or anything.

She chuckled loudly. 'Do you think if we were neighbours we wouldn't have got to know each other before this?'

'If it was up to you I suppose we would.'

She wrinkled her nose at him. The freckles stood out against her skin like little golden dots. There was a look of challenge in her eyes. 'Nothing wrong with being friendly, is there?'

He sidestepped the question. 'I've never been friends with a girl.'

'Why not?'

He eyed her frankly. A bit small for his taste. He liked his women taller. But her figure was okay. And she had nice eyes. That hair probably meant she had a quick temper. 'I don't know. I just don't think of them in that way.'

'Oh, you're that sort, are you?' Again her eyes challenged him. 'Just after the one thing?'

'No!' He felt his face grow hot. 'No, of course not.'

'Waste of a night,' Donie hissed. 'They live somewhere out in the wilds.'

'So?'

'Great birthday you're having, that's all.'

'Fat lot you care about my birthday.'

Fran looked interested. Like a terrier pricking up its ears, he thought. 'When is it?'

'Sunday,' he said reluctantly. 'The twentieth.'

'How old will you be?'

He didn't bother to lie. 'Nineteen.'

'Is that all?' She gave a triumphant laugh, counted on her fingers. 'I'm five months older than you.'

He wished he *had* lied. God! She looked such a kid. 'That's nice for you.'

'Don't be like that. Come on, I'll buy you a drink.'

'You don't have to.'

'Yes I do. Do you hear that, Freda? It's Mick's birthday.'

'Happy birthday,' Freda said unenthusiastically. It was obvious she was not enjoying her night. Beside her, Donie raised his eyes to heaven and gave a resigned shrug.

'What did I tell you?' Huddled in his overcoat, he stared in disgust after the departing taxi. 'But you wouldn't listen, would you?'

'Sorry Donie. Looks like you're going to have to sleep in your own bed tonight. Anyway, I thought you said she wasn't your sort.'

'You better believe it, boy.' Donie shook his head and laughed. 'Ah well, you win some, you lose some.'

'Yeh.' He rubbed his hands together before shoving them into his coat pockets. 'You could say that.'

'Mick?' Suspiciously. 'Was there some talk of phone numbers back there?'

He was evasive. 'There might.'

'You're not going to, are you? I'd think long and hard before I – '

'Bit late for that.' Mick gave a sheepish smile. 'I'm going to the cinema with her on Sunday.'

'Ah, Jesus, no!' Donie was aghast. 'What would you want to do that for?'

'Look, there's no big deal about it – we're only going to the pictures.'

He gave a wolfish grin. 'Is that right, Mick?'

'That's right, Donie. There's nothing more to it than that.'

'God bless your innocence, Mick.' The black eyes mocked

him. 'There's no doubt about it but you've an awful lot to learn.'

'Did you enjoy the film?'

'It was sad,' Fran said. 'I prefer ones with a happy ending.'

'Girls usually do.'

She gave him a mock-innocent look over the edge of her teacup. 'I suppose you're an expert?'

'On girls or films?'

She grinned at him. '*You* tell *me*.'

You're on shaky ground here, he told himself as he returned the grin. 'Maybe I'll pass on this one. Would you like another biscuit?'

'No thanks. You know what they say: "A moment on the lips, a lifetime on the hips".'

He laughed in surprise. 'I never heard that. But you don't have to worry, do you?' He leaned back in his seat and appraised her openly. 'You've a lovely figure.'

And skin the colour of thick cream, a powdering of pale gold freckles across the bridge of her nose.

'Oh, go on!' The cream was suffused with pink. 'You're just saying that.'

'No, honestly, I mean it.' Then, without thinking, he heard himself say: 'Did anyone ever tell you your hair is the exact colour of a brand-new penny?' He rooted through the change in his pocket and found a bright coin. 'Look!'

She pulled at a few tendrils, tried squinting at them. 'I can't. It's too short.'

'You should wear it longer. It would suit you all around your face in curls like the girl in the film. You know the one I mean, the singer.'

'But she was beautiful.' Fran was half-laughing, half-incredulous.

'You could be too.' He stopped himself, aghast. 'Look, I didn't mean it like that.' In his embarrassment he stumbled over the words. 'What I meant was – '

To his relief she didn't take offence. 'It's okay, I know what you meant.' She stared at him thoughtfully. 'Maybe I *should* grow my hair.'

'You don't mind me saying it?' He exhaled in relief. 'I thought you'd fly off the handle.'

She grinned. 'I don't know why I haven't. But don't push your luck. Next time I mightn't be so – '

He found himself warming to her cheeky grin. He wanted to reach across the table and touch her hand. Instead he glanced over at the counter, where a bored-looking woman stood behind a steaming tea-urn. 'Like another cup?'

'I can't. My bus. But, before we go – ' She picked up her shoulder bag and began rummaging in it. As he watched, mystified, out came a large blue envelope which she slid towards him across the Formica table top. 'Happy birthday!'

Embarrassment gripped him. 'You needn't have.'

Her face coloured up again. 'It's just a card.'

'Okay, thanks.' He made to shove it into his pocket.

She looked disappointed. 'Aren't you going to – ?'

'If you want me to.' He opened it awkwardly, tearing the corner of the envelope. A pig in a paper hat with a glass of champagne clutched in its trotter grinned up at him. Another pig teetered on the edge of a bar stool. *Live It Up On Your Birthday.*

She had neat handwriting. *Hope you have a great time, lots of love, Fran.*

'Is it all right? It's hard to choose when you don't really know someone.' She looked at him doubtfully. 'Maybe I shouldn't have?'

'No, no. It was really nice of you.'

She glanced down at the shiny-topped table with its cheap crockery, ketchup bottle, stainless-steel sugar bowl and milk jug and then around the café, where other customers sat at identical-looking tables and a boy with vermilion streaks in his cropped hair bent over the jukebox in the corner. Mick's gaze followed hers. Then back to the champagne bubbles and the streamers on the card. The incongruity of it struck them both at the same time.

She gave a wry grin. 'You'd hardly call this living it up, would you?'

'No, but – '

There was the familiar knot of excitement at the base of his stomach as he looked into her eyes. Tawny eyes, lion-coloured, with gold flecks. But what he saw there made him hesitate. It was as if, for one split second, he glimpsed her soul. He turned away in a kind of panic, glanced down at the neat handwriting, read again the artless message. It touched him, made him feel protective. He looked up again, met her gaze and, this time, didn't look away. 'It's okay, Fran. I *am* having a great time.'

Her face was eager, doubtful. 'Do you really mean that?'

He took her hand. It felt warm and firm as it fitted comfortably into his larger one. 'Yes, Fran, I really mean it.'

To his surprise he realised that he did.

The bread shop was only five minutes' walk from his house. On Saturday mornings he would see her behind the display cases, her bright hair hidden under a white cap.

'French bread? Buns?' Ma was puzzled the first time he brought stuff home. 'What's come over you, Mick?'

It was the only way he could get into the shop to talk to her. The woman in charge didn't encourage followers.

'Followers!' Sitting with her in a nearby park during her lunch break, Mick didn't know whether to be amused or indignant. 'You'd think we were some kind of *animals!'*

'Maybe she's got something there.' Fran gave him a meaning look as she bit into the last of her burger.

He felt his face redden. 'Come on, Fran, you think if a man puts his arm around you he wants to rape you.'

Her lips tightened. She discarded the greasy wrappings into a nearby litter basket and wiped her fingers on a piece of tissue with an air of deliberation. 'Last night went a bit further than wanting to put your arm around me,' she said sternly.

He was hurt by her tone. 'Don't be like that.' He took her hand, held it between his. For a moment it looked as if she was going to pull away but she changed her mind and left it there, staring reluctantly back at him, her breath puffing out in the icy air. The tiny park was deserted except for themselves and a white-haired old man in a shabby overcoat slouched on the bench opposite, his head lolling on his chest.

'Look,' he said patiently, 'it's only natural.'

She didn't answer, tried to glance away. But he held her gaze.

'This is the eighties, Fran.'

'I don't care if it's the twentieth-first century.' There were sparks in her eyes. 'Look, Mick, we've only known each other a couple of weeks.'

'You mean,' he asked eagerly, 'if we knew each other a bit longer, you'd – ?'

She bit her lip. 'I didn't say that.'

'But it's what you meant?'

'No.' Her gaze faltered. She looked up at the leaden sky. 'I think it's going to rain, or snow, or something.'

'Don't change the subject.'

'I'm not.' She pulled her hand free so abruptly it took him by surprise. 'I've got to get back. That old biddy will take it out of my wages if I'm late.' She stood up, dusted the crumbs off her anorak. 'Will I see you tonight?'

'What?' He got up disconsolately. 'Yes, I suppose so.'

It was her turn to look hurt. 'Don't be like that.'

'What way do you expect me to – ? Oh, Fran!' He pulled her towards him suddenly, buried his face in her hair. 'I'm sorry. You're right. I *am* a bit of an animal.'

'I didn't mean it, Mick.' Her voice was muffled against his heavy jacket. The old man on the bench opposite emitted a loud snore, his greasy white locks falling over his face. The sound took them both by surprise; they drew apart hastily, then laughed, glancing at him with pity and disgust.

'Oh God!' Fran jumped as an empty sherry bottle rolled away from her foot. The old man slept on, oblivious.

At the gate she slipped her arm through Mick's and said almost pleadingly, 'Look, I've seen what happened to my sister. He's a grand little kid but she has no life.'

'It doesn't have to be like that.' He was stung. 'I wouldn't – I'd make sure – '

'Those things don't always work.' She might look young for her age but her chin had a stubborn line to it. To clinch the argument she said, 'Anyway, we both live at home. Where would we – ?'

'Donie has a flat. I know he'd – you could say you were spending the night with a friend.'

'Are you joking? Freda lives down the road from me. My mother would never buy that. After what happened to Sandra she watches me like a hawk. And my Da would kill me.' She grinned suddenly. 'As for what he'd do to *you!*'

He grinned back. 'Don't worry. I'd run so fast he'd never catch up with me.'

'Meeting the folks? Bit soon, isn't it?' Donie's words echoed through the empty classroom. Paint-spattered sheets covered the desks and the varnished floorboards. A crayoned red Santa beamed at them from the blackboard. Artificial snow glittered on the glass of the high, uncurtained windows.

Mick put down his brush and eased the tension from his shoulders. 'It isn't what you think.' His voice was stiff as he turned to face his friend. 'It's a party. No need to look like that. There'll be other people there.'

'Of course.' Donie's face was suave. His black eyes looked solemnly at Mick. 'A party. It's the season for it, after all. A great way of using up the cake and the Christmas pudding.' The eyes gleamed suddenly. 'A party? Why didn't you tell me? I'll bring a bottle.'

'It isn't that kind of party.'

'What? No booze?' Donie looked sardonic. 'Now that sounds great craic!'

'No, no, what I meant was: it will just be family, a few

neighbours. Married couples mostly, Fran says. Except for her and her sister.'

'Doesn't sound like my scene.' His eyes narrowed. 'What's the sister like?'

'You wouldn't be interested. She's – well – she's got a kid, a little boy.'

'Living with someone, is she?'

'Actually, no. Fran doesn't say much but I gather the fella did a runner after the child was born. Bit of a chancer, apparently. She lives at home with the parents.'

'I see.' Donie slapped a large brush laden with emulsion against the wall in front of him and watched thoughtfully as pale green rivulets ran down its surface. 'Better watch out for her old man's shotgun, Mick.'

'What's that supposed to mean?' He found he was getting irritated by the other's air of omniscience.

'Figure it out for yourself.' Donie began working the brush into the paint with slow, deliberate strokes. 'Boyfriends probably aren't too popular in that house.'

'See what you mean. But what's it got to do with me? It wasn't my fault.'

'People can be funny sometimes. When I came to Dublin first I went out with a girl for six months. Her mother always looked at me like a bad smell had just walked in the door. The father never addressed a word to me, just grunted. She told me they called me "that mad Kerryman" behind my back.'

Mick forgot his irritation. 'That was rough. What happened to her?'

Donie shrugged. 'Life's too short to put up with that kind of shit.'

'You gave her the push?'

'Let's say it was mutual.' Another shrug. 'She was no loss.'

'I'm sorry, Donie.'

'Yerra, that's life, boy. You wouldn't need to take it too seriously.'

He thought for a moment. 'But Fran's not like that.'

The other man made no reply, working with an air of concentration, humming tunelessly to himself as the colour spread over the surface. Mick watched him uneasily, his own brush idle in his hand.

'Did you hear what I said?'

Footfalls echoed in the corridor outside. Someone whistling. Then a voice called through the open doorway, 'Brewin' up, lads.'

'Okay.' Mick didn't turn his head, still watching Donie's back and the sweeping movements of the brush. 'Donie – ?'

The brush broke its rhythm, then stopped. Donie turned around, a wide grin on his face. 'Did you ever see anything like it, Mick?'

'Like what?'

He raised his eyebrows and pointed at the wall. 'Jesus, Mick!' He gave a derisive cackle. 'Aren't you glad you're not still at school? Imagine having to sit here day after day looking at walls the colour of dried snot.'

He laughed reluctantly. 'Very funny. Did you hear what I said?'

'You never give up, do you? Yes, boy, I heard.'

He eyed Donie steadily. 'Fran's not like that.'

The other man shrugged. 'I've only your word for it, Mick, *but* – I believe you.'

'What's the problem, then?'

He put down his brush and wiped his hands on a piece of rag. 'No problem. No problem at all. Look, are we going for the tea?'

Mick didn't move. '*Donie?*'

'Okay,' Donie said. He looked earnestly at him. 'I may be all wrong but – I just wouldn't want you to be disappointed. All I'm saying is – don't expect the red carpet.'

'You've nothing to worry about,' she said. In the light cast by an overhead street lamp he saw a slight frown between her eyes. 'They won't eat you.'

Earlier, when the bus had left behind familiar streets and had begun rattling through housing estates, past dimly lit anonymous semi-detached houses and shadowy gardens, he had felt he was being borne inexorably into the unknown. Now, as they reached the front gate of her house, the feeling intensified. 'I nearly didn't come,' he confessed.

She paused in the gateway. Behind her, lights glittered and danced in a downstairs window. A garland of berried holly decorated the front door. A small, cold hand touched his. 'I had a *feeling* – what made you change your mind?'

He took the hand, pressed it against his face. Kissed the palm gently, smiled down at her. 'I didn't want to let you down.'

Her eyes gleamed in the darkness. 'You'd never do that, Mick.'

'Bit skinny, isn't he?' Her mother had a laugh that reminded him of water running too quickly out of a bath. It cut across the noise in the crowded front room right through to the archway to the back room, where he could see people looking up from their conversation and staring at him expectantly. 'I like my men with more meat on them.' Maisie Hennessy was a sharp-featured blonde with plucked eyebrows and a glittery pants suit twenty years too young for her. She held Mick's arm in an embarrassingly tight grip as she thrust him forward into the room. 'But – give him time.'

'Big fella, isn't he?' another woman said admiringly. She looked even older than Maisie, with a gash of red lipstick pasted onto a network of wrinkles. He felt his own face flame with embarrassment amid the barrage of guffaws, introductions and handshakes that followed.

'You don't have to remember everyone's name,' Fran hissed.

Some hope of that! As long as he remembered which fat, balding man was her father and which her Uncle Charlie. Or was it Uncle Jim? No, Jim was her father. You could see the resemblance to Fran. Only it looked different on her. She was pretty. He looked like that carved figure of the laughing Buddha the Joyces had on their sitting-room mantelpiece. Except for the clothes, of course. But if the Buddha wore a cardigan and drank pints, he'd be the –

'What are you laughing at, Mick?'

'Nothing, Fran. Just – '

'I told you it'd be okay, didn't I?'

Then there were the two brothers. Denis was another one who looked like Fran. No, that was Tony. He'd be the image of the Da in another twenty years or so. Denis, the younger fella, was the dead spit of Maisie, his mother. The same loud, confident manner. Remind you of Henno, only sharper and better dressed. Well, you couldn't expect to like everyone belonging to Fran, could you? Which was just as well because he hadn't known what to make of Sandra at all.

'That your sister?' he couldn't keep the incredulity out of his voice. 'The one with the – ?'

'It's okay, you can say it.' Fran's smile was resigned as she looked around the packed sitting room. 'Everyone here knows about Jason.'

'And that's *her*, the girl in the leather skirt and the spiky hairdo?'

'What's wrong with her?' Fran asked tensely.

'Well – nothing.' Nothing wrong with her figure, anyway. Even Donie would have been impressed. Legs that seemed to go on forever under that short, little skirt. Pointed breasts in a skinny-rib sweater; you could see the nipples, for God's sake. Eyes like –

'*Mick?*' Fran's face was beginning to flush indignantly.

'Wipe off that make-up and she'd be a – ' Even with the garish make-up she was a stunner. 'What I mean is – ' He saw Fran's face grow pinker. ' – she's not what I expected, that's all,' he said lamely.

'And just what were you – ?'

'Is this a private fight or can anyone join in?' A sharp, spicy scent engulfed Mick and he encountered a darker version of Fran's eyes, set among spidery black eyelashes. Eyes that examined him with cynical amusement. 'Not bad. Better than the last fella, anyway.'

He felt his face grow hot and smiled back, saying nothing. Beside him, Fran scowled. She said reluctantly, 'Mick, this is Sandra, my *older* sister.'

'Didn't know you had a younger one.' She had a way of standing disturbingly close. He took a step backwards but the wall was behind him. Fingertips, nails the colour of dried blood, brushed lightly against his hand, sending tremors up and down his spine. She pursed her red lips provocatively. 'Definitely better than the last fella.'

He stared back at her, trying not to show his embarrassment.

'Don't mind her, Mick.' Fran's voice came sharply from the other side of him. 'Leave him alone, you!' she said angrily to her sister.

'Fuck off!' Sandra turned away and reached for her cigarettes. As she bent to rummage in her handbag for matches he saw that the ends of her short, black hair were dyed bright green.

'What's the matter, Mick? Are you not enjoying it?'

'Of course I am. It's a great party.' He had to shout to make himself heard above the din. 'It's just – look – why don't we go out into the hall for a bit?'

Fran looked dubious. 'People might notice.'

'You must be joking. Look – only to talk, Fran.'

'Okay. Just for a while.'

It was dark in the hallway. And cooler. The noise of the party sounded like the roar of a huge furnace through the sitting-room wall.

'I see what you mean.' Fran was laughing as he drew her down beside him to sit on the bottom stair. 'Did you ever hear anything like it?'

'It's not just the noise.'

Her hand gently touched his face in the darkness. 'What's wrong, Mick? You looked so sad in there.'

He said nothing for a moment.

'You wouldn't understand.'

'Maybe I would. Try me.'

He sighed. 'It'll probably sound stupid.'

He put his arm around her shoulders, felt her nearness to him, the warmth of her body. 'It's – ' he hesitated. 'It's your family.'

He sensed her stiffen. 'What's wrong with them?'

'Nothing. It's just – they look so like each other.'

'No they don't.' She laughed suddenly. 'Well, maybe they do, just a little bit. But what's wrong with that?'

'I told you. Nothing. It's just me.'

It had hit him suddenly when he had looked around the room at her family. She could look at any one of them and say, 'That's where I come from. I'm a part of these people and they're a part of me.' Unlike Mick, Fran knew who she was. And then the sadness had hit him.

Her voice was puzzled. 'I don't understand, Mick.'

'I told you you wouldn't. Look, it's no big deal.' His arm tightened around her shoulders. He pulled her almost roughly to him and nuzzled her face. 'Mm, you smell nice. Let's not go back in. Let's stay here for a while.'

He could hear her heart beating, her breathing grow a little faster. His mouth found hers, his fingers gently probed her breast, felt the nipple grow firm under the thin stuff of her blouse. Felt himself becoming aroused. 'Fran – '

Abruptly she pushed him away. 'We'd better be getting back. Someone might – '

'Ah, Fran!'

'Look, Mick,' her voice was unexpectedly firm, 'you've got the wrong girl. I'm not my sister, no matter what *you* might think.'

'When are we going to meet the girlfriend? Come on now! Don't be doing the innocent. You can't fool your Aunt Lizzie.'

'I don't know what you're talking about,' he muttered, darting a wicked glance at Ma behind Lizzie's back.

'That's not what I heard.' Lizzie gave a cackle of laughter. 'You know what they say, "In the spring a young man's fancy lightly turns to thoughts of love." They don't be long growing up, do they, Nan?'

'What did you tell her?' he demanded fiercely of his mother after Lizzie had gone.

'I told her nothing, Mick. How could I? Considering you never tell me anything any more.'

He felt a pang of guilt. 'There's nothing much to tell.'

'You were *seen,*' Ma said. 'And to think I had to hear it from Lizzie.'

'I'm sorry, Ma. I was going to tell you.'

'So it's true?'

'Yes, there is a girl,' he admitted. 'Her name's Fran. You'd like her.'

Ma's face gave nothing away. 'When are we going to meet her?'

'One of these days,' he said airily. 'There's no rush.'

'I can't believe I'll be twenty next month,' Fran said one bright, blowy Sunday in May, as they were walking through the Botanical Gardens. 'Can you believe it? *Twenty?* I won't be a teenager any more.'

'Next stop the old folk's home.'

'Easy for you to laugh. You'll have another six months of it.'

'What's so great about being a teenager? I can't wait to be twenty.'

'I don't know; a part of me wants to stay one a bit longer. It's as if I won't be young any – '

'But Fran, we've the whole of our lives ahead of us.'

' – and then another part of me feels as if life is rushing by and I've nothing to show for it.'

He stopped walking and stared at her. 'How do you mean – nothing to show for it?'

'Well, I don't know.' Under his scrutiny her face went pink. As if seeking inspiration she glanced quickly at a bed of perfectly matched crimson tulips swaying in the wind. 'Well, look at Sandra, she had Jason when she was nineteen.'

'But – ' he couldn't hide his bewilderment. 'Sandra? Don't tell me you'd want – ? After all you've been saying – ?'

'No, no,' she said quickly. 'Not that. I wouldn't want a kid. Not without being married. Look, that isn't what I meant at all.'

'What, then?'

'Oh, nothing, Mick.' She grinned at him. 'Forget I said it, will you. I don't know what gets into me sometimes.'

'Women! Who could understand them?' He stopped and glanced around him. The gardens were thronged with people out for the afternoon. There wasn't a seat to be had among the wrought-iron benches placed at intervals along the edge of the pathway. He checked his watch and said, as if the idea had just occurred to him, 'This place is useless. Why don't we go back to my house, have a cup of tea?'

Surprise, followed by doubt, chased across Fran's face. 'But what about your folks?'

'That's just it. They won't be there. They've gone to my uncle's for tea. Mostly he and Auntie Carmel come to us on a Sunday. But today Ma and Da are visiting them. We'll have the place to ourselves.'

'I don't know, Mick.' She was still doubtful. 'Maybe we'd better not.'

'Ah, come on, Fran. I'll show you my books. We'll play a few tapes. It'll be great.'

She smiled suddenly. 'Well okay. Why not? But only for a little while. I won't stay long.'

The house lay very still as he let himself in the front door. 'Anyone home?' he called, although he knew he would have had a heart attack if someone had answered. The evening sun illuminated the living room, the fire set in the grate, Da's slippers beside his armchair, the Sunday papers folded neatly on the table. It glanced off the photographs on the china cabinet, Mick's First Communion and Confirmation pictures, his parents' wedding, the papal blessing, framed and hanging on the wall overhead. Fran squinted at Ma, tiny and dark in her ballet-length dress, Da, solid-looking even then, in a double-breasted suit.

'You don't look a bit like either of them.'

'You'd hardly expect me to, would you?'

'Sorry, I forgot. It's silly but I keep forgetting you're adopted.'

'I never do,' Mick said.

'Look.' He kept his tone casual. 'While we're waiting for the kettle to boil why don't I show you my room?'

She gave him a long, considering look. He felt his face flushing up. Dodging her gaze, he went out into the kitchen and filled the kettle at the sink. As he lit the gas he looked up to see her standing in the doorway examining the room with interest.

'It's so tidy.' She looked around her in awe. 'Not a thing out of place.' Ran her hand over a worktop. 'You could eat your dinner off this.' She gave a quick sigh. 'You should see our kitchen.'

'I have. And it's bigger than this.' He turned away to open the door of the refrigerator. 'Everything in your house is.'

'You wouldn't think that if there were six of you. Of course it's easier now that my brothers moved out.'

'Are they both married?'

'Yes. Tony has two kids. Denis got married last year.'

'Bit young, isn't he?'

'Not really. He's twenty three. Sandra's a year older. Course she should have been married first – '

He sighed inwardly. Not Sandra again. Change the subject fast. He searched the fridge for inspiration. Saw a plate of cold ham surrounded by lettuce and wedges of tomato. Good old Ma! 'There's enough for two here, Fran.'

'I think you're a bit of a Mammy's boy, Mick.' Her voice held a teasing note. She had come up behind him. He could smell the warm, clean scent of her.

'Want to bet?' He left the plate where it was, straightened up cautiously, felt the fridge door shut behind him as he turned to pull her into his arms. Brought his mouth down hard on hers.

'Go easy, Mick!' But she didn't push him away. Her arms went around him and she kissed him back.

The handle of the fridge was pressing into the small of his back. He could hear the kettle coming to the boil nearby. 'It's early yet,' he whispered. 'Why don't we – ? I could show you my books.'

A moment passed. They stood close together, saying

nothing, their bodies touching. Another moment. Then, 'Okay, Mick. But just for a little while.' She loosened her hold, smiled up at him. 'Better lower that gas.'

His heart soared. He smiled joyously back at her. 'I'll turn it off altogether.'

'I like it,' Fran said. 'It's small but really neat. And you've places for everything.'

Now that she was actually there, he felt awkward, embarrassed almost. 'My Da's a carpenter. He did the shelves and presses himself. And the desk.'

'You're lucky.' She sighed enviously. 'Daddy's no good with his hands. Mammy always says all he's good for is delivering sacks of coal.'

He pictured Jim Hennessy's heavy, stooped frame, his big hands wrapped around a pint glass. 'Is that what he – ?'

'Yes. And my mother works in the foodmarket down the road from us.' She inspected the books on the shelf above the desk. 'Have you read all these?'

'There's not that many.' He felt an impatience mounting inside him, a sense of urgency. 'We can look at the books later.'

'Poetry?' Fran said. 'And what's this? *The Quest of The* – ?'

'That's part of a trilogy.' He took the book from her and put it back in its place on the shelf. 'It's a fantasy book. You wouldn't have – '

'I *have* heard of fantasy.' She sounded aggrieved. 'I'm not stupid, you know.'

'I never said you were. Look – ' His impatience couldn't be contained. He sat down on the bed, drew her down beside him. 'Fran – '

'The kettle – '

He placed a finger against her lips. 'I turned it off, remember.'

She gave a reluctant laugh, her eyes sliding away from his.

'So you did.'

The evening sun streaming through the window had turned her skin golden. Her eyes, a darker gold, met his uncertainly at first, then grew more confident. The curve of her shoulder had a silken sheen to it, warm and smooth when he pressed his lips against it. Her breasts were round and firm, the nipples springing to life under his insistent fingers. He felt his own body respond so urgently he was afraid he wouldn't be able to control it.

'God, Fran, you're beautiful! I love you so much! Don't be afraid, I won't hurt you.'

'No, Mick!' She began pushing away his probing fingers, pressing her knees together, fending him off as she scrambled up against the pillows, trying to shield her naked body with her hands, her eyes dark pools of fright. Anger sharpened her voice.

'I said *no*, Mick!'

'But – ' He heard her words but his body didn't want listen. His heart and his loins were pounding, his breath coming in gasps, damp patches of sweat between his shoulder blades. Disappointment fought with disbelief. 'You don't mean it, you can't.' He reached out frantically but she evaded him, backing away until the wall behind the bedhead prevented her from going any further. This time he managed to catch her arms. 'Fran, please!'

'*You're hurting me!*'

The cry brought him to his senses. Suddenly aware that his fingers were digging into the soft flesh of her upper arms he released his grip and stared in horror at the marks his hands had left, at her tear-stained face.

'Fran, I'm sorry.' He was overwhelmed by remorse. 'I'm really, really sorry.'

The clock on the mantelpiece struck six. Was that all it was? It seemed like a lifetime ago that they had left to go upstairs. The kettle would be boiled dry by now. When he went out to the kitchen to check he found the gas ring cold. Of course, I forgot, he thought. As he went back into the living room he heard the strains of the Angelus sounding from the parish church a few streets away.

'They're always late.' He tried to sound jocose. 'Or is that clock fast?'

She didn't answer, sitting gingerly on the edge of a chair as if about to leave at any minute, her lips moving in prayer. Abashed, he waited.

As the bells died down he motioned in the direction of the sound and asked diffidently, 'Is that why you wouldn't?'

'Maybe,' she said coldly.

He was bewildered. 'In that case why did you let me go so far?'

She stared at him without answering.

A thought struck him. 'According to the priests everything we did was wrong. So why stop then?'

She said reluctantly, 'It's not just because of religion.'

'What then?' Comprehension dawned on him. '*I* know. It's

because of Sandra, isn't it? Because of what happened to your sister?' He felt exasperated suddenly. 'But we've been through all this before. There's no way I'd ever get you pregnant.' He looked at her closely. 'You do believe me, don't you?'

She hesitated. 'Yes, I suppose so.'

'So if it isn't that?'

Fran made to get to her feet. 'I think I'd better be getting back. I won't wait for the tea.'

A painful suspicion occurred to him and began to gnaw at his heart. He tried to ignore it but he knew he had to ask. 'You didn't want to, did you? Because you don't fancy me.'

She threw him a startled look. Sat down again abruptly. Gave an embarrassed laugh, her face turning pink. 'Don't be stupid.' Her voice sounded stern almost. 'Of course I fancy you.'

The pain around his heart eased, but his bafflement remained. 'But why, Fran? Why did you let me down like that?'

Her expression softened. 'Look, Mick, I wasn't leading you on. I really do like you. But – ' He saw the stubborn line of her chin. 'Well – it's a promise I made to myself.'

'What kind of a promise?'

She looked down at the table, fiddled with the edge of a newspaper, twisting a little curl of paper between her fingers. 'Do you really want to know?'

'Tell me!'

Fran's lips tightened. 'After Sandra's fella dumped her I swore to myself I'd never let any man use me.'

He was stung. '*Use* you? How can you say such a thing!'

Again that stubborn look on her face. She stared at him and said nothing.

'*Use* you?' He shook his head in disbelief. 'When you know

how I feel about you!'

Her expression didn't change. The clock on the mantel-piece ticked away the seconds in unison with the thumping of his heart. Suddenly he saw her eyes flash fire. But when she spoke her voice was soft.

'Do I, Mick? Do I *really?*'

His heart began to thump even faster. He sat down beside her and took her hand in his. He looked earnestly at her. 'Okay, Fran. Tell me what I can do to convince you?'

'Get married, Fran?' Mick was so stunned he let go of her hand. 'You mean *us?*'

'Who do you think I meant?' Her face went pink but she held his gaze steadily. 'You did say you were serious about me. Of course,' she gave a little shrug and half turned away, 'if you didn't mean it – '

'Oh, Fran. Of *course* I did.' He reached out and took possession of her hand again. 'But marriage, Fran? It's such a big decision.'

'Do you think I don't know that,' she said earnestly. 'But I love you, Mick. I want to be with you always.'

It took a moment for the words to sink in. 'Do you really mean that?'

He felt the pressure of her hand in his. 'Yes, Mick, I do.'

Despite the joy that began to rise up in him he felt a sudden doubt. 'But what about upstairs when you wouldn't – ?'

'I've told you, Mick.' Her voice was patient. 'It wasn't because I didn't want to. I just didn't feel right about it.'

'I wouldn't want you to do anything you didn't feel right about, Fran. You must believe that.' He hesitated, the pain of the recent rejection still raw. 'But you do *want* to, don't you? I mean – if we were married you would want to do it, wouldn't you?'

'If we were married?' Fran's smile put him in mind of the sun bursting through a rain cloud. 'Well of course I would.' She looked at him almost shyly. 'That is, if you still want me?'

'*Want* you?' He thought with awe of the first sight of her naked breasts and the way the sunlight had turned the triangle between her thighs to molten gold. Remembered the satin touch of her body against his. His voice grew suddenly husky. '*Want* you, Fran? I'm crazy about you. And if you want us to get married, then that's what we'll do.'

'Engaged?' Ma looked aghast. 'But you hardly know the girl.'

'Six months.' He hid his own doubts under a show of confidence. 'I wouldn't call that "hardly knowing her".'

'Well *I* would. Besides, we haven't even met her.'

'Well, we can soon fix that.' Mick said briskly. 'How about next Sunday?'

'Now don't you try steamrollering me, Mick Cleary,' Ma said sharply. 'Nothing's settled yet. You're too young to be thinking of marriage.'

'We're not getting married till September. I'll be nearly twenty by then.'

'September! But that's only four months away.' Her eyes narrowed. 'What's the hurry? Mick, have you been – ?' She looked at him with suspicion. 'Whose idea is it?'

He gave an embarrassed laugh. 'What kind of a question is that?'

A look of alarm crossed her face. 'Oh, God, Mick, you

haven't – ?' She turned beseechingly towards Da. 'Jesus, Mary and Joseph, Maurice, he hasn't gone and got this girl into – ?'

'No I haven't.' Mick was indignant. If she only knew. 'What do you take me for?'

Ma gave a sigh of relief. 'Well thank God for that!' A look of puzzlement crossed her face. 'But what's the hurry then?'

'We love each other. We want to be together.'

'Love!' Ma sighed. 'You haven't an idea.' A pleading note came into her voice. 'You're young, Mick. You've the whole of your life ahead of you. And you're bright; your teachers all said you were. You could do things with – '

Resentment rose up in him suddenly. 'If I was that bright why didn't you let me finish school? Why did you make me go to work in Hennigans?'

She opened her mouth, closed it again and looked at Da, who was puffing away at his pipe, pretending that it had nothing to do with him. After a quick glance at Ma, he said equably, 'That's all water under the bridge, Mick.'

'It might be for you.' He was amazed at the bitterness that welled up inside him.

His mother found her voice suddenly. 'This is all your fault.' She glared at his father. 'I wanted to give him his chance but you said, "No, he'll only look down on us. A trade was good enough for me and my father."' Her face twisted in distress. 'If you'd listened to me none of this would have happened.'

'Hold hard, Nan. No need to be going on at me like that.' His father's tone was reasonable although his face had reddened slightly. 'The boy has a trade. He's *earning*. Mightn't be much. But it'll get better. If I'd let him go to college like he wanted, if he was a student without tuppence to his name and started talking about marriage, where would we be then?' He wiped the stem of his pipe on the sleeve of his cardigan and pointed it at her. 'Answer me that?'

Ma looked nonplussed for a moment. Then she said eagerly, 'If Mick had gone to college, this never would have – '

'We don't know that, do we?' Da's logic seemed unassailable. 'Anyway, maybe it's not such a bad thing.'

'Maurice!' Mick was surprised at the anguish in Ma's voice. 'He's only nineteen.'

'Maybe it's about time he settled down.' His face brightened as he warmed to the idea. 'Might knock a bit of sense into him.'

'What do you mean *sense?* Mick was never wild.'

'Maybe not wild,' Da conceded, 'but he was full of airy-fairy nonsense. All that poetry and stuff.' He looked at Mick. 'Hennessy, did you say? Is she from around here?'

Strange to have his father on his side for once. 'She lives out near the airport.'

'A northsider, anyway.' A thought struck him. 'She is from *Dublin*? Not a culchie?

Mick sighed to himself. 'No, Da, she's not a culchie.'

'Well, thanks be to God for that.' He slapped his lips around the stem of his pipe and sucked contentedly. 'Come on down to Foley's with me, son, and I'll buy you a pint. This calls for a celebration.'

Da wasn't the only one to feel that way. Fran's father couldn't hide his delight at the news; her mother immediately began making plans for the wedding reception.

'You haven't given us much time.' Maisie Hennessy's

plucked eyebrows rose upwards to meet the blonde curls that always reminded Mick of a Sindy doll's wig. 'Most places need a year's notice.'

'A year?' Mick hid his relief. 'As long as that?' Disappointing for Fran, he thought. But maybe it was just as well. His relief was short-lived.

'Don't mind Maisie.' Jim Hennessy exuded reassurance as he handed Mick a brimming beer mug. 'She's talking about the bigger places. A mate of mine owns the Boeing Bar. He'll look after us. We put enough business his way, God knows. As for the church, Fran's Auntie Phil and Father Doran are like *that!*' Fingers, thick as two pork sausages, gestured briefly. 'He'll fit you in somewhere.'

As he listened to his future father-in-law Mick had a sense of things being taken out of his hands, of a process, once started, gaining momentum, like a train gathering speed. Panic clutched him. He tried to catch Fran's eye. Her face pink with excitement, she sat beside her mother on the imitation-leather sofa poring over the pages of an illustrated magazine. 'What do you think of that colour for the bridesmaids?' he heard her ask.

As he watched her his panic began to subside, to be replaced by a fatalistic calm. With a mental shrug, he sat back and took a long swallow of his beer.

'Leave it to the women, Mick.' Jim Hennessy's eyes were the same colour as Fran's but, unlike hers, they were small and piggy-looking, buried in folds of flesh. 'No place for a man in that kinda talk.' His future father-in-law smiled broadly. 'All *you* have to do is turn up on the day.'

'When you put it that way –' Mick took another swallow of

beer and tried to return the smile. As he stifled his doubts his sense of fatalism grew. They had pulled out of the station by now. It was too late to ask himself if he had got on the right train.

To his relief his parents approved of Fran once they had met her. 'A grand, sensible girl,' was Da's verdict. 'Just the sort to keep Mick's feet on the ground.' Although Ma expressed some fleeting doubts about the wisdom of marrying a redhead. 'No offence, Mick, but she's not the kind to fly off the handle, is she? Redheads can be awful fiery.'

'Ah, *Ma* –' Mick was beginning when Da asked with a sly grin, 'What about black-haired women, Nan?'

'Oh, *you*,' Ma bridled. 'I'm not that bad, am I, Mick?'

He laughed, deciding not to take offence. 'It takes one strong woman to know another, Ma.'

She looked at him doubtfully. 'She's a lovely girl, Mick, I'm not saying she isn't. I just don't want you to go making a mistake.'

He thought of the soft places inside her thighs, the clean, flowery smell of her hair, the way the sun turned the freckles on the bridge of her nose to gold. 'No mistake, Ma. Everything will work out for us, you'll see.'

'Only a few weeks of freedom left, eh, head?' his cousin Pete said a few months later when he called one August evening to bring Da to the pub. He sniggered and dug Mick in the ribs. 'Are you comin' for a few scoops while you still have the chance?' Well into his twenties, Pete seemed to have got his pimples under control but he still retained his adolescent sense of wit. His hands, always ready to pinch and thump when he was a boy, had grown hard in the practice of his trade as a fitter. Mick moved hastily out of their reach and shook his head. There was something he needed to ask Ma and, as he wouldn't be seeing Fran that night because she was going to the dressmaker for a fitting, he wanted to make the most of the opportunity.

'Gettin' into practice for the ball and chain.' His cousin grinned knowingly. 'He's all yours, Auntie Nan.' He pulled a lugubrious face. 'But not for long.' As Da followed him out into the hallway, Pete's voice could be heard singing, '*Be nobody's darlin' but mine.*'

Ma's face darkened as the front door slammed behind them. 'He was always a young pup.' She reached for her cigarettes and lit one. 'But he's right about one thing: I'm going to miss you, Mick.'

'Ah, Ma.' He felt guilty suddenly. 'I'm not going far. And you'll see plenty of us.'

'That'll make a change,' she said tartly. 'I've barely seen you all summer.'

'I haven't had a minute, *you* know that. What with all the arrangements for the wedding and trying to find a flat. *And* I've been taking all the overtime I can get. Money's going out hand over fist at the moment.'

'Didn't I tell you that's how it would be?'

'Ah, Ma, don't start that again.' He fought down his annoyance. 'Listen, there's something I want to ask you.'

'Do you need more money? Is that it, Mick?'

'No, no, it isn't that.' He felt ashamed of his irritation. 'Look, you've been very good helping us with the deposit for the flat and everything. That isn't what I – '

'It's there if you want it, Mick. I have savings.'

'I know, Ma, and I'm grateful but this isn't to do with money, it's to do with *me*.' He saw a guarded look come over her face. 'You've never really told me what happened when I was a baby. How you came to adopt me.'

Her head snapped up. 'Yes I did. We went through all that years ago. I don't know any more than what I told you then.' She gave a quick shrug. 'It's all in the past, Mick.'

'Why won't you talk about it, Ma?' He refused to be put off. 'Is there some mystery about my birth?'

She laughed shortly. 'Isn't it all a mystery? They tell you nothing. That's the rules. Anyway, what difference did it make to *me* where you came from? Do you know how long your father and me were waiting to have a child? If it wasn't for this nun –'

His breath quickened with excitement. 'This nun? Tell me about her –'

To his disappointment he saw her shake her head. 'I've said enough, Mick. The past is past. Anyway, why this interest all of a sudden? This is no time to be worrying about things like that. And you getting married next month.'

'Maybe it's *because* I'm getting married that I'd like to know where I came from. But to be honest, Ma, I've always wondered. Don't tell me you haven't.'

'Well –' she hesitated, obviously reluctant, then suddenly relented. 'Maybe I did. When I seen you growing up so refined.'

'Refined? Come on, Ma, what kind of a word is that?'

'Don't laugh, son. You've always been that bit – different to the other young fellas around here.'

He said slowly, 'I've always *felt* different. But I never thought you –'

'Oh yes.' Ma nodded her head vigorously. 'I seen it early on. Of course the baby clothes gave me a clue too. All new stuff. No washed-out hospital hand-me-downs there. And the best of quality. Wherever you came from, Mick, it wasn't from nothing. That much was obvious.'

'Oh, Ma.' He felt his voice falter. 'Ma, why didn't you tell me this before?'

She looked shamefaced. 'Me and your father, we're ordinary people. We hadn't much to offer. I didn't want you growing up dissatisfied.'

He said with a touch of bitterness, 'Do you think I haven't?'

She looked sad. 'We done our best, Mick.'

'I know you did. But – '

Her face was a mixture of emotions, as if some inner battle was going on. As he watched, she seemed to come to a decision. 'Wait here.' She left the room and he heard her feet on the stairs. A few moments later she returned, carrying a parcel wrapped in tissue paper. 'I've never shown this to anyone before. Switch on the light, Mick.'

He did so, bursting with curiosity. His mother parted the folds of tissue with careful fingers to reveal a tiny blue jacket crocheted in silken yarn.

'You were wearing this the day I got you.'

He fingered the matinée coat gently. 'It looks so new.' He glanced at her in surprise. 'As if it's never been worn.'

Again that shamefaced look on her face. 'God forgive me but I didn't want anything to remind me that you had belonged to someone else. I didn't want talk or questions from the neighbours. I don't know why I kept it, really. But it was too pretty to throw away.'

He felt a sudden surge of anger. 'So that's what I was wearing? Did she dress me herself, I wonder, the day she gave me away?'

Ma looked distressed at the bitterness in his voice. 'Don't talk like that, Mick. We're not in a position to judge. That poor woman must have had her reasons to do what she did.'

His anger grew. And with it came a resolve. 'One of these days, Ma, I'm going to find her and ask her what they were.'

A look of anxiety crossed her face. 'Will you listen to me, Mick.' He felt her hand tug at his arm. 'Forget the past. What's done is done. You're going to be married soon. That's what you should be thinking about.'

'Okay, so I'm getting married. What difference does that make?' He felt his resolve strengthen. 'Wherever she is, whatever she's doing right now, I want her to know – one of these days I'm going to come looking for her. And I hope she has her answers ready.'

Ma looked startled. 'But Mick – '

'One of these days,' he said firmly. '*Soon.*'

PART TWO

The phone call came like a bolt from the blue. A thunderbolt from the gods. Nemesis.

The day had started pleasantly enough, apart from a slight sensation in the pit of the stomach. A clutch of panic? Or was it excitement? Sometimes it's hard to tell the difference.

No need to panic, Margaret. She kept her hand steady as she applied delicate foundation to her smooth, unlined skin. It was only another birthday. Forty wasn't old in the scheme of things.

No need to get excited, either. Her life was uneventful, safe, *predictable.* Not a bad way to be, after all. Being forty wasn't going to change that.

She fluffed on powder with a big brush and reached for eyeshadow.

But it was still a milestone.

As she applied mascara to her lashes with even, upward strokes, she remembered something she had heard her father say years before.

'The forties? The old age of youth, the youth of old age.'

'Welcome to the club!' Her husband threw an envelope at her across the breakfast table. Eight years older than she, his sandy hair already thinning on top, he seemed to relish her new status. 'Let's face it, you're getting long in the tooth. Have to hand it to you, though, you don't look your age.'

Although his tone had been envious rather than admiring, she decided to accept it as a compliment. A rare thing from Vincent nowadays. 'Thanks,' she said.

Caroline, their daughter, hunched over a bowl of low-calorie cereal, emerged from her usual early-morning cloud of resentment to hand her something loosely wrapped in silver paper. 'I ran out of Sellotape.'

'It's fine.' Margaret took the lumpy parcel with some trepidation. Caroline's presents were always near misses. Aware that other mothers might feel touched by the bits of sticky tape stuck haphazardly and ineffectively to the paper's surface, she fought down a pang of irritation. Then she was visited by her usual sense of guilt where her daughter was concerned. The contents of the parcel, a sequinned evening top, did nothing to dispel this feeling.

'If you don't like it, I have the receipt.' She was conscious of Caroline's eyes anxiously scanning her face.

'It's lovely,' Margaret lied. 'Of course I don't want to change it.' Her sense of guilt deepened. Nothing wrong with it. Not *really*. Just too glittery for her taste. Guilt made her say, 'I might wear it tonight.' Although she knew she wouldn't when the time came.

Caroline must have known this too. Her green eyes narrowed, admitting defeat. 'You don't have to.' She lapsed into silence and went back to her cereal.

'The table's booked for eight.' Vincent watched Margaret as she opened the envelope he had given her. 'I've only asked a few people. You said you didn't want any fuss.'

'That's right.' She hid a wry smile. Although she had rejected the idea of a big party, for her own reasons, she had sensed at the time that he had not been too disappointed at having his offer turned down. From what she knew of her husband, she guessed he would be claiming tonight's meal on his expense account. As managing director of his own company he had a generous one. And, being Vincent, he would be able to justify it on the grounds that most of the couples invited would be business contacts anyway. It was all grist to the mill. She took out the birthday card. It was covered in roses and had *Life Begins at Forty* emblazoned on it in red letters. His secretary had probably bought it, she decided. The brief signature inside bore this out. She pictured him scrawling it impatiently between business letters. Another scrawl for the cheque. Not a lavish sum but big enough by his standards.

'Thanks.' Although a present might have been nicer.

'Didn't know what to get you,' he grunted, spreading marmalade on his toast. 'Hadn't time, anyway. Up to my eyes in work.'

He didn't say that to Caroline on *her* birthday. She thought of the expensive radio and CD player that he had given their daughter the previous week when she had celebrated her seventeenth birthday. Celebrated was the appropriate word. Vincent had taken time off work to help her choose her present. And there had been other gifts too. Her favourite pop group's latest. A large box of Belgian chocolates. A cuddly toy to add to her collection. The kind of things he had given Margaret when they were first married.

Still, a cheque was better than nothing. She read the

message on the card again. 'Do you think that's true? About life beginning at – ?'

'A load of bullshit.' Vincent gulped tea hastily. 'You make your own life. And the earlier the better. If I had sat around waiting for life to begin I'd never have made anything of myself. Do you know what I sometimes think about you, Margaret? You never knew hardship. You had it too easy.'

'Thanks,' she said again, this time ruefully. It's your own fault, she chided herself. You should never have given him that opening. She poured a cup of coffee and tried to coat herself in a protective armour off which his words would bounce harmlessly.

'Of course, it probably explains why you have so few wrinkles.' Vincent looked thoughtful as he chewed the last of his toast. 'A lot to be said for being born with a silver spoon in your mouth.' He glanced over at Caroline, who stared morosely back at him. 'Isn't that right, sugarbush?'

She yawned and pushed tangled, blonde hair out of her eyes. 'Oh, Daddy, don't start all that stuff about growing up the *hard way.* I can't take it at this hour of the morning. I've a double period of French at ten and I don't mind telling you I'm not looking forward to it.'

'Sorry, darling.' Vincent looked penitent and patted her hand. 'Don't worry. Six weeks in France will do wonders for your language.'

'Maybe.' Caroline shrugged as she got up from the table. 'The family Karen was with last year insisted on practising their English. Even the grown-ups. Not very fair.'

'You won't let that happen to *you*.' He stood up too, rapidly brushing crumbs off his business suit. 'No one takes advantage of my daughter. Come on, I'll drop you off on my way to the office.' As Caroline shot out of the room, he turned to Margaret and gave a little smile. Some instinct made her tense up, armour in place against the shaft that she suspected would come. She hadn't long to wait.

'I hope you're not going to mope around the house all day feeling sorry for yourself?'

'I don't intend to,' she said stiffly.

He looked unconvinced. 'I hope not.' Vincent always liked to have the last word. Unerringly, his shaft found the chink in her armour and shot home. 'It won't bring thirty-nine back again, you know.'

No point in getting angry with him. A waste of time. Not that she felt angry – more depressed really. His sallies had that effect on her sometimes. She tried to shake off a slight feeling of unease as she stacked the breakfast dishes into the dishwasher and hastily swept the tiled floor, anxious to leave the sombre kitchen. Being west-facing, it would not get the sun till later in the day; then it would come alive with its presses of golden pine, gaily patterned tiles, the glint of copper pans. She loved the room then but now it had a gloomy, waiting air which oppressed her, intensifying her unease.

In the hall, early-summer sunlight poured in through the glass on both sides of the heavy front door and down from the huge stained-glass window at the turn of the stairs, catching the gleam of polished mahogany, the richness of the thick-piled stair carpet. When Margaret reached the upper landing, she found herself sighing as she glanced in at her daughter's open doorway. As usual, the room looked as if it had been ransacked by thieves: contents of drawers spilling out, clothes draped over chairs, the carpet covered in shoes and boots. No point in getting worked up about that either. Leave it to Mrs Canvey, her three-times-a-week treasure, to sort out the mess. Besides, Vincent always said that Caroline was just passing through a phase. All teenagers are untidy, he used to say. Maybe he was right. She closed the door firmly and moved on.

And he was right, too, about not feeling sorry for yourself. But he was wrong in thinking she wanted to turn back the clock. The past was a country she never wanted to revisit. That much she was decided on. *No looking back, Margaret. The past is gone.*

Her spirits began to lift as she thought this; and when she entered the sunny bathroom attached to the bedroom she shared with Vincent they began to lift even further. As she cleaned her teeth at the pale, primrose handbasin, she began to make plans for the day. Shopping first. Get a few summer things. It was bound to be hot in Cannes in August. Have a bite to eat. Hair appointment in the afternoon.

The face that looked back at her from the bathroom glass bore a look of determined gaiety. Life is what you make it, after all. She was just trying to decide on which of her acquaintances she could bear to meet for lunch, today of all days, when, from the bedroom, the phone began to ring.

Mummy, with birthday greetings? She was tempted not to answer.

No, it wouldn't be Mummy. She never surfaced before ten.

'I'd like to be sure I have the right person,' the woman's voice said.

A deep voice. Lower than Mummy's high, light cadences. 'You *are* Margaret St Clair?'

'No – I mean – yes. It was my maiden name.' A thought struck her. 'Are you from St Celeste's? The past pupils' union? I'm afraid I've let my membership lapse.'

'No, not the –' A pause, a slight hesitation, as if the person at the other end was choosing each word. 'Your father was Julian St Clair? Your mother's name was Maeve?'

'Is. She's still alive. My father's –' What was she doing discussing her affairs with a stranger? 'Look, who is this? What's it about?'

'It's a delicate matter,' the voice said carefully. 'There's confidentiality involved. That's why we have to be sure.'

'I see.' But of course she didn't see. Baffled would be a better word. And a bit intrigued. 'It's not money, is it? Has someone left me some?'

'No.' A little rueful laugh. 'Not money.'

It was that little laugh that alerted her. Something about it that sent the first thrill of fear shooting through her body. She felt the hand holding the receiver begin to tremble.

But this was ridiculous. What was there to fear? She was at home, sitting on the edge of her bed in her own bedroom, the May sunshine pouring into the room. No shadows. No dark corners. What could happen to her? She was quite safe. She gripped the phone more firmly, tried to keep her voice at a comfortable pitch. 'What, then?'

And then they came.

Words dropping out of the blue, like stones shattering

the surface of a calm pool.

Words that were to change her life. The fact that they were delivered with some sympathy made them no less cataclysmic.

'Does 20 November 1965 mean anything to you?'

The phone jerked uncontrollably in her hand. The blood rushed to her head. The room sang around her, the ground falling away from her, chasms opening at her feet. Her breathing seemed to stop as she fell back against the pillows, grateful for their support. A deafening silence came from the other end of the phone, as if the other person had stopped breathing too.

After what seemed like aeons, she found her voice – a small voice she hardly recognised as her own. 'I think there must be some mistake.'

But there was no mistake.

Many years before, Margaret had taken the past and buried it deep, the way you hear of nuclear waste being buried in layers and layers of concrete, in bunkers of steel, deep down in the ocean. Deep down deep. Locked and padlocked. Out of sight and out of mind. Buried it deep. And had thrown away the key.

And now someone had found that key.

'I thought you'd be gone by now.' Her mother's brittle tones crackled over the line.

If you thought that, why did you ring?

'I'm on my way out.' A lie. But Mummy wasn't to know that she had spent the last hour, half-sitting, half-lying against the pillows, staring into space. And would probably have spent the next hour like that if the ringing phone hadn't broken through her reverie. The panic engendered by the previous phone call had subsided, to be replaced by a dull ache in her stomach. With an effort of will she sat up, swung her legs over the side of the bed and forced her voice to sound calm, pleasant even. 'How are you this morning?'

'As well as can be expected.' Maeve St Clair, a young-looking sixty-four who seldom missed her regular golf game or frequent bridge sessions with like-minded cronies, always spoke as if her health were a matter for grave concern, needing constant monitoring by her doctor son. 'Peter has put me on new tablets.'

'Good.' They were probably placebos, Margaret thought, cynically. Peter would do anything to keep his mother happy and preserve the harmony of his household. Not for the first time, she wondered how he could bear to have her under the same roof as himself and his family. But then his wife, Beatrice, probably bore the brunt of the arrangement since Peter, as a busy surgeon, seemed to spend more time in the operating theatre than he did at home. He happily left the running of their large house in Dalkey to Beatrice, who was one of those women that everyone calls a 'saint', managing to cope uncomplainingly with the demands of a growing brood of unruly children and of a mother-in-law who had been used, all her life, to having people at her beck and call and saw no reason for this ever to change, despite the death of a devoted husband thirteen years before.

'Your father's anniversary last week – ' Mummy was saying.

'I know, I know.' The ache in Margaret's stomach intensified. Not now, not now, she pleaded silently, wishing she had the courage to slam down the phone. It was still impossible to think of Daddy without pain. 'Look, I must go.'

'Oh, by the way –' Mummy suddenly seemed to remember the purpose of her call, 'Congratulations.'

'Oh?' Of course, the *birthday*. Somehow it no longer seemed important. 'Thanks.'

'I have a present for you.'

Not another cheque. When she was growing up, Mummy had usually given her money. Less trouble for both of them.

No, surprisingly. 'Jewellery. Just a small piece.' She sounded almost coy. 'It *is* a special one, after all.'

Margaret felt touched. Then guilty for having ungrateful thoughts. For a moment she was tempted to unburden herself. If only Mummy were the kind of mother you could confide in. But that had always been the trouble, hadn't it?

'I don't want to entrust it to the post,' the high, confident voice went on. 'Perhaps Vincent would call out for it?'

Margaret smiled wryly. Mummy always spoke as if Vincent were some kind of lackey, always ready to do her bidding. 'You're not coming tonight, then?'

'Oh, darling!' Her mother was all regret. 'It's the bridge tournament. I can't let my partner down. I'm not sure if Peter can make it, either. Some committee meeting or lecture he can't get out of. But he said to be sure and give you his regards.'

'*Quelle surprise!*'

'Now, Margaret, don't be like that.' Her voice was suddenly icy. 'You know what a busy life he leads. As a surgeon's daughter you should –'

'Yes.' Resignation settled over her. 'What's Beatrice's excuse?'

'Well, you know *Beatrice!* The children come first even if it's nothing worse than a head cold.' Maeve St Clair made no pretence at loyalty to her daughter-in-law. 'The truth is she hates socialising. No manners, whatsoever. *Not* an asset to an up-and-coming man. But she's a good mother, I'll say that for her. Mind you, that said, I think she indulges them too much.'

'Like you did Peter.' It was out before she could stop it.

'Now, Margaret.' Maeve's tone was razor sharp. 'You know I never made any difference between you.'

Margaret sighed. Mummy was so good at ignoring reality. Any thoughts of confiding in her faded rapidly. Madness to have ever thought she could. If she were to tell her about the phone call her reaction would probably be to pretend not to hear the words. Or deny that there was any truth in them. As far as her mother was concerned, the past wasn't just buried, it had never happened. Not by as much as a raised eyebrow or curled lip had she ever alluded to it in all those years.

'Just as you like, Mummy. And now I really *have* to go.'

'Don't let *me* keep you.' Her mother sounded so like an offended child that Margaret began to feel guilty again. Not wishing to end the conversation on a sour note, she found herself prolonging the conversation so that another half-hour elapsed before she could extricate herself. At that point Mummy, finally restored to good humour, released her with the benediction, 'Be sure and enjoy your special day.'

Her special day? Oh it was special, all right. Exceptional might be a better word for it. But what made it a day to stand out from all others was not that she had clocked up another birthday, however much of a milestone it might be, but that this was the day that the past had finally caught up with her.

But how had they found her? How had they picked up a trail that had been cold for almost twenty-two years? The voice on the phone had not been forthcoming. Confidentiality, you understand.

'But what about *my* confidentiality? *My* privacy?'

'Well of course.' The voice was reasonable. 'That's protected too. Nothing will be done without your consent.'

Well that was something. *If* you could believe it.

'Okay.' From somewhere she got the courage to say, 'I don't *give* my consent.' Felt a rush of relief. That's it then. I'm going to put down the phone, get on with my life, pretend this conversation never took place.

'You're under no obligation, of course.'

'That's fine, then.' Her fingers tightened on the receiver, ready to replace it on its cradle.

'You're under no obligation, of course. But – ' The 'but' made it clear that the voice wasn't going to give up *that* easily. 'Look – ' It grew persuasive suddenly. 'You've had a bit of a shock – it's understandable – you don't have to have to decide now. Think it over. Sleep on it.'

Sleep on it? It was the stuff of which nightmares are made. Sleep on it? If she ever made it till night-time she doubted very much if she would be able to sleep. But the voice was difficult to refuse. Reluctantly, very reluctantly, she had allowed herself to be persuaded to take down the telephone number.

It was a beautiful day outside. Mummy, not normally given to enthusing about the weather, had remarked upon it, had grown nostalgic, even. 'Our Lady's month. I can never think of May without remembering the procession in St Celeste's. All the little girls dressed in white. Do you remember it, Margaret?'

How could she forget? It had taken place every year all through her schooldays. Banks of white flowers in the corridors, the hothouse smell of chrysanthemums, the shuffle of rubber-soled feet on polished wooden floors. 'O Mary, we crown thee with blossoms today,' the nuns and the girls had sung. 'O Mary, I give thee the lily of my heart. Be thou its guardian forever.'

Be thou its guardian forever? When she had buried the past she had thought it would be forever. Forever was a long time. But not long enough.

And now there was a crumpled piece of paper staring up at her from the bedside locker. A piece of paper with numbers on it that would open a Pandora's box.

O Mary, I give the lily of my heart.

The lily was the sign of purity. Virginity, the most prized possession of a St Celeste girl. Lose it at your peril.

Those days are gone, Margaret. Put them behind you.

Easier said than done. She eyed the piece of paper with a kind of fascinated horror. Into the wastebasket with it? It would be the best solution. But she couldn't bring herself to do this. As a compromise she thrust it into a drawer, where it slid out of sight between the folded layers of scented underwear.

Out of sight but not out of mind. With a tremendous effort of will she tried to push it to the back of her thoughts.

Harden your heart. Put your emotions on ice. The only way to get through the next few hours.

The day wasn't completely ruined, she told herself, locking the front door behind her. She must salvage it somehow. Petals rained gently down on her from the cherry tree overhanging the driveway as she crunched across the gravel; birds sang in the branches of other trees in neighbouring gardens; and along the avenue the sun shone down from a cloudless blue sky. Early summer was here in all its glory. But to Margaret, sliding behind the wheel of her BMW, it might as well have been the dead of winter. A frozen band had tightened itself around her heart, encircling it in its icy grip.

'You look as if you had spent all day in the beauty parlour.' Susan, Margaret's friend from childhood days, looked at her admiringly as they sat together on a huge sofa in the lounge of the discreetly luxurious hotel where the meal was being held. 'But knowing you, I suppose you didn't need to.'

'I went shopping.' Wandered the shops would be a better way of describing it, staring unseeingly at racks of beachwear, unable to decide on anything.

'Bought anything nice?' Although Susan wasn't interested in clothes – hadn't been for years – in her career as a concert pianist, a career which had taken her all over the world, she was expected to dress with formal elegance. Once out of the public eye, she tended to slop around in whatever casual outfit came to hand. Tonight, however, she seemed to have made a special effort and wore an understated black dress that cleverly glossed over the shortcomings of her dumpy figure.

Noticing this, Margaret remembered how, when they were girls together, growing up in the Square, the other would wail,

'Nothing ever looks well on *me*. It's not fair! With *your* looks and *your* figure you can wear anything.' A slighter friendship might have perished at that point, she thought, looking affectionately at her friend. But Susan wasn't the jealous type, thank God. And her life was so successful nowadays she had no reason to be jealous of anyone.

'I'm so glad you could make it tonight. I thought you'd be away on one of your tours.'

'I nearly didn't. I'm off to Amsterdam on Tuesday. Then Berlin. Poor Tom – ' Susan glanced over at her lanky, bespectacled husband, who was making conversation with Vincent. ' – He's getting withdrawal symptoms already.'

'He can hardly complain, though. Doesn't the orchestra travel quite a bit?'

'Around the country mostly, although they're based in Dublin. He doesn't go to foreign parts as often as I do. But we grudge every minute we spend apart. You don't know how lucky you are to be able to see your husband every day.'

'You're only two years married.' Margaret's voice was dry. 'Will you say the same after eighteen?'

'It's such a miracle that Tom and I found each other at this stage of our lives.' Susan shook her head in wonderment. 'Another sixteen years would be bliss.' Her face changed and she looked more closely at her friend. 'Nothing *wrong*, is there, Margaret?'

Her heart missed a beat, then steadied itself. She wondered what Susan had read in her face. 'Between me and Vincent? No, of course not.' She glanced across the room and saw Caroline wending her way towards them through the tables scattered around the huge lounge. 'Did *we* spend as much time as that in the Ladies when we were that age?'

'Longer, I should think,' Susan said, laughing. 'Remember all that back-combing. Girls nowadays have simpler hairstyles. But we lived simpler lives, don't you think? I never remember being brought out to meals in places like this, do you?'

'Sometimes.' Margaret was reluctant to reminisce. 'Lunch, mostly.'

'Of course your parents lived a much higher lifestyle than mine,' Susan said without envy. 'There were five of us, after all. And my father was just a humble dentist.'

'Humble dentist, indeed. He had a very good practice.'

'Well it didn't run to cooks and scullery-maids, like yours. I suppose we were what you would call comfortable. But compared to you we were only in the ha'penny place even if we *did* live three doors down from you.'

'Cooks and scullery-maids!' Margaret laughed. 'What an exaggeration. I get enough of that from Vincent. He tries to make out we had a butler.' She shook her head and tried to look amused. 'Poor Mrs Roberts with her shower-of-hail pinny and her varicose veins. A *butler?*'

'Well, compared with Daddy you seem to have been very lucky,' Caroline said as she sat down on a nearby chair. 'Losing his father so young, his mother having to take lodgers and ruin her eyesight making clothes for the neighbours. Poor Daddy.' Her face softened as she glanced over at Vincent, who was lecturing a bemused Tom on the wisdom of Thatcherite economics. 'He really had it hard.'

Was Margaret supposed to feel guilty about that too? She smiled at Caroline and said nothing.

'Well it has all worked out for the best, hasn't it?' Susan

said comfortably. 'Tell me, Margaret, who else is coming tonight? Will we know anyone?'

'*You* might but I don't think Tom will. Couples we know through business, mostly.'

'No family?' Susan was disappointed. 'I haven't seen your mother in ages. And Peter? I don't think we've met since my wedding.'

'They're busy people,' Margaret said. 'A bit like yourself. When have you and I had a good chat lately?' When she saw Caroline turn away to follow the men's conversation, she whispered, 'Listen, I really need to talk to you. Is there any chance we could meet before – ?'

' – I go to Amsterdam?' Susan's face fell. 'Oh, Margaret, I wish I could. I'll be back in a fortnight. Will it wait till then?'

Could she last out till then? Getting through the next few hours would be difficult enough. She shook her head. 'It's okay. It isn't that important.'

'Well if you're sure – '

'I'm sure.' This was neither the time nor the place. 'I see some of our guests arriving.' Just before several couples converged on the group, she impulsively squeezed Susan's arm and felt its warm, comforting solidity. 'I'm so glad that you're here tonight.'

'I am too. But Margaret – ' she looked at her thoughtfully, ' – this is your special night. Why don't you just sit back and enjoy it?'

'Why not, indeed!' Margaret picked up her half-empty glass and drained it with a flamboyant gesture. 'Let's eat, drink and be merry.'

'For tomorrow we diet.' Susan laughed. But the glance

she threw her friend was a puzzled one.

'That went off well.' Vincent settled back in the taxi between Margaret and Caroline, threw an arm around each of them and gave a huge sigh of satisfaction. 'How did my two girls enjoy themselves?'

'Oh Daddy, you're drunk,' Caroline giggled as he nuzzled her face. 'Stop it, your moustache tickles.'

He took his face away. 'But had you a good time, sugarbush?'

She shrugged. 'All those *old* people. What do *you* think? Anyway, it wasn't *my* party.'

'True, true.' He turned to Margaret. 'How about you?'

Thank God it was over! Despite Susan and Tom's presence and the anaesthetising power of alcohol, the evening had been an ordeal. In the midst of the jollifications she had longed to crawl away into the darkness somewhere, away from the toasts and the banter – and the pretence. Away from the voice that kept sounding in her head, saying the same words, over and over.

She felt Vincent's arm tighten around her shoulders and smelled garlic and whiskey on his breath as he pulled her face close to his.

'Yes, it was lovely,' she lied.

'I think it went off very well.' He was behind her as she was cleaning her teeth. 'Service might have been better at times but I feel, all in all – ' His hands were warm against her naked shoulder blades. She saw her face looking back at her, vague, unfocused in the strip lighting over the mirror.

'Yes.' She felt his hands brush past the narrow straps of her nightdress and reach downwards to cup her bared breasts, forcing the nipples upwards. His lips were hot on the back of her neck. The start of a headache began to gnaw at her temples.

Does 20 November mean anything to – ?

Oh God!

She pushed his hands away and saw his affronted face in the mirror. 'Ah, come on, Margaret.'

She pulled her straps up. 'I'm a bit tired.'

'Lovely! That's bloody lovely!' His face reddened. 'After all I – '

'I'm sorry, Vincent, I – '

'That's just typical of you. Do you know what your trouble is, Margaret? You're all take, take, take. And no give.'

'That's not true.' No match for his sudden fury, she was overcome by the unfairness of it.

He glared at her. 'Isn't it?' He pushed past her into the bedroom.

'I'm sorry, Vincent. She followed him and, almost timidly, put a hand on his arm.

He shook it away angrily. 'Go to hell, Margaret. Look, I'm tired too. I've to work in the morning even if you haven't.' He climbed into bed and turned his back on her. His snores soon filled the room.

Sleep was a long time coming that night. She lay staring into the darkness, her head thumping, Vincent snoring, her thoughts hammering away at her.

Does 20 November mean anything – ?

20 November – ?

'After all these years,' Susan said, staring blankly across the restaurant table at her, 'you get a phone call out of the blue. Just like that?'

'Yes.' She sipped a glass of mineral water glumly. 'Just like that.'

'But how did they – ?'

'I don't know.' The anxiety that had been gnawing at her stomach for the past fortnight turned to nausea in her mouth. She pushed her Caesar salad away, uneaten. 'They didn't – '

The other woman's brow furrowed. 'They didn't tell you much, did they?'

'It was difficult over the phone.'

'Must have been. Must have been *awful*. But you can't leave it just like that. You've got to talk to someone, find out more.'

Panic clutched at her. 'I don't want to find out *more*. It's in the past, *dead, buried*.'

'Not now it isn't. Look, Margaret.' Susan's face was sympathetic. 'I know this is terrible for you – I mean, the shock alone – but – ' she hesitated. ' – But, don't you think, before you make up your mind – '

'I *have* made up my mind.'

' – that you should find out a little bit more of what's involved. Margaret, will you listen to me – '

She stared back unwillingly at Susan and tried to ignore the plea in her voice.

'You owe it to yourself,' the other woman said urgently. 'And to *him*.'

'You never thought of trying to trace him?' the social worker asked. By now she had a face and an office, a discreet, featureless room in a building run by some charitable religious organisation with an acronymic name. Sunshine glinted on the plain gold cross she wore on the lapel of her dark blue blouse. Her flat, comfortable shoes were of the kind that Mummy would never be caught dead in.

'Well, I – ' There had been no hint of accusation in the question, yet she felt accused. She who excuses herself accuses herself!

'Of course,' the other woman's tone was reasonable. 'It was a closed chapter for you, after all.'

A closed chapter? If she thought that, why had she made the phone call? For that matter, why had Margaret agreed to a meeting?

This was all Susan's doing. For a moment, sudden anger flared up in her against her friend. But why blame Susan? She had no one to blame but herself.

'I could show you some photographs.'

'I'd rather not – ' her voice was so shaky she thought it would die in her chest. Her stomach grew hot with fear. 'I think it's better this way.'

'It's your decision, dear.' Her eyes seemed kind. It was easier when nuns wore habits and you knew exactly what they stood for. A print skirt and a Marks and Spencer blouse tended to confuse the issue. Kind eyes or judgemental eyes? In her confusion Margaret didn't know which was the truth. She saw the other woman give a resigned smile. 'Not everyone wants to rake up the past.'

What past? How could it ever be past? Some things had been buried and forgotten, it was true, but not the fact of his existence, not the knowledge that somewhere her son lived and breathed and went about his daily life.

Not a day goes by that I don't think of him. She wanted to say it but didn't, fearing the look of scepticism she felt sure would cross the listener's face. Bad enough to be thought an unfeeling monster who had abandoned her child. To be judged insincere on top of that was unthinkable. She got to her feet. 'As you say, it's my decision. I really think it's for the best.'

They reached the door. 'You know where we are, Margaret, if you should change your mind – '

The open doorway beckoned. Another few steps to freedom, and she need never look back. 'I'm not likely to.'

'A pity, though.' There seemed a note of genuine regret in the social worker's voice. 'He's a lovely young man. I think you'd be pleased at the way he's turned out.'

God damn her! Why did she have to say that? Why, oh why, did she have to say that?

In the anonymity of the car park, safe from prying eyes, she leaned her head against the steering wheel and let the tears of longing come.

She held out for most of the summer. Luckily Caroline was staying in Bordeaux for July and most of August. No one to comment on preoccupied silences, inexplicable memory lapses. Vincent didn't seem to notice at first. He was planning to open a second factory in Wexford. The arrangements took up most of his attention.

'I want to get everything sorted out before we go on holidays.' A couple they knew had rented a villa near Cannes and had invited them to stay for the first fortnight in August. She'd been looking forward to it but now the prospect filled her with alarm.

'You look peaky.' He was momentarily diverted from his absorption with business matters. 'Not sleeping any better? You should get something from the doctor.' With Vincent there was a solution to everything.

'I have but it doesn't seem to work. Nothing seems to work.'

'More exercise is what you need. A few rounds of golf would do wonders for you. Look at me, I never have any problem.' He patted his taut midriff complacently. '*And* can eat anything I want. What you'll do is get a few lessons.' His voice was brisk, brooked no dissent. 'See Seamus at the club.'

When had he first started ordering her around? Or had he always been like that and she just hadn't noticed? She felt too tired to remember. To hide her growing irritation she gave a light laugh. 'Now why didn't I think of that?'

'It's no joke.' Vincent hated anyone poking fun at him, however gently. 'And remember, my sleep is being disturbed too. His voice took on an aggrieved note. 'All that tossing and turning. *And* you're back on the cigarettes again,' he added accusingly.

Guilt put her on the defensive. 'Maybe you'd like me to move out to the guest room. I'd hate to be the cause of you losing your beauty sleep.'

'*My* beauty sleep!' he shot back at her. 'I'm not the one who looks like death warmed up.'

'Thanks. Thanks very much.'

'No, but seriously, Margaret.' He gazed at her appraisingly.

'You look awful. You'll start losing your looks if you don't watch it.'

With a husband like that, who needed enemies?

'Maybe I *will* move into the guest room.'

'Please yourself.' Vincent began putting some papers into his brief case. 'I suppose a couple of nights apart won't do either of us any harm. Anyway we're off to France next week.' He sighed as he snapped the lock shut. 'God knows, I could do with the break.'

They came back from Cannes and she still hadn't made up her mind. The holiday had turned out better than expected. The other couple had been good company. Despite the fact that Vincent spent part of each day on the phone to his personal assistant – daily contact with the office having been an essential component of any holiday as far back as Margaret could remember – she managed to enjoy the break. Sun, Mediterranean food and lots of wine helped to keep the past safely in its box. It was only when the plane glided over the tarmac at Dublin Airport and she glimpsed the blue sweep of mountains in the distance that the memories began clamouring to get out.

'It's no use, Vincent,' she said next day. 'I'll have to move into the spare room again. I didn't close my eyes all night.'

'Off you go, then. Don't leave it too long, though. ' He smiled sourly at her. 'I mightn't want you back.'

Caroline returned from Bordeaux morose and critical. 'This place sucks.' Even her appearance, hair bleached white from the sun, limbs evenly tanned, failed to lift her spirits. 'It's so *boring* here.'

'You've grown.' Vincent was delighted to have her back.

'Nearly an inch.' She brightened momentarily, then her face fell. 'But still not as tall as *her*. I'll never be as tall as her.'

'Being tall isn't everything,' Margaret said.

Caroline scowled at her. 'You *would* say that.'

'Your mother's right.' This was so unusual that Margaret stared at him in surprise, waiting warily for the sting in the tail. It wasn't long coming. She saw Vincent put his arm around Caroline's shoulders and smile at her. 'You take after my side of the family, sugarbush. Some of us may not be all that tall. But we have *drive*. We get things *done*.'

She might have known. Margaret smiled ruefully to herself as she watched the two of them together. For a moment the two faces looked so alike. Then Caroline's eyes filled with tears. 'Oh, Daddy! Even you can't mend a broken heart.'

Vincent looked resigned. 'I know, I know, don't tell me. There's a Bertrand or a Gaston back there?'

'Thierry.' Caroline gave a sob. 'Oh, Daddy! I wish you could have met him. You'd just love him.'

'I'm sure I would, pet.' It was amazing how kind Vincent could be when it suited him. He stroked Caroline's hair. 'Tell Daddy all about it.'

'You should spend more time with her. A girl her age needs her mother.'

'Yes.' Margaret smiled faintly. 'Maybe that's why she's been on the phone to her friend Karen for the last hour.'

'Come on, you know what I mean. I wish you and she got on better.'

'You make it sound like my fault.'

'Well you could make more of an effort.' Vincent's tone was judicious as he picked up his newspaper. 'You can't expect Caroline – they don't know what they want at that age. One minute she thinks she's a woman, the next minute she's a child. The trouble with you, Margaret, is you've forgotten what it was like to be seventeen.'

It was a wonder he hadn't said, 'Sweet seventeen'. Although some of the memories were sweet.

A boy and girl sat together on a park bench. Skeletons of trees stood silhouetted against a wintry sky, a cold breeze ruffled the surface of the duck pond. They didn't touch each other but her body was acutely aware of his nearness. With his white skin and dark, dreaming eyes, he had the face of a poet, she thought. She longed to reach out and touch his black curls where they strayed over the collar of his Aran sweater.

> *Márgáret, are you grieving*
> *Over Goldengrove unleaving?*

His soft western cadences evoked nameless longings in her – and unfulfilled hopes.

'What's that from? It sounds really sad.'

'A poem by Gerard Manley Hopkins.'

'We did "The Wreck of the Deutschland" at school but I don't know that one. Did she lose her lover or something?'

'No, it's to a young child. It's about the loss of innocence.'

She felt his eyes on her face as she watched the grey water

lap against the concrete edge of the pond and felt her cheeks grow warm despite the cold air. '"Margaret, are you grieving?" I'm not grieving.'

'I thought you looked sad for a moment.' His fingers brushed her cheek. 'You have beautiful skin, do you know that. I wish –'

Her face tingled as if the fingertips had been charged with electricity. 'What do you wish, Martin?'

'Nothing. I –' He gave a hopeless shrug. 'You and I, we come from such different worlds, Margaret. I can't expect you to understand.'

'But I do,' she said eagerly. 'You've told me so much about yourself.' His story was like something out of Walter Macken, she thought, picturing his father's shop at the crossroads with its sides of bacon hanging from the rafters, the black-shawled women customers cashing money orders from husbands over in Coventry and Birmingham, the sawdust on the floor. When the wind was blowing in the right direction, he had said, you could hear the voices of the children chanting spellings and multiplication tables in the little stone schoolhouse where his mother taught. And then there were the long, straight roads cut through the bog where you could travel for miles without meeting a soul. And, towering over it all, the bare, bleak mountain. An unfamiliar world, true, but one she wanted to share. 'We're not that different, Martin, *underneath*.'

'Do you think so?' A touch of bitterness in the laugh he gave. 'Me, a boy from the arse end of Mayo? And you, a wealthy surgeon's daughter?'

'It's what people are underneath that counts,' she said

earnestly, 'not how much money they have. Besides, you're not poor, are you? I mean – the business?'

'It isn't *that* good. And money doesn't go far when you have five kids to clothe and feed. But my mother is determined to give us all our chance.'

She was surprised to feel a stab of jealousy for a woman she had never met. 'You think a lot of her, don't you?'

'Yes. She's a remarkable woman.' His face grew solemn. 'She wants me to make something of myself. I'd never want to do anything to let her down.'

'But that won't happen. You're clever and you work hard –'

'Not hard enough,' he said ruefully. 'Not since I met you.' He jumped to his feet. 'Look, we'd better get back to college.' He took her hand. 'I've a lecture in ten minutes.'

'Me too. Wish I didn't.' She felt his warm hands around hers as he pulled her to her feet. 'Wish we had nothing to do but sit here all day.'

'And freeze our backsides off.' He gave a sceptical laugh.

'Don't be so crude.' She laughed too as they walked away from the pond. 'We could keep warm by feeding the ducks.'

'With what?'

'When I was little we collected stale bread in a paper bag. We came here most days. Did you never – ?'

'Isn't this what I've been trying to tell you, Margaret.' He gave her a wry smile. 'Where I come from, we *eat* the ducks.'

'I'm dying for Christmas,' Margaret said later that day when he was walking her home. As the Square gardens came into sight she felt a familiar rush of excitement at the sight of holly wreaths on doors and the sparkle of fairy lights behind lace curtains. 'It's such a magical time.'

'Do you think so?' She heard Martin make a sceptical noise beside her.

'Well of course. It's like being a small child again. You feel something wonderful is going to happen.'

'It's a long time since I felt like that about Christmas. If I *ever* did.'

'That's a shame.' As they came up to her front steps she turned towards him impulsively. 'It must be awful for you.' She saw him look bleak for a moment, then shrug.

'You get used to it.' He pulled the collar of his jacket up over the neck of his sweater and blew on his hands to keep them warm. 'I'm no great pity, anyway.'

'Why's that?' Margaret was puzzled.

The sweetness of his smile took her by surprise. 'Something wonderful has already happened to me,' he said. 'I've met *you*.'

She smiled back at him. 'Something wonderful has happened to me, too.' She felt her whole body tingle with excitement. What could be more wonderful than to be seventeen and falling in love?

'I hate being an only child,' Caroline said from her seat at the kitchen table. 'Why couldn't you have had more children?'

Margaret, gazing out at the garden, most of which lay in the shadow cast by the back of the house, said nothing for a moment. On the strip of lawn which the sun had managed to reach, a blackbird patrolled its territory, his bright beak reminding her of a crocus she had seen at the end of winter bravely thrusting its spike up through the snow. Oh to be still in February, with the promise of the year spread out in front of her, instead of dragging her days through August, racked by indecision!

Reluctantly she turned to look at Caroline. 'What brought this up?'

The girl pushed tousled strands of hair away from her eyes with nail-bitten fingers and yawned hugely. 'I always wanted a brother.'

'I had a brother – *have* a brother.' Margaret's voice was detached. She went over to switch on the electric kettle. 'Judge for yourself how well that worked out.'

'Oh, Uncle Peter's a dry stick, I'm not denying *that*.' Caroline inspected a carton of low fat yoghurt before stripping off its foil cover. 'But at least you *have* a brother. You have nieces and nephews. Not like me. Just think, when I get married my children won't have any cousins.'

'How do you know that? Your husband might have brothers and sisters.'

Her face brightened. 'I never thought of that.' All the same, I still wish –' She looked accusingly at her mother. 'Why didn't you? I'm sure Daddy wanted more.'

'Yes,' she sighed, without thinking. 'He'd have liked a son.'

'I *knew*.' Caroline's voice was triumphant.'

'But why do you assume it was *my* fault?' Margaret was bewildered.

'You don't mean –?' The girl looked shocked. 'You're not saying Daddy couldn't – that he –?'

'No, of course not.' She found herself lowering her voice as if afraid that Vincent might overhear, although he was not in the house. 'Nothing like that.'

'So it *was* you? So you *didn't* want any more.'

She suppressed another sigh. Caroline could be difficult to take at times. 'It wasn't as simple as that.' She hesitated, unsure of whether to continue, and then decided. 'I lost a baby a few years after you were born.'

'Oh!' The girl was suddenly full of sympathy. 'Was it a boy?'

'They said it would have been.'

'They *said?* You mean you didn't see him?'

'No, they said it would be too distressing – there were complications. Maybe I was better off.'

'How awful!' Caroline shuddered. 'To have had a son and never to lay eyes on him. It must be the worst thing that could happen to you.' Her expression softened as she looked at her mother. 'Do you still think about him?'

A sudden fierce longing wrenched at her gut. With an effort of will she kept her face blank and stopped herself from doubling in two from the pain.

'About *him?* No.'

She was conscious of Caroline's eyes, so like Vincent's, watching her curiously. 'But didn't you try again? Couldn't you – ?'

She turned away from those prying eyes back towards the window. The blackbird had been joined by a thrush. As the sun gradually reclaimed the lawn, each bird strutted peacefully on its own section of grass, ignoring the other.

'You're so passive!' Caroline's voice sounded behind her in disgust. 'If it was *me* I'd never have given up.'

After her daughter had left the kitchen Margaret waited until she heard pop music blaring from an upstairs room before quietly lifting the telephone receiver down from the wall. Taking a crumpled piece of paper from her pocket, she carefully tapped out the digits and then heard the ringing tone. Her long fingers drummed nervously against the counter-top as she waited for someone to pick up the phone at the other end.

She thought of what Caroline had said.

The worst thing that could happen to you?

What about having a beautiful, perfect son you saw just once? Never to set eyes on him again?

When the discreet voice answered, she fought the temptation to hang up. Never was a long time, after all.

PART THREE

I've been waiting all my life for this moment, Mick told himself. All my life.

He stared at the woman sitting across the table from him and shook his head in disbelief. He just couldn't take in the reality of it. Even though he was trying to believe that what she had said was true, a part of him was still doubtful.

There had to be some mistake. It just didn't fit. *She* didn't fit. None of it fitted. She just wasn't the person he had been expecting to meet. Although what he *had* expected was difficult to put into words.

Ma's ignorant country girl taken in by some city slicker? Grown older, run to fat, maybe? A comfortable-looking, ageing woman with children at home, ready to enfold him in a motherly embrace? Tears spilling down her face, protestations of love? Pleas for forgiveness on her part, magnanimity on his?

Forget about it, Mick. As he looked at the elegant, slender woman who sat quietly watching him, he squirmed inwardly at the emotion-laden scenarios that he had built around their imagined reunion. Tear it up and start again. Say something. Anything. The trouble was the words wouldn't come. A part of him wanted to laugh at his own foolishness.

How wrong could you be? This was no earth mother ready to clasp him to her comforting bosom. Nor was she some poor, downtrodden creature in need of a champion. She was –

She was beautiful. She had class. He could tell by looking at her that she came from another world. A world he could only dream about. Oh God! She was *La Belle Dame Sans Merci* of his adolescent fantasies. Beyond his reach. Remote. Untouchable.

Instead of the elation he had expected to feel, he felt dismay. He felt let down, tricked, cheated in some way. And a part of him, a huge part of him, wanted to weep.

To hide his sadness he began to laugh.

The last time she had seen him he had been so tiny. Just newly arrived in the world yet ready to take it on. A tiny, aggrieved scrap of humanity, fists waving wildly. At least that was how she remembered him. Blue eyes, black hair, indignant red face. But it had been only a glimpse. Such a brief glimpse. Not much to keep you going for nearly twenty-two years.

And she had never even held him! The regret she had been holding at bay for so long stabbed at her stomach. But she wasn't going to cry in front of this young man, with his eager, questioning face. This stranger who was not quite a stranger.

His eyes were no longer blue, if they ever had been. They were dark brown now. Martin's eyes. Those dark, dreaming eyes of his. Poet's eyes. His hair, too, was dark, but not as black as Martin's had been, and he was a bigger man altogether, more Daddy's build, but slighter, on account of his youth. His mouth looked familiar but she couldn't place it. And his hands –

As she examined him hungrily, she was startled to hear

him laugh. She looked enquiringly at him. 'Is there something funny?'

'The joke's on me,' the young man said.

She felt herself flinch at the pain and anger in his eyes.

'Don't get me wrong.' His voice sounded harsh to his own ears. 'I've nothing against people of your – class.'

He heard her sharp intake of breath, saw her wince.

He was appalled. Had he really said that? Had he put himself with Uncle Thomas, with people like the Hennessys, Da, for God's sake? *People of your class.* Where had the words come from? He felt his face redden but it was too late to call the words back.

She said stiffly, 'I don't quite know what you mean?'

'Yes you do. Don't pretend. You know very well what I mean.'

He saw her face tighten. 'Well, now that you mention it.' There was frost in her voice. 'You're not what I expected either.'

The barb found a home. He felt the blood rush to his cheeks.

Her eyes widened. 'I shouldn't have said that. I'm sorry.'

'I'm the one to be sorry.' He had been wrong. And they had been right. Ma, the social worker, Fran. It had been one big mistake. He jumped to his feet. 'I should never have come.'

'No, wait.' She rose too. He saw that she was tall for a woman but not as tall as he was. 'Don't go. I've been so nervous. Like you, I didn't know what to expect.' She put out her hand almost pleadingly. 'Why don't we sit down. Start all over again. Get to know each other.'

It took a moment for her words to sink in. 'You were nervous too?'

'What do you think?' She gave a breathless laugh. 'I nearly changed my mind at the last moment.'

He felt the edge of his disappointment begin to soften. Felt himself warm to her.

'I'm glad you didn't,' he said.

'What does your husband do?'

'He's a businessman. He's doing quite well. We have a good life.'

'Are you happy?'

She shrugged. 'As happy as most people, I should imagine. You're married too, aren't you?'

'Yes. It's our second anniversary next week. *And* I have a son, Sean.' He couldn't keep the pride out of his voice. 'He's six months old.'

'A son.' He saw the shock in her eyes. 'I hadn't realised – ' It was obvious the news wasn't particularly welcome. 'Imagine me being a grandmother.'

'I can't, really.' He shook his head in wonder. 'You don't look old enough to be my mother, actually.'

'Thanks.' She seemed unimpressed by the compliment. 'I was only eighteen, after all.'

'When I was born?'

'Yes.'

He wanted to pursue the subject but the flat monosyllable discouraged him. 'Have you other children?'

'I've a daughter, Caroline. She's seventeen.'

'You only had the one?' He didn't hide his disappointment.

She frowned. 'Don't tell me you were hoping to discover brothers and sisters? A ready-made family?'

He sighed. 'Something like that.' Now that he'd met her it seemed a foolish notion. 'But it doesn't matter,' he said quickly.' You're the one I – '

'That's true.' She offered him a cigarette, which he refused, and lit one for herself. 'What do you do, Michael?'

'I'm a house painter.'

She looked surprised. 'But I thought – '

'The suit?' He gave an embarrassed grin. 'I wanted to make a good impression. It's the one I got married in. I don't usually – '

'I see.' She pondered this for a moment. 'Is it a job you like?'

He shrugged. 'Not particularly. But it pays the rent.'

She looked troubled and seemed about to say something but he interrupted her.

'Look, I'm more interested in hearing about you.' So many questions on the tip of his tongue, he didn't know where to start. 'You said you were eighteen when I – ?'

'That's right. I was eighteen in May. You were born the following November.'

'What happened? I mean – why did you – ? Who was my father? *Tell* me.'

She sighed gently. 'There isn't a lot to tell, Michael. I was in my first year at university. Martin was a year ahead of me. He came from the west of Ireland. His father was a shopkeeper. We met at a student hop and fell in love. Then I – I became pregnant. My parents wouldn't hear of our getting married. When you were born I had to give you up for adoption. There's not much more to it than that.'

He was puzzled. 'And the fella? Did he do a runner?'

'Not exactly. It's a sad little story.' She gave a wry smile. 'I don't really want to talk about *that*. I believe he finished college, got his degree and emigrated to America. Or so I heard, anyway.'

'You *heard?* But I don't understand; you said you were in love. If he loved you – ?'

'I told you my parents were against it. This was the early sixties, you must remember; attitudes were different then. And he was nineteen, a penniless student.'

'I was twenty when I got married.'

She looked blankly at him. 'I don't think we can compare – '

'Just out of my time as a painter. The money wasn't great at first, still isn't, but we're managing. Course Fran worked for a bit – '

He saw she was only half-listening to him. 'His people were against it too. They must have made sacrifices to send him to college; didn't want him to miss his chance.'

He thought of the little blue matinée coat Ma had shown him. 'But *your* people had money, hadn't they?'

'Well, yes – '

'Well then – ?'

'You don't understand.'

He felt his anger return. 'Why did you do it, then? The rich don't have to give their kids away.'

Her face had gone pale. She said again, 'You don't understand.'

'No, I don't understand.' His voice sharpened. 'I don't

understand any of it. You don't even have to be rich to hold on to your child. Take Fran's sister, Sandra. She had a son a few years ago. She didn't marry the guy but she kept the baby. Her parents stood by her. I don't even like the girl but I will say this about her: she held on to her child.'

'Unlike me?' Something about the rigid way she sat made him pause. To his horror, he saw that her eyes were bright with unshed tears. But his anger drove him on, made him pitiless.

'I could understand it if you were poor, if you had no choice.'

'Is *that* what you think?' Her voice barely rose above a whisper; he had to strain his ears to hear it. 'That I *had* a choice?'

He looked at her doubtfully. 'I don't know. *Had* you?'

A tear slid down her cheek. She shook her head wordlessly.

He was moved to pity. His anger died down. Impulsively he reached his hand out to her. 'Margaret, I'm sorry. I didn't mean to –'

She ignored the hand, pulled hard on her cigarette, shook away her tears and stared into the middle distance. Her face was remote, unapproachable. In the silence that followed he felt she had retreated deep inside herself, where he couldn't follow. He watched her uneasily, aching to ask more questions yet afraid to break in on her mood. The waitress came up suddenly to ask if they wanted more coffee and Margaret shook her head slowly like someone coming out of a trance. She stubbed out her cigarette and glanced at her watch.

'I must go.'

'But you can't – ' To his surprise his own watch told him they had been talking for nearly an hour. 'There's so much I want to ask you. Can't you stay, have lunch with me?'

'No.' She avoided his eye and began collecting her belongings. 'I have to go. I'm on a parking meter.'

'But we'll see each other again?'

'If you want to.'

Although he was chilled by the offhand way she said it, he refused to be put off. 'Well of course I do. Will you give me your phone number?'

She hesitated for a moment, then wrote the number down for him, and made a note of his. 'I'll ring you.'

'No,' he said. 'We share a phone. The old biddy downstairs isn't good at passing on messages. I'll get in touch.'

As his eyes followed her tall, slender figure moving away from the table his heart began hammering with excitement. He couldn't believe it had really happened. It was like a dream. If he pinched himself he'd probably wake up.

But he didn't want to wake up. He wanted to rush home and phone her immediately. Not a good idea, he cautioned himself. Better wait a few days.

Thank God that was over! As Margaret hurried up Grafton Street, weaving her way through the Saturday crowds, she felt her legs tremble violently under her. It was just the reaction, she told herself; it would be okay once she got to the car.

That was that, then. She backed out of her parking place in front of the railings of the Green and slipped into a gap in the traffic heading past the Shelbourne. She had seen him, and that was an end to it. She could get back to her life again. It was over.

But was it ? As she followed the stream of cars up Merrion Row, doubt set in. Why on earth had she given him her phone number? That had been a mistake.

Maybe he wouldn't ring.

'*You* look happy.' When he got back to the flat, Fran was in the big front room that served as a kitchen-cum-living room, mixing baby food in a bowl. She threw him a cautious look. 'It must've gone well, then?'

'It was a bit strange at first but – ' he went over to where Sean lay gurgling in his Baby-Relax. 'Hey, Fran, I see now where he gets his colouring from.'

'Is that right, Mick.' Her face was inscrutable. 'Will you bring him over to me. I want to feed him.'

'Yeh, okay, in a minute. And his hands, Fran – do you remember when the nurse in the labour ward said he had my hands?' As he picked up one of Sean's plump little hands he remembered the thrill he had felt the day of his son's birth when he had examined the tiny, wrinkled fingers and discovered that they were miniature versions of his own. What a moment that had been! This was his son! The only person he knew of his own flesh and blood. The only one to share his genes.

'Just as well our hands looked alike. Because it was the only resemblance I could see.' He recalled the tiny form, wrapped, papoose-like, in a blue blanket, saw again the raw little face with its neat features, the pale eyebrows and the blond fuzz just like an American serviceman's crew-cut. 'Do you know, Fran, he just didn't look like anyone I *knew*. And now he does.'

'That's great, Mick.' Fran smiled at him as he placed the baby on her knee. 'But your mother – what's she like? To talk to?'

'Well –' He watched Sean's eager mouth open like a bird's as Fran spooned the cereal in. 'She's –' How did you capture beauty like hers? How did you sum up the impact it had? For the first time in his life he was at a loss for words.

'*Well*, Mick?' Fran said impatiently. 'What are you sitting there for with your mouth hanging open like an eejit? Go on, tell us?'

He felt a sudden reluctance. 'She's a nice woman. A real lady.' Better not say too much. She mightn't understand. 'But wait till I tell you.' Elation rose in him suddenly. 'She has a daughter, Fran! I have a sister!'

'That's nice, Mick.' Her face was expressionless as she wiped food from around Sean's mouth with the edge of his bib. 'I'm very happy for you.'

'Does she know about you?' The baby had been fed, and Fran was bent over the table, changing his nappy. 'This Caroline? And the husband – what's-his-name – Vincent? Have they been told?'

His elation began to fade. 'I don't know, she didn't say.'

'She didn't tell you much, did she?'

He felt a sudden resentment. 'Don't ruin it for me, Fran.'

'I'm not trying to ruin it for you, I was just *asking*. Here.' With a grin she handed him the soiled nappy. 'Put this out, will you. Mind you don't drop it.'

He grimaced at her. 'Thanks very much.' The less attractive side of fatherhood, he told himself, as he went out on to the landing, where the black refuse sack was kept.

'If the bag's full, will you put it out,' Fran called after him.

'That's right, give me all the dirty jobs.' But he didn't mind, not really. He felt his elation returning and, with it, a kind of nervous energy that needed some outlet for expression. Even if it was only dashing downstairs to put the rubbish out.

'Watch out for the nosy old wagon down below,' he heard Fran warn as he picked up the refuse bag. 'And whatever you do, don't encourage her. That one probably checks the bin to see what we had for breakfast.'

'That won't give her much of a thrill.' He grinned to himself as he went down the gloomy staircase. Fran was always moaning about the disadvantages of living in the top half of this bay-windowed, red brick terrace house but, let's face it, compared to the flat which they had rented when they were first married, this place was a palace. Their first flat had been over the hot-bread shop where Fran was working at the time. It had been poky, the living room looking out onto a sunless backyard bordered by a high wall, which in its turn was overshadowed by the blind side of a supermarket. The bedroom had faced a busy street. Traffic noises had persisted into the small hours and the neon sign from the pub opposite had cast shifting patterns of red and blue against the bedroom wall for most of the night. It was a real luxury to live in a quiet road in a house with a garden front and back – even if the gardens were untidy and the grass neglected.

And Mrs McGrath, the landlady, wasn't the worst, Mick

thought as he tiptoed past her quarters on his way to the back door. Okay, she was an inquisitive old thing and drove Fran mad with her questions but anyone could see the woman was lonely. Mind you, he didn't feel like talking to her today but, with any luck – uh-oh, that sounded like her! As he locked the back door behind him and headed back up the passageway he felt her presence just before he saw her. A kind of fusty smell. A mixture of old clothes and fried grease. She was dressed for going out, a battered felt hat pulled carelessly over her wispy white hair, hemlines dipping below a not-too-clean raincoat, a face that looked as if it hadn't been washed in weeks.

'I seen you go out this morning, Mick.' Although how she could have was a mystery to him since her rooms faced the back and the front room was let out in a bedsitter. Her cunning old eyes took in his shirt and tie, the crease on his pants. 'Were you goin' to a weddin', love?'

'No, not a wedding.' He grinned as he hurried past her. 'But now that you mention it – ' As he took the stairs two at a time, he recalled how it had struck him when he was leaving the house earlier that day that he was possessed with the same kind of excitement he had felt on another September morning just two years before, the morning he had gone out to marry Fran.

It was difficult to settle to anything. He threw his tie onto the back of a chair, opened the neck of his shirt, sat on the threadbare couch that faced the empty fireplace and stood up again. 'Have we any beer, Fran?'

'There might be a can in the fridge. Have you had anything to eat, Mick?'

'I'm okay.' Whatever he was hungry for, it wasn't food. Or beer either. He grinned at her. 'Sean gone down for his nap?'

'Yes. He's sound.' She looked up from the baby clothes she was folding and caught his eye. 'What are you looking at me like that for, Mick Cleary, at this hour of the day?'

'Your hair looks nice, Fran.' She was wearing it longer these days; it stood out from her head in a sunburst of curls, reddish-gold like the leaves that were beginning to drift down from the trees in the neighbourhood gardens.

'Thanks.' She went on folding the clothes, a thoughtful look on her face. He watched her for a moment, picked up a newspaper and tried to interest himself in an article. Then he threw down the paper, went over to the bay window and gazed down at the featureless garden. Next door, an elderly neighbour pottered among his roses. Across the road, beyond a row of parked cars, a man was painting his front railings, watched by a small child sitting on a tricycle. A peaceful scene, one that was at variance with the tumult Mick harboured within. He heard Fran behind him, smelt her perfume, felt her fingers touch his back.

'How'd it really go, Mick? Are you happy now you've met her?'

'Yes. No. I don't know.' He turned and pulled her into his arms, buried his head in her hair. 'I don't know what I feel, Fran. One minute I'm all excited, the next I'm – oh, I don't know.'

'It's only natural – ' she was beginning when he brought his mouth down on hers. Hard. His hands sought her breasts.

'Come to bed, Fran.'

'At this hour of the – ?'

'Yes, Fran, *now*. I want you.'

'But not here.' Her voice was shocked. 'Come in to the bedroom.'

'No, *here*.' He began to undress her, breathing hard as he unzipped her jeans.

'You're an animal, Mick Cleary, that's what you are.' There was laughter in her voice. 'Come over here. Anyone could see us in the window.'

'Who cares?' But he allowed himself to be led over to the couch. Then began to remove her clothing, piece by piece, until she was completely naked. His passion mounted as he caressed her warm body. 'Oh, Fran, you're beautiful. I want you so much.'

'Mick. Wait!' She began to unbutton his shirt. 'Your good clothes, you'll ruin them.'

'Who cares about them.' He allowed her to undress him, barely able to control his impatience. And then he was naked too. Her breasts were soft under him, as were her lips. When he felt her body opening to receive him his excitement rose to a crescendo. And as he came to climax, everything he had experienced that day, his hopes, his fears, his elation, all came together to take part in one overwhelming explosion of release.

'I haven't time for dessert.' Caroline pushed her plate away and got up from the table. 'I'm meeting Karen at nine and I have to get ready first.'

'I thought we agreed to cut down on discos this year.'

'The Leaving's not till next June, Mum. And anyway it's not a disco. It's a party in someone's house. And Daddy said it would be okay.'

Margaret looked enquiringly at Vincent, who said impatiently, 'The odd Saturday night out won't hurt her. If you have any problem getting a taxi home be sure and ring me, sweetheart.'

Caroline threw Margaret a triumphant look. 'Thanks, Dad.' The kitchen door slammed behind her.

'She hardly touched her dinner.' Vincent looked perturbed. 'Not turning into a picky eater like you, I hope.'

'Girls her age are always watching their figures,' Margaret said. 'How did the golf go?'

'Fine. What kind of a day had you?'

He mustn't have won his game. Otherwise she'd be hearing all about it. 'I didn't stay long in town this morning. Too packed.'

'What did I tell you?' Vincent was pleased at being proved right. 'Never go near the place myself on a Saturday. Do anything interesting in the afternoon?'

She hesitated. 'I went out to Dún Laoghaire. Walked on the pier.' Walked and walked. But still didn't lay any ghosts. Not that she expected him to understand. 'Are you playing golf again tomorrow?'

'What? No. Wish I could but I've a bit of work to do. Matter of fact,' he drained his wine glass, 'there's some stuff I want to go over tonight. You'll be okay, won't you? Get a video for yourself, or something.'

'I'll be fine,' Margaret said. 'As always.'

Vincent frowned. 'I don't like the way you said that. Anyone would think I was neglecting you. Look, we'll go out tomorrow night for a meal – no – I can't – I've a meeting first thing Monday, I need to be at my best. Another night, then.

Next Saturday. How about that? I'll get Jane in the office to book a table, invite what's-his-name in that new company I was telling you about.' He smiled to himself. 'Better keep an eye on the opposition.' Got up from the table. 'That's settled then.'

She looked at him and felt a sense of despair. If only they could have talked. If only she could tell him.

Vincent looked at her sharply. 'God, what is it *now?* What are you putting that face on for?'

'I haven't got a face on,' she said hurriedly. 'Honestly. That will be fine. Next Saturday will be fine.'

'Well okay, then.' He grimaced. 'But sometimes I get the feeling that you're never satisfied. No matter what I do to please you.' He stared hard at her for a moment. 'What do you *want* from me, Margaret?' There was something intimidating about his stare.

She felt at a loss, wrong-footed. 'I – it's no use if I have to tell you.'

'Oh God!' He threw up his hands in despair. 'Isn't this just what I've been talking about? I'll be in the study if you want me.' At the door, he turned and said, 'You don't think I want to spend my Saturday night working, do you?'

Why do it, then? But she hadn't the courage to say it. She sighed to herself as she gazed after his departing back. Just as long as he didn't tell her that he was doing it all for her.

As she poured herself another glass of wine her sense of despair deepened. Where did I go wrong? she wondered and found herself yearning back to a time before Vincent, before Martin. Back to a time when life had been safe and uncomplicated and she had been loved just for herself. Truly loved.

But had there ever been such a time? And had there ever been such a person?

Not Mummy, certainly.

Daddy? Before the betrayal? Before he had closed ranks with Mummy? Daddy had loved her, hadn't he?

Maybe. But she didn't want to think about that now. Further back? Yes, there had been someone. Someone who had truly loved her. Someone she hadn't thought about in years.

But who? She reached back into childhood, and up floated a name.

Delia.

Delia was great at playing games, I Spy and This Little Piggy Went to Market. And a marvellous one she had invented herself which involved lifting you up onto the kitchen table when Mrs Roberts's back was turned. You could peer up through the bars of the basement window and count the legs of the people going by on the street outside.

'I see two, no, that's four! And look, Delia, a dog. Don't people look funny when – '

'My clean table!' Mrs Roberts gave an outraged cry behind them as she examined the scrubbed board for marks. 'You'll have to do it again.'

'What harm, 'tis only clean dirt.' The girl laughed as she swung the child down to the floor. With her shiny black hair and rosy cheeks Margaret though she looked just like Snow White in the story book. 'Will we go to the Green and feed the ducks today, alanna?'

The little girl's eyes shone. 'Yes please!'

'Don't forget, madam wants that hat to go back to Switzers.'

'I know. She told me. *And* she wants a cake from Fullers.' Delia winked at Margaret. 'One of them walnut ones with the coffee icing.'

'What does she want to do that for?' Mrs Roberts looked distressed. 'She knows the doctor loves my walnut sponge.'

'But does the doctor have the say?' Delia winked again at Margaret. 'You know what her nibs is like.'

'You've no call to talk about madam like that. Even if – ' The housekeeper turned away, biting her lip.

'Ah, now.' Delia relented suddenly. 'I was only coddin' you. You don't really believe her nibs would be eejit enough to go buying a shop cake when she has a cook as good as you. I'm telling you, I was only coddin' you.'

'That sense of humour of yours.' Mrs Roberts looked vexed but Margaret saw she was relieved too. 'I suppose I can take a joke.'

'Of course,' Delia couldn't resist saying when she saw the older woman's face relax. 'You're the bigger eejit for believing me.'

'God give me patience.' Mrs Roberts threw up her hands. 'I don't know how I put up with you.'

She was to say that many times over the next few years but, looking back, Margaret remembered that, after Delia went and Mrs Roberts had to cope with a succession of serving girls who never measured up to her exacting standards, she often heard the housekeeper lament that none of them were 'a patch on *poor* Delia'.

'Who do you love best? Peter or me?'

'Let's see now – ' Solemn-faced, she would pretend to consider. Then, just when Margaret was beginning to get uneasy, Delia would throw a quick glance at the boy who sat poring over his sums copy, pencilling figures into little blue boxes with a careful hand, and then she'd turn and give Margaret a quick hug. 'You're my girl, Mags, you know that.'

'And you won't ever go away?'

'Now why would I do a thing like that?'

'What about tomorrow, then?'

'Ah now, that's different. But I'll be back before you know I'm gone.'

'Promise.'

'Cross my heart an' hope to die.'

Mrs Roberts lived with an unmarried brother in Harold's Cross and came in every morning on the first bus, but Delia was from a place called 'the country', where cows were liberated from the pages of picture books and hens perched on garden walls and told you when to get up in the morning. Peter, who knew about most things, being a boy and three years older, said 'the country' was miles and miles away. She went home to her family once a month and, when she did, she left very early in the morning. Margaret always meant to wake in time to see her go but she never did. She always felt a bit lost for a while after she woke up and found Delia gone. And Mrs Roberts, grumbling on about having to climb stairs 'and me with my veins' was *no* help. 'I'm up to my eyes here, child. Go and bother someone else.'

'Don't tell me it's the girl's day off? *Again?*'

'Can I come into your bed, Mummy? Just for a little bit? *Please?* I'll take my sandals off.'

'No darling. You'll only get marmalade on the sheets again.'

Margaret's lip quivered. 'But you always let Peter.'

'Peter knows how to behave. Play quietly while I make a phone call. If you're a very good girl, I might take you shopping later.'

Mummy's dressing table was crowded with jars full of cream and bottles with interesting smells. And look at all those lipsticks, like pink and red crayons. If Margaret wore lipstick she'd look just like Mummy.

'My dear, we can't rely on Julian,' the high voice said behind her. 'Someone will decide to have a burst appendix in the middle of the first act.' A crackle of agreement at the other end of the line. 'Yes, it is very awkward. Oh no! What *is* that child up to?'

And then Mummy was beside her, prising the sticky container from her fingers, her voice sharp with anger. 'You're a very naughty girl. Just *look* at the mess you've made of yourself. And there's powder *all* over the carpet. Peter! Where's Peter? Oh there you are, darling. Take this bold girl down to Mrs Roberts. And bring a dustpan and brush back with you, there's a good boy.'

'Yes, Mummy.' Peter's fingers took her arm in a painful grip as he hustled her downstairs to deliver her into the old woman's care. 'She's been bad,' he said with relish. 'And she's not coming out with us. Mummy *said.*' He took on a look of self-importance. '*Anyway,* most shops don't allow small children, isn't that right, Robbie?'

Mrs Roberts's lips tightened.' Doesn't Madam know I'm on my own?' But she accepted her charge with resignation, washed the lipstick from Margaret's face and hands and settled her down on the faded carpet of the little sitting room beside the kitchen to play with the doll's house Santy had brought last Christmas. And every now and then she'd pop her head around the door. 'Are you all right, child?' Knowing that she was in disgrace, Margaret would nod mutely and concentrate on placing the furniture neatly on the shelves of the house. It was always a long day when Delia was away but she knew it wouldn't last forever.

After lunch, which they ate together at the kitchen table, Mrs Roberts would put Margaret down for a nap on the sofa in the sitting room while she, herself, relaxed in an armchair with a newspaper, her feet up on an old leather pouffe that had seen better days in the upstairs drawing room before being banished to the basement. Soon the paper rose and fell to her snoring. The sofa cushion felt prickly under Margaret's cheek; it had a smell off it that was a funny mixture of cigarette smoke and rasher rinds but it was a familiar, comforting kind of smell. As she moved her head on the cushion to find a more accommodating spot she heard the old woman's snores, like bees buzzing in the sunshine, the laughter of children, a car starting up on the street outside, and then dreams that were shadowy and dark. In this shadow world she ran to the kitchen door, heard the sound of Delia's feet coming down the area steps and waited for her to come bustling in, laden with home-made butter and a cardboard shoebox full of brown eggs, each one carefully wrapped in its own little newspaper nest.

'I'm back,' she'd say. 'Did you miss me?'

And then it was evening and Delia really did come. As well as the butter and eggs she brought with her two sticky lollipops shaped like spinning tops.

You weren't allowed play with toys in St Celeste's, not even in the playground. On Margaret's first day there Mummy said, 'Doesn't she look lovely in the uniform?'

And Daddy said as he kissed her goodbye, 'You're going to love school, princess.'

But Delia was the one who brought her there.

'We must always change into our indoor shoes first thing.' Sister wore a black dress down to her ankles, a kind of white bonnet that hid her hair and a black veil over the bonnet. The only bit of flesh showing was the circle of skin between her forehead and chin and the pale fingers with which she indicated the shoe lockers and the numbered coat hook in the cloakroom which from now on would belong to Margaret. 'The floors must be protected.'

'Of course, Sister, the floors.' Delia's voice was unusually subdued as she admired the polished boards. She squeezed Margaret's hand as they followed the nun out into the corridor. 'Are you all right, lovey?'

Margaret said nothing as she tried to make sense of her surroundings. Everything in St Celeste's seemed to be made of hard surfaces: the wooden lockers in the cloakroom, the vast shining floors, the bare high walls of the corridors. There was a clean, cold smell to the place that was not unpleasant but was unlike anything she had ever known. A cheeky-looking boy in the middle of a line of small boys and girls which was forming in the passageway stuck his tongue out at her. Tears sprang to her eyes. Home seemed very far away. Then Sister beckoned to her to join the line. Margaret felt sudden panic. She tightened her grip on Delia's hand. 'Don't go!'

'It'll be all right, lovey,' Delia's voice whispered. 'Look, here's someone you know. Isn't that Susan Miller from down the street?' She pointed to a vaguely familiar-looking small girl with untidy brown curls and a tear-stained face standing at the end of the line. 'There y'are.' She prised Margaret's fingers loose and wrapped them around the other child's hand. 'You're to take care of each other, do ye hear?'

The two little girls nodded dumbly. As the line started moving away, Delia said, 'I'll be back for you at lunchtime, I promise.'

They followed the other children up a narrow staircase. Margaret tried to look back but a nun came up behind them out of nowhere and shooed them up before her. In a daze of bewilderment, she clung tightly to Susan's hand. But despite her bewilderment she held on to one certainty.

Delia would come back for her. She had promised. And Delia always kept a promise.

'Margaret's settling in at school quite well.' Mummy was pleased.

'Yes, Pidgie Miller says she and Susan have made friends.'

'Pidgie Miller? There's something foolish about that woman, Julian. I don't know why you encourage her.'

'They're patients of mine, Maeve. Besides, they're neighbours.'

'Well we don't have to be friendly with all our neighbours, do we? I hope Margaret makes other friends besides the Miller child.'

'It's early days yet, Maeve.'

Days turned into weeks, then months. There were summer holidays when they took a house in Skerries. Christmas came and went. But every day during term-time the routine was the same.

Hand in hand, she and Delia walked to school together while Peter ran ahead of them, rattling a stick against area railings, firing his schoolbag across cracks in pavements. Around the Square gardens they'd go, down the quiet street past the rows of houses, their scrubbed steps leading up to front doors with neat fanlights overhead, the sun glinting off well-kept paintwork and polished brass plates. When they reached the wide street, on the other side of which could be seen the three tall houses which comprised St Celeste's, Delia would call to Peter, who waited impatiently, scuffing his shoes against the kerbside, 'Don't you dare cross that road by yourself!' Although the traffic wasn't heavy it was sporadic and unpredictable, and she was taking no chances.

'*Now* you can cross.' Off he'd go like a shot, across the street, up the steps and through the door of the Junior School while she and Margaret would follow at a more sedate pace. Because *everyone* knew that boys might be made of 'slugs and snails and puppy dogs' tails' but little girls were made of 'sugar and spice and all things nice'. And little girls who went to St Celeste's would grow up to be ladies someday. And ladies didn't run across streets. When Margaret became a lady she would have a house of her own and she and Delia would live in it always.

Always.

But there's no such thing as always, is there?

It was Peter who told her. He prided himself on knowing everything that was going on. Mrs Roberts said he listened at keyholes. 'Delia's leaving.'

'She can't be! You're making it up.'

He gave her a look of triumph. 'Ask her yourself.'

'I will.'

She found Delia mopping out the scullery floor. 'Mrs Roberts's veins are at her again. I don't know how she's going to manage.' She twisted the cloth head of the mop between reddened hands, and grey droplets ran into the sink.

Margaret stared at her, aghast. 'It's not true. Say it isn't true.'

Silence, while Delia shook out the strands of the mop until they resembled a heavy grey wig. She didn't meet Margaret's gaze. 'I'm going on Thursday.'

'But my First Communion next month? You said you'd be there.'

Delia said nothing, her fingers idly separating the strands of the mop. Margaret felt a stab of alarm. She had never seen her like this before.

'But you promised.'

The mop gave off an acrid smell as it was stood up against the wall. Perhaps that was why Delia's eyes were red when she turned to her. 'I know, lovey. I'm sorry.' She tried to smile. 'But you'll be grand. You'll have such a great day, you won't even miss me.'

'But who's going to look after us? Bring me to school?'

Delia washed her hands and dried them carefully on the roller towel at the back of the scullery door. She pulled down her turned-back sleeves and straightened her apron. When she turned to Margaret, she was her own laughing self again.

'Haven't you a mammy and a daddy? And what about Mrs Roberts? Anyway, a big girl like you will soon be walking to school on her own. Peter will see you across the road on his way to the Marists. I don't want to hear another word out of you. You'll be grand.'

Tears welled up into her eyes. 'But you promised.'

'Look,' Delia sighed, 'if I can come, I will.'

'It's an ill wind as they say.' Mummy pursed her lips as she sorted through her embroidery silks. 'We'd have had to get rid of her sooner or later. Margaret was beginning to pick up all sorts of unsuitable expressions. I'd hate to think of what kind of accent she'd have ended up with.'

'It's a bad business, all the same, Maeve.' Daddy's voice was regretful.

'*Pas devant les enfants*, darling.' Mummy threw a warning look in Margaret's direction. She found the colour she was looking for and threaded the silk with precision through the eye of the needle. 'As I said, it's an ill wind. I never liked the girl. Too pushy for her own good. Didn't know her place. I can't say I'm too surprised at what's happened.'

'I think you're being a bit hard, Maeve.'

'Sometimes you have to be, darling. But then, if you don't mind my saying so, you're always inclined to think too well of people.'

'Maybe.' He lifted Margaret onto his knee. 'You look pale, chicken.' He felt her forehead. 'Let's see the tongue. Mmm, *looks* all right.' It felt safe sitting on Daddy's knee. His hands were warm and gentle. His voice was kind. She wished she could stay there forever. 'Maybe we should keep her at home for a day or two.'

'It's a bad time, Julian. I'm really busy with this Friends of the Hospital charity concert. Besides, she's not sick, just sulking because that *creature* is gone. You know darling, it's not good for children to get too attached. It only leads to trouble in the long run. She's better off at school, anyway. Take her mind off things.'

'Maybe you're right,' Daddy said doubtfully.

'Of course I am.' She finished off a perfect rose petal and held the tray cloth away from her to admire her handiwork. 'Take no notice of her. She'll have forgotten the whole thing in a few days.'

'What are you doing sitting here in the dark?'

She was startled back into the present as the sitting room sprang into light. She saw Vincent glance at the half empty glass on the coffee table near her chair as he went over to draw the floor-length curtains at either end of the large room. 'Don't you know that drinking on your own is the first step on the slippery slope?'

'Really? You surprise me.'

'No need to be sarky,' he said equably. 'You shouldn't

drink if it puts you in bad form. I think I'll have a nightcap, though.' He headed for the drinks cabinet. 'What are you on? Vodka?' His tone was conciliatory. 'Like a top-up?'

She recognised the peace offering and accepted it as such. 'Okay, thanks.'

'What were you sitting in the dark for, anyway?' he asked as he poured out the drinks. 'I thought you'd be gone to bed by now.'

'I was thinking.'

'Oh.' He glanced at her warily. 'What have I done now?'

She hated the way he was beginning to cast her in the role of the nagging wife. 'I wasn't thinking about you. I was thinking of someone who promised to be there for my First Communion and never came.'

'Your First Communion!' Vincent exploded with laughter as he sat down beside her. 'What put that into your – ? How many drinks have you had tonight?'

'It's got nothing to do with drink. It's just – oh, I wouldn't expect you to understand.'

'Damn right I don't. But then I never know what's going on inside your head. What brought all this on?' He glanced at her curiously. 'It's not like you to start talking about your childhood.'

'True.' She took a sip of her drink and felt the edges of her irritation soften. 'I – I met someone today who reminded me of the past.'

'Anyone *I* know?'

'No.'

'Oh, well then.' His interest faded. 'Tell me, are you sleeping any better?'

She sighed. 'Not really. I'm beginning to think I'm a hopeless case.'

'I could have told you that years ago. No, no – only joking.' He held out his hands in a supplicatory manner. 'I hope this doesn't mean you're going to take up permanent residence in the spare room?'

'Well – I – '

'Ah, Mags. Have a heart.' It was amazing how charming Vincent could be when he wanted something. He smiled at her and ran his finger along the inside of her wrist. 'That big bed of ours can be awful lonely at times.'

The guest bed was lonely too. Once in it, the memories could no longer be kept at bay. And Vincent was going out of his way to be pleasant. Tomorrow he would be his usual, critical self. But tonight he was pretending to be Prince Charming. Why not go along with the pretence? Who could it harm? Anything was better than being left alone with the past. Or to have to start worrying about the future.

She took another swallow of her drink. 'Well maybe, just for tonight.'

Vincent grinned, dipped a finger in his own glass, then smoothed down his little sandy moustache with the wetted finger. When he kissed her she tasted the whiskey on his lips.

'That's my girl,' he said. 'Finish that up and we'll go to bed. And listen, I don't need to spend all day tomorrow on those reports. Maybe we could go out somewhere, get a bit of fresh air. Pity to waste a Sunday.'

Tomorrow he could be singing a different tune, she thought. But who cared about tomorrow? As long as she could get through tonight, tomorrow could take care of itself.

'Here's to another Sunday.' Jim Hennessy raised his arm and half a tankard of beer slid effortlessly down his throat. He smacked his lips and gave a belch of satisfaction.

'Another Sunday,' Mick echoed unenthusiastically. Although it was early September and the weather was mild, the imitation coal fire in the grate was going full blast and the room was stifling. He shifted Sean to his other knee, took a half-hearted sip of his beer and sighed inwardly. God! He'd only just got here and already he was wishing it was time to go. He looked around for Fran but the minute they'd arrived she'd vanished through the archway leading from the sitting room to the dining room, and on into the kitchen, saying she had to help her mother with the lunch.

She did this to him every time, he told himself, leaving him to hold the baby, abandoning him to the clutches of Jim, the laughing Buddha. Not to mention the advances of Jason, Sandra's six-year-old, who was swarming all over the couch, trying to use Mick's shoulder as a launching pad for a space ship.

'Vroom, vroom,' went Jason, ramming the edge of the spaceship into Mick's arm.

'Christ!' He recoiled in pain. Startled by the sudden movement, the baby on his knee began to wail. Mick tried to soothe him, rub his own arm and fend off the little boy with his deadly toy all at the same time. 'It's okay, Sean. Will you go easy, Jason.'

'The joys of fatherhood, eh Mick?' Jim Hennessy's little piggy eyes gleamed. He laughed, his big belly heaving and his double chins wobbling in unison as he enjoyed his son-in-law's predicament.

'Well look who's here!' To Mick's dismay, Sandra irrupted into the room, with the careless bonhomie of one who has just spent the past hour in a packed pub. 'Mickser, the answer to a maiden's prayer. And Sean, the wonder baby.' She advanced on the couch, chased her son from it with a 'Feck off outa there' and slid onto the shiny, imitation leather surface, her tight skirt riding up over her thighs almost to the crotch of her flesh-coloured tights. Her sharp, spicy scent reached his nostrils and her dark, tawny eyes met his. 'Howya doin', Mick? How's that sister of mine treating you?'

As always, she made him feel like an awkward sixteen-year-old. As always, his senses were stirred by her perfume and by the sight of her pointed breasts. In an effort not to look at her legs, he couldn't help noticing that, as usual, she wore no brassiere under her clingy sweater. To hide his growing discomfort he clutched the baby to his stomach.

'Brilliant,' he muttered. 'Couldn't be better.'

She raised a cynical eyebrow and gave a disbelieving smile. 'That's your story and you're sticking to it.'

'That's right.' He looked her firmly in the eye, praying that Fran would come back into the room soon; she generally had a radar-like instinct for knowing when Sandra was around and would suddenly materialise out of nowhere to rescue him.

But not just yet. Sandra's thigh brushed against his and he found himself backing into the corner of the couch, holding the baby between them like a shield.

'Will you look at him.' She let out a hoot of laughter.

'Anyone would think I was going to rape him. Don't flatter yourself, Mick. You're not my type.'

He felt his cheeks flame up. You bitch! One of these days I'll get you up against a wall. He glared at her. 'Don't flatter yourself, either.'

'Why don't you give your mother a hand.' Jim Hennessy was getting tired of being left out of the conversation. Sandra shrugged and lit a cigarette.

'Shut up, Da,' she said without animosity. She turned to Mick again. 'How's that friend of yours, that fella who was your best man? Do you ever see him?'

'Donie?' Mick was surprised. 'Yeh, I see him on the job most days.'

'On the job? You can say that again.' Sandra gave a cackle of laughter. 'That fella's never off the job, if you ask me.'

He cast his mind back to his wedding day and remembered Donie's appreciative comments after he met Sandra. 'Jesus, Mick. You're marrying the wrong sister. Listen, boy, if a man were to get a leg over there – '

Had Donie – ? No, he'd have said something. Wouldn't he?

'That fella?' Jim Hennessy frowned, no longer the laughing Buddha. 'Wasn't he some kinda Kerryman?'

'Nothing wrong with that, is there?' Mick said stiffly. He glanced over at his father-in-law's huge hands cradling his pint mug. God, he hoped Donie hadn't been that foolish.

'He was a bit of craic, anyway,' Sandra said, blowing smoke carelessly in his direction. 'More than I could say for some.'

'Who's a bit of craic?' Fran suddenly appeared at Mick's elbow. 'If I've told you once I've told you a hundred times,

Sandra Hennessy, I don't want you smoking in front of my child.'

Sandra shrugged. '*You're* no craic, little sister, that's for sure. What's this *child* stuff, anyway? You'd think you were an expert. Wait till you've had one as long as me.'

'You're nobody to talk.' Fran's face flushed suddenly. She almost snatched the baby from Mick's arms. 'At least I waited till I was married.'

'Marriage,' Sandra snorted. 'You didn't waste any time getting the ball and chain on that fella.'

'Now, girls,' Jim Hennessy said. 'That's no way to – '

'Is that pair at it again?' Maisie Hennessy appeared in the archway, wooden spoon in hand, frilly apron over her shiny pink and purple shell suit, a lighted cigarette dangling from her lips. 'God, I don't know who they take after. Listen youse two – ' She waved the spoon threateningly at her daughters. 'I don't know what youse are on about but I don't want to hear any more about it. We'll be sitting down to dinner in a minute.'

'And then nobody's going to get a word in edgeways,' Sandra groaned mockingly. 'Once *you* start.'

'Cheeky bitch!' Her mother gave that laugh that always reminded Mick of water running too quickly out of a bath. 'Just don't *you* start.'

How in the name of God did he ever get mixed up with that lot? His heart sank as he followed his in-laws into the dining room. Was there no escape from them? The day stretched endlessly ahead of him. Just don't let it rain, he prayed. And maybe there was a chance he could persuade Fran to come out for a walk after lunch.

As they left the house a gleaming shape skimmed the nearby rooftops and soared cloudwards in a deafening burst of sound.

'One of your mother's crack fighter planes.' Mick threw up his hands, dodging imaginary bullets. 'I knew I'd pay for not taking that second helping of roast beef.'

'You're a real comedian.' Fran strapped Sean into the buggy and straightened up. 'That plane's probably taking people off for a fortnight in the Canaries.'

'Or to a villa in Cannes,' he said, without thinking. 'That's in the south of France, Fran.'

Her eyes gleamed. 'Oh, excuse *me*. I thought it was what beans came in.'

He reddened. 'Who's being the comedian now?'

She grinned. 'Sometimes I think *you* think I'm stupid. But a villa in the south of France, for God's sake?' She threw him a curious glance. 'Who do *we* know who could afford something like that?'

A picture of Margaret came into his mind; he saw the flash of diamonds as she lit a cigarette, heard her quiet voice.

'Nobody – a customer,' he lied. 'She said something about having gone there last month. It sounded – oh, I don't know – it sounded exciting.'

'If you like that kind of thing. Give me a fortnight in the Canaries, any time.'

He was stung by her dismissive response and found himself getting annoyed. 'More our style, do you mean?' His voice was crisp.

'What's wrong with the Canaries? Fran threw him a puzzled look. 'My brother Tony and his wife had a great time there last year. Maybe we'll be able to afford it some time.'

His annoyance grew. 'While we'll never have that villa, is that what you mean?'

She shrugged. 'No need to jump down my throat, Mick. No, I can't see us ever getting a villa, can you?'

He found himself glaring at her. 'So you're only going to wish for something that you think you've a good chance of getting, is that it?'

'It makes sense, doesn't it?

'Does it?' He looked at her bleakly. 'The world would be a very backward place if everyone thought like you.'

She frowned and slowed her pace. 'What's that supposed to mean?'

'Well, there'd be no progress if everyone settled for less.'

'I'm not settling for less. I just don't see the point of hankering after something you can't have.'

He fought down his irritation and said coldly, 'Well, that's the difference between us, then.'

'Oh is it? Right.' She turned and glared back at him. 'We're different. Big deal. I could have told you that for nothing. Are you happy now that you've made this great discovery?'

Happy? He stared at her, baffled, unable to respond. Fran shrugged, and they resumed their walk in silence.

On their way back to the house they had to pass a piece of ground which the neighbourhood children used for a playground. One section of it contained goalposts and a small pitch on which a few teenage boys were desultorily kicking a football to each other. Not far from the youths a man, with two small children and a dog, was attempting to launch a kite but the breeze was fitful and the kite kept dipping and falling to the ground, where it trailed in the long grass. The children ran around shrieking with merriment, the dog yapping frantically at their heels.

'It'd be nice for Sean to have somewhere safe to play when he gets older.' Fran's face was thoughtful as they stood and watched them.

'We have the use of the garden, Fran.'

She shook her head quickly. 'I mean – a place of our own.'

A sudden gust of wind caught the kite and flung it up into the air, where it hung quivering against the sky, a black and yellow demon's mask, with streamers fluttering. The children cheered in triumph.

'We'll get a house of our own,' Mick said as they moved away.

'This year, next year, some time, never.' He was surprised at the bitterness in her voice. Ashamed of his earlier anger, he felt an impulse to comfort her.

'Don't be like that, Fran. It's not the same as the villa in France.'

'Isn't it?' She looked at him morosely.

'Course it isn't. Wanting to have a house of your own isn't an impossible dream.'

'Do you really mean that, Mick?' Her face lit up. 'Like one of these?'

'Well – not *exactly*.' He surveyed the row of semi-detached houses without enthusiasm. As they came up to Hennessys he noticed that the house next to it had crazy paving on its front path, a plaster gnome peering from behind a clump of dahlias and a hedge cut into bird and animal shapes. His in-laws had contented themselves with a square of lawn and a tired-looking rose bush near the door. An ornate wooden plaque nailed to the wall proclaimed *'Sans Souci'* in Gothic lettering. Without care? That was a laugh. Once into one of these houses, a man's whole future would be mapped out for him. Once he took on a mortgage and bought a lawnmower, there would be no escape

'What then, Mick?'

'I don't know,' he hedged. 'I haven't given it much thought.'

'I have,' Fran said. 'I want a nice, safe neighbourhood. A house big enough for a family. And a garden at the back, with room for a swing.'

'We all have our dreams, Fran.'

The trouble was, he thought, as he manoeuvred the baby buggy into the Hennessys' narrow hallway, they dreamed of different things.

Her voice sounded distant on the phone. For an awful moment he thought he might have to remind her who he was.

'I said I'd ring.'

'I know you did.' But he had the feeling she had been taken by surprise.

Better keep this casual. 'How does Saturday afternoon suit you?'

'Next Saturday? Well, I – ' He sensed her trying to think up some excuse.

'It's okay if you can't – ' He kept his fingers crossed. 'Maybe another – '

'No, no.' Her voice was suddenly decisive. 'Saturday will be fine.'

Yess! He put his hand over the mouthpiece so that she

wouldn't hear his sigh of relief.

'Did you hear what I said, Michael?'

'Yes, yes. That's great.'

'The only thing is – I won't be able to stay long. It might not be worth your while.'

His confidence came back in a great surge. 'Let me be the judge of that.'

As he left the telephone box his heart thumped loudly against his ribs. He found himself smiling foolishly at people passing by on the street.

'Going into town?' Fran was surprised. 'It's such a nice day, I thought we'd take Sean for a walk.' She lifted the baby out of his feeding chair. 'Who's this mate you're meeting, anyway? Is it Donie?'

'Just a fella I used work with. Nobody you know. Ran into him the other day. Said we'd have a drink.' He knew he should tell her the truth but something stopped him. As the lies built up he took Sean from her and hid his face in the baby's soft curls, avoiding her eye. What she didn't know wouldn't hurt her. But guilt tugged at him. It made him suggest: 'Look, why don't you get a babysitter tonight? We'll go out somewhere.'

Fran looked dubious. 'It's awful short notice. She mightn't be free.'

'Try anyway. If all else fails, there's always Mrs McGrath.'

'That oul' biddy!' Fran bridled. 'I don't want her up here going through our stuff.'

'Sure, what secrets have *we*, Fran?' He held his breath as their eyes met over the baby's head.

Fran grinned and looked at him speculatively.' *You'd* better not have any secrets from *me.*' Then she asked, half laughingly, 'How do I know it's a mate you're going to meet and not some girl?'

'You've got me dead to rights.' He grinned back at her and stifled his guilt. 'Actually I'm going to meet a gorgeous blonde. I was afraid to tell you.'

'A blonde, hmm. I might have guessed.' Her eyes narrowed as she reached out her arms for Sean. 'What has she got that I haven't?'

He pretended to consider this as he relinquished his hold on the baby. 'A good question, Fran. A good question.'

'Oh, *you*!' She wrinkled her nose at him. 'Well, whoever she is, don't stay all day with her. There's a tap leaking in the bathroom you promised to fix.'

'That's what I love about you, Fran, you're so romantic.'

'*One* of us needs to keep their feet on the ground, Mick. And it isn't *you.*'

He took the steps up to the entrance of the hotel two at a time, pushed through the revolving doors into the opulent foyer past the bored-looking commissionaire and crossed the thick pile carpet into the panelled bar. Bet the drinks here cost a bomb. Just as well Donie wasn't with him. Donie was another person that what he didn't know wouldn't hurt him. He could just imagine his comments. 'Jesus, Mick, this isn't our kinda place. Careful you don't lose the run of yourself.' He banished his friend firmly from his thoughts. What did *he* know, anyway?

Apart from a man reading a newspaper up at the bar and

a couple of expensively dressed women with high voices sitting at one of the tables, the place looked deserted. Not to worry. She'd be along soon. He *was* ten minutes early, after all. He went up to the bar, ordered a beer and tried to quell his nervous excitement. Was he dressed properly? The mirror behind the bar cast back his image, clad in casual sweater and pants. Too casual, maybe? Should he have worn a tie? No, the open-necked shirt looked okay, although a suit wouldn't be out of place in these surroundings. Would he ever get it right?

He was halfway through his beer before he caught a movement in the mirror, turned and saw her enter the bar. He forgot his worries about his appearance, forgot his doubts about Donie, forgot everything in the excitement of seeing her again.

'I was afraid you might have changed your mind.'

'No, no. I was held up. It's been that kind of day, having to dash from one thing to another. I hope I don't look too ragged round the edges.'

'You look great.' It was an understatement. He could have written a poem about the way she looked. As he pulled a chair out for her at a table he asked, 'You didn't get all dressed up just for me, did you?'

'Not exactly. I'm going on somewhere afterwards.'

Stupid to feel disappointed. 'Yeh, I remember now – how long have we – ?'

She took off her jacket and placed it on an empty chair; he saw the curve of her breast under the thin stuff of her blouse. She glanced at her watch. 'About an hour.'

He looked at her in dismay. 'Is that all?'

'I'm sorry, but I *did* say.'

The waiter came up with her drink. Mick paid him, irritated at the interruption. It was difficult for him to take his eyes off her. 'That outfit. It really suits you. Must have cost a bomb, though.'

She smiled, said nothing and sipped her drink.

'Of course,' he gestured briefly, 'it goes with a place like this.'

She looked at him thoughtfully. 'Not your kind of place?'

It could be. It could be.

'You can say that again.' Pride made him shrug, adopt a hard-boiled tone. 'I'm one of the plebs, remember. I'm usually in places like this as a humble worker, not a paying customer.' In case she thought he was overawed by his surroundings, he leaned back and crossed his legs. 'Still, it's no harm to see how the other half lives.'

'Yes.' He saw the corners of her mouth twitch.

'I think you're laughing at me.' He didn't know whether to be offended or not.

'Not *at* you,' she said gently, '*with* you. You *were* being funny, weren't you?'

'Yes. I'm noted for it.'

This time she laughed outright.

He felt himself beginning to relax and felt safe enough to ask, 'Did you and my father laugh a lot together?'

Her smile vanished. 'Yes, I suppose we did. It was a long time ago.'

'It's not something you'd forget unless – '

She looked at him blankly.

' – unless you wanted to put it right out of your mind.'

Her blank stare unnerved him. 'You don't want to talk about it, right?'

'Something like that.' She fumbled for her cigarettes.

'You've one lighting already.'

Margaret gave an embarrassed laugh as she picked up the cigarette from the edge of the ashtray. 'I'm always doing that. It infuriates my husband.' She inhaled shamefacedly. 'Awful habit. But what would we do without them?'

'My ma smokes. I'm always at her to give them up. They're bad for her chest.'

She looked at him closely. 'You sound fond of her.'

'Yeh, well, I suppose I am.' He felt embarrassed suddenly. 'She's okay.'

'And your father?'

'Da?' What could he say about Da? And the Clearys? 'All right, I suppose. Means well, but – '

'But they're good people?'

'Yes, I suppose they are. I never really thought – '

'I'm glad, Michael. I've often wondered.'

'I've wondered, too.' Why did he always have the feeling with her of blundering up blind alleys, one-way streets? 'All my life I've wondered.' He stared at her in frustration. 'This is the second time we've met. And still I know nothing.'

'But I've told you,' she said, almost pleadingly. 'It's such a slight story, so little to tell.'

'Look, I realise you don't want to talk about *him*. It's too painful for you, isn't it?' When she nodded, he asked, 'But what about *you*? Can't you tell me something about yourself. You went to college, didn't you? What was it like?'

Her face came alive when she spoke about her time at university.

'I couldn't get over the freedom of it after school.'

'It sounds great.'

The way she told it, it sounded a magical place where life seemed to consist of parties and barbecues, leisurely strolls through the Green and gossip sessions with girlfriends to discuss who was 'doing a line' with whom and how long a particular romance was likely to last.

'I thought students spent their time discussing heavy stuff like nuclear disarmament and acid rain and holding protest marches and things.'

'There were those sort of conversations too, although pollution wasn't so much of a problem in those days. People argued a lot about religion – '

'Religion?'

'Don't laugh. There was rather a lot of it about then. On the surface, anyway. It was a different society, much more closed. It was okay as long as you kept the rules – or pretended to.'

'What about study? Didn't anyone do any work?'

'Most people seemed to fit it in somehow. And coming up to exam time there would be a mad dash to cram in as much as possible. Of course, there were the usual casualties.' Her face lost some of its animation. 'I didn't finish my studies. I had other things to think about. I was often sorry afterwards that I didn't take my degree.'

'Why didn't you go back later on? Or is that a stupid question?'

'No. I could have if I wanted to. That wasn't the problem. No, it was – ' She shrugged. 'I suppose it would have called for a certain amount of commitment – determination. I just didn't have it, that's all.' She bit her lip suddenly and looked away into the distance.

He hated to see that bleak look come back into her face.

'It's okay if you don't want to talk about it,' he said gently. Without thinking, he touched her hand. Then he saw the look of surprise on her face and took his hand away quickly in embarrassment.

'It's time I went.' She looked around for her jacket.

'Do you have to?'

'I *told* you.' A quick glance at her watch. 'I think I'd better take a taxi.'

'He won't kill you if you're home a bit late.' He tried to sound jocose. 'After all, it isn't every day you meet your long-lost son.'

He saw her face change. Suspicion dawned on him. 'He *does* know about me? You *have* told him?'

'He does and he doesn't,' she said reluctantly.

'What's that supposed to mean?' He stared at her in dismay.

She avoided his eye and got up from the table hurriedly. 'I really have to go. We'll talk another time.'

'When?'

'Ring me next week.'

It seemed like an eternity to wait.

On the bus home he tried to imagine to himself how she spent her time, and tried to picture her with her husband, her daughter. But it was a futile exercise. He gave up in disgust. He knew so little about her, after all.

'Everyone is coming back to our place for drinks.' A dumpy woman in an expensive dress pulled at Margaret's sleeve as they left the hotel restaurant. Swaying slightly on stiletto heels, she said archly, 'Now, I won't take no for an answer.'

'It's awfully kind of you but – ' Exhausted from making conversation with strangers over a meal for which she'd had little appetite, her only desire was to get away as quickly as possible. To her relief, she heard Vincent behind her.

'Another time, love.' Glancing back, she saw him bend and whisper in the woman's podgy ear. A loud peal of laughter rang out.

'Aren't you an awful man!'

'And she's an awful woman,' Vincent muttered, hurrying Margaret away across the hotel car park. 'Hate these bitches who can't hold their drink.'

'You surprise me. Considering the way you were playing up to her all night.'

'Her husband's one of our biggest customers; what do want me to do?' he said as they got into the Mercedes. 'Don't tell me you were jealous? That'll be the day.'

'No, just a bit disgusted sometimes. Do we have to be so nice to these people?'

'Business is business. Puts the bread on the table. Look, your father had customers too. They were called private patients.'

She was affronted. 'Not quite the same thing. Anyway, he didn't have to – court people, didn't expect Mummy to – '

'Want to bet?' He threw her a knowing smile. 'On the way up there must have been arses they had to lick: professors, senior consultants, the nuns. Your mother was well got with the nuns, wasn't she?' He adopted a falsetto tone. 'Yes, Reverend Mother, no Reverend Mother. I bet she could arse-lick with the best of them.'

'God, you're crude.'

'And you're naive. Will you grow up, like a good girl. Get your head out of the clouds.'

Head in the clouds? That was the way Mummy used to go on. As the car pulled out into the night-time traffic she found herself thinking back to her teenage years. She heard her mother's amused voice. 'Margaret walks around with her head in the clouds. Sometimes I wonder how she manages to find her way back from college.'

The hedges bordering the Square gardens were sepia against a colourless sky. The street lights came on as she turned the corner and saw what she hoped was the last of the bridge crowd coming down the front steps of the house. Old Dr Lavin and Mrs What's-her-name, the one who tried to dress like Mummy but hadn't the figure for it. Although her husband worked in the hospital and had taken out Peter's tonsils, she could never remember the woman's name. You couldn't mistake those legs, though. Just like Christmas hams. As she approached them Margaret pinned a smile on her face. If you weren't polite to Mummy's friends you heard all about it afterwards.

The old gentleman raised his homburg, softening the formality with a friendly nod before shuffling away but the woman stared at her with about as much warmth as that displayed by the glass eye of the dead fox nestling against the shoulder of her Chanel two-piece.

'Oh, it's you, Margaret,' she said with a marked lack of enthusiasm.

I suppose they've been talking about me again. I wonder what sin I'm supposed to have committed this time? 'Hullo Mrs – er – O'Reilly. How did the cards go today?'

'Bridge is a game of skill not chance,' her mother's friend informed her frostily. Small, unfriendly eyes took in the girl's sheepskin coat and fur-lined boots. 'You're well wrapped up, anyway.' Plump shoulders quivered visibly under the fine wool of her jacket. 'I wouldn't mind but I had to leave the car on the other side of the Square.' Her voice had a high, querulous tone. 'The parking gets more ridiculous every day.'

'I'm sorry,' Margaret found herself saying. Then she wondered what she had apologised for. She frowned to herself as she headed down the area steps towards the kitchen door. How could Mummy be friends with an old trout like that and have no time for a lovely woman like Susan's mother?

'Madam likes to mix with the right people.' Mrs Roberts deftly trimmed the edge off a piecrust and long, curling strips of pastry fell away on to the floured boards of the big kitchen table. 'Mrs Miller's a nice woman but – '

'Not grand enough for Mummy.'

'I'm not saying that, now.' The old woman's voice was careful. 'But she wouldn't have the right connections.' Mrs Roberts had been in service with a titled family in her younger days and knew about these things. 'It's important to mix with the right people, child; that way you'll make a good match.'

Margaret gave a hoot of laughter. 'Nobody bothers about

that kind of thing nowadays. Do they, Mrs Kavanagh?' She turned to the cleaning-woman, who had just come in from the scullery.

'Now what would I know about things like that?' Mrs Kavanagh had a raucous voice, roughened by many cigarettes. She pushed in beside the girl at the table. 'God, Mags, you're gettin' as big as a house.'

'I'm not *that* tall.'

'Compared to herself, anyway.'

'Of course madam is what you call fine-boned.' The housekeeper wiped the table clean and began putting cups and saucers out. 'Margaret gets her height from the doctor's side. You'll have a cup of tea, child?'

'I shouldn't.' She glanced at the little gold watch Daddy had given her for her seventeenth birthday in May. 'I had coffee in Bewley's with Susan when lectures were over. But – ' there was something comforting about the fragrance of hot tea when you came in out of the cold. And freshly baked scones. Her hand shot out towards a golden mound bursting with currants. 'These look delicious.'

'You'll spoil your dinner,' Mrs Roberts warned.

'It's always late on bridge evenings. No butterfly buns? Did they all go upstairs?'

'You'll be lucky if there's a sandwich left,' Mrs Kavanagh grimaced. 'Not with them priests.'

'Father Tim brought a friend. A monsignor.' Mrs Roberts threw a repressive look at the cleaning-woman, who winked at Margaret.

'I never seen a priest yet that didn't like his grub. The older they get the worse they are.'

The housekeeper patted the sausage of grey hair coiled under the wispy hairnet at the back of her head and darted a quick glance in Margaret's direction. 'You've no call to be talking like that, Mary.'

'Oh, excuse *me*.' The other woman pinned an expression of false humility on her freckled face and waved a packet of Woodbines at Margaret. 'Want a fag, Mags?' She laughed hoarsely at her own wit.

Margaret never knew whether to be amused at Mrs Kavanagh's insouciance or to be repelled by her coarseness. 'They're a bit strong for me.'

Mrs Roberts frowned. 'If madam knew you were smoking.'

'Ah, Robbie, you wouldn't.'

'I was only saying.' She gave Margaret a reassuring look. 'Don't worry, child. She won't hear it from me.'

'Ah, for God's sake.' Mrs Kavanagh dragged pleasurably on her cigarette. 'Doesn't she take the odd one herself?'

'It's not the same thing.' Margaret's tone was wry as she made her way to the door.

'Wouldn't you *know*.' The cleaning woman gave a guffaw behind her. 'It never is with *her*.'

She heard the sound of her mother's laughter even before she opened the door of the drawing room. Not that she had a loud laugh. Far from it. 'Refined' was a word that came to mind when you heard those tinkling cadences. They had a polished quality to them, the sort of polish the nuns in St Celeste's had been anxious for Margaret and her classmates to acquire. And something else too. Without having to be told, before she put her head around the door, Margaret knew from the sound of her laughter that she would find her mother among male company.

Sure enough, there were three men with her, two of them in clerical garb. The younger of the priests was helping the third man to fold up one of several card tables arranged in the bay window that overlooked the darkening garden. The other priest, an elderly man with thinning hair and a ruddy complexion, was sitting on the sofa beside Mummy.

'Oh, there you are, Margaret.' Her mother looked brightly at her. You're just in time to help. Leave that, Father Tim. Margaret will do it. Sit down and finish your tea.'

Father Tim threw up his hands obediently, grinned engagingly at Margaret as he abandoned his task, and resumed his seat, studying a nearby cakestand with renewed interest. He was a handsome man in his thirties with a slightly rakish air who always reminded Margaret of the character in Hollywood costume dramas who loses the girl to the hero in the last reel. Not that priests were interested in that kind of thing, she admonished herself as she went over to the window, recognising the other man, who had been left to wrestle with a hinge that was stubbornly refusing to close, as one of Mummy's tame doctors from the hospital, a bachelor of unspecified age, with an abrupt manner and a passion for bridge. Between them they dismantled the remaining tables and stacked them away in a cloakroom at the back of the hallway.

The doctor looked at his watch. 'Tell your mother I had to run. I'll see her next week.'

Back in the drawing room, someone had drawn the curtains and switched on a few lamps. The room looked warm and welcoming. She was introduced to the elderly priest, who turned out to be Father Tim's uncle. As the younger priest was some kind of a cousin of Mummy's, that must make him a relative too. Maybe that was why he held on to the handshake longer than most people normally did. 'A fine, tall girl.' His faded blue eyes studied Margaret as he reluctantly relinquished his grip. 'She's a credit to you, ma'am.'

'The trouble is, *Monsignor*', – Mummy pronounced the title with a kind of relish – 'she doesn't seem to know when to stop growing.' Then he said, in a concerned way, 'It's not good for a girl to be too tall.'

'In some parts of the country, there's a saying.' Father Tim picked a sponge wing off a queen cake, catching a blob of cream on its point before popping it into his mouth. ' "Beef to the heels like a Mullingar heifer."' He licked a stray crumb off his bottom lip and grinned at Margaret.

She felt her face flame up.

'*Honestly,* Father Tim!' Mummy giggled a genteel protest.

'It's all right.' The older priest patted Margaret's hand. 'They mean it as a compliment.' His hand lay heavily over hers.

She withdrew her own hand cautiously, fumbling in her cardigan sleeve for a hankie so as not to make the rejection obvious. She said doubtfully, 'Doesn't sound like one.'

'Where's your sense of humour?' Mummy dismissed Margaret's feelings with a wave of a manicured hand. A slim, dark-haired woman in twinset and pearls, her shapely legs crossed under a fine wool A-line skirt, it was obvious she would never be the butt of male quips. 'But he's right, you know. Men don't like girls to be taller than themselves.'

Father Tim looked taken aback, half-opened his mouth

to say something, thought better of it, glanced half-apologetically at Margaret and then shrugged, disavowing all responsibility. It was the older priest who spoke, with the air of one pouring oil on troubled waters. 'I think maybe what you meant was cleverer?'

'Oh well! In *that* case.' Mummy's laugh was like the tinkling of glass chandeliers. 'We've nothing to worry about. What do *you* think, Father Tim?'

'I – ' He was saved from the necessity of replying by the sound of the door from the hall being opened. All eyes turned to watch the tall figure of Margaret's father as he came swiftly into the room. He came to a sudden stop, a look of mild surprise on his face. 'I hadn't realised – '

'It's all right, Julian.' Mummy laughed soothingly. 'You're quite safe. The bridge crowd are gone.' She turned to the other men, inviting their laughter. 'He goes into hiding on Thursdays. I sometimes think he uses the patients as an excuse. Father Tim's uncle is up for a few days, darling. He has a parish in Kerry, you know.'

Margaret thought Daddy looked tired but by the time the introductions were over he had his social manner in place. 'You'll have something, Monsignor? Father Tim?' He went to the cabinet to get out the bottle of Jameson, the Waterford crystal tumblers. 'How are things in the – where's this you are now, Father Tim?'

'I'm still in Dublin.' The younger priest looked bland. No one was quite sure about what he did. He seemed to be loosely attached to the university. There was vague talk of a chaplaincy with a convent. Whatever work he had, it seemed to give him plenty of free time. 'I'm kept busy.'

'Fine, fine.' Daddy always seemed at a bit of a loss to know what to say to Father Tim. 'No, no, I won't have anything just yet,' he murmured when he had attended to the priests' needs. 'What I'd like is a cup of tea. Anything left in that pot, Maeve?'

'There should be.' Mummy lifted the quilted tea cosy, patted the gleaming flank of the teapot with a reluctant hand and looked around vaguely for a clean teacup.

'That tea will be stewed,' Margaret said. Daddy liked the second cup out of the pot, hot and not too strong. She jumped to her feet. 'I'll get more.'

Mummy frowned. 'There's a perfectly good pot here. Yours was all right, wasn't it, Father Tim?'

'It was, Maeve. A good strong cup.' He looked across at his uncle for corroboration.

'Aye.' The old priest took a thoughtful swallow of whiskey. His face looked rosy in the lamplight. 'Tea and whiskey should be poured strong.'

'Well, then – ' Mummy gave a satisfied nod, and lifted the teapot.

Margaret watched Daddy's face. 'I'll go,' she said again.

Mummy gave her a reproving smile. 'Mrs Roberts will be up to her eyes getting the dinner, darling.'

'*I'll* make it.' Margaret felt her face growing pink. 'I know how to make tea.'

Her mother said nothing, just smiled.

'Good girl.' Daddy sat down on the sofa beside the old priest in the place Margaret had vacated. He stretched his long legs out in front of him with a sigh. He gave her a trusting smile. 'While you're at it see if you can get a piece of Mrs Roberts's shortbread.'

The smile gladdened her heart. 'Leave it to me.' She reached for the teapot with eager hands.

Mummy looked baulked for a moment. But her voice when she glanced over at Daddy sounded indulgent. 'Well, if that's what you want, dear.' She surrendered the teapot to Margaret with a resigned smile. 'Now don't take all day, darling, And whatever you do, don't forget to warm the pot.'

As she left the room, she heard her mother say, 'I don't suppose she heard a word I said. Poor Margaret walks around in a daydream most of the time. Julian will tell you.'

Daddy's reply, if any, was lost in the closing of the door.

'Feel like a nightcap?' Vincent asked as they entered the hallway of the house.

'Why not?' She knew she had probably drunk enough but the thought of another vodka was very tempting. 'I'll just go up and see if Caroline's home. I saw her light on but I'd better check before you lock up.'

She tapped gently on her daughter's bedroom door and peeped inside. 'Are you asleep, Caro?'

'If I was I'm not now,' came the ungracious response. As Margaret looked in she saw the girl lift her head from the pillow, dislodging a magazine, which slid off the bed onto the carpeted floor. 'What do you want?'

'I'm sorry. Your light was on.' She felt the usual pang of guilt that Caroline engendered in her. 'I thought you were still awake. Did you have a good night?'

'Not really,' she scowled; for a moment she looked just like Vincent. 'School discos are *so* gross. Irish boys are just *pathetic*.' A familiar refrain since the summer. '*Juvenile*. At my age you had started college. You don't know how lucky you were.'

Yes. She had a sudden memory of the floor packed with couples at the Saturday-night hop. A saxophone wailing out 'Stranger on the Shore', two dark eyes on a level with hers and a hand pressed firmly against her back as they swayed in time to the music.

'Lucky? Funnily enough,' Margaret said, 'at the time I thought I *was*.'

'Come back from wherever you are.' Vincent's tone was caustic. 'That's the third time I – '

'Sorry, I was miles away.' She glanced at him over the rim of her glass. 'You were saying something about the trade exhibition. It was a success, then?'

'Great to see you take such an interest.' His smile was sardonic. 'Since you ask, yes. It went off very well. Of course you'd have known this if you'd bothered to turn up, like you said you would.'

'I *did* come.'

'Dead late. I was expecting you all afternoon. Where were you, anyway?'

She thought back to the hotel bar, saw a young man's eager face, remembered the anxious way he had asked, 'He does know about me? You *have* told him?'

She tried to banish the memory. 'I was held up at the hairdresser's.' It sounded a lame excuse but she couldn't think of anything more convincing.

'Till that hour? You barely made it in time for the drinks.'

'I know. I'm sorry. They were very busy.'

'You shouldn't put up with that kind of service, Margaret. Tell them you'll go elsewhere if it happens again.'

She began to regret being so specific. 'It won't happen again.'

'It better not. You shouldn't let people walk all over you. You don't see me putting up with that kind of shit.'

'No,' Margaret said. 'You never have.'

She could still see the look of incomprehension on Michael's face when she had answered, 'He does and he doesn't.' She thought back to that time years before when she had tried to tell Vincent, had tried to make him understand.

It had been in their first house, the modest semi in which they'd lived after they'd got married. It was early August, one of those close nights with all the windows left open to catch a breath of wind and that sense of apprehension in the air that sometimes precedes a thunderstorm. Just the two of them at the table, Caroline, little more than a baby, sound asleep upstairs. They had sat late over their meal and it was beginning to grow dark.

'You married me under false pretences.' She could still see the angry flush which had stained Vincent's neck and spread rapidly upwards until his whole face seemed to be on fire. 'You deceived me.'

'That's a bit strong, isn't it?' Already half-regretting the confidence, she tried to keep her voice light, although she felt the ground being cut away from under her feet.

'Is it?' A stranger's voice, hard and unforgiving.

She stared back at him, aghast. Then anger came to her rescue. Except that in her case, anger always came out as coldness. 'Why should it concern you? It all happened before I met you.'

'Why should it – ?' It was difficult to read his expression in the twilight. Over his shoulder, she could see the black shapes of small bats as they whirled and darted in the darkening garden. His voice was incredulous. 'You had a child by another man before we met and you say it was none of my business?'

She said nothing, played nervously with some cheese crumbs on the plate in front of her. Oh, God! Why did I have to tell him?

'All the time I thought you were so pure, so cool.' His voice rose. 'So *unapproachable*. It was all an act, wasn't it?'

She recoiled. 'No, it wasn't. I never claimed to be a virgin when we got married.'

'You never claimed otherwise. It was taken for granted. Oh, I know I suspected you had some experience but I didn't think it was anything serious.'

'Some experience?'

'Oh, all right – maybe I knew I wasn't the first – I just didn't want to enquire into it too closely, as long as it was over before I met you.'

'I've told you – it *was*.'

The room had grown dark. She could no longer make out his face.

'But – to have a child – ' he made an anguished sound. 'That's a different matter.'

'I can't see what's so different.' But she knew her voice lacked conviction. She got up abruptly and switched on a couple of table lamps.

'Who else knew about this?' Vincent blinked like a cat in

the lamplight. 'Besides your parents, I mean? Your brother?'

'Peter? Yes.'

'Anyone else?' His voice was like a whiplash.

'Susan. Nobody else.'

'Susan?' He stared at her. 'You mean *she* knows.'

'Of course, she's my friend. But she would never tell anyone.'

He finished off what was in his glass and reached out for the bottle. 'Well, that's something, I suppose – to know that half Dublin wasn't laughing at the eejit who thought he was marrying unblemished goods.'

The blood rushed to her cheeks. 'Is that how you thought of me? Like a piece of property – something you'd buy?'

She saw him pour out more wine for himself without offering her any. 'So that was why they had no objection to us marrying? I've often wondered. Someone with your background should have got herself a doctor or a barrister – at the very least, a college graduate. Not someone like myself, from the wrong side of the tracks.'

'No one says things like – '

'No? Not in so many words, maybe – ' He put his head in his hands and groaned suddenly. 'God! What a fool I've been.'

'It wasn't like that,' Margaret said. But was it? Had Daddy ever said he liked Vincent? And Mummy's attitude at the wedding, now that she thought about it, had been downright condescending. Especially towards Vincent's family. 'That wasn't why I married you.'

He looked at her bleakly. 'Why, then?' Noticing her hesitate, he added, 'It wasn't for love, was it?' The words had a harsh sound to them.

Love? Passion? Call it what you will. Whatever it was it was a trap. You fell into it without thinking. And it always let you down. She stared at him, dry-eyed, a band of pain around her heart. 'What about you? If you loved me you'd understand.'

'Understand?' Vincent's face contorted suddenly. 'I understand, all right. You really took me for a sucker, didn't you?'

'No, I didn't. It wasn't like that.' She put a hand out towards him. 'Vincent, please try to understand.'

He shook the hand away viciously. 'Get away from me, you slut! I never want to touch you again.'

The pain around her heart tightened. 'In that case,' she said, with as much dignity as she could summon up, 'there's nothing more to be said.'

'Suits me.' He glared at her. 'I don't care if I never speak to you again.'

'Margaret?' His voice reached across the no man's land between them as she lay staring into the greyness that comes just before dawn. 'Are you awake?'

Her head ached after a night without sleep. 'No.'

'Look, I shouldn't have spoken to you like that.'

'No, you shouldn't have.'

'But it was a hell of a thing to hear. A terrible shock, no point in pretending otherwise. I mean, what do you expect? Any man would have reacted in the same way.'

'Would they?' she asked dully.

'You know they would. But look, I've had time to think. Maybe I was a bit hasty. I can't pretend I like what you told me but, as you said yourself, it happened before we met. I think I can be big enough to overlook – '

'Overlook?'

'Well, maybe that's not the right word but – you know what I mean. Don't be like that.' She felt a hand reach out towards her under the sheet that covered them. 'Look, no man wants to hear a thing like that from his wife. There are men who wouldn't want to have anything to do with you after this. But I'm not like – ' The hand caressed her bare arm. 'Look, Mags, I think the best thing to do is forget the whole thing. Pretend you never told me. That way we can put it behind us, get back to the way we were.'

Was that possible? 'Pretend it never – ?'

'Yes, Mags.' His hand had reached her breast now, gently stroking her nipple through the thin cotton nightdress. 'Under the circumstances, I think it's for the best, don't you? Come on, Mags, I don't want to fight.'

'I don't want to fight, either. But – '

'What do you say? We'll forget all about it.'

She sighed. Under the circumstances, maybe it was for the best. But it was not what she had wanted to hear.

'Well – okay.' It had been stupid of her to think that things might have been different. 'We'll pretend it never happened.'

'Good girl.' His hand moved downwards over her stomach. 'We'll never mention it again.'

And they never had.

Mick waited till Wednesday to ring her. A strange woman answered and he rang off without speaking. Then he gathered his courage and tried again. This time, to his relief, he heard her voice at the other end.

'Was that you the first time? My daily woman thought you were a heavy breather.' Although she laughed, he thought she sounded as nervous as he felt. 'Don't worry. She's not inquisitive.'

'Must have been a wrong number,' he said gruffly, hiding his embarrassment. 'Look, I haven't much time. Are you okay for Saturday?'

'Well, actually, no,' Margaret said.

His heart sank to the floor of the phone booth. Then zoomed up again when she added, 'I need to see you before that. Are you free tonight?'

Despite his eagerness to see her, he hesitated. 'Saturday would be easier.'

'Saturday's out.' Her voice was firm. 'But there are a few things I have to explain.'

He was puzzled. 'Like what?'

'I can't over the phone.'

He made up his mind. 'Okay, tonight.'

He wondered what excuse he could make to Fran.

As it turned out, there was no need.

'This evening?' He looked blankly at her, unable to believe his luck.

'Yeh, I told you about it. Haven't seen Freda for ages, she's coming over for a chat.' As she whipped a pile of baby clothes off the airing rack, Fran sounded on the defensive. 'Suppose you weren't listening, as usual.'

He ignored the jibe and hid his delight. 'You want me to make myself scarce?'

She looked at him doubtfully. 'I know the way you feel

about Freda. Do you mind, Mick. There wasn't anything on telly you – ?'

'I'll watch it in the pub.' In his relief he put his arms around her and smiled down at her. 'You girls need a good natter now and then.'

Her face lit up. 'Do you know, Mick, you can be a real dote at times.'

He stifled his guilt. What she didn't know wouldn't hurt her. 'Enjoy your night, love.'

'I will.' She studied his face. 'Are you sure you don't mind?'

'No,' he said. 'I don't mind a bit.'

She was wearing the trench coat she had had on at their first meeting, with her hair worn loose around her face and a scarf at her neck the same blue as her eyes.

'Nice car.' He gazed admiringly at the silver BMW parked near the doorway to the pub. Behind them the car park was beginning to fill up although it was Wednesday, and early in the night.

'Yes.' She avoided his eye; she seemed uncomfortable with the compliment. 'It's the smaller engine, of course.'

He couldn't help smiling. 'Of course.'

Why did she always have to play down her wealth? A waste of time, as far as he was concerned. Because that car said it all. This year's model. Metallic finish, sleek lines, black upholstery. God! What he wouldn't give to own a car like that! If they were in a movie, she'd hand him the keys and suggest he drive. They'd leave the top down, and then they'd go bombing along, her sitting beside him in the passenger seat, her bright hair streaming in the wind.

'Michael.' He came out of his fantasy to find her looking at him enquiringly. 'It's too nice an evening to stay indoors. Do you feel like a walk?'

He fell into step beside her, they crossed the bridge and turned away from the canal down a side road. The colour had drained from the sky behind the small terrace houses and the street lights were beginning to come on. Although the breeze was gentle on his face he could feel a crisp hint of autumn in the air. 'You said you had things to explain?'

'Yes – well.' She didn't look at him; she seemed to be finding it difficult to start. 'I – the other day when I was leaving, you got a bit upset.'

He felt himself redden. 'I wasn't upset.'

'Surprised then – '

'That you hadn't told your husband you were meeting me? Look, I've had time to think about that. Maybe I was being a bit stupid.' After all, who knew what kind of character the husband was? 'Can't be easy bringing up the past again. How much does he know about me, anyway?'

No answer from Margaret. Just the ring of their footsteps on the pavement, the hum of traffic in the distance.

A suspicion tugged at him. 'But you told him when you got married that you had a kid, right?'

She gave a little laugh. 'That's the trouble.'

Anger fought with disbelief. Anger won. He turned towards her, his face furious. 'That's just great!'

'Look at it from my point of view.' She met his gaze reluctantly. 'You were something that happened to me when I was very young. There was no need for him to know anything about it.'

'*It?* So that's all I was, an "it"?'

'Don't be silly, Michael. You know what I mean.'

'No, I don't know what you mean.' He stopped walking and glared at her, heard his voice rise. 'I don't know anything about you.'

'Michael.' It had grown dark but there was a street lamp nearby and he could see her face clearly. 'Can't you see this is no good? We should never have met.' Her eyes were sad in the lamplight. 'I should never have agreed to it. It was against my better judgement.'

His anger gave way to alarm. 'Why *did* you, then?'

'I was curious.'

'*Curious!*' He felt as if someone had kicked him in the gut. 'Is that all? Curious?'

'I often wondered how you'd have turned out.' She began walking again and he followed blindly, falling automatically into step with her. 'I just couldn't resist the chance to find out. And now I have – you're all I wanted – all I hoped you'd be. But it's no good.' She slowed down and looked away from him into the darkness. 'We can't see each other any more. It won't work.'

The pain in his gut had spread through his body. It was all he could do to stop himself from doubling in two. He opened his mouth but the words wouldn't come.

She kept her face turned away from him. 'I think it's the best solution, don't you?'

He came to a sudden halt and found his voice. 'No, I don't! It's not the best solution. You can't leave it like this. I won't let you!'

'Keep your voice down,' she said quietly as a man and a woman came towards them out of the darkness. 'Let's keep walking. We don't want to draw attention to ourselves.'

'Well – okay.' He subdued his impatience and waited till they had passed the other couple. 'But I thought we were getting on so well. Don't you want to see me again?'

They came to a point where the road intersected with another. 'Let's go back this way.' She began turning the corner. 'It's quicker.'

'*Margaret*, will you answer me? Don't you want to – ?'

The traffic was heavier here. He had to strain his ears to hear her voice above the noise of the cars. 'Of course I want to see you again. I just don't think it's a good idea. I'm sorry.'

As they went back across the bridge, he said: 'But I'm your *son*.' He could hear the desperation in his voice. 'You can't just turn me away like that.'

'I gave you away a long time ago, Michael. I've no rights to you now.'

But what about his rights?

When they reached the car he tried again. 'We were just getting to know each other.'

He heard her fumble for her keys. 'Don't make it harder for me, Michael.' Lamplight from the gable wall of the pub glinted on her hair as she bent over the car door. When she straightened up she turned towards him. 'You have parents who love you. They need you. I don't.'

Despair filled him. He said nothing. As she turned away he saw something glisten on her cheek. 'Goodbye, Michael. God bless you.'

Long after the car had driven away he stood in the semi-darkness of the car park, feeling nothing, thinking nothing.

Sensation came flowing back slowly like life into a frozen limb.

The bitch! Oh, God! The bitch!

They need you. I don't.

How could she? Christ! How could she?

My own mother. To take me up like that and then drop me as if I were someone she'd picked up in a bar. I just don't believe it. It didn't happen.

The pub was noisy and cheerful. He saw an empty seat in a corner beside a young couple engrossed in each other, and took his drink over to it, resisting the temptation to bury his head in his hands.

How could she do it to him? Her own son. Her only son, come to think of it. How *could* she? God forgive her! Because he couldn't. God damn her! She was nothing but a – no, he couldn't say it – not his own mother – but that's all she was with her fancy ways and her perfume, and those expensive clothes. And that car she took for granted. Stupid of him to think he could mean anything to a woman like that. How could he have expected her to like a guy like him?

But she did like him. They had got on great the last time they'd met.

He thought of the way her face had lit up when she had spoken of her college days. She had been warm, and funny. And so likeable. They had been a man and a woman enjoying each other's company. Not like tonight.

Oh God. Why did they have to meet tonight? Why? Why? Why? He had known something was wrong. Sensed it. If only he had put her off. Said he couldn't get away till Saturday. If they had waited till Saturday it would have been all right. He knew it would.

Don't be stupid. She had her mind made up. What difference would a couple of days have made? Not much, he supposed. But he'd have had a few more days of hope. Now he had none.

Suddenly the beer he was drinking began to nauseate him. He looked at the couple beside him chatting quietly to each other, at the cheerful group opposite whose voices were getting louder by the minute, at the barmen with their professional smiles. And he wanted to smash all their silly grinning faces. Smash them and grind them on to table tops in pools of spilt beer and broken glass. And rip the hangings away from the windows and the lights from the walls and –

Abruptly, he put down his half-empty glass and pushed his way through the crowded tables towards the exit.

'What is it, Mrs McGrath?' His heart missed a beat. 'A phone message?'

The old woman smiled her gap-toothed smile. 'No love, that wasn't what I wanted you for. Will you have a look at me toaster. It's after going again.'

'No problem.' He hid his disappointment under a cheery smile. 'I'll just get a screwdriver. But if anyone rings up, you won't forget to tell me?'

''Course I won't, love.' She gave him a roguish look. 'Girlfriend, is it?'

'God forgive you.' He forced a laugh. 'Don't let Fran hear you say that. Girlfriend, indeed!'

There were days when he told himself that even if she were to go down on bended knees he'd have nothing more to do with her.

Bended knees? You've got to be joking!

Listen, Mick Cleary. If you've any sense you'll put it all behind you. That's the name of the game. Look, you met your mother and found out who your parents were. Isn't that enough? She's right; there's no place in her life for you. You don't belong. So why don't you get on with your life? Do all the marvellous things you've been promising to do for years? Make something of yourself.

What for? She wouldn't want me anyway.

'You're all I ever wanted or hoped for.' She had said it. He hadn't just imagined it. And he hadn't imagined the tears either. She doesn't want to stop seeing me, he told himself. I know she doesn't.

After a week went by and there was no word from her, it hit him. If he ever wanted to see her again it was up to him to do something about it.

'And that's it?' Susan looked closely at her. 'You won't be seeing him again.'

'No,' Margaret said. 'It just wouldn't be worth it. When I think of Vincent's reaction when I told him years ago. I just couldn't go through all that again.'

'But what about you? You'd like to go on seeing him, wouldn't you?'

She hesitated. 'I don't know. In a way I would. But it would mean having to go back over the past, talk about things I haven't thought of in years. He asks so many questions, you see.'

'It's understandable,' Susan said. 'In his position I think I'd be the same. But I can see why you wouldn't want to open things up again. As long as it's what *you* want, though, and not just to keep Vincent happy.'

Something in the other woman's tone of voice made Margaret look quickly at her. 'You never really liked him, did you?'

'Vincent? Well, I never thought he was good enough for you,' Susan said bluntly.

She sighed and looked down at her hands. 'Maybe better than I deserved, under the circumstances.'

'Don't put yourself down like that, Margaret. You were young, very young. You made a mistake, that's all. It could have happened to any of us.'

'Not to you, Susan.'

'Maybe that's because I never got the opportunity.' Her friend gave a wry laugh. 'Boys never looked at me in those days. If they had, who knows how I might have ended up. Don't punish yourself, my dear. You were unlucky, that's all. But remember, you put it behind you and got on with things. You didn't let it ruin your life.'

'And it's not going to ruin it now.' Margaret's voice was firm. 'I feel bad about Michael. He's such a lovely fellow. I don't want to do anything to hurt him but I really feel this is for the best.'

'Maybe you're right.' Susan didn't look wholly convinced. 'I've never had a child but I think that if I had one somewhere and he turned up out of the blue, I wouldn't want to let him go.'

Margaret's face grew bleak suddenly. 'I didn't say it was

easy, Susan. But it's not just my feelings to be considered, you know. There are other people involved in this too.'

'You're quite a stranger.' Ma tried to frown but she couldn't hide her pleasure at seeing him. 'Look, Maurice. It's Mick.'

'Mick who?'

'Come on, Da, it hasn't been that long.'

'A fortnight, near enough.' His father's gaze strayed back to the sports programme he had been watching. 'We thought maybe you'd emigrated.'

'I've been working hard.' He took the cup and saucer Ma handed him and sat down at the table. 'Never seem to get a minute these days.'

'Don't let Hennigans catch you doing nixers,' Da warned as he slurped his tea.

'Don't worry, I'll keep my nose clean.' Nothing changes, he thought. He turned to his mother. 'Everything okay with you?'

'We're fine, Mick.' She looked at him keenly. 'I met Fran at the shopping centre yesterday. She seemed a bit down.'

He looked at her guardedly. 'She was fine when I left her just now.'

Ma sighed. 'Maybe it was just my imagination.' She absently crumbled a piece of fruit cake on her plate. 'Mick – do you remember in March just after Sean was born when I gave you the name of that nun?'

'Yeh. I remember I had to fight very hard to get you to tell me.'

'What could you expect?' Her voice was tart. 'It doesn't do no good to go raking up the past. God knows I said enough to you about it at the time.' She looked at him almost hopefully. 'I don't suppose you changed your mind about that?'

'No.' He was tempted to lie but he couldn't do that with Ma. 'No, I didn't. I went to see her like I said I would.'

Ma's eyes narrowed. 'And?'

'There were a few hiccups. But – to cut a long story short – they were able to get in touch with my birth-mother. We met a fortnight ago for the first time'

She gave him a tentative look. 'What's she like, Mick?'

There was something vulnerable about Ma's face. He kept his voice casual. 'A nice woman, actually. Very respectable. Not a bit what I was expecting.'

'From down the country, maybe?' she probed.

'No, that's the funny thing about it. It all happened just a few miles away, the other side of the Liffey.'

'You're not serious? You mean – all these years – ?'

'Yeh, there she was, living her life, getting on fine without me. It's a funny old world, Ma.'

'Isn't it, Mick?' She shot him a quick look. 'How did she –' Was she glad to see you?'

Trust Ma to get to the point straight away. He thought back to their first meeting. 'She's not the emotional type but – yes, I think she was. Wouldn't *you* be?' He moved quickly to safer ground. 'She told me a bit about my father. They were at college together. Doesn't sound like he was much good. I gather he did a runner before I was born.'

'Poor girl.' Ma shook her head. 'Did she marry since?'

'Yes. She has a daughter doing the Leaving.'

'I see.' She hesitated. 'Will you be meeting her again?'

'Not much point, really.' He kept his voice casual. 'We haven't much in common. Different backgrounds, if you know what I mean.'

He thought he saw relief in her eyes but she was puzzled too. 'Tell us, Mick – '

'Another time, Ma. Not now.' If he gave her any more clues she wouldn't be long figuring out the truth. He made a show of looking at his watch. 'Got to run.'

To his surprise, when he bent to kiss her goodbye, she held him tightly for a moment, something she hadn't done in years. When she took her arms away she said quietly: 'I'm glad things worked out the way they did, son. Glad it's all over.'

The phone book was no help: she was obviously ex-directory. But he did have her phone number. And hadn't Donie a friend who worked in the telephone exchange?

'Jesus, Mick, they're not supposed to give out information like that. And anyway he mightn't be in the way of getting it.'

'Ah, come on, Donie, it's worth a try. Tell him there's a couple of pints in it for him.'

'I can't promise anything, now.' The black eyes looked at him speculatively. 'Who's this woman whose address you're so anxious to get? Have you been holding out on me, Mick? Has she a friend, maybe, that I might like?'

'God, Donie, it's nothing like that. It's this oul' one I did a job for, doing up a couple of flats. She still owes me some money, never gave me an address.'

'The old bitch! Pity, though. I thought you were beginning to show a bit of initiative. Marriage doesn't have to be a straitjacket, Mick.'

'For God's sake, Donie! If Fran heard you say that – '

'Wouldn't do her any harm, boy.' His friend shrugged. 'Keep her on her toes.'

'Donie! You know I'm not like that.'

'We're *all* like that, Mick, if we get half a chance. Don't fool yourself, boy.' He gave a wolfish grin. 'And don't worry about that other thing. We'll make sure you track the old bitch down.'

It was a large, detached house set well apart from its neighbours. A hedge of copper beech hid most of the lower storey from the roadway. He was relieved to see only one car, the silver BMW, parked on the gravel driveway in front of the double garage. He had made good time on the motorbike through the early-evening traffic. With any luck he could be in and out before the husband got home. That is, if he was let into the house in the first place.

It was a big 'if'. He took a deep breath as he came up to the front door, noticing the black and white carriage lamps on the porch walls, the bright-leaved plant trailing from the overhead hanging basket. He glanced at the brass knocker shaped like a wriggling fish and decided to ring the doorbell instead. A chime sounded somewhere inside the house. This is it, Mick. Another deep breath as he waited.

'Yes?' A teenage girl in a school uniform, fair hair in a thick plait over one shoulder, gazed at him enquiringly.

The daughter! He'd forgotten the daughter. He was tempted to make an excuse and turn away. Instead he mentioned Margaret's name.

'Just a minute.' She went away. And almost immediately

Margaret appeared, looking relaxed and friendly in a casual sweater and pants. Her smile vanished when she saw Mick.

'Dear God, it's you.'

His heart in his mouth, he said, 'I had to see you.'

She glanced around her with an almost furtive air and said reluctantly, 'I suppose you'd better come in.'

As he cautiously stepped onto the thick pile carpet he had a confused impression of light and space, shot through with coloured patterns from the huge stained-glass window which dominated the mahogany staircase. He had just time to notice a sunburst of flowers in a formal arrangement in front of a gilt-edged mirror and, in complete contrast, a grubby, denim bag overflowing with schoolbooks thrown carelessly on a chair beside it, before she hurried him through a doorway into a dining room.

'I won't be a minute.' She disappeared through another doorway, and he was left alone to examine his surroundings. Not that it took long. It was an amazingly uncluttered room. Pale walls, plain beige carpet. Slender-backed mahogany chairs stood around an oval table, bare but for a bowl of golden chrysanthemums on its polished centre. Ma would have found it stark, he knew. No photographs or ornaments jostled for space on the gleaming sideboard which took up the length of one wall, just a silver tray containing a cut-glass decanter and matching tumblers. Not her style at all. But Fran would have liked the curtains. Floor-length, on either side of the patio doors, their colours echoed the signs of autumn in the garden outside. He was studying the brown and gold leaves that clung like tattered bunting to the upper branches of a couple of birch trees on the windswept lawn when Margaret came back into the room, closing the door quietly behind her.

She sat down at the end of the table farthest from him. 'How did you find me?' Her voice sounded breathless, as if she had been running.

His own voice felt suddenly shaky. He tried to grin. 'I should have been a detective.'

She looked at him bleakly. 'You shouldn't have come here, Michael. Can't you see you're putting me in an awkward position?'

'I forgot about your daughter,' he said hastily. 'I'm sorry. She doesn't know either, I take it?'

'No, she doesn't. And I'm not going to – ' The bleak look intensified. 'What am I going to tell her?'

He reddened. The conversation was not going the way he had planned. He felt wrong-footed, on the defensive. The unfairness of it hit him. 'How do I know what you should tell her?'

She glared across the table at him. 'You don't have to shout.'

He glared back. 'Look, I didn't come here to spend the time talking about the lies you're going to tell people.' When he saw her wince he immediately regretted what he had said but it was too late to take the words back.

'Why *did* you come?'

'I wanted to see you again.'

Her face softened. 'Couldn't you have rung first?'

'I was afraid you'd hang up on me.'

Margaret sighed. 'Could you blame me if I had?'

'Yes, I would.'

'You blame me for a lot of things, don't you?'

He met her gaze squarely. 'It's hard not to. Maybe, if you told me. If I knew more about – '

She looked down at her hands. 'It's not easy. I'm not that free. There are other people to be considered.'

He felt a gleam of hope. 'So it's not because you didn't want to see me any more?'

'Oh, no!' She looked up, startled. 'Never think that, Michael. It's so cruel to have met you after all these years only to have to let you go again. But I did think – *do* think it's for the best.'

'No! It doesn't have to be that way.' His voice was urgent. 'We'll think of some way that we can meet. Margaret! I've waited a long time too. The whole of my life. Please don't send me away.'

He watched her face as she thought it over. Kept his fingers crossed. Please God, don't let it end like this.

She gave him a reluctant smile. 'I'll probably regret this.'

'You mean – ?' His sense of relief was enormous. He wanted to rush across the room and throw his arms around her, but he fought down the impulse. 'You won't regret it,' he said eagerly. 'I promise you.'

'I hope not. I hope I'm not making a terrible mistake.'

'Look,' he said earnestly. 'Nobody need know about it. I wouldn't want to do anything to make life difficult for you.'

She looked at him doubtfully. 'Are you sure?'

'I'm sure.'

It was not wholly what he wanted. But half a loaf was better than no bread.

'You managed to get away all right?'

'He had a meeting.' Margaret looked down over the sea wall, smiling ironically. 'He usually has a meeting.'

'Lucky for me.' He watched a seagull investigate a greasy paper bag thrown down on the rocks below. 'And Caroline? What does she do on a Saturday?'

'She's supposed to be studying.' She gave him a quick look. 'What did you tell your wife?'

They were like a couple of conspirators. The thought excited him. He shrugged away the faint guilt he felt at the mention of Fran. 'She thinks I'm meeting someone about a painting job. A nixer.'

The gull had broken through the paper bag to reveal a congealed mass of potato chips. It began probing it with a greedy beak. 'Isn't that disgusting?' Margaret said. 'People can be so careless. I hate mess.'

'So that's where I get it from!' He grinned at her. 'Fran always says I'm far too tidy for my own good. It isn't natural, she says.' He pointed at the gull, which had been joined by several others amid angry shrieks. 'Now, *that's* natural.'

They both laughed. As they walked away, leaving behind them a noisy battle for possession of the paper bag and its unappetising contents, Margaret turned to him.

'Michael, I wouldn't want to cause any trouble between you and your wife.'

'What trouble?' He smiled disingenuously. 'It's okay. Fran knows about you – that we've met. It's no problem. She wouldn't grudge me a few hours spent with my long-lost mother.'

'Well that's okay then.' They reached the entrance to the pier. 'I've always loved this place. Ever since I was a child. I suppose you know it well.'

'I'd know the other side of the bay better. Although when Fran and I were married first we often took trips on the bike down along the coast. Of course Sean put a stop to all that. Not that I'm complaining,' he added hastily.

But Margaret was following her own train of thought. 'It's not looking its best today.' The sea had a look of cold menace to it: the boats in the harbour seemed massed together for their own protection. 'You should see it when the sky is blue, the sun dancing on the water. Heaven to be out sailing.'

'Do you sail much?' he asked eagerly.

A shadow crossed her face. 'Not now. I'm talking about years ago, when I used go out with my father.'

'I suppose you had your own yacht?'

She glanced quickly at him. 'Daddy always had a boat. Not the sort you're thinking of, though.'

'What sort would that be?'

'You know. Something rather grand, with servants. It wasn't like that at all.'

'It's all the one to me, anyway.' He began to walk briskly, the wind in his face.

'Michael!' Her long legs matched his strides. 'I don't blame you for resenting my way of life, my background.'

'I don't resent it.' He felt the wind blowing the words back against him. 'Why do you keep pretending there's no difference? That's what I resent.'

'But – ' she sounded bewildered. 'It's all in your mind.'

'Is it?'

'Nobody pays any attention to social differences any more.'

'Want to bet?' He stopped walking, dug his fists into the pockets of his anorak and turned to face her. 'What did you tell Caroline about me the other day?'

'I said you'd come about a painting job.'

'There you are.' He was surprised at his own bitterness. 'Do you see what I mean?'

'What was so wrong about that? Painting's what you do, after all.'

'You mean I looked the part? What if I came to the door wearing a suit, talking in a fancy accent?'

'There's nothing wrong with your accent. But – ' she began to smile. 'I'd probably have said you were trying to sell me insurance.'

'Oh, what's the use!' He found it hard to stay angry with her for long. 'You've an answer for everything.'

She said in a jokey voice, 'That's what mothers are for, son.'

'Yes,' he said.

They stood and looked at each other for a long time.

He felt something wet spatter against his face and saw other walkers hurrying back towards them. 'It's going to rain. Maybe we should – ?'

'Okay. But let's stop a moment and look at the view.'

'What view?' Beyond the mouth of the harbour a grey sky was closing down towards the horizon. He turned away from contemplation of the cold expanse of water. 'I wouldn't fancy being out in a boat on a day like this'

It was easier to talk with the wind behind them. Droplets of rain trembled at their backs but the sun was shining on the shore ahead of them. It lit up houses, rooftops, spires of churches, a patch of green on Killiney hill. An insistent chinking sound that grew louder as they walked made him think of cowbells tinkling in Alpine pastures.

'It's the wind moving through the stay wires.' Margaret pointed at the boats at anchor in the harbour. 'Although I must say I like your *Heidi* image. My parents took us skiing once but it was a bit of a disaster. My brother broke his leg. Mummy was terribly put out; Peter was always her favourite.'

He was shocked. 'You mean she wouldn't have minded if it had been you?'

'She'd probably have said it was my own fault. "Margaret's so awkward."'

He thought about this grandmother whom he had never met. 'She's still alive?'

'Yes, she lives in Dalkey with Peter and his family.'

His interest quickened. 'He's got children?'

'A whole mob of them. Oddly enough, doctors don't seem to go in much for family planning. Mind you, there were only *two* of us. But that was Mummy's wish, I should think.'

'They'd be my cousins?'

'Now that you mention it, they would be.'

'And none of them know of my existence?'

'How could they?'

'Your mother – my grandmother – does she ever mention me?'

'Never.' She gave him a troubled look. 'Don't let it bother you. You haven't missed much where she or my brother is concerned.'

'But they're my relatives.'

She gave a helpless shrug. 'I know.'

'It doesn't sound as if you like them very much.'

'They're not very nice people.'

'But they're your flesh and blood,' he stammered.

Her face clouded over. 'Should that make a difference?'

He couldn't think of anything to say to that.

'Margaret?' He looked back to see her standing at the low wall that edged the promenade. She was too absorbed in following the course of the waves as they crashed against the shingly beach below to notice when he came up beside her. He stood watching her aloof profile and trying to guess her mood. With some misgivings he touched her sleeve. 'Margaret, it's starting to rain.'

She turned abruptly. To his surprise, she was smiling.

There was something heartstopping about that smile. He looked at her uncertainly. 'Margaret?'

'Isn't this marvellous?' She held her face up to the wind like a child and began to laugh as big drops of rain began to spatter against her cheeks and run down her chin. He watched her, without speaking, uncertain how to deal with this new mood of hers. When she turned back to him her eyes were dancing.

'I've made up my mind,' she said.

'What about?'

'About us. You and me, Michael.'

'And?' He gave her a cautious look.

'And. You're my son. I'm your mother. We have a perfect right to see each other.'

He stared at her dumbly, unable to take in what she was saying.

'And – ' her chin lifted bravely. 'If Vincent doesn't like it, he'll just have to lump it.'

He didn't believe her at first. He was afraid to believe. He searched her face anxiously but her smile didn't waver. And then it hit him suddenly.

'You really mean it, don't you?'

'Yes, I do.'

He knew then it was safe to let himself smile back. Safe to let himself laugh. *And cry.* It was as if something tightly knotted inside him had unravelled suddenly. And at last he was free of it. Tears filled his eyes. Not caring what the passers-by might think he put his arms around his mother and hugged her to him.

I'm your mother. You're my son.

How good the words sounded.

PART FOUR

Vincent's car was in the driveway when she arrived home. She found him sorting through some papers in the study.

'Are you in long?'

'No. The meeting dragged on.' He looked at her closely. 'Where have *you* been?'

Why did she have the feeling he was checking up on her? 'I went for a walk – by the sea.'

'Getting to be a habit with you, isn't it?'

She felt put on the defensive. 'I've always liked the sea.'

He looked unconvinced. 'You hardly ever visit your folks in Dalkey.'

'They have their own lives to lead,' Margaret murmured, hoping to deflect an argument. The fact that they saw so little of her relatives had long been a point of contention between them. She often felt that Vincent had a higher regard for her family than he had for his own, whom they seldom met any more. After his mother died, the links between him and his brothers and sisters had become tenuous and his desire to leave behind his working-class background had strengthened, along with his anxiety for Caroline to mix with what he called 'the right crowd'. And Margaret's relatives were definitely the right crowd, in Vincent's book. She sometimes suspected that it was one of his chief reasons for marrying her. 'But I'll have them over some evening soon,' she said placatingly. Tonight was a night for getting Vincent on to her side, not for antagonising him.

'Okay.' He was satisfied to have won his point. 'Caroline home?'

'No, she's gone to Karen's.'

He looked disappointed. 'No wonder the house is so quiet. So it's just you and me, then?'

'Afraid so. Steak all right?'

'Fine. Open a bottle of Chateauneuf du Pape, will you. Open it now, give it a chance to breathe.' For someone who had never tasted wine till his twenties, she thought, Vincent was good at giving the impression he was an expert. 'And get me a whiskey, like a good girl.' He went back to the balance sheet he had been studying. 'I've had a rough day.'

Hope it won't be a rough night. Maybe she should put off telling him till tomorrow. Or never, even. But she had promised Michael. It would have to be tonight.

The steaks spat and sizzled under the grill. Better give Vincent's another minute or two. He liked his done more medium than rare and would turn snotty if it wasn't cooked exactly right. No point in giving him any excuse. She mixed some salad dressing and cut the crusty bread he was so fond of into thick slices. When the meal was ready she took it into the adjoining dining room, where bright napkins, gleaming glassware and the bottle of red wine gave the table a deceptively festive air. The room itself, with drawn curtains and overhead lights dimmed, looked intimate, almost romantic.

She heard him behind her in the doorway. 'Oh, we're in

here, are we? What's wrong with the kitchen?'

'Nothing. I just thought – ' Maybe it had been a mistake? Would he see through her ploy; would the whole thing backfire on her?

To her relief, he smiled. 'Actually, this is nice.' He glanced at the table approvingly. 'Should do it more often.'

Apprehension robbed her of any pleasure she might have felt in the unexpected compliment.

'How was your steak?'

'Fine, fine.' Then, as if he realised how abrupt this sounded, he added quickly, 'Actually it was – delicious, the whole thing was. You're a good cook, Margaret.'

That was the second time tonight. She glanced at him doubtfully. What had got into him? He sounded conciliatory, ingratiating almost. Not words one would associate with Vincent. Even with a client he was trying to impress he would employ a hustling, abrasive sort of humour which swept all before it. When she met him first she had been bowled over by this mixture of drive and self-confidence but had learned over the years that it had a less attractive side to it. It was quite a surprise to see him hesitate over words, anxious to choose the right ones. Nor was it like him to linger over a meal when there were only the two of them at the table. At one time, maybe, but not recently. What was behind it, she wondered.

Maybe it was the wine? It was a particularly good one. Or could it be the dress she was wearing? It was one he had always liked. Whatever the reason, she had better make the most of it. Get in with her story. Present her case. But she would have to do it soon. Before his mood changed and he escaped back to his precious sales figures, leaving her with nothing but a bottle of vodka and her thoughts to keep her company. Do it now, Margaret, before your courage fails you.

Fingers crossed under the table, her heart pounding against her ribs, she said, 'I have something to tell you.'

To her amazement, he listened intently, without interrupting. When she had finished talking she bowed her head and waited for the storm to break.

But sometimes things don't turn out the way you think they will.

Silence for a moment. Then she heard what sounded like a relieved laugh. She looked up in astonishment.

'I thought you'd be angry.'

'By rights I should be.' He shook his head and laughed again. 'You little bitch! You really had me worried. I knew you were meeting someone – '

'You were spying on me!' She felt her face flush.

'No I wasn't. You were *seen*. What did you expect? Dublin's not that big and you didn't exactly go out of your way to hide it, did you?'

'Since it wasn't what you thought,' she said stiffly, 'I had no reason to hide it.'

'But you didn't tell *me*, did you.' His face tightened. 'I don't like things going on behind my back, Margaret.'

As always she felt wrong-footed. 'I know – and I'm sorry. I should have told you but I didn't think things would turn out the way they did, that I would want to see him again.' It was hateful to have to put herself in a position where she practically had to beg from him. But, for Michael's sake –

She dug her nails into her palms and forced herself to sound penitent. 'Please believe me.'

'Well, okay.' Vincent began to look mollified. 'I suppose it could have been worse. But no more lies, Margaret. I need to be able to trust the people around me. You're my wife, for God's sake. If I can't trust my own wife – '

'I'm sorry – '

'Don't let it happen again.' He was very much the managing director ticking off a subordinate. 'Now about this character – this fella – don't tell me I'm expected to meet him?'

'Well – yes – he wants to – and Caroline too.'

'Caroline?' His brows snapped together. 'That's one person who hasn't been mentioned here. Have you given any thought to her feelings?'

'Well, obviously – ' But, as she said it, she realised that in the excitement of the afternoon's events she had given very little thought to Caroline or her feelings. 'But I don't think it will be a problem. She might even be pleased. She's always wanted a brother.'

Vincent looked sceptical. 'You don't think it'll be a problem. That's the trouble with you. You don't *think*. Look, if you want to bring this character here – '

'My son.'

'Okay.' A look of distaste crossed his face. 'Your son. If you want to bring him here I can't stop you. I suppose I could but there'd be no living with you if I did.'

'That's not fair, Vincent.'

'Why not? It's the truth. But you're one of those people who don't like the truth. As I said, you can bring him here. I'll even feed him, give him my drink. He *does* take a drink? That's *something*, I suppose. But you're to leave Caroline out of this. I'm not having her upset. She's my daughter – '

' – she's my daughter too.'

'Well, don't you forget it. She's not to be told anything about this. It's her Leaving year, and I don't want anything to upset her studies.'

'But what are we going to tell her?' Margaret was distressed. 'How will we – ?

'You'll think of something.' He got up from the table to show that the discussion was over. 'As long as you don't upset her you can tell her any damn lie you want.' His smile was mirthless in the dim light. 'You're good at that.'

'You needn't think I'm coming with you on Wednesday.'

'That's okay,' Mick said quickly. Too quickly. He saw Fran's eyes narrow.

'I wasn't invited, was I? What's the matter? Am I not good enough for her?'

'She's not like that. But we thought – the first time – '

'We?'

'Look, I thought you'd understand.' He felt resentful suddenly. 'Why are you trying to spoil it for me?'

'I'm not the one trying to spoil things.' Her voice was laden with meaning.

'I don't want to go through that again. I thought you'd be happy for me.'

'I am, I am.' She sighed. 'I just wish you knew what you were getting yourself into.'

So do I. Believe me, so do I. Aloud he said, 'Don't worry,

Fran, I think I'm old enough to know the score.'

Know the score? He didn't even know the ground rules.

It wasn't just a question of what to wear. Or of which knife to use. Although that did worry him a bit. It was the feeling of venturing into unknown territory that scared him. He had no stomach for his breakfast on Wednesday morning.

'Wish me luck, Fran.'

'Yeh, sure.' She yawned sleepily and began to butter a piece of toast. 'Don't be too late tonight.'

'Don't worry.' He tried not to show his disappointment at her lack of interest. 'My Ma taught me not to wear my welcome out.'

'Good for her.' She smiled faintly and went on with her breakfast.

As he left for work his mind leapt forward to the evening. Instead of the joyful anticipation he had expected to feel, he knew what it must be like to be a soldier facing into a minefield without a map.

'But who is he?' Caroline was intrigued. 'Some distant relative? Of Granny's, is it? From County Waterford? Is she coming too?'

'No.' She seized the red herring gratefully. 'It's a bridge night, and you know how Mummy is about – ?'

'I know.' The girl giggled. 'Nothing short of a death in the family. And even then – '

'Set the table for me, will you.' Margaret sliced a melon in half and began scraping out the seeds. 'We'll eat in the dining room.'

'Okay.' Caroline watched her curiously. 'You're going to a

lot of trouble, aren't you? What's he like, this old cousin, a bit of a stickler for etiquette? If he's a relation of Granny's that wouldn't surprise me.'

'It was your father's idea to eat in the dining room.' Margaret suspected that it was part of Vincent's plan to keep their guest at arm's length. 'And Michael's not old. He's quite young, actually. Not quite twenty-two.'

'Oh?' Caroline's interest was aroused. 'In that case, I think I'll change out of my school uniform.'

Margaret hid a feeling of unease. 'Do the table first.' She forced a laugh and tried to sound gently humorous. 'And don't start getting any ideas. He's married. With a child.'

Caroline's shoulders slumped. 'Typical! I might have known you wouldn't invite anyone interesting.'

'He *is* interesting.' For a moment she was tempted to brave Vincent's anger and tell Caroline the truth. It was what she wanted to do. But she had agreed to his conditions and had given her word. She couldn't go back on it now. 'I hope you'll like him.'

'Don't count on it,' the girl said ungraciously. 'You and I have very different tastes.'

'We'll see.' Although she kept her voice light she was filled with sudden apprehension. Please God, don't let this be a mistake, she prayed.

The sitting room struck him as being huge. You could have comfortably fitted the whole ground floor of Ma and Da's house into it and still have room over. Despite its size it had a welcoming air, with its soft carpet, comfortable couches and the log fire blazing in the huge brick fireplace. Attractive table lamps dotted at intervals around the place provided a soft, mellow light. Although darkness had fallen outside he noticed that the long window curtains at either end had not been drawn and that the two glass chandeliers overhead were unlit. He had just time to take in these details when he heard Margaret say, 'Caroline, this is Michael.'

'Hi!' The girl, lounging on one of the couches had long, blonde hair the same colour as Margaret's. She looked up from the magazine she was reading and gave him an amiable nod. Then her eyes narrowed. 'Haven't you been here before?'

'I –' He was taken aback. He looked at Margaret and waited for her to explain.

To his surprise, she said quickly, 'No, this is the first time Michael has been invited.' As he stared at her in puzzlement her eyes slid away from his. 'Sit down, make yourself comfortable.' She headed over to the well-stocked drinks cabinet. 'You'll have a beer?' Her voice had a determined gaiety to it. 'I'm going to have a vodka myself.'

'A beer would be great.' Still puzzled, he sat down on one of the couches to find Caroline watching him over the edge of her magazine. Her eyes were an unusual colour, not blue like Margaret's but green, with amber lights, the kind that normally went with red or sandy hair. She frowned at him, obviously trying to work something out.

'It's funny. You're awfully like someone who came to the door last week – of course I only saw him for a minute. Must be just a coincidence.'

'Must be. They say we all have a double.' He hid his discomfort under a show of humour. 'Hope he was good looking?'

'It was more the height than anything else.' Caroline pursed her lips. She struck him as someone who didn't let things go easily. Maybe they had that in common. She was his sister, after all. 'Probably just a coincidence. Funny, all the same.'

'Life's full of coincidences, darling.' Margaret still managed to avoid his eye as she handed him his drink. 'Isn't it, Michael?'

He was saved from the necessity of replying to this by the sound of car wheels on the gravel outside. Margaret went over to draw the curtains as headlamps lit up the big front window.

Caroline's face brightened. 'Dad's home.'

He felt a tightening in the pit of his stomach.

One down, he told himself. And one to go.

He wasn't at all what Mick had been expecting. Didn't measure up to the picture he had formed in his mind. He had been expecting someone taller, for a start. Taller and more – ? Glamorous was a funny word. But yes, glamorous was the one that occurred to him. Someone sophisticated, handsome in a mature kind of way. Cultivated. Someone *worthy* of Margaret. Not an ordinary, five-eight type of bloke, a couple of inches shorter than her, with thinning hair and a little sandy moustache which he touched occasionally as if to reassure himself it was still there. He looked fit enough; there was no sign of a paunch under the well-cut suit. But he was much too old for her. Fifty if he was a day, with a lot of lines on his sharp, alert face.

'So you're the famous Michael?' His voice was another

surprise. Harsh, with none of the well-modulated cadences he had grown used to hearing in Margaret's voice, which were echoed in Caroline's. Eyes, the same colour as his daughter's, examined Mick shrewdly. 'Well, well.'

He felt himself redden but decided not to take offence. No point in getting off to a bad start. 'I'm not famous. Not yet, anyway.'

'Do you expect to be?' His eyes were more amber than green. Like a cat's. He struck Mick as the sort who pounced on words, making you explain yourself even when he wasn't particularly concerned with the answer. Obviously a tactic with him. The thing was not to let him know you were rattled.

'Who knows.' He kept his voice light. 'I'm young. I've plenty of time.'

The other man's eyes narrowed. But before he could say anything, Margaret broke in hurriedly. 'Michael's a northsider like yourself.' It hurt Mick to hear the nervousness in her voice.

'That right?' Vincent lost interest suddenly. The cat no longer wanted to play. 'Get me a whiskey, Caroline, like a good girl.' As she scrambled to obey, he took her place on the couch, stretched his legs, and yawned hugely. 'Traffic gets worse every evening. Time something was done about it.' He glanced at Mick. 'Maybe you have the right idea. That your motorbike outside?'

'It is, actually.'

Vincent grunted. 'Looks a bit shook. What mileage are you getting out of it?'

'I'll leave you two to get to know each other.' Margaret stood up. 'Dinner won't be long.'

Both men watched her as she crossed the room. But when she turned at the door, Mick felt that the little smile she gave was just for him.

'If there is an election – '

'Oh, Dad, not that again.'

Mick felt himself in sympathy with Caroline. Vincent liked the sound of his own voice, he thought. Either that or he had some reason for keeping up an endless flow of talk on impersonal matters. The history of every car he had owned – or driven – going back to the elderly Morris Minor which had been his first, had occupied them through most of the meal. Now it was the turn of politics.

'The business community will certainly welcome an election.' Vincent warmed to his theme. 'This present crowd haven't a clue how to manage the economy.'

Mick glanced over at Margaret. She gave him a startled look as if he had interrupted her thoughts. 'More of anything, Michael?'

'I think I've enough, thanks.' The meal had been delicious. He was surprised to see that she had barely touched her own. He caught Caroline looking at him and saw her frown.

'Don't get started on the economy, Dad. I want to ask Michael something.'

Vincent gave a resigned laugh. 'Okay, the floor's yours. Fire away, honeybunch.'

'Just how are you related to us?' The girl's green eyes were puzzled. 'I thought I knew all of Mum's relatives. Where exactly do *you* fit in?'

'You mean you don't know?' He stared back at her in

astonishment. 'I thought your mother would have explained.' He looked at Margaret. Tell her, he pleaded silently.

She gave him an apologetic look, then turned to Caroline. 'There's no secret about it.' Her voice sounded faintly amused. 'Michael's distantly related on my father's side.' As Mick stared at her in growing disbelief she explained that they'd always known of the connection but had lost touch over the years. It sounded plausible enough the way she told it, provided you didn't dig too deep.

'For God's sake,' Vincent said impatiently. 'What difference does it make? Second cousin, third cousin. It's all the one.' He gave Margaret a peremptory look. 'What about a cup of coffee?'

'Won't take a minute.' She got up with alacrity. 'Is coffee okay for you, Michael? Or would you prefer tea?'

'I don't care,' Mick said. He stared after her departing back. So that's the way it was? He might have known there'd be a catch.

He looked dully at Caroline, who had been listening intently. 'Have you brothers and sisters?' she asked.

'No. I'm an only child.' That bit was true at least.

'We have something in common then.' She looked pretty when she smiled.

You don't know the half of it. He forced himself to return the smile. 'Yeh, maybe we have.'

He caught Margaret's eye as she returned with the coffee pot, and he read the unspoken plea. Try to understand, it said.

He didn't understand. He felt weighed down with disappointment. He didn't understand any of it.

'Why didn't you tell her?'

'I think maybe the time isn't right yet.'

He felt a sense of frustration. 'What's that supposed to mean?'

'These things take time. Look, Michael, I don't want to get into this over the phone. We'll talk about it the next time.'

'Is there going to be a next time?'

'Well, of course. I thought you understood. You can come and visit me any time you like.'

His spirits rose. He put his doubts to one side. 'That's great. Maybe you're right about Caroline. We'll give it a bit of time.' After all, she wasn't the only one. Fran needed a bit of time too. 'We'll work things out, Margaret. You'll see.'

'Mum, there's a meeting on Wednesday for the parents of the Leaving Certs,' Caroline said over her shoulder as she began rooting through the refrigerator.

'Wednesday's a bit awkward. I've invited someone over.'

'Not *him* again?' Her sharp eye had already spotted the pencilled initial on the kitchen calendar. 'Must you?'

'Don't you like him?'

'He's okay,' the girl shrugged. 'Is all the low-fat cheese gone?'

'You should know.' Her mother smiled faintly. 'Unless we have a resident mouse in the fridge.'

'Ha, ha! Very funny.' She gathered together the ingredients for a hearty snack and dumped them down on the kitchen table. 'Want some?'

'No thanks. I'll just have a cup of coffee.'

Caroline wrinkled her nose. 'Do you have to smoke?'

'Sorry,' Margaret said but she didn't put out the cigarette. She moved away from the table and took up a position near the window. Glancing out at the rain-drenched garden she fell into a thoughtful silence.

Caroline was used to these silences but they still had the power to irritate her. She could never decide whether her mother possessed enormous reserves of patience, enabling her to sit out an argument, or whether she was merely indifferent, thinking other thoughts, perhaps, while waiting for a response.

Don't let it bother you, she told herself. Pretend not to notice. She sliced a tomato with swift downward strokes and arranged the slices carefully on the roll between layers of lettuce and cheese. Now for the tiniest smear of mayonnaise. She checked the label on the jar, made sure it was Lo-Cal. Sometimes life seemed to be a constant battle with calories but Caroline felt it was worth the effort. She might not be as tall as her mother but at least she could try to be as slim. She studied her sandwich and decided to replace some of the cheese with cucumber. Less fattening. As a reward for such self-discipline, she would allow herself a glass of Diet Coke. And maybe a tiny piece of that yummy gateau left over from last night. She glanced, half-guiltily, across the room. But Margaret, head slightly averted, seemed more interested in the progress of raindrops moving sluggishly down the window-pane than in what her daughter was having for lunch. Relieved, Caroline nibbled at a piece of lettuce and returned to the attack.

'About Wednesday, Mum.'

Margaret turned reluctantly. 'I've told you – '

'Can't you put him off?'

'I'm afraid I can't.'

Caroline was incensed. 'Are you telling me this – this Michael person is more important to you? More important than my whole future?'

'Of course not.' She was surprised to see her mother's face colour. 'I – it's not that easy to get in touch with him.'

'That's ridiculous.' As she bit into the roll a piece of tomato escaped and dribbled down her chin. She wiped it away irritably. 'Why do you have to have him over so often?'

'He's only been here twice.'

'And Wednesday will make three times. In a *fortnight*. Come on, Mum. You've never bothered about relations before. Even Granny doesn't come that often. What's so special about *him?*'

Margaret's eyes flew open. She was obviously startled by the question. An uncertain look crossed her face. Some intuition told Caroline that her mother was on the brink of a disclosure. She felt a sudden sense of excitement. At last she was going to be taken seriously, treated as an adult to be trusted with a confidence. She put down the half-eaten roll and looked eagerly at her mother. 'Tell me, Mum?'

To her disappointment she saw Margaret draw back from the brink. The blue eyes grew evasive and studied the tip of her cigarette. A slender finger tapped out ash meditatively. 'Why on earth should you think that?'

Disappointment struck Caroline like a blow. Undeceived by the other's light tone, she said petulantly, 'Fine! Don't bother to tell me.' Running her hands through her hair until it fell untidily, half-hiding her face, she began to cram pieces of food into her mouth. Keep your stupid little secret, for all I care, she thought savagely. Probably something utterly unimportant, anyway. Grown-ups were always making a fuss about very little. 'It doesn't matter.' But, as she stared at her mother, she was overwhelmed by a sense of loss.

'Don't be like that, darling,' Margaret said quickly. 'There's nothing to tell.' It was her turn to run her hand through her hair, pushing it back from her face in a characteristic gesture. 'I'm being nice to Michael because – because I owe it to his mother.'

'Really?' Caroline's lip curled. It was clear to her that what was now being offered was merely a substitute for whatever information was being withheld. The moment for truth was gone. 'Was she a friend of yours?' she asked without any real interest.

'I knew her – a long time ago.' Margaret's face was sad suddenly. She turned away and went back to studying the raindrops.

Another stupid silence. Any sympathy Caroline might have felt for her mother vanished abruptly, to be replaced by exasperation. What about me?

Glancing down at her plate, she saw it was empty. She must have finished the roll without even noticing. Worse still, she couldn't even remember what it had tasted like. Well, she knew who to blame for that. She started to throw angry, accusing looks across the room until it dawned on her that they were having no effect on Margaret, who seemed to have retreated into a private world of her own. Life was so unfair. Denied her right to be an adult, she relapsed into childish-ness.

'You needn't bother about the school meeting. I'll ask Dad. He takes more interest, anyway.'

'Who's this, Margaret? Is that your mother?'

'Yes. Doesn't she look young? That dark hair, not unlike yours, really. Oh, look, there's one of me and Peter – Skerries, I think.'

They were in the big drawing room, curtains drawn at each end. Firelight. And a few lamps lit here and there. To the girl watching from the doorway, the couple sitting on the sofa, heads bent over the photographs, seemed to be on an island in a sea of darkness. Or on a lighted stage. The two heads, one fair, the other dark, seemed very close together. They were both laughing as Margaret pointed out some detail, her voice eager. Caroline thought she had never seen her mother look so animated before. So *beautiful*. With a queer little stab of jealousy, she thought, She looks like a young girl.

'That was taken the summer I left school, just before I started college. Aren't the dresses strange? Skimpy somehow. And the patterns! Did you ever see anything so gaudy? That's Susan Miller, my best friend.'

He studied the holiday snap with interest. The two girls blinked at the camera, the sun in their eyes, wispy grass sprouting from sand dunes in the background.

'She wasn't as pretty as you.'

'Perhaps not then.'

'Not ever, if you ask me. What happened to her?'

'She's a concert pianist, travels quite a bit.'

'I know the sort. Dedicated to her art. No time for a man in her life.'

'You're wrong, as it happens.' She laughed gently. 'She's happily married to a violinist. Looks aren't everything.'

'Still.' He grinned at her. 'I bet *you* had all the fellas after you.'

Caroline saw her mother reach out for another album, look up and catch sight of her in the doorway. 'I'm showing Michael some old photographs.'

'Is that what you're doing?' Her voice dripped sarcasm. 'I'd never have guessed.'

The young man smiled at her. 'Why don't you join us?' He had a pleasant smile. In other circumstances she might have found him attractive. 'These old photographs are great stuff.'

'Boring, you mean.' She gave a look of disdain. 'I have to study, anyhow.'

'A pity.' He seemed genuinely disappointed. But maybe he was only being polite. He had good manners for someone from the northside. He smiled again. 'Maybe next time?'

She refused to respond to the smile. 'Maybe.'

As she closed the door she heard Margaret make some remark but couldn't catch the words. The young man laughed and Caroline was convinced they were talking about her. With burning cheeks, she took the stairs to her bedroom two at a time.

She hated him. She wished he had never come there.

'That's the house in Ballsbridge.' Margaret smoothed out a curled-up corner of the photograph. 'We moved there in

January. You were born the following November.'

He did a quick calculation. 'So you didn't move because of *me*?'

She looked surprised. 'Is that what you thought? That we had to leave the Square because I was pregnant? No, no, the decision was made long before that. The reason given was that Daddy wanted to be near the new hospital but Mummy had been going on for years about how the Square was going down. A lot of families had sold and the houses were turned into flats and offices. When they put a photographer's studio into the basement next door to us, it was the last straw, as far as she was concerned. I suppose she had a point but I hated leaving our house. It affected me quite badly. I often thought that if we'd never left, things might have been different.'

He touched her arm gently. 'Tell me about it. But only if you want to.'

'You mightn't like what you hear.'

'I'll take that risk.'

She smiled wryly. 'He was a good listener too. In fact, at the time, I felt as if he was one of the few people who really cared.'

'It must be rough having to move.' Martin's dark eyes were sympathetic. 'Like you, I've lived in the same house all my life. I missed the place something awful when I came to Dublin first.'

'But you know you can go back for weekends and holidays. *My* house has been sold. I can never go back to it.' She felt inconsolable. 'It's not the same thing.'

'No.' He took one of her cold hands between his two warm ones and smiled into her eyes. 'Poor Margaret.'

'And the worst of it is Mrs Roberts didn't come with us. She said all the years of climbing stairs had caught up with her. Even though there's only two storeys in the new house, she didn't want to work any more. We've got someone else but it's not the same. And Mummy doesn't even *care*. She says Robbie was past it, anyway. You'd think she was talking about an old horse put out to grass. If she *was* a horse, Mummy would probably have had her put down. I know that's an awful thing to say about someone but my mother can be very hard sometimes. She *uses* people.'

'Sounds a bit like my old man.' Martin nodded. 'All over them to their face when it suits him, not a good word to say behind their back.'

'That's it exactly.' She looked at him eagerly. 'I knew you'd understand.'

He said earnestly, 'You were great that time I told you about him having too much to drink over the Christmas. There's not many girls you could tell that to. You'd be afraid they'd turn up their noses at you, wonder what kind of a home you came from, at all.'

'I'd never do that. I always think, "There but for the grace of God – " Thank goodness Daddy isn't like that. But if he *was* – '

'God forbid! I wouldn't wish that on my worst enemy let alone someone as nice as you,' Martin said, with feeling. 'It's not so bad for me. It's much worse for the ones at home. And I don't know how my mother puts up with him. Tell you what – ' he glanced at the bare, windswept trees and at the duck pond with its inhabitants swimming disconsolately around in the grey afternoon light. 'It's cold enough here to freeze a brass monkey. I've finished lectures for today. Why don't we go back to the house I'm in? It's not that far to walk, about fifteen minutes. We can make coffee and talk.' He smiled into her eyes and tightened his grip on her hand. 'How about it, Margaret?'

Go to his house? It was the first time he had suggested anything like that. Usually he was rushing back to study. As she returned his smile she could feel her body react to the pressure of his hand against hers. Butterflies in the pit of her stomach, a sudden moistness between her legs. Her cheeks burned. To hide her confusion she spoke quickly. 'Why not? I'd love to see where you live. I'll have to skip French but I can get the notes from someone in my class.' A thought struck her. 'Will there be anyone there?'

'No, the other three lads are doing engineering. They have lectures all day. That's the beauty of arts. You have more time for the books.'

She stifled a pang of guilt. 'I wish I were more like you. You're so dedicated you put me to shame. But it's only the end of January. Early days yet. I'll really get down to it soon.'

'Of course it's not so important for you,' Martin said as they went through the gateway of the Green and began crossing the street. 'It never is for a girl. You're only going to go and get married. And, anyway, your folks are well off.'

'I hadn't given it much thought,' she admitted. 'But I really feel too depressed at the moment to talk about the future. I'm more worried about how I'm going to get through the next few months in the new house. It's like a madhouse at the moment. Mummy goes around looking distracted, measuring everything. And Daddy keeps saying he can't find anything, and why did we have to move. And the phone never stops ringing.'

'That's something the house lacks.' He grinned at her. 'One of the *many* things, if the truth be known. God knows, it's a bit of a kip. And it can be a bit of a madhouse too when the lads start arguing about politics and the like. But at this hour of the day it'll be nice and quiet.'

'I know it isn't what you're used to.' Martin's voice was apologetic as he showed her into the shabby, musty-smelling hallway. 'Bit rough and ready. But it does us lads. And the rent is reasonable.'

'It's grand.' Margaret glanced around her with interest. 'I like old houses.' Although, if she were to be completely honest, its age was about the only thing the place had in common with the house on the Square. The kitchen, for instance, with its dingy cupboards and sink half-full of dirty pots, would never have passed Mrs Robert's scrutiny. No prizes for guessing her reaction to the greasy gas cooker and the ancient fridge. As for the peeling wallpaper and cobwebs in corners only half-guessed at because of the uncertain light, she could almost hear her mother's shriek of disgust. She pushed all thoughts of Mummy from her mind and turned her attention to the moss-covered patio glimpsed through a grimy window-pane in the kitchen. 'The garden has a lot of old-world charm. Could be nice if it was tidied up.'

'If they cut down those trees,' Martin agreed as he filled a kettle at the crowded sink. 'As it is, those trees cut off the light from the back of the house. You should see my bedroom. It's caught in a perpetual twilight.'

At the mention of his bedroom she felt a twinge of embarrassment, avoided his eye and looked out at the garden again. 'You have a nice way with words, Martin. But that's because you're a writer. Can I ask you, what kind of things do you write?'

'Poetry mostly. I don't usually show it to anyone but I wouldn't mind with you. But – ' she heard the hesitancy in his voice ' – maybe you wouldn't be interested?'

'Well of course I would. I'd be really honoured.'

'Do you mean that?'

'Yes.' She turned to find him watching her eagerly. 'I really mean it. I've never met a poet before.' Her gaze faltered under his intent scrutiny and she felt her face getting warm. It was a relief when the kettle suddenly came to the boil with a high-pitched whistling sound. They looked at each other and laughed.

'We'll have this first.' Martin reached into one of the dingy cupboards and took down a jar of instant coffee. 'Then I'll show you my room.'

'Is this where you write?' She averted her eyes from the untidily made single bed, avoiding the mournful gaze of the Sacred Heart picture on the wall overhead, and tried to concentrate on the books and papers on his desk. 'Are you working on something at the moment?'

'Just finished this.' He proffered a foolscap sheet. 'I'm not that happy with it.'

'Why not?' She glanced at the neat handwriting. 'It has a

clarity about it. The rhyming couplets remind me a bit of – '

'Pope or Dryden?' His face flushed suddenly. 'But they do it better.' He took the sheet from her, crumpling it in his hand. He then threw it into a waste basket, which was already overflowing with paper.

'Ah, why did you do that?' Margaret was disappointed. 'I thought it was really good.'

He shook his head. 'I have this picture in my mind of how it should be. But it always falls short.'

'I thought it was good.' She felt abashed suddenly. 'But maybe you think I'm not much of a judge?'

'No, no, I didn't mean it that way. It's just that I get a bit frustrated sometimes. My mother says I'm impatient. I want too much too soon.' He stroked her hand and she felt electricity tingling up and down her arm. 'You can't blame me. When I see someone like you – ' They were standing very close now, their faces almost touching. 'Oh, Margaret!' She closed her eyes as his lips met hers. 'You don't know how beautiful you are.' His arms went around her and she felt the rough coverlet on the bed scrape against the back of her legs as he urged her gently downwards.

His lips were soft at first, then became more demanding. They had kissed several times before but they had been gentle, goodnight kisses, not urgent, probing, exciting ones like these. She felt the weight of his body pressing against hers. And then his hand under her sweater, caressing her breasts, sending tremors throughout her body. His two hands moved around to her back and began fumbling with the catch on her bra.

'No!' Margaret pushed his hands away although a part of

her wanted him to go on. She struggled to sit up. 'I think I'd better go.'

'Maybe you should,' he said in a low voice. He rolled away from her and sat on the side of the bed, his chest heaving. As she pulled down her sweater and straightened her skirt, she saw him turn and meet her gaze. 'I'm glad you stopped me.' His eyes were solemn. 'Before we went on and committed a serious sin. Next time we'll stick to the couch downstairs.'

'Yes,' Margaret said. 'Next time.'

The springs in the living-room sofa were loose and poked painfully into her spine, and the base creaked and swayed so alarmingly under the weight of their bodies that it seemed as if it were in danger of disintegrating under them at any minute.

'This is no good,' Martin muttered. 'My bed is rock-solid compared to this. And we've no privacy here. If one of the lads walked in – '

Margaret was suddenly conscious of buttons open on her blouse and a skirt that had worked its way above her knees. Nothing *wrong* had happened. But it would be embarrassing to be caught like this. 'Maybe you're right. If we just lie on *top* of the bed.'

It was dark in the bedroom. A raw February day outside. Rain spattered against the window panes. The two-bar electric fire gave out a feeble glow.

'Leave the light on,' she said.

'Of course, whatever you want.' He pushed back her blouse and kissed her throat until her whole body began clamouring for the touch of his hands.

This time when his fingers sought the catch on her bra, she didn't try to stop him.

'But it's only a fortnight since we were there last,' Susan objected. 'We'll be late for the film. Won't it wait till next Saturday?'

'No.' Margaret dipped her finger into the stone font outside the church door. 'I want to go to Holy Communion tomorrow.' She felt her cheeks go pink. 'I was out with Martin the other day.'

'Oh, is that the way it is?' The other girl nodded wisely. 'Wish I had something to tell like that.' As they entered the echoing building, she hissed, 'Better be careful which priest you get.'

' – Passionate kissing and immodest touches,' she whispered into the darkness.

'How many times?' The man on the other side of the wooden partition had a sonorous voice, the kind that could carry a sermon into the four corners of the church.

'Um – several times.' Wish he'd keep his voice down. A whole row of people waiting outside. Hope he doesn't ask for details.

'Anything else, my child?' To her relief, he didn't sound too interested.

'No, Father.' She fell back on formula. 'And I'm sorry for all the sins of my past life.'

'Ten Hail Marys for your penance. Now make a good Act of Contrition.'

'Yes, Father.' She sighed with relief and gabbled out the prayers, falling over the words in her haste to get it over and done with.

The priest said in a bored voice, 'Go, and sin no more.'

'We'll probably burn in hell for this,' Martin whispered as his hand moved up her thigh and began stroking the soft inside of her leg.

What was another sin among so many?

'Ten Hail Marys. *And* a Hail Holy Queen.' This priest, more inquisitorial than the last one, had sought particulars. 'Remember you are a temple of the Holy Ghost,' he informed her sternly. 'It's your duty to avoid occasions of sin.'

'Yes, Father.'

That means don't go to his house any more. But, as she joined the evening crowds hurrying up Grafton Street in the rain, she knew that nothing was going to be able to keep her away.

'How's the study going, Margaret?'

'Fine, Daddy, fine.' How could anyone be expected to study when they were in love? Her body tingled at the memory of his hands. She could hear his voice murmuring in her ear and could smell the special smell of him. She stood at the dining-room window and savoured the thought of his lips tasting hers as she watched a man planting a small tree at the edge of the newly seeded lawn.

'I told him he should do that first.' Mummy's voice sounded plaintively behind her. 'But he just wouldn't listen.

Sometimes I wonder will we ever get this place to rights.'

'It will be grand, Maeve,' Daddy said soothingly. 'It's just the one tree. Everything else is in place. Rome wasn't built in a day.'

The daffodils would be beginning to bud in the back garden of the house in the Square. Last year she had had a bet with Daddy over which one would flower first. Now someone else would enjoy their beauty. She felt a wave of homesickness suddenly. She missed that house so much. And nobody understood.

Except Martin. She felt her spirits lift at the thought of seeing him later that day.

The house had a secluded air to it. When you walked through the neglected garden to the front door it was easy to forget that a short pathway separated it from the busy road outside. The back bedroom was a haven that belonged to just the two of them. With the key turned in the lock they were safe from interruption and could ignore the occasional footfall on the stairs or the clatter of pots in the kitchen down below. The wind prowled through the trees outside and rattled against the ill-fitting windows. Although the room was chilly she let him remove her sweater. And then the skirt.

He stroked her bare arm. 'Don't be afraid.'

Was it cold or excitement that made her body tremble? 'Maybe I should put my jumper back on.'

'No, don't do that.' He had stripped down to his underpants. She saw his body glimmer whitely in the poor light as he pulled back the coverlet. 'We'll get inside the bed clothes.'

She hesitated. The bed looked warm and inviting. 'Maybe I shouldn't.'

'Ah, come on, Margaret. Just for a little while. We don't have to do anything.'

Without clothes his body looked leaner, harder. He had little black hairs around his nipples. She averted her eyes from the bulge in his underpants. 'Okay. Just for a little while. And I'll leave my slip on.'

'The path to Hell is paved with good intentions.' Sister Baptista at school was very fond of quoting that. And, of course, the catechism said, 'He that is unfaithful in small things will fall by little, by little.' And – But who cared about Sister Baptista and St Celeste's? Forget them, they don't matter.

The path to Hell. Little by little. She gave the slip up without a struggle. Then the bra. And gasped with pleasure as he caressed her breasts and felt the nipples blossom and grow huge under his fingers. When his hands moved downwards she found herself shuddering with desire.

'Oh God!' His voice was awed as he explored her body. 'Oh God Margaret, you're beautiful.'

And he was beautiful too. She felt the muscles in his back, the lean curve of his buttocks, stroked the nipples on his chest, felt them harden in a miniature parody of her own. Then shyly, tentatively, her hand moved downwards over his flat stomach, felt the coarse, dark hairs on his body, and then –

'Oh God, Margaret!' he moaned. 'Oh God!'

And then things seemed to happen very fast.

Passion took her by surprise. The way her body responded to his. She hadn't expected it to be like hunger. A hunger they had for each other so that nothing less than complete capitulation would satisfy either of them. They were like two swimmers competing in a race. He was the stronger of the two, and try as she would she could not keep up with him. When he reached the finish line first she wept with disappointment. And *pain*. Nobody had told her to expect pain.

'I'm sorry, I'm sorry.' He tried to kiss away her tears. 'I'm a clumsy fool.'

'It's okay.' She forced a smile. 'It wasn't your fault. Did you – did *you* like it?'

'*Like* it?' She could barely make out his face in the dusk of the room. 'It was the most *wonderful* – you're a *fantastic* girl! Next time I'll make sure you enjoy it too.'

'Next time?' She felt a mixture of joy and doubt. Thought of the priest in Confession. But she couldn't go back there again, could she?

'I love you, Margaret,' he whispered.

She put her doubts aside. It was too late for regrets. What was done was done.

'I love you, too.'

'You're just in time for a cup of tea.' Susan's mother put down the book she had been reading by the fireside and smiled at the two girls who had come into the kitchen by the area door. She was a small, plump woman in her late forties with a good-humoured face and untidy brown curls streaked with grey. 'Well, Margaret, have you met the father of your children yet?'

It was a stock greeting of hers ever since the girls had started going to dances, and Margaret's usual response was to give a protesting laugh and a shrug but today she felt at a loss for an answer. She glanced for inspiration around the Millers' kitchen, an untidy room which bore only a passing resemblance to the one in her old house, a few doors down the Square. Although it wouldn't have matched up to Mrs Roberts's exacting standards with its cluttered table, football gear slung in a heap on the floor near the scullery door, and the lingering odour of cooked cabbage vying with the smell of damp laundry on a rack beside the fireplace, it was a room in which she had felt comfortable ever since she was a child. But there was nothing new to comment on; even the old dog asleep in his basket near the door looked exactly the same as he had been the last time she was here. But she wasn't the same, was she?

Still at a loss, she abandoned her scrutiny of the kitchen and brought her gaze back to the novel lying open in Mrs Miller's ample lap. 'What's the book, Pidgie?'

'Oh, what do you think? A historical romance, what else?' Pidgie rolled her eyes comically and mocked her own foolishness. 'Rubbish, really. But it's a great read. But tell us – ' She was suddenly more interested in present-day romance. 'Who's this new boyfriend you've met?'

Margaret felt her cheeks grow pink. 'How did *you* know?'

Pidgie Miller's plump, good-natured face crinkled up. 'Oh, a little bird – '

'Don't look at me,' Susan said hastily from her position by the Aga cooker. She splashed boiling water into a teapot. 'Don't mind her. She's only fishing.'

'I wasn't wrong, though.' Pidgie gave a comfortable laugh. 'There *is* someone, isn't there, Margaret?'

'Well, I don't mind *you* knowing. But – '

'Now there's little danger of me telling your mother.' Mrs Miller laughed again, this time drily. 'Who is he? Do we know him?'

'He's a year ahead of us in college.' She could feel her lips shaping into a smile. 'He's – '

' – from the country,' Susan said, plonking two steaming mugs down on the table between them. 'A culchie!'

Margaret felt her smile fade abruptly. She took a long drink of tea, and avoided her friend's eye.

'What's wrong with that, for God's sake? I went out with a country fella myself. From Tipperary he was. Farming people.' A reminiscent smile on Pidgie's face. 'God, but he was romantic. The letters he sent. And *poems.*'

'A farmer who wrote poetry?' Susan looked sceptically at her mother. 'You've been reading too much Mills and Boon.'

'This one had a soul.' Despite her greying curls, Pidgie looked girlish suddenly. 'I couldn't tell you whether he wrote them himself or copied them. Not that it mattered. He looked like a poet even if he wasn't one. He had the eyes of a dreamer.'

'I know what you mean.' Margaret nodded eagerly.

'The eyes of a dreamer!' Susan scoffed. 'I don't know which of you is worse.'

'Listen to little Miss Sensible.' Pidgie gave a tolerant smile. 'No imagination. Takes after her father.'

Margaret thought of Frank Miller, balding, pot-bellied, hairy hands smelling of disinfectant. Being married to him must be a fate worse than death. Did he say 'Open wide' in that curt way when they made love? She repressed a giggle. 'What happened to the poet?'

'Nothing happened to him. We met too young, that's all. It would never have worked, anyway.' Pidgie shrugged fatalistically. 'Poets don't make good husband material.'

'Not like dentists.' Susan looked smug as she munched a chocolate biscuit.

'No, love.' Did she detect a wistful look on Mrs Miller's face? 'Not like dentists.'

'You're wrong,' Margaret said eagerly. 'It doesn't have to be that way.'

They were safe, the pair of them, in their own little cocoon. Safe and warm. Nothing could touch them as long as they stayed there. As long as the wind prowled through the trees in the overgrown back garden. And the rain rustled against the window-pane, the sounds weaving an invisible barrier to shut out the rest of the world.

If only it could always be like this. If only this moment could last forever.

'It's a fortnight late?' Susan looked puzzled. 'Well, there's nothing to worry about, is there? Or – ' her gaze sharpened suddenly. ' – *is* there?'

Margaret bit her lip. 'Well – maybe.'

She saw surprise and something approaching awe in the other girl's eyes. 'You *haven't* – ? You *didn't* – ?'

Despite the worry that niggled at her she found herself laughing with excitement. 'Yes, yes, I *have*.'

'Oh, *Margaret!* What was it like? *Tell* me.' Susan was laughing too. 'Did you do it just the once, or – ?'

'Twice so far. The second time was better than the first.'

'And was it the *whole hog*, or everything *but*?'

'The *whole hog*.'

'Oh my *God*! But he *did* – ' Susan lowered her voice discreetly, ' – pull it out, didn't he? Before he – ?'

She felt her face grow scarlet. 'Well no, actually. How do you know so much, anyway?'

'I don't really but my mother says – '

'Your *mother?* She stared at her friend in astonishment. 'You can talk to her about things like *that*?'

'You know how outspoken Pidgie is.' Susan sounded half-apologetic. 'Sometimes I don't know where to look.'

Not for the first time Margaret wished that she had someone like Mrs Miller for her mother. The niggling worry sharpened. 'And she says – ?'

'That it's one way of – well, *you* know – it's safer. But not foolproof. *She* says the best contraceptive is the word "No!"'

'Thanks.'

Susan looked apologetic again.' She only *sounds* progressive. Underneath she's just as conventional as other people's mothers. But maybe she's right about this.'

'Thanks, thanks a *lot*!'

'I'm sorry, I didn't mean – ' Her friend's face showed concern. 'You *are* worried, aren't you?'

'No, I'm not,' she lied. 'I'm just a bit late, that's all. I mean – everyone knows it's not that easy to get pregnant.'

'No, no, of course not,' Susan said staunchly. But, practical as always, she added, 'All the same, if your period doesn't come soon, aren't there tablets you can take to bring it on? But you can only get them from a doctor.'

'Old Dr Murphy?' Margaret stared at her in horror. 'I can't do that. He'd tell my parents.'

'There are other doctors. Peter's a medical student. He's bound to know someone.'

'You can't be serious? You know what a dry stick my brother is.'

'In that case – ' Susan's eyes slid away from hers. 'My cousin Felicity has the name of a woman.'

'Are you sure it was that simple?' Margaret asked. Darkness was falling as they got off the bus and began walking down a shabby backstreet. 'She gave her this bottle and it – '

' – did the trick. It happened about a year ago. Don't you remember me telling you about it?'

'A year ago I was more interested in trying to get a good Leaving Cert.' A year ago this kind of conversation would have been unthinkable. 'It doesn't sound very safe, though. I mean – who knows what would be in the bottle?'

'It didn't do Felicity any harm,' Susan said firmly. She took a piece of paper out of her pocket and consulted it. 'It's around here somewhere.'

'Are you sure?' Margaret glanced uneasily into a dingy shop window, where several dead flies shared the space with a pyramid of empty cigarette packets balanced on some sheets of yellowing newspaper, and then further down the street at a couple of youths in ill-fitting jackets leaning against the wall of the end house, smoking cigarettes. 'This looks like kind of a rough area.'

'Don't pay any attention to them.' Susan peered at the address in the fading light. 'Come on, it's just around the corner.'

Her heart sank. 'Okay then.'

The youths glanced at them as they hurried by and one of them made a comment under his breath, but neither made any attempt to accost them. Margaret breathed a sigh of relief as she and Susan rounded the corner. A relief which almost immediately turned to apprehension when she saw the grim outlines of the Corporation flats ahead of them.

Although daylight was fading rapidly, a number of small children still played in the forecourt of the flats, their shouts ringing out in the cool March air. They all stopped to watch the two girls as they approached the entrance; curious eyes appraised the long raincoats, the headscarves pulled low over the forehead. One of the boys sniggered. A small girl, with uncombed hair and no stockings, took charge, directing them to an upstairs flat reached by a dark, damp flight of concrete stairs smelling of urine.

Margaret hesitated, her foot on the bottom step. 'I don't think this is such a great idea.'

'I know what you mean.' Susan wrinkled her nose. 'What a pong! Look, we've come this far. The sooner we go up, the sooner we'll be out of here.'

The landing seemed bright after the stairs. They were faced with a row of numbered doors, all of them needing a coat of paint.

Susan consulted her piece of paper. 'Number thirty-seven.'

She felt her stomach begin to heave. 'I can't do it.'

'But – '

'I told you this was a rotten idea,' Margaret said in a rapid undertone. 'I've changed my mind. I should never have listened to you. Look, I'm going to be sick if I don't get out of here this minute.'

'What will you do?' Susan's short legs tried to keep pace with Margaret's long ones. Around them, children flitted like hobgoblins through the half-darkness. The night air was full of whispers. The streetlamps had come on. The two girls headed for the lighted street with the speed of travellers trying to reach an oasis in the desert.

'I don't know,' Margaret said as they hurried through the narrow streets. 'I'll think of something.' She tried to hold back the tears that were threatening to engulf her. 'Maybe I'll wake up and find it's all been a bad dream.'

Mick was silent after she stopped speaking. He watched the logs crackling and spitting in the big fireplace and saw the shadows dancing on the chimney breast. He felt her eyes on him but he didn't look at her.

'Do you blame me?' she asked.

'For wanting to – ?' He turned and met her eye. 'No, I don't actually. If it had been anyone else, I'd have said, "Go ahead, good luck to you." But when I think, if you *had*, *I* wouldn't have existed.' He exhaled a long shudder of breath. 'I – it's just mind-blowing. Doesn't bear thinking about.'

'I don't know if I thought much about that at the time,' Margaret said. 'It was just the awfulness of the place, the sordidness of the whole thing. I just couldn't go through with it.' A thought struck her. 'Maybe it wouldn't have worked. It's not always that easy, despite what Susan's cousin said.'

'All I know is that you didn't go through with it.' His voice was fervent. 'God! I'm so glad you didn't.'

She smiled, and he thought he had never seen her look so beautiful, the lines of her face – what few she had – softened by the lamplight, her bright hair hanging to her shoulders. 'I'm glad too. But I didn't see it that way at the time. And I still had to tell Martin.'

'That's something I don't understand.' Mick frowned. 'Why *hadn't* you told him? How could you make a decision like that without consulting him?'

'I suppose I panicked. I didn't really think. Besides, this may seem strange but I didn't know him that well. I wasn't sure what his reaction would be.'

His interest quickened. 'How did he take it?'

She gave him a sombre look. 'Not well.'

'This'll kill my parents.' He buried his face in his hands and groaned.

She watched him anxiously. It was lunchtime and the Green was crowded but they had found a seat beside a high hedge out of earshot of the packed deckchairs and the lawns covered with sprawling bodies. It was cold away from the sunshine and she shivered in her light jacket. She saw him lift his head, hope flicker in his eyes.

'Are you absolutely sure?'

'I'm not positive. But I've been getting sick in the mornings.'

'Oh God.' Hope died swiftly. He thought for a moment.

'You should have got the stuff from that woman.'

She stared at him, aghast. 'You don't mean that.' She shuddered at the memory of the dark staircase and tried to banish it from her mind but it lingered in the background like an accusation. 'Say you don't mean it.'

'I don't know what I mean.' He ran his hands distractedly through his hair until the black curls stood up like a halo round his head. 'Oh God! How could we have been such *eejits*?' He looked at her accusingly. 'Why didn't you stop me? Why did you let me?'

She felt as if a knife had entered her heart. Tears stung her eyes. 'Why are you blaming *me*? We both – '

'I know, I know.' He tried to smooth down his hair. 'I'm sorry, I shouldn't have said that. It's the shock of it. I can't think straight.'

'I understand,' she said. 'I've been that way too. I couldn't sleep last night thinking of this but – look – ' she touched his sleeve tentatively. 'It's not the end of the world, you know.'

'No?' He gave a short laugh. 'It's not exactly the best news of the century.'

'I know you feel that way now but once you get used to the idea – ' she took a deep breath and hurried on ' – it just means we'll have to get married a bit sooner, that's all.'

'Married?' He looked at her blankly. 'How could we get married?'

'I know we're a bit young but people do get married at our age and make a go of it,' she said eagerly. 'And Daddy would help us. I know he would.'

'Your father?' He shot her a startled look. 'Does he know?'

'No, no, not yet. I thought maybe you – that we – '

'Oh God!' He looked distraught. 'How can we – ? And my parents? My mother! What's my mother going to say?'

'Wallpaper or paint?' Mummy sat in the big, airy sitting room surrounded by pattern books and colour samples. 'I just can't decide.'

'Surely all that should have been settled before we moved in?' Daddy had been in the operating theatre all day and wanted to read his newspaper in peace.

'You know how difficult it is to get anyone to do anything on time, Julian. Besides it's only the guest room, nothing for you to worry about. Oh, there you are, Margaret. What kept you so late?'

'I had a tutorial,' she lied. Her feet ached from wandering aimlessly around the streets. Despair was lodged like a heavy lump in her stomach. 'I'm sorry.'

'You might have told me.' Mummy's voice was petulant. 'Your meal's keeping warm in the oven. It's probably spoiled by now.'

'It doesn't matter. I'm not hungry.'

Daddy looked up from his paper and smiled at her. 'Hello, Margaret. How's the study going?'

Feeling like Judas, she smiled back at him. 'It's okay.'

'That's the girl. Keep it up, won't you?'

'Yes, Daddy.'

Despair clutched at her suddenly.

Oh, God! What am I going to do?

The phone rang. 'Will you get that, Margaret?' Mummy said. 'It's probably for you anyway.'

She thought it was a wrong number at first. It seemed ages before anyone spoke.

'Is that you, Margaret?'

'Oh, it's you,' she said coldly.

'Look – ' his voice was hesitant. 'I think I got in a bit of a panic today. It was the shock. I just couldn't take it in.'

She said nothing,

'Are you still there? Listen, I haven't much time. I'll be cut off in a minute. I just want to say – we're in this together – we'll work something out.'

'That isn't what you said earlier.'

'Don't mind what I said then. I told you I was – '

Abruptly the pips began to sound.

'I love you,' he said.

Margaret found her voice. 'I love you too,' she whispered. But the line had gone dead.

Hope welled up in her as she replaced the receiver,

'Who was that on the phone?' Mummy was on her way upstairs, her arms full of pattern books.

'No one. I mean Susan.' She wondered how much of the conversation her mother had heard.

'You girls spend too much time on the phone.' Her mother gave an exasperated laugh. 'How you get any work done I just don't know. If you can spare a minute you might help me pick out the curtains for the guest room.'

'Of course.' She was feeling so much better after Martin's phone call she could afford to be generous. 'Not the blue, Mummy. That pattern would be too much with the wallpaper. What about this pink?'

As they leafed through the pattern books, discussing and comparing colours, she had a sudden urge to blurt the whole thing out and get it over with. Anything would be better than carrying this awful secret on her own. But she knew it was madness to even think of it. If she had a different kind of mother, someone like Pidgie Miller, maybe? No, better to say nothing until she had discussed it further with Martin. The two of them could tell her parents together.

'I think I should sound out my own people first,' he said next day when they met after lectures. 'Break it to them gently.'

How did one do that? 'But when?'

'What about when I go home for Easter?'

'But that's nearly three weeks away.' She looked at him in dismay. 'I can't wait that long. Besides, Easter is late this year.' How long would it take to organise a wedding? How long before she began to show? She gave a laugh that was part desperation, part hysteria. 'I don't want to walk up the aisle with half the world *knowing*. No, you'll have to tell them before that. This weekend.'

He shook his head and looked embarrassed. 'I'm not sure if I can.'

'Why not? Is it the money? Don't worry about that. I'll pay for the train ticket.'

He opened his mouth, closed it again and gave a little shrug of defeat. 'Okay. But I'll pay you back as soon as I – '

'The money's not important,' Margaret said. 'Now, when can you meet my parents? What's the matter? Daddy won't eat you. He's not like that.'

'Listen, Margaret.' Martin's face wore a stubborn look she

had never seen before. 'It's bad enough having to tell my own parents. Don't ask me to face yours as well.'

'If that's the way you feel.' She had no choice but to agree. 'But I still think my way would be better.'

'In the meantime,' he said, 'I think we should act as normally as possible.'

Easier said than done. How could she behave normally with this momentous thing happening inside her? How could she sit through lectures, her mind seething with plans for the future? It would have to be a quiet wedding. Just the two families, a few friends. And the honeymoon? She had always wanted to go somewhere exotic but under the circumstances it might be wise not to be too ambitious.

'A honeymoon?' He looked at her uneasily. 'Margaret! The exams start in six weeks' time.'

'Well, maybe later on. Who needs a honeymoon, anyway? It's more important to find somewhere to live.' They'd have to get a flat. Unless, of course, Mummy and Daddy suggested they live with them at first. No, not a good idea. These things never work. A flat would be more sensible. Besides, when the baby came –

'Maybe we'd better wait till we hear what they have to say before making any plans,' Martin cautioned. 'I mean – you're taking for granted that your father will agree to support us till I graduate. Supposing he doesn't? Supposing he tells me to shag off?'

'He'd never do that.'

'How do you know? And if he does I'll have to forget about my degree, leave university, get some kind of a job. Oh God!'

He gave her a stricken look. 'How the hell did we get ourselves into such a mess?'

The station was full of jostling, hurrying people, long queues at the ticket counters.

'Just as well we came early. It's always like a cattle market on Fridays.'

'I got you some magazines.'

'You shouldn't have bothered.' He took them awkwardly. 'But thanks, anyway. Look, I'll have to go if I want to get a seat.'

'Yes.' Would it be like that every time they parted? This feeling of desolation? She tried to smile while tears stung at her eyes.

'Don't be like that.' He put his arms around her and she clung to him gratefully.

'I can't bear to let you go.' Was it the same for him? When he went away on the train would he feel as if he had left a part of himself behind?

'I hate to go too.' But she knew by the tension in his body he was impatient to be gone. 'Wish me luck. I'm going to need it,' he said as they drew apart.

'Oh Martin! Will they be awful to you?'

He frowned. 'They can't say anything to me that I haven't told myself already. But the worst part of it is that I've let my mother down. After all she's done for me.' He looked at her helplessly. 'In the name of God, how am I going to face her?'

She watched him stride down the platform, duffle bag over his shoulder, dark blue anorak already beginning to blend with the shadow cast by the waiting train. Her eyes followed him until he was swallowed up by the crowd, until there was no point in staying at the barrier. Yet she lingered, waiting until the last latecomer had breathlessly gained his compartment, the doors were slammed, the whistle blown. Then, with the swiftness and finality of death, the train was gone from under the high, echoing vault of the station and rapidly dwindled to a speck in the distance. She turned away reluctantly. As she made her way to the exit she pictured Martin's face when he spoke of having to face his parents.

With a little thrill of fear she thought, Now it's my turn.

'Are you out of your mind?' Her mother looked away from the mirror in which she had been studying herself and stared at Margaret in amazement. 'You're too young to get married. Much too young. And even if you weren't, he doesn't sound remotely suitable. A young man from a little huckster shop in the middle of nowhere.'

'His mother's a teacher; she's the principal.'

'Of what?' Mummy gave a tinkling laugh. 'Some little country school where the pupils have to bring in a sod of turf for the fire and the roof leaks in the winter. Really, Margaret, I thought you had more sense.'

Trust her to try and spoil everything with that tongue of hers. 'It's not like that.'

'No? They probably have to fetch water from the pump. Can you see yourself queuing up with your bucket every morning?'

Margaret winced at the contempt in her voice. 'Nobody lives like that any more. But, anyway, it wouldn't make any difference to us. We wouldn't be living there.'

'No?' Raised eyebrows. 'Where, then?' Her mother wore a slight smile of amusement as if determined not to take any of it too seriously.

'In Dublin, of course. Martin has plans – he's ambitious.' Despite her anxiety she couldn't help beaming with pride. 'He sees his degree as a passport to a better way of life.'

'Does he indeed?' Mummy pursed her lips. 'And, of course, marriage to the daughter of a well-known surgeon – '

' – It's not like that.' Margaret recoiled. 'He's not some kind of fortune hunter.'

'He has money of his own, then?'

'Well – no, but we thought – ' The conversation just wasn't going as planned. Why oh why hadn't she waited till Daddy came home? He would have been more understanding. 'It would be just a loan,' she said desperately, 'to get us started. We'd pay you back when – '

'Isn't that just like Margaret.' Mummy seemed to be inviting comment from some invisible third person. 'She wants to marry some penniless student without a clue as to how they're going to live. It makes no odds, anyway.' She turned back to her dressing table and examined her reflection with satisfaction. At forty-two she was still a handsome woman, with thick, dark hair and good cheekbones. 'You're too young to get married.'

'I'll be eighteen next month.'

'Eighteen? My dear, you are getting on.' She was inspecting her eyelashes now, removing a loose one with a wetted finger. 'But it's still too young.'

Margaret sighed in frustration as she watched her. This

wasn't getting them anywhere. There was only one way to get through that barrier of self-absorption. Feeling like someone about to toss a hand grenade at an unsuspecting target, she said quickly, 'Not too young to be a mother.'

Silence except for the clock on a bedside locker ticking away the seconds. It was like the silence before the explosion goes off.

She saw her mother's face frozen in the mirror and almost laughed at the stunned expression on it. She heard the front door slam. Daddy's voice in the hall. Hurried footsteps on the stairs. Saw the bedroom door open. The faint smell of antiseptic, that whiff of the hospital he always brought home with him.

'Sorry I'm late, Maeve. Is there a clean dress shirt for me? We haven't much time.'

She saw him stop, switch his gaze to her and then back to the motionless figure in front of the dressing table, a look of mild enquiry on his face.

'How many times?' Her voice was razor-sharp.

The atmosphere in the study was tense, inquisitorial. Mummy was the Grand Inquisitor. Daddy watched helplessly, leaning against his desk in a bewildered manner.

Margaret squirmed under her mother's hard, brown-eyed stare. But she stood firm. If her mother wanted chapter and verse, times and dates, she wasn't going to get them from her. 'What difference does it make?'

Mummy's lips tightened. Before she could say anything, Daddy asked in a puzzled voice, 'Are you sure you're not making a mistake, Maeve? I mean, what you're suggesting is unthinkable. Margaret would never – '

'Ask her yourself,' she shrugged,

He turned beseechingly to Margaret. 'Tell me it's not true, dear?'

It was easy to be defiant with Mummy. Her attitude almost invited it. But Daddy was a different matter. She hung her head and avoided his eye.

'Oh my God!' He stared at her in disbelief. Walking behind his desk, he sat down heavily, as if he could no longer trust his legs. 'How could this have happened?'

'I don't know.' Margaret was close to tears. They had only done it twice. It just wasn't fair.

Silence for a moment. Her father stared down at the big ink blotter on his desk, studying the smudges on it as if they might furnish an explanation. Finding none, he looked pleadingly at Margaret. 'Did this boy – did he force you?'

'Force me?' She recoiled from the implication. 'Martin isn't like that. You don't understand. We love each other.'

'*Love!*' On Mummy's lips the word was an obscenity.

Her father looked dismayed. 'So it wasn't – against your will?'

'No,' Margaret cried. 'Of course not. I keep telling you, we love each other. We want to get married. I thought *you'd* understand.'

'Understand?' He gave her a stunned look. 'How could I be expected to – ?' He passed a trembling hand over his face. 'Oh, Margaret, why have you done this to us?'

'And what about Peter?' Mummy said dramatically. 'I don't suppose you gave him a moment's thought. In case it has escaped your notice, he is training to be a doctor. He has a brilliant career ahead of him. Do you think he'll be able to show his face anywhere when word of this gets out?'

'Peter?' she stammered. 'But what about *me*?'

Her mother looked at her coldly. 'It's a bit late now to be worrying about *your* reputation. You should have thought of that before you lowered yourself, before you shamed us like this.' She glanced at her watch. 'If we don't go now, Julian, we'll be late for this dinner.'

He looked at her distractedly. 'I'd cancel if I could but I'm one of the speakers.'

'Although how he can go through with it after this I just don't know,' Mummy said bitterly. 'You have a superb sense of timing, Margaret.'

'I thought they'd understand,' she said to her bedroom ceiling. 'I really thought they would.'

Downstairs, the grandfather clock in the hall struck the hour. A sound she never heard without being reminded of the house in the Square. A sudden picture of it came into her mind, vivid and sharp like a stab to the heart. A picture so immediate that her eyes filled with tears and she buried her face with longing into her pillow.

If only they had never left there. If only she could be a child again, feeding the ducks in the Green or playing with the big doll's house in the basement sitting room while Delia sprawled on the sofa, engrossed in the latest copy of *True Romance.* That old sofa! Although it was years since she had laid eyes on it she could see its balding velour arms and shiny cushions, could feel the harsh prickle of horsehair under her cheek and smell that familiar smell of cigarette smoke and rasher rinds which had clung to it as far back as she could remember. She held on to this comforting vision for a few moments until it faded into nothingness.

With a sigh she returned to the present. The old house and all its associations belonged to childhood. She could never go back there. Not since that cold, windy day in February when, without a thought, she had put childhood behind her.

'I'll drop this off at the lab.' Daddy took the bottle in the brown paper bag from her and stowed it away in his pocket. 'With any luck we'll have a result by Monday.' He avoided her eye, shuffled papers around on his desk and glanced elaborately at his watch. 'Is that the time? Must go. Expected at the hospital.' Although it was Saturday, he liked to do a quick round of the wards. If nothing urgent cropped up he'd have an early lunch before heading off to the golf club for his weekly four-ball.

'But nothing's been settled yet.'

'We can't settle anything till we know for certain.' His manner was detached, impersonal. Gone was the distraught, disbelieving father of the previous night, in his place the calm professional. 'It's not my field, of course, but I understand something like this could turn out to be a false alarm.'

For a moment she saw him as his patients must see him. A big, pleasant-faced man, fair hair going a bit thin, but still youthful-looking, with a gentle voice and an air of imperturbability that most people found reassuring. But for once she was not reassured by it. For the first time in her life she saw it as one of the tools of his profession, a part of the façade, like the well-cut suit, the discreet tie, the highly polished shoes. She had never before thought of him as being cold – all her life she had enjoyed the warmth of his approval – but now she felt he was keeping her at a distance, hiding behind his professional manner, using it as a shield against her.

A false alarm? Please God let it be.

'And if it's not?' But even as she asked it she had a premonition that, whatever the outcome of the test, things between them would never be the same again.

The morning sunlight etched lines of tiredness on his face.

'I'm afraid we'll just have to wait and see.'

'This must be the longest weekend of my life,' she said to Susan over the phone. 'Will I ever last out till Monday? The atmosphere's pretty grim here. They're behaving as if there'd been a death in the family.'

'Does Peter know?' The other girl's voice was sympathetic.

'He's away for the weekend with some friends from college. Not that he'd be any help. He always sees things from Mummy's point of view. And of course, if his precious career is going to be affected – ' Tears filled her eyes. 'Oh, Susan! She says it's all my fault. You'd think I'd done it on purpose to shame the family.'

'She doesn't mean that,' Susan said soothingly. 'It's just the shock of the whole thing. Once she gets over that you'll find she'll start seeing your side of it.'

'Do you think so?' Margaret was doubtful. 'I hope you're right.'

'And maybe things aren't as bad as you think. Maybe the

test will turn out to be negative.'

'If only – ' her spirits lifted slightly. 'Susan, say a prayer for me, will you?'

'I will,' her friend said, 'and I'll light a candle for you too.'

Dear God, let me not be pregnant.

I'll do anything.

I'll say the Rosary every night. I'll give up going to dances. I'll study hard. I'll keep my room tidy, be nice to Mummy (not that she deserves it), give all my pocket money to the poor.

Please let my period come.

If my period comes I promise I'll be good. I'll never, ever do it again.

I'll never let him touch me again.

I'll never see him –

No, don't ask me to do that. Don't ask me to stop seeing him. I love him too much.

But if you listen to my prayer, I'll never do it with him again.

I promise I'll wait till we're married.

Sunday evening. Crossing the landing after another fruitless trip to the bathroom, she heard the phone ring downstairs in the hall.

Her heart gave a great leap. Martin was back! She put her hand on the banister, ready to run downstairs. Then she heard Daddy say, 'I'll take it in the study,' and her elation died. The hospital, probably. She hoped he wouldn't stay on the line too long. Martin would be trying to get through. She glanced down the stairwell and saw her mother emerge from the shadows and follow her father into the study, clicking the door shut behind her. Definitely not the hospital. But who, then? She was tempted to go into her parents' bedroom and listen in on the extension but knew it would only make matters worse if she were discovered. Back in her own room, she threw herself down on the bed and resumed her contemplation of the ceiling, her thoughts going round and round in her head like mice on a treadmill.

Why doesn't he ring?
Please God don't let me be pregnant.
I'm too young to have a baby.
Mummy's right. I'm far too young to get married.
But if he doesn't marry me I'll have an illegitimate child.
Oh God, let it be morning soon.

She was having a dream. A nightmare. She and Martin were quarrelling. 'I hate you,' he said. 'You're the cause of all my troubles.'

'No! No!' Margaret stared at him in hurt and bewilderment. 'Please! I don't want to fight.' But nothing she said would persuade him to make up.

She awoke, stiff and trembling, in the grey light before dawn.

It was only a dream, she tried to comfort herself as she rubbed her aching limbs. Something I ate. She shuddered at the memory of the dream. Martin, so harsh and unloving, so determined to take offence. Martin's not like that. He's good and he's sweet and he's kind. It was just a dream. And I'll be seeing him soon. Only another few hours, thank God. Once she met him and felt his arms around her, everything would be all right. She *knew* it would.

'Not go in to college!' She was aghast. 'But I have to. What about my lectures?'

'Your mother and I feel it would be better – till certain matters are sorted out.' He glanced at her in a kind, professional way. 'You look as if a few days in bed wouldn't do you any harm.'

'But I've arranged to meet Martin. No, I must go in.'

Her father's expression hardened. 'Just do what you're told, like a good girl.'

Tears sprang to her eyes. She had never heard him use that tone with her before. 'I've got to – he's expecting me – '

'You needn't worry too much about that.' Her mother looked up from the breakfast table with a knowing smile.

'What's that supposed to mean?' Margaret glanced warily at her.

A look of tight-lipped triumph crossed Mummy's face. 'You'll find out soon enough.'

What a strange-looking couple! She gazed out her bedroom window, too dispirited to read. There were several houses still in the process of being built farther down the cul-de-sac but the two people who had just got out of the taxi didn't seem the type who would be looking to buy a house in this neighbourhood. The stoutish, middle-aged man, his shiny dark suit straining at the seams, finished paying off the driver and came to join the dowdy, bespectacled woman who stood awkwardly on the pavement, smoothing the creases from her skirt. As they stood there gazing uncertainly around them, it struck her again how out of place they seemed. Which one of the neighbours was in for a visit from their country cousins?

To her surprise, they walked up the short, curving driveway, past her father's car – which, unusually for that time of the afternoon, was parked in front of the house – and disappeared into the porch. The doorbell rang. There was a rumble of voices down below. She heard what sounded like the study door being shut.

Who on earth? No, it couldn't be.

Martin's parents? No, it – but who else could it be? So that's what Daddy had meant by 'certain matters being sorted out'. They certainly hadn't wasted any time. Martin must have done a good job in convincing them that speed was essential in getting the arrangements for the wedding under way.

But why the study? Wouldn't the drawing room be more suitable? And why wasn't Martin with them? Lectures, of course. She knew how he hated to miss one. He would be along as soon as he could, she told herself. And they would want to meet her too. She had better tidy herself up, make herself presentable.

Half an hour went by. Still no call came from the study. And no sign of Martin arriving. Suddenly she heard voices in the hall, the unmistakable sounds of departure. And then the two visitors were gone down the garden path and out the gate without a backward glance. As she watched in bewilderment from the window, it seemed to her that they were walking straighter and taller than before, like people relieved of a burden. There was no time to dwell on the implications of this. The housekeeper was knocking on the bedroom door to tell her that her parents wanted to see her. Unable to contain her impatience, Margaret rushed eagerly downstairs to learn her fate.

'Not see each other again?' She gave him a stunned look. 'You can't be serious.'

'You've been a very foolish girl,' Daddy said. 'Foolish and thoughtless. You've jeopardised your future, ruined your good name – '

'*All* our good names,' Mummy cut in.

' – and brought sorrow on the family. However – '

'Not see each other again? But the wedding – '

'There's to be no more talk of marriage.' Her father's voice was firm. 'It's simply out of the question.'

'But you don't understand,' she said frantically. 'If I'm going to have a baby – '

'We don't know that yet. We haven't got the results of the test. If it's positive we'll have to face that, make plans. But, in the meantime, you're not to have anything more to do with the young man. We're all agreed on that.'

'All? Who's *all*?' She stared at him in angry disbelief. 'What about Martin and myself? Don't *we* have any say?'

He sighed. 'In this case you'll have to be guided by your parents.'

'But – '

'It's in your own interest.' Mummy's tone was impatient.

Daddy said, more gently, 'Believe me, Margaret, we're doing this for your sake.'

'My sake! I know whose sake it's for.' She felt a sudden hatred for him. 'The only thing you're interested in is appearances. All you care about is what people will think.'

Daddy looked at a loss and said nothing. But Mummy was not disconcerted by the accusation. 'Somebody has to, considering *you* seem to have lost your wits completely.'

Ignoring her mother, she looked accusingly at her father. 'Is that what you think too?'

'Margaret,' he said earnestly. 'Will you listen to me – ?'

'No, I won't listen.' Never again would she listen to him. Her beloved Daddy was gone forever and in his place was a middle-aged stranger who had judged her and found her wanting. Trembling with rage and disappointment, she stood up and rushed from the room. Not see each other again! The very idea! She paced her bedroom in a fury. Martin would have something to say about that!

She saw his familiar figure walking ahead of her up the main steps of the university, books under one arm, black curls bouncing off the collar of his shabby tweed jacket. She caught up with him rapidly and touched his sleeve.

'Martin! Thank God you're back!'

He turned. For one startled moment their eyes met. And then he was gone, up the steps and plunging through the pillared doorway.

'Martin!' She stared after him in disbelief.

He hadn't seen her. He couldn't have.

Oh Margaret, don't be such a fool. Of course he saw you.

This couldn't be happening! Heedless of the people pushing past her on the steps, she stood staring at the porticoed entrance.

'Are you all right?' a girl out of her class asked. She noticed several others checking their strides to look over at her.

She wanted to scream, rush after him, beg him to come back. She wanted to throw herself down the steps, crying out her anguish.

'Is something wrong?' The other student's face showed concern.

Pride came to her aid. 'I'm fine, really, I'm fine.' Brushing away the girl's friendly enquiries, she hurried down the steps and out through the gates of the university, like a wounded animal bolting for cover, unable to trust in anyone but herself. The sun was shining; the trees were heavy with cherry blossom; all around her was the scent of betrayal.

'Bad news, I'm afraid.' Her father's face was sombre. Beside him, Mummy managed to look martyred and self-righteous at the same time. Their sitting together on the sofa like that increased Margaret's sense of isolation. She had the feeling that they were ganging up on her, shutting her out.

Not that it mattered any more what they said or did. Nothing mattered now. All she could think of was what had happened that morning in college. The scene kept repeating itself in her head. Would she ever get over the shock of it? As her father talked, she stared at him with indifference, barely listening to what he had to say, his words flowing over her without touching her.

The important thing was to tell no one, to behave as if nothing had happened. In order to avoid talk, she was to finish the term out. Later on, before her condition became obvious, they would arrange for her to go away to some safe place to wait till the baby was born. The child would be put out for adoption. When it was all over she would be able to put it behind her and get on with her life. But it was essential that she do nothing to draw attention to herself. 'And keep away from that boy. He's brought you enough trouble already.'

'Don't worry, Julian. I don't think we need worry about that,' Mummy said with grim satisfaction. 'He's already been warned to stay well away from her.'

Margaret pricked up her ears at this. That explained it, she thought. And she felt a small stirring of hope. If she could just talk to him they could still work something out. She knew they could.

'He's not here.' Although they had met before, the tousle-haired young man in an Aran gansey and grubby corduroys showed no sign of recognition. As he peered out the door the smell of cooking filled the narrow hallway. 'Try the arts library.'

'He wasn't – when are you expecting him home?' Behind her, raindrops rustled in the overgrown garden. 'I have to talk to him.' Desperation robbed her of pride. 'Maybe I could come in and wait.'

A look of alarm crossed his face. 'That's not a good idea.' He had a soft, western accent similar to Martin's. 'Look, I've got to go. I'm sorry.' The door began to close.

The truth hit her suddenly. 'He's in there, isn't he?'

His eyes slid away from hers. 'Nothing to do with me,' he mumbled. 'Sorry, now, but my fry will be destroyed.'

The door slammed shut.

She stumbled down the weed-infested pathway.

How could he do this to me? How could he? After all we meant to each other?

As she went through the narrow gateway into the street, two things dawned on her simultaneously.

I've lost him.

Oh God! I'm pregnant!

She gazed blindly at a double-decker bus pulling away from a stop. For one panicky moment she thought of throwing herself under its wheels. She clung to the concrete gatepost and the moment passed. But the panic remained.

Oh God! How was she going to get through this without him?

'I think I need another drink.'

She looked at him, bright-eyed. 'I said you wouldn't like it.'

'Nobody likes to think his father was a rat.' Mick took their empty glasses and went over to the drinks cabinet. 'A dirty, cowardly rat.'

'More of a mouse, really.' She gave a short laugh. 'I suppose he was thinking of his future.'

'What about your future? Okay, maybe marriage wasn't the right thing, just then. But he didn't have to do a runner, did he? You could have had the child, got married later on when you were ready. It happens all the time. I heard of a wedding recently where the couple's daughter was a flower girl.'

'Attitudes have changed in the last few years, certainly. People are getting more tolerant. But it was different then.'

'I thought it was called the Swinging Sixties?'

She shook her head. 'In London, maybe. Not here. Not in the circles we moved in. The stigma attached to having a baby outside marriage – ' She bit her lip. ' – you've no idea what it was like.'

'And he left you to go through with it on your own?' Anger rose up in him as he placed the refilled glass in front of her. 'I'd give a lot to tell him what I thought of him. If only I knew where he was – '

'If you knew how many times I said that to myself. How many times I cried – '

'It must have been pretty rough on you.' He glanced at her sympathetically. 'What happened then?'

She picked up her drink. To his surprise, he heard the ice cubes rattle against the glass and realised that her hand was shaking. 'Not just now, Michael. I think I've talked about it enough for one night.'

'I've upset you.' He was full of remorse. 'I didn't think – I should never – we won't talk about it again if you don't want to.'

'I'm okay, really I am.' She took a long swallow of her drink and smiled at him. 'In one way, it's a relief to tell someone after all these years. But it's enough for now. We *will* talk about it again, I promise you.'

She saw the line of light rimming the study door. On an impulse, she turned the handle and looked in. Vincent glanced up from his desk.

'That bloody fella still here?'

'He's just left.'

'Nice to see him keep decent hours for a change.'

Why did he have to take that attitude! 'I wish you could be nicer to him – talk to him more.'

'Why? He's not coming to see *me*.' He gave a dry laugh, yawned and stretched himself. 'I think I'll pack it in. Want a nightcap?'

Suddenly she hated him for his obduracy. It was like a wall he had built around himself. She felt like beating against that wall with angry fists. Not that it would make any difference. Nothing would. 'No thanks.' She kept her voice colourless and tried to hide her anger. 'I'm a bit tired. I'm off to bed.'

Vincent looked up. Something – a corresponding anger perhaps – stirred in the eyes that met hers. Cats' eyes, she thought, their colour shifting between green and amber. As with the cat, you could never tell which way he would jump. 'Suit yourself,' he said curtly and began sorting papers on his desk.

'Goodnight, then.' When he didn't reply she turned on her heel and went upstairs.

'Are you awake, Fran?'

'No.' She screwed her eyes up in protest against the bedside light. 'Go away, Mick. I'm too tired.'

'Sorry.' He angled the lamp away from her. 'I just wanted to talk.' His mind was swarming with images. He felt keyed-up, excited, and wanted to share with her the story he had just heard. 'Margaret's been telling me – '

'Not her again?' Fran yawned and buried her face in the pillow. 'Can't it wait till tomorrow? It's all very well for you but you didn't have to listen to Sean whingeing all evening. I only just got him to settle about half an hour ago.'

He looked at her in alarm. 'What's the matter with him?'

'I rang Mammy and she said it sounds like he's getting another tooth. He got the first one no bother. But this time he's having it harder.'

'A tooth?' He was relieved. 'That's great. He's not sick, anyway?'

'Fat lot of use you'd be if he was.' Fran was wide awake now. She sat up and glared at him. 'You're never here, anyway.'

'That's not true.' He was stung by the unfairness of it. 'I was home last night and the night before.'

'Yeh, yeh. But you're seeing an awful lot of that woman. How much longer is it going to go on? That's what I'd like to know.'

'She's not *that woman*. She's my mother. And she's a terrific person. If you knew the full story – '

She gave a resigned shrug. 'Oh, go on, then. Tell me.'

He hesitated and felt a sudden reluctance. It was between Margaret and himself, after all. 'Maybe it would be better if you met her first.'

'Oh?' The look she threw him was suddenly alert.' And when's that going to be?'

'Soon, Fran, soon.' He hid his doubts under a show of confidence. 'But first we have a bit of catching up to do, my mother and I.'

'Now remember,' Mummy said. 'If any of Maud's friends ask, your husband is on board ship; he's a wireless officer – it sounds better than an ordinary sailor.'

Margaret sighed. 'Why don't you make him the captain while you're at it?' What a snob Mummy was. And what a waste of time concocting a cover story that anyone of normal intelligence would see through the minute they heard it.

'No. You're too young for that.' Her mother looked regretful. 'Wireless officer sounds more plausible. All Maud's family were in the armed forces – British army, that is. She's used to uniforms and –'

'But who is she?' Margaret fought down a feeling of panic. After a summer spent skulking around the house, making excuses not to play tennis or go swimming, a summer in which her every movement was queried and her telephone calls monitored, it would definitely be a relief to get away from Mummy and her constant pleas for secrecy. As if she needed any reminders! Still, the prospect of being banished to some remote spot to spend the next few months with some dotty old relative of her mother's was beginning to fill her with alarm. 'I never even *heard* of this Aunt Maud till now. Why do I have to go and stay with her?'

'Maybe you'd prefer to go to the nuns in County Limerick?' There was an edge to Mummy's voice. 'Or there's a very good Home over in Liverpool. That, in my opinion, would be the best solution. But your father, for reasons known only to himself, won't hear of it. However –'

'It's okay,' Margaret said hastily. Anything was better than one of those mother-and-baby homes, where, according to Susan, the nuns made you scrub floors and treated you as a fallen woman. *And* you had to go to Mass every day. Besides, living with Aunt Maud couldn't be any worse than living with Mummy, could it?

'One thing in Maud's favour – she's got so terribly vague. Half the time she probably won't know who you are.'

Aunt Maud's house was on the edge of the village, just a short walk from the harbour. An old country house with plain sash windows in walls so thick that the windowsills were deep enough to hold large pots of geraniums. It must have been built around the same time as the nearby whitewashed cottages that were let out to summer visitors, and long before the bungalows which appeared occasionally in the gaps in the blackberry hedges lining the narrow, twisting road. Summer still lingered among the rose bushes in the small front garden but the blackberries were colouring in the hedgerows and the lower branches of the surrounding trees had begun to shed their leaves. As they walked up the narrow pathway they heard the mournful call of a pigeon and, in the distance, the soft sigh of the sea.

'It's so peaceful here,' Mummy said enthusiastically.

Peaceful? A shudder went down Margaret's spine. As peaceful as the grave.

'Poor Charles and Eddie were killed in the Somme, you know.' Aunt Maud waved a mittened claw at the tarnished medals, the fading letters of commendation preserved under spotted glass. 'We were always loyal to the Crown, of course.' The old woman was delighted to have a new audience, her cheeks flushed with the excitement of recalling the military balls of her youth, the glittering receptions at Dublin Castle.

Watching her, Margaret found it hard to tell just how old she was. Her face was crumpled rather than lined, like a rose that had faded while still in bud, with washed-out blue eyes and thin, pursed lips. White hair pulled back from a high forehead was coiled in place under a delicate hairnet. Only the bony, blue-veined fingers protruding from the woollen mittens she wore, despite the mildness of the weather, gave any clue to her age.

Nutty as a fruit cake, the girl thought. As for the room! Her heart sank as she examined her surroundings. Antimacassars on high-backed chairs, padded footstools with tassels on them, sepia photographs on the walls. It was straight out of *Jane Eyre*. Only there was no Mr Rochester. Just dotty old Aunt Maud and Bridie, the gnomelike housekeeper, who had brought in the tea tray but was still hanging around, joining in the conversation whenever she felt like it. And Mummy, of course, perched on the edge of her chair, drinking tea from the Royal Doulton with little, delicate movements, obviously dying to leave as soon as she decently could.

Aunt Maud, blithely unaware of her audience's lack of interest, pointed at a group photograph of young men in officers' uniforms hanging on the faded Regency wallpaper. 'Solid, true blues,' she announced proudly. 'Loyal to the last.'

'Much good it did them.' Bridie, stacking cups and saucers on the tea tray before taking it out to the kitchen, gave a contemptuous laugh. She had obviously been with the family for so many years that the fine line between servant and confidante had long ago been blurred and overstepped. 'King and country, how are ye!'

Maud stiffened, pushing out her sloping chest like a pouter pigeon's. 'Some of us knew where our duty lay. *And* we knew our place.' She caught Mummy's eye and gave her a meaningful look. '*Some* people seem to have forgotten theirs.'

Bridie laughed again, unimpressed. It was obviously an old game played out over the years but Mummy, who had been casting covetous looks at a satinwood occasional table instead of following the conversation, nodded vaguely. 'The sea air will be so good for Margaret. You know how you've always loved the sea, darling,' she added with the false brightness of a grown-up trying to make a dull treat attractive to a five-year-old.

'Yes.' The girl shrugged. 'If you could go for a swim. Or take a boat out.' She saw a look of alarm cross her mother's face. 'Don't worry, I wasn't going to. I know the rules.' As well she might, since Mummy had talked of nothing else all the way down in the car. 'I won't show my face in public till all the summer visitors are gone.'

And then, all too soon, Mummy had to go, murmuring something about the traffic and the need to get home in time for some unmissable social engagement. 'I'll ring at the weekend, darling. Aren't you lucky? All that lovely fresh air. I wish I had time to take a holiday by the sea. I know you and Maud are going to get on like a house on fire!'

She stood at the gate and watched the little grey Volkswagen reverse and turn in the narrow roadway. Then, with a quick wave and a beep of the horn, Mummy sped away without a backward glance.

The road seemed quieter than ever after the car had gone. Reluctant to go back into the house, Margaret kept her eyes fixed on the bend of the road. At that moment she would have given anything to have her mother back. She felt abandoned – a child on her first day at school. Her eyes swam with tears.

How could they? How could they leave her with those two dotty old women? How would she ever last out the next few months in that awful house? A sharp longing came over her for the scent of Mummy's perfume, for Daddy's reassuring presence.

How could they do this to her? She would never forgive either of them as long as she lived.

The days formed their own pattern. As the mornings grew progressively chillier, she heaved herself reluctantly out of bed – usually missing the woolly floor rug, toes recoiling from the hard linoleum – and felt her way into the icy bathroom, where there was always a shivering wait for the water to run hot, the pipes banging and shuddering as in the engine room of a ship. Then a quick sponge-down over a body which was increasingly becoming unfamiliar terrain to her, her mind bemoaning the destruction of a waistline while her hands explored the growing mound of her belly with a mixture of dismay and wonderment. At the precise moment when despair was beginning to set in, a bawled command would carry up the staircase. 'Don't be all morning in there. The tea's wet.'

Aunt Maud always breakfasted in bed and seldom appeared downstairs before midday. Other meals were eaten with the old lady in the gloomy dining room at the back of the house but, to save the housekeeper's legs, Margaret usually breakfasted at the kitchen table. Bridie's breakfasts were simple but substantial: thick, spicy sausages, bacon rashers cooked till the fat was brown and brittle, fried eggs with black lace collars and doorsteps of mottled toast made with the help of what looked like a lacrosse stick from a Chalet School story pressed against the hot plate of the Aga. Tea was hot and strong, with tea leaves floating on its surface. It was a foolish person who would refuse one of these feasts, as Margaret soon found out.

A simple request for, 'Just coffee, please, and a thin slice of toast,' on her second morning there, unleashed such a fury of reproaches concerning the waste of good food, not to mention the time spent preparing it – 'And what about the importance of eating right in your condition? Had you thought about that, at all?' – that she decided to take the easy way out in future. Any food she couldn't eat was fed to Jess, the aristocratic Wicklow collie, when Bridie's back was turned. Failing that, because Jess was a temperamental dog, it was sneaked out in a handkerchief to be emptied later into the ditch outside the front gate before Margaret headed off on one of her solitary walks.

Even her walks had a pattern to them: there was so little choice. She could go out the winding road past the last of the bungalows, with nothing to see except hedge and ditch on either side and the odd glimpse of cattle through a barred gate, meeting an occasional horse and cart, and the very occasional car, until she grew tired and turned back. Or she could walk into the village past the houses, the pub, the shop-cum-post office, to head for the tiny harbour to check which fishing boats were in and listen to the sound of water lapping against the jetty.

Sometimes she'd trudge the small, stony beach, trying to imagine what it must be like in the summer months with the sun shining, people in swimming, families building sand-castles. And sometimes she'd take the narrow road up the headland and gaze down at the sea dashing itself against the rocks below. But wherever she went in the village, she always felt eyes watching her. People nodded the time of day to her but that was all. She didn't get to know any of them or learn anything about their lives. Yet she always had the feeling they knew everything about her.

If the days were lonely, the nights were even worse. Very often, lying there in the blackness, her legs shifting restlessly, she would picture his face, the way his black curls strayed down over his collar, and would see the brightness of his brown eyes. *Oh Martin!* A wave of longing would come over her. She heard the soft cadences of his voice, his reluctant laugh, that way he had sometimes of loping along with his head down, what he called his 'mountainy walk'. If only he were here. If only. But along with the longing would be a terrible feeling of hurt.

As she grew heavier it was getting more and more difficult to find a comfortable position. She yearned for her own bed at home and her own possessions, longed to hear a familiar voice and feel the touch of a friendly hand. At times like that the blackness seemed to close in on her. She was marooned in space, the only being left in the universe.

Susan wrote a couple of times. Short, careful letters, saying very little. Nothing much was happening in college, apparently. Just boring study and hours of boring practice at the piano. Margaret wasn't missing much, she said, but *she* was missed. Can't wait to see you. Her only other contact with the outside world was Mummy. Every week, there was a phone call. As regular but not as frequent as the trains that passed through the tiny railway station on their way to and from Dublin. Short, stilted conversations, her mother doing most of the talking. Are you getting enough to eat? Remembering to take your iron? Getting enough rest? Your father sends his love. Let us know if you need anything. You could almost hear the sigh of relief as she put down the phone, her duty done for the week.

And every Sunday, Aunt Maud dragged her off to a different kind of duty. Eleven o'clock Mass in the small parish church, where more eyes followed their slow progress up the aisle to the old lady's favourite seat. The eyes probably noted Margaret's failure to receive Holy Communion but she didn't care. Let them think what they want, she would say to herself as she sat back and watched Aunt Maud totter prayerfully up the aisle. It was her one act of defiance, even if the only ones to witness it were strangers.

Some Sundays the old lady had visitors. A middle-aged man and a woman would arrive by car in the afternoon, sometimes accompanied by a younger man and a girl around Margaret's age. On those days she kept to her room. Bridie would bring her evening meal up on a tray, wheezing and grunting as she negotiated the narrow stairs. She hated those Sundays, having to stay upstairs, hearing the sounds of conversation and laughter drifting up from the parlour. The sounds of normal people leading normal lives. People with nothing to hide. People who didn't have to be hidden away from others like something to be ashamed of. Who, when the visit was over, were free to go away and get on with their lives – go to parties, ride openly on buses, walk through the city streets. Free. Not in prison like she was.

But it wasn't the house that imprisoned her, although it always seemed like that on the Sundays Aunt Maud's relatives came. Nor was the old woman who toiled upstairs with the tray of food her jailer. It was her own body that was the prison. The creature who kicked inside her, disturbing her sleep and weighing her down as she walked, was the real jailer, the one responsible for her misery. She knew it was wrong to think like that but she couldn't help it.

'Everything is coming along nicely,' the local doctor would say every fortnight after her check-up. He was a middle-aged man with a brusque yet jovial manner, a bit like Susan's dentist father, she thought, only nicer. Although he was utterly professional in his approach she could never get used to his hands on her body and only managed to get through the examination by staring into the middle distance and pretending it was happening to someone else. 'You're a strong, healthy girl,' he'd say briskly, putting his notes back into her file with a satisfied flourish. Mercifully, he asked few questions.

Aunt Maud had other visitors, but these she didn't have to hide from. A couple of genteel old ladies from the village, a retired solicitor, an elderly doctor, uncle to the one whose surgery she visited. Far from having to hide, it was a question of needing to escape from them. Old eyes would light up with pleasure at the sight of a young face, bony hands would detain her while their owner delved into the intricacies of family relationships, recounting the exploits of grand-children, nieces or nephews. The old men paid her gallant compliments, the ladies were solicitous for her health, the seafaring husband was enquired after punctiliously. Only when the preparations for the bridge game were complete was she free to make an excuse and leave.

'That's right, dear; you go for a nice walk.' The rings on Aunt Maud's mittened fingers winked in the lamplight as she shuffled the cards. 'Very good for you in your condition.'

'That oul' one doesn't know the difference between night and day.' Bridie, who had fought a losing battle to prevent Margaret from going out after dark, followed her into the hall and pressed a flashlight into her hand. 'You watch yourself, now. You wouldn't know what kind of go-boy would be out at this hour.'

'Don't be such a fusser, Bridie.' At home, people would be getting ready to go out for the evening, queues would be forming for the cinemas, streets would be lit up. 'It's quite early.' But she took the torch with her. There was a short, unlit stretch of road between the house and the village. No sense in catching one's ankle.

A crisp autumn night, the scent of turf smoke in the air. It was peaceful walking at that hour. No watching eyes to assess her bulky shape. As she passed the lighted pub, there was no one about, except for a man with two greyhounds on a lead. The harbour looked different at night, romantic somehow, like a scene waiting to be peopled by actors. A cold moon hung in a starless sky; the light from the lamps on the quayside plunged and wriggled through the dark water like glittering worms.

How deep was the harbour? Deep enough to jump in and not come up again? How simple it would be to slip in over the side and feel the waters closing over your head. She pictured herself being borne on the tide out to sea, her long hair floating behind her like Ophelia. How simple. And somehow attractive. It would mean she need never go through the ordeal that lay ahead.

Then another picture came to mind. Her body trapped by weeds in the murky waters beside the jetty, her face bloated, eyes staring.

She shuddered. The child lurched violently inside her. It's okay, she whispered, I didn't mean it. I wouldn't do it to you. She felt protective, yet resentful. There was no escape. No way out. Whatever was ahead would have to be gone through. As she made her ponderous way back along the dark road, she comforted herself with the thought that in only another few weeks it would all be over.

The nursing home was a rambling affair spread out over several tall, narrow terrace houses with a distant glimpse of the sea from their top windows. Her room was small, the carpet worn in places, but it looked clean. The fire blazing in the grate struck a welcoming note in the dull November day. After the uncomfortable car journey it was a relief to climb into bed and lean back against the pillows.

'You need have no worries. Your daughter will be in good hands here.' The matron was a large woman in a blue dress and a wide, starched white veil. When she moved, her corsets creaked and floorboards shuddered under her feet. It had been quite a squeeze coming up with her in the ancient wrought-iron lift. 'My nurses are first-class. And very discreet.'

'Yes, yes, of course.' Mummy didn't seem as comfortable with the situation as Matron. She kept smoothing imaginary creases out of the fingers of her gloves and darting quick glances at the door. 'Don't let me keep you. I know how busy you are.'

'Not at all, dear. Only too glad – ' She paused in the doorway, her voice dropping conspiratorially. 'Don't forget now. Nothing to worry about.'

'I only hope she's right,' Mummy said, turning to Margaret after Matron had gone. 'You know how these nurses gossip.'

'She seemed kind.'

'Oh, I'm sure she's *kind*. That's not what I'm worried about.'

'I can see that.' Was it possible to hate anyone more than she hated her mother at that moment? She picked up a magazine and began to leaf through it.

'Don't take me up like that. You know I didn't mean it that way.'

'No?' The printed letters danced on the page, making no sense. 'Does it matter?'

She heard Mummy sigh. 'Look, darling, I'll have to go. I'll try to get out to see you tomorrow. But if I can't, I'll definitely telephone.'

She kept her eyes on the page. 'You do that.'

Still her mother lingered. 'You'll be all right, won't you?'

'Don't worry about me.' She gave a short laugh. 'I'll be fine.'

She was climbing a hillside up a narrow twisting path. On one side, the ground dropped away steeply towards the sea. On the other, the hill was covered in brambles which kept trailing across her path. It was difficult to make any progress; the ground kept sliding under her, tilting her towards the edge. Resisting the pull of the incline, scratching her hands on brambles, she tried desperately to avoid being sucked over the side. Below her the sea glinted evilly, boiling and frothing against the jagged rocks. She had to keep climbing but it got harder and harder as the path rose higher and higher, twisting and turning around the face of the hill.

'I can't go on.' But it was impossible to turn back. A fierce dog was behind her, snapping at her legs. She could hear its breath panting and could glimpse its sharp teeth. If she stopped she knew it would fall on her and devour her.

Suddenly a woman appeared on the path in front of her. A young woman with dark hair and a rosy, smiling face. 'Take my hand.'

'Is it really you?' Margaret looked at her in wonderment. 'I thought you had gone forever.'

'Yes, lovey, it's me.' The woman held out her hands and the girl knew that once she felt those warm, comforting arms around her, she would be safe.

She stretched out her own arms. 'I'm coming, Delia!' But, just then, the animal following behind sprang. She felt its sharp teeth tearing her flesh and biting into her.

She came up into the darkness. A hard, unfamiliar bed. The sheet soaking wet under her. The dog still gnawing away at the pit of her stomach. And someone screaming at the top of her voice.

They were very kind. And encouraging. 'Good girl!' they said. 'It won't be much longer,' they said.

But it seemed to go on forever.

It was the cliff path all over again. You knew you had to keep going. There was no turning back. Oh God! Would it ever end?

Would it ever – ? The cliff. The path. The cruel rocks.

The pain that mounted to a crescendo and then mercifully died away.

The relief of it.

But no! It was coming back again. The dog snapping at her heels. The cliff path. But where was Delia? Or was it Mummy she wanted? It was impossible to think straight. It was like bedlam in the room. The pains coming so fast, the voices calling out. The exhortations, the rallying cries. Just one more push, dear. Try a little harder. That's it. That's it! Good girl! Oh, good girl!

And then it was over. It was finished.

Thank God, it was over!

'But aren't you going to hold him?' The nurse's round, cheerful face looked bewildered.

'No.' She was utterly drained. All she wanted to do was crawl away into a hole and hide. She turned her head away, but not before she glimpsed two tiny fists waving in the air and damp tendrils of dark hair above a red, aggrieved face.

'Will you *look* at him!' The nurse was ecstatic. 'Isn't he a little dote?'

Something lit up inside her at the words. But she shook her head.

'Ah, come on. Just one look.'

What's the use? They wouldn't let me keep him anyway. A clean break, was what Mummy had said. She shook her head again, screwing her eyes up tightly to hold back the tears.

'It wasn't easy getting up here.' Susan was indignant. 'This *enormous* woman interrogated me. Talk about the Gestapo!' She flung her duffel coat on a chair and sat down on the end of the bed. 'Was it awful?' Her voice was a mixture of sympathy and eagerness. 'Really awful? Worse than getting your appendix out?'

'Much worse.'

'Tell me about it.'

Margaret hesitated. There was so much to tell; where did you begin? And how did you explain to someone who hadn't been through it? Suddenly it seemed an impossible task. She felt as if the two of them were on different sides of a gorge. She was being asked to bridge the distance between them with nothing but words. The beginnings of a headache gnawed at her forehead.

'Not now. I'm a bit tired.'

Her friend's face fell. 'I thought you'd want – '

The gorge grew wider until she seemed to be looking at

Susan from a long way off. 'I will, sometime. But not now.'

'I see.' The other girl sighed. She got off the bed, wandered over to the mantelpiece, picked up a card and read the message on it. 'Get well soon! Honestly! You'd think it *had* been your appendix.'

Margaret laughed painfully. 'That seems to be the general idea.'

'It's not here, then?'

'*It?*' She wished Susan would stay still for a moment. All that wandering around was making her headache worse. 'Do you mean the baby? I've no idea.' She made her voice sound indifferent. 'He's not here, anyway.'

'Oh.' Susan looked uncertainly at her and went over to the window. 'You can see the sea from here.'

'I know.'

'What's going to happen to him?'

'You'd better ask Mummy.' The pain in her head grew tighter. All she wanted was to be left in peace. 'Look, Sue, this way is best for everyone, believe me.'

'Yes, I suppose it is.' The other girl turned around, her face wistful. 'But I can't help feeling – '

She felt her control snap suddenly. 'Don't say it, Susan! Please don't say it.' Tears began rolling down her face. 'I know what you're thinking but please don't ever say it.' If only she'd held him in her arms. Just for a little while. Just so she'd have something to remember. If only she'd looked at him properly.

'There, there.' Susan put an awkward arm around her shoulders. 'Don't cry. Look, I brought you a present. I made it myself.'

'It's beautiful.' She gazed through her tears at the tiny, blue matinée coat. 'It's so delicate. It must have taken you ages.'

'Not really. Pidgie helped with the buttonholes. I'm glad you like it.' Her friend beamed with pride. 'I took a bit of a chance with the colour, though. Just as well it turned out to be a boy.'

'Oh Susan!' The tears sprang out again. 'I'll never see it on him.'

'Of course you will. Just tell the nurse –'

'But I sent him away.'

'You didn't know what you were doing,' Susan said comfortingly. 'It'll be okay. They're not going to stop you seeing your own child.'

'Your baby?' The young nurse looked blankly at her. 'You want to see him? But I thought –' Her head around the door, she had a hurried air as if the bell had taken her away from a more important task. 'You said –'

'I changed my mind. I want to see him.' Her voice was firm. Whose baby was he, after all? She reached for her dressing gown. 'Where is he? I'll go with you.'

'I'll have to ask Matron.' The nurse was gone before Margaret could say anything.

Five minutes went by. Then ten. No sign of Matron. No sign of the nurse.

She rang the bell again.

'Why can't I see him?'

'It's Matron's evening off. We need her permission. You'll

have to wait till tomorrow.'

The next day, a litany of excuses.

He's being fed.

He's having a nap.

He'll be along shortly.

She became tired of excuses. I'll look for him myself. Wait till the corridor is clear, then slip along to the nursery. But where was the nursery? The corridor was narrow, dimly lit. Nothing in sight but closed doors. She opened one at random. A woman, propped up against pillows, looked at her without curiosity.

'Have you seen my baby?' Margaret approached the bedside.

The woman said nothing. Seen up close, she looked too old to be having a baby. Confused, the girl withdrew and stumbled down the passageway, where she met another woman. She was old too but quite alert. 'The nursery? There's no nursery here, child.'

A nurse appeared from nowhere and urged Margaret back to her own room.

Matron came. She stood at the end of the bed.

'Don't be upsetting yourself, dear. Calm down. Getting all worked up about it won't do any good.'

She looked out through swollen eyes. 'I want my baby.'

What a big woman Matron was. Such unshakeable calm. Nothing would ever upset Matron. The old people must find her very reassuring. 'I'm afraid that's not possible, dear.'

Mummy had thought of everything. No point in blaming Matron or the nurses. They were only following instructions. It was her own fault, anyway. She had made it so easy for them. Why hadn't she held him? Why hadn't she insisted? She tried to recall what he had looked like. Dark hair. It looked as if it might be curly. Eyes? What colour eyes? Try to remember, Margaret. I can't. Oh God, she couldn't remember. She had only seen him for a moment.

Her arms ached with longing. Her breasts were sore and heavy. Her head felt as if it would burst. She couldn't speak without breaking down in tears. She was quite sure that she was losing her mind.

Nonsense, the nurses said. The third-day blues. Perfectly natural. Everyone goes through it. Take these tablets. Cut down on fluids. You'll be all right in a day or two.

'People think you're in France.' Mummy looked positively lighthearted. 'You're expected home for Christmas.'

'But why can't I go home now?' She longed to have her own things about her, to sleep in her own bed.

'It's better this way, darling. Gives people less time to ask questions. It's only for a few weeks, and I'm sure Maud will be glad of the company.'

Daddy visited her before she left the nursing home. It was almost three months since they had seen each other. When he removed his scarf and overcoat she thought he looked thinner and had more grey in his hair than she remembered. 'What's the food like? Are you getting enough to eat?' His hand when he shook hers was icy cold.

'It's okay. I'm fine.' She avoided his eye and went to the window.

'You must put all this behind you,' he said. 'Concentrate on the future.'

She wiped the condensation from the glass with her fingertips. If you looked very hard you could just make out the sea, a faint smear against the skyline.

'You've done the right thing, Margaret. In years to come you'll realise – '

The right thing? What did that mean? They were just words. The right thing. She saw again the raw, bewildered face, the fists waving helplessly. If only she had held him. Just once. If only she had felt his tiny fingers in hers.

'It's too late now.'

'No, never say that. You have your whole life ahead of you.'

What do you care? You can't even bring yourself to say what happened. You'd think it was a bad flu that you had to get over. Wrap up well when you go out.

As if he guessed what she was thinking, he said quietly behind her, 'If it's any consolation, he's gone to a good home.'

No, it wasn't any consolation. A good home! Like something you'd read in the newspaper. 'Good home wanted for loveable puppy.' A tear slid down her cheek but she kept her face turned towards the window. She would never see him now. Already she was beginning to forget what he looked like.

She felt a gentle touch on her shoulder and heard the plea in his voice. 'You could have ruined your life.'

She shook his hand away.

What makes you so sure I haven't?

The day was closing in. It was no longer possible to make out the sea. Funny how cold and grey the sea could look at times. And at other times it looked so blue. When she was a child she could never get over how blue it was. Of course, that was it. He had blue eyes. How could she have forgotten? It wasn't much to be going on with, was it? Not to last you a lifetime.

How was she going to get through the rest of her life without him?

Mummy couldn't understand why she didn't want to go out much that Christmas, why she refused invitations to parties and stayed in her room reading. Daddy said she was far too thin and prescribed a tonic, which she threw down the sink when no one was watching. She wanted no favours from either of them. It was not as if they really cared for her. It was all an act, a pretence. Just like the pretence that the last nine months had never happened.

'How was Paris?' Father Tim asked her one day after Christmas.

He was just as much a fixture in the drawing room of the new house, she thought, as he had been in the Square. And as handsome as ever. Although it looked as if he was getting a bit of a paunch. Not enough exercise. And too many cream cakes. Her amusement faded as an anxious thought struck her. Had Mummy told him anything? They were as thick as thieves. 'I haven't had a chance to see much of it,' she hedged. 'Maybe when the weather gets better – '

She watched him alertly but he gave her a guileless look as he handed over his teacup for a refill. 'When you go back make sure you visit the Sacré-Coeur. In my opinion, even more beautiful than Notre Dame –'

' – and what about the Champs Elysées!' her mother cut in, her voice soaring with enthusiasm. 'And the *Louvre*! How I envy you, darling. What a marvellous opportunity for a young girl. Am I right, Father Tim?'

'As always, Maeve.' He gave her an eager, boyish look, then turned to Margaret. 'You should listen to her, you know. When all's said and done, a girl's best friend is her mother.'

Resentment rose up in her like bile. She stared back at him stonily.

You wouldn't say that if you knew the truth, she thought.

They couldn't wait to get rid of her. That much was obvious. Wasn't it convenient, her mother said, that someone in St Celeste's knew of a French family needing an au pair? How well it had all worked out. No need for any more lies. No need for Mummy to invent stories of letters home and what the weather was like in Paris. No more having to explain to her friends why Margaret wasn't going on with college. Really, darling, I envy you. Paris in the spring! Those marvellous shops. The style! Parisian women are so chic! Maybe some of it would rub off on Margaret. And think of what it will do for your French.

Really, things could have been a lot worse. Mummy was almost philosophical as she helped Margaret with her packing. Disaster had been averted, but only just. *She* had done her best. 'It's up to *you* now. If you've any sense you'll put it behind you and get on with your life.'

It was obvious that Daddy was of the same opinion although he was kinder about it. 'Give it time,' he said when he left her at the airport. 'There's a wise saying that time heals all ills.'

How much time would it take? As the plane rose higher through the blackness of the January evening, she gazed down at the lights of Dublin growing smaller beneath her. How long before you were able to forget?

PART FIVE

'I usually dread this time of year.' Margaret's face was sombre as she drew the long curtains to shut out the dark November night. 'That awful, low feeling for weeks beforehand. And then the birthday itself – '

'God, yes.' Imagine if it were Sean! Mick thought. Imagine every March coming around and you knew you were never going to see him again. 'It must be worse for the woman. I mean – after going through the whole birth experience – '

She nodded without speaking.

'And it wasn't just the birth itself, was it? It was all the months before, especially the last three. Margaret!' Impulsively he put out his hand and touched hers. 'I'm haunted by the thought of you wandering around that fishing village at night. Those three months must have been the loneliest ones of your life.'

'They were.' She took his hand and pressed it briefly before letting it go. 'And the first few months in France were lonely too, in a different way.'

He could still feel the touch of her hand against his. 'Tell me about it.' He watched her face eagerly as she talked.

'The language, the people. It was a real culture shock. I think I must have gone around in a kind of trance. I felt quite numb, you see, as if my feelings were dead. I keep thinking of this bird I saw. It was very cold in Paris when I got there, much colder than I expected. Snow on the ground. We lived out in a suburb and one morning we found a frozen bird lying in the front garden. It was dead but the children insisted on bringing it in to the kitchen to try to revive it. It was no good, of course. Even when it had thawed out it was still dead.' She stared thoughtfully into the distance. 'And that was the way I was inside. For a long time.'

Neither of them spoke for a while, the silence broken only by the crackling of the flames in the fireplace and the wind stirring the trees in the garden outside.

Then Mick asked, 'Did you ever get over it – completely, I mean?'

'I don't know.' Her voice was pensive. 'On the surface, maybe, but a part of me never has. And of course every year on your birthday – '

'But this year will be different, won't it?'

'Oh yes.' Her face brightened. 'This year I won't be tormenting myself, wondering.'

'And I won't be either,' he said with feeling.

'Oh Michael, it must have been hard for you too.' There was regret in her voice. 'I never realised – '

'It's okay.' He was full of compassion as he patted her hand. 'You weren't to know. And it wasn't your fault, anyway. I realise that now.'

'I can hardly believe it but this year I can give you a present.' There was a note of wonder in her voice. 'What would you – ?'

He grinned. 'How about a Porsche?'

She laughed suddenly, blue eyes sparkling with amusement. 'Why not a Rolls while you're at it?' Sitting beside him on the couch, she looked like a young girl, her long legs tucked under her, soft hair hanging loosely around her face.

God! She was beautiful!

For a split second his heart seemed to stop.

'What's the matter, Michael?' Her smile faded.

'Nothing,' he stammered. 'Nothing's the matter.' It was his turn to shake his head in wonderment. 'Sometimes I find it hard to believe you're my mother.'

'I find it hard to believe, too. You're my *son*.' She said the words with a kind of joy. 'Oh, I wish I could throw a party for you, show you off to everybody.'

He was pleased, astonished. 'Do you really mean that?'

'Yes. I *really* wish I could.'

The sadness in her voice pulled him up short. He said cautiously, 'If wishes were horses – ' An old saying of Ma's, it always brought him down to earth. 'That's not on, is it?'

'No,' she said. 'I'm afraid it's not.'

Alarm tugged at him. 'Not just for now, you mean? Or not *ever*?' When she said nothing his alarm grew. 'There's something you haven't told me, isn't there?'

She met his gaze briefly. 'I'm afraid there is.'

'But *why*? *Why? Why?*' His voice rose in bafflement. 'Why does Vincent not want Caroline to know who I am?'

She looked at him helplessly. 'He says he doesn't want her upset.'

'*Upset*? But why would she – ? I'm her *brother*, for God's sake. You'd think she'd be glad. I know I am.'

'It's not as simple as that, Michael. He was never happy about having you here in the first place. The truth is, he doesn't want you to be part of our lives, doesn't want people to know that I had a son before I met him.'

Realisation dawned suddenly. 'And if Caroline isn't told, nobody can be told. Not your mother, your brother, my cousins, your friends, even.'

'That's about it.'

'But what about you?' His voice rose again. 'How could you agree to such a thing? How could you!'

He saw her flinch. 'I – I didn't have much choice.'

'Yes you did!' he raged. 'Of course you had a choice. All you had to say was – '

She shook her head. 'It's not that simple.'

'You said that before. Maybe *I'm* simple but I just don't understand. Unless – ' a painful suspicion occurred to him. 'Unless you agree with him. Maybe you don't want people to know about me.' He looked at her accusingly. 'You're ashamed of me, is that it?'

'No!' She shook her head vehemently. 'Before I met you, maybe, but not now. Not since we've got to know each other. Now, I'd be happy to tell the world.'

'I wonder how true that is?' He felt bitter suddenly. 'You seemed happy enough with things the way they were.'

'I suppose I was being selfish. It gave us so much more time together. But you must admit we needed it; we needed that time to fill in the past.' Her face softened. 'You've no idea how much the last couple of months have meant to me.'

'And to me.' Although he longed to respond to the plea in her voice he hardened his heart and kept his voice firm. 'But you know we can't go on like this.'

'Why not?' She seemed taken aback. 'Nothing's changed.'

'For me it has. Now that I know. Look – you don't expect me to keep coming here on sufferance, do you? Like some kind of hanger-on?'

'You were never that, Michael.'

'No?' He couldn't keep the bitterness from his voice. He got to his feet. 'I'd better go home.'

She looked alarmed. 'But when will I see you again?'

'I don't know. I have a lot of thinking to do.'

'Michael!' She put her hand out to him. '*Please* don't go like this.'

Again he hardened his heart, ignored the hand. 'I'll be in touch.'

'I'm sorry for the short notice,' Margaret said. 'But I just had to see you.'

'Of course.' Susan held the door open welcomingly. 'Come on in.' She led the way into the living room of the flat, where a half-filled suitcase lay on the dining table surrounded by piles of folded garments. 'Excuse the mess. As I told you on the phone, packing for this American trip is a bit of a headache. Not my own stuff; I have that down to a fine art by now. It's Tom. He's terribly disorganised. I don't know how he ever – ' She laughed as she cleared a chair for Margaret to sit down. 'When I told him you and I wanted to chat, he was only too delighted to abandon the packing and go for a pint. It's okay, we're not flying out till the day after tomorrow. Plenty of time to sort things out. Now, why don't you relax by the fire while I get us both a drink.'

'Sounds lovely.' She eased back into her armchair, enjoying the warmth of the blazing coals. As she gazed around her, Margaret marvelled at the changes that had been wrought in the room since Susan's father retired and the house had been converted into flats. When Frank and Pidgie Miller had moved out to Dalkey three years before, they had given Susan and Tom one of the flats as a wedding present. What had once been the dentist's waiting room was now a comfortable sitting room. Like her mother before her, Susan's taste in furniture was practical rather than elegant. Except for the baby grand in one corner, the furniture was not valuable – stuff picked up mostly in auction rooms or inherited from relatives – but it was a pleasant room, with the same air of casual comfort that had characterised Pidgie Miller's kitchen all those years ago.

And Susan had the same knack as her mother, she reflected as her friend returned with a bottle of wine and two glasses, that lovely talent for making you feel instantly welcome the minute you walked in the door. And comforted in some way. She was such a solid, *safe* person to be with. 'I'm glad I caught you before you went away.'

'I'm glad too.' Susan gave her a considering look. 'You sound as if you need a shoulder to cry on.'

'You don't know the half of it.' Margaret smiled wryly. 'I have a problem and I can't see any way out.'

'It's been a week now, and no word.' She stared at her friend in dismay.

'Why not ring *him*?' Susan said in her sensible way. 'Is he on the phone?'

'I have a number I can contact. But what good would that do? What could I say to him? Vincent isn't going to change his mind. In fact, he's been insufferable over the last week, making pointed remarks about it being a relief to have the house to ourselves. He keeps asking if Michael and I have quarrelled. He's positively gloating at the thought of it. Not that I've told him anything.'

'I don't know how you put up with it.' There was distaste in Susan's voice. She looked quickly at Margaret. 'I don't mean to interfere but – '

'It's okay. You're not saying anything that I don't know already.' She sighed heavily. 'I just can't keep pretending about myself and Vincent any more. It's been difficult enough these last few years but since Michael came on the scene it's been intolerable.'

'But I thought you were so happy to have your son back?'

'I am. I was. It's been wonderful getting to know him but, as I told you, he doesn't want to come to the house any more unless Vincent will accept him. Which he isn't prepared to do, of course.'

'Why not just tell Caroline the truth?'

'I'm afraid to do that. I don't know how she'd react. She takes her line from Vincent so *she* doesn't want Michael around either. Besides, Vincent would never forgive me – '

'A pity about him.' Susan's voice was scornful. She looked closely at her friend. 'You're not afraid of him, are you?'

'No, of course not,' Margaret said quickly. 'He's not violent, or anything. But he can make life pretty difficult when he – '

'There's more than one kind of violence.' Susan shook her head. 'Oh, Margaret, what are you going to do?'

'I don't know.' Her voice trembled. 'I'm so afraid he won't come back.'

'Of course he will. If Michael really cares for you he won't let something like this put him off. You're his mother, after all.'

'We know each other only a couple of months,' Margaret said sadly. 'The ties don't go very deep. Oh Susan.' Tears filled her eyes suddenly. 'I've only just found him. I can't bear the thought of losing him again.'

'It won't come to that.' Her friend's voice was firm.

But Margaret thought she saw doubt in Susan's eyes.

'What do you want to do for your birthday, Mick?'

'My birthday?'

'Yes, Mick, your birthday next week.' There was a look of amused exasperation on Fran's face. 'Don't tell me you've forgotten. Although you've been acting so strange lately I wouldn't be surprised at anything.'

'No, I hadn't forgotten,' he said dully. 'I have a lot on my mind.'

She looked at him alertly. 'Like what?'

Wish I hadn't said that. She'll be like a terrier after a bone until she finds out.

'Oh, nothing – work,' he mumbled.

Another mistake. He saw Fran's eyes narrow.

'Not laying people off, are they?'

'God, no!' What had possessed him to put that idea into her head? 'The job's safe enough, as far as I know. But it's all indoor work this time of year. And the light isn't good. Gets a bit depressing at times.' Which was true enough. 'November's a dreary month at the best of times.' But this year it was worse.

'Pity about you.' She had no sympathy for him. 'How would you like to be me, cooped up in this dump all day with old Nosey Parker downstairs wanting to know your every move? If we had our own house – '

He sighed. 'Some day, Fran. But not yet. The job doesn't pay enough.'

'I could get work. There's notices up in some of the shops.'

'But who'd look after Sean?'

'Maybe your Ma – ?'

'She has her job in the hospital canteen. It's only part-time, I know, but Ma isn't getting any younger and – '

'Probably wouldn't work, anyway.' She dismissed the idea as quickly as it had arisen. 'Now if we lived near my mother – ' Her eyes gleamed. 'I know Mammy would be only too happy – '

I bet she would. He shuddered inwardly at the thought of living near the Hennessys. 'You don't know that. She has her own job, after all.' He looked at her uneasily. 'How did we get on to this subject, anyway?'

Fran thought for a moment. 'I know. Your birthday,' she said triumphantly. 'Have you thought what you'd like to do?'

'No, I haven't.' It came out more curtly than he intended.

She looked taken aback. 'No need to bite the head off me.'

'Sorry, didn't mean to,' he muttered.

'I don't know what's got into you lately.' She looked affronted. 'I'm only thinking of *you.*'

'I know, I know,' he said wearily. 'Just leave it for the moment, will you.'

'But Mick – ' She had a stubborn look on her face.

He felt his control snap. 'Leave it, will you. It's no big deal. It's only a friggin' birthday, after all.'

This year will be different, she had said, and her whole face had lit up. This year I won't be tormenting myself wondering.

And I won't be either, he had said.

This year 20 November was going to be different for both of them. A real celebration.

How wrong could you be!

And now Fran was talking about making plans. All he knew was he didn't want to be a part of them.

'What are you doing today?' Vincent asked at breakfast.

What did he care? She looked at him with lacklustre eyes. Lately she was finding it more and more difficult to be polite to him. 'The Friends of the Hospital are running a coffee morning in aid of the new dialysis machine. And then I've a meeting this afternoon – '

'Yeh, yeh – ' Although he liked the idea of his wife being involved in charitable committees, he had no interest in hearing about them. 'Should keep you happy for a bit.'

'Happy?' The day's commitments were like leaden weights hanging around her neck. She just wanted to crawl back to bed and sleep forever.

'Sorry, my mistake,' he grunted. 'You don't know the meaning of the word.' He frowned as he studied her face. 'Still not sleeping? I thought that was the whole point of your taking up residence in the spare room. Get something from the doctor, for God's sake. Or – ' A thought occurred to him. ' – go back to that shrink you saw a few years ago. Get her to fix you up with some happy pills. They did the trick the last time.'

As always, she was stung by his lack of sensitivity. 'Vincent, that's nearly thirteen years ago. I went to a psychiatrist because I was depressed after the miscarriage. Don't you remember?'

His face went blank. 'That's all water under the bridge.' He put down his teacup and stood up. 'I want to look in to the office before I drive to Wexford. I've a meeting with the architects on the site. The builders are dragging their heels. We'll be lucky if we have this factory up and running by the end of next year.' He glanced at the apple core and empty yogurt carton marking Caroline's place at the table. 'She got off to school all right?'

'She took an early bus. Talking of Caroline – ' She summoned up her courage to say, 'There's something I wanted to – '

His interest caught, he turned back. 'Nothing wrong, is there?'

'No, no, she's fine. But – it's about her and – and Michael.'

'*That* fella! What about him?' His voice was curt.

'Him and Caroline. I think we should – '

Vincent's features seemed to harden as he looked at her. 'If you're asking what I think you're asking,' he snapped. 'The answer's still " No !".'

'I need a favour,' Susan said over the phone. 'You know we're going to be away on tour until the end of March – ?'

'In America?'

'Where else? Margaret, are you listening?'

'Yes, of course.' She forced a note of interest into her voice. 'What can I do to help?'

'Do you remember I told you that we'd arranged for someone to stay in the flat while we're away? Well, that's fallen through and it's too late to get anyone else.'

'You want me to keep an eye on it for you?'

'Oh, would you? Margaret, you're a dear. I'll leave the keys in an envelope with the woman in the basement. It's just a question of coming in occasionally, the plants only need watering once a week, the bills are all taken care of – '

'Don't worry.' She tried to sound cheerful. 'I'll look after things while you're gone.'

'I knew I could rely on you. And listen, if you want to use the place yourself, stay the night or – '

'Why would I want to do that?' Margaret was puzzled.

'If you needed a break, a bit of space, maybe.' She sounded diffident suddenly. 'Look, it was just a thought.'

'Thanks, anyway. But Susan, I can't believe you're going to be away for four whole months.' Her heart sank at the prospect. 'You've no idea how much I'm going to miss you.'

'I'll miss you too. Although I have to admit I'm really looking forward to this trip.' Margaret could hear the excitement in Susan's voice. 'It's the first time Tom and I have gone on tour together. The first time I won't mind being away from home for Christmas.'

'I'm very happy for you,' Margaret said.

But when she put down the receiver she was close to tears.

Another phone call. Mummy's voice on the answering machine. 'If you're there, Margaret, pick up the phone.'

It was gloomy in the hallway. Rain spattered against the stained-glass window at the turn of the stairs. She shrank back into the shadows, holding her breath, as if her mother could somehow sense her presence. I can't talk to her now. Please, please go away.

'Oh, very well. You're never there when you're needed. It's not you I want, anyway. I was trying to contact Vincent but he's not in the office today.'

Vincent? What does she want Vincent for? Has someone told her about Michael? Has Vincent – ?

But Mummy's thoughts were running on different lines. 'Don't worry, darling,' she said archly. 'I'm not trying to steal your husband; he's quite safe. Just a few business matters to discuss. Get him to ring me.' And then she was gone.

Thank God for that. She pressed the playback button on the machine and listened to the message again just to make sure. It was okay. Mummy knew nothing, that was clear. It had been ridiculous to suspect Vincent of having told her. She was the last person with whom he would have discussed it. And, if Caroline had mentioned something to her about a new long-lost relative turning up, Margaret would have been the one her mother would have questioned.

Business matters, she'd said. Which was no surprise, come to think of it; she occasionally consulted Vincent about investments and suchlike. Margaret pictured her husband's reaction this evening when she would pass on the message. 'Picking my brains again,' he'd sneer. 'Saving herself the cost of an accountant.' But at the same time he would preen himself on the fact that her mother thought enough of him to ask his advice. 'Better give the old girl a ring,' he'd say.

'Put her out of her misery.' And then he'd fawn all over her on the phone, trying to lose his harsh accent and being careful about his endings.

She felt a sudden sense of revulsion as she pictured this performance. Contrasting it with the curt way he had spoken to her that morning, she found her stomach churning with dislike and resentment. The day after tomorrow was her son's birthday and, because of Vincent's attitude, she wasn't allowed celebrate it. Because of Vincent she had driven Michael away. Despair settled over her. He wouldn't come back. And Vincent would never change. What was she going to do?

If only she could get away for a bit. Get away from Vincent and the pressures of her life. Go somewhere where she could get her head in order, think things out.

But where? There was nowhere she could go.

It was then she remembered Susan's offer.

'Going away? At this time of the year?' Caroline looked baffled. 'Is Daddy going too?'

'No. It's not a holiday really, more a short break. I need some time to myself. I've a few things to think over.'

The girl nodded. 'One of these health farms, is it? Lucky you! The mother of a girl in my class went on one last year. She lost half a stone in three days, can you imagine! Not that you need – '

'Not exactly,' Margaret said hurriedly. 'Anyway I've left your dinner in the oven and Mrs Canvey will come in every day. There's plenty of food in the freezer and you might give this note to your father when he gets back from Wexford. I'm not sure what time he – '

'A note?' Caroline frowned as she took the envelope. 'Doesn't he know?'

'There hasn't been time. It was all a bit spur-of-the-moment-ish. Look, I have to dash. You'll be all right, won't you?'

'Of course we will.' She looked uncannily like Vincent as she scowled at her mother. 'I'm not a *child*, you know.'

'No.' Margaret looked thoughtfully at her. 'I never said you were.'

'Daddy and I will manage perfectly.' Caroline's eyes lit up at the thought. 'So there's no need for you to rush back.'

'By the way, there was a phone message for you,' Fran said just after they had got into bed.

His heart gave a great leap. 'Why didn't you tell me?'

'I'm telling you now, amn't I? Some woman – '

'Yes?' He sat up and looked at her eagerly.

' – a friend of Mammy's – wants her kitchen painted. I said you'd ring back.'

'I see.' He hid his disappointment, switched out the bedside light and lay with his back turned to her. 'I don't know if I – '

'Please yourself.' Fran yawned and burrowed her head into her pillow. 'Although with Christmas just around the corner we could do with the money. And my mother's not going to keep recommending you to people if you keep turning them down.'

'I haven't turned anyone down yet, Fran.'

Except his mother. And, for the life of him, he would never know why he did it.

In the darkness he could hear her voice: 'This year will be different.' Saw her face light up as she sat on the couch with her feet tucked under her like a young girl. This year would be different, all right, with each of them knowing that only a few miles of city was keeping them apart. That and his stupid pride. Because that's all it was. Pride. Suddenly the reasons why he had kept away from her didn't seem to make sense any more. Against all the odds he had found his mother and now he was about to lose her again because he couldn't have everything his own way in the relationship. How childish could you be? He wanted to kick himself for his own stupidity.

But it wasn't too late, was it? His birthday wasn't till the day after tomorrow. There was still time to do something about it.

His heart raced with excitement in the darkness. He'd telephone as soon as he got to work in the morning.

'Gone away? Are you sure?' He couldn't believe that he had heard aright. 'Did she say when she'd be back?'

The voice at the other end of the phone exuded amiable indifference.

'No, love, she didn't.'

He hung up, cursing his own stubbornness.

That was it, then. He *had* left it too late.

He was up a ladder working away at an office ceiling when someone told him he was wanted on the phone.

'Margaret! How did you know where to find me?'

'I rang the firm you work for.' Her voice was high, with an underlying note of excitement. 'They gave me this number.'

He felt excited too, yet bewildered. 'They said you'd gone away?'

'That's right. But I haven't gone far. I'm staying in a flat belonging to friends of mine. I'll give you the address in a moment.' He had never heard her so brisk and decisive. 'Have you anything planned for tomorrow?'

'Nothing important.' His excitement grew to match hers. 'Does this mean we'll be able to celebrate it together after all?'

'It most certainly does. That is – ' Her voice was suddenly unsure. ' – if you want to?'

'What do *you* think? Oh, Margaret, I've missed you.'

'And I've missed you, darling. You don't know how much.'

'Look.' He kept his tone patient. 'There's no way I can let her spend tomorrow evening alone.'

'But we had plans, Mick.' Fran's expression was taut as she spooned sieved vegetables into Sean's mouth. 'Had you forgotten we're going to the cinema?'

'We can go to a film any night, Fran. But this is important. It's a very emotional day for her. You've no idea how much it means to her.'

'But it's your birthday, Mick!'

'That's just it. It's *my* birthday.' He looked at her firmly. 'Surely it's up to me to decide how I want to spend it?'

She made an exasperated noise and pushed Sean's hand away as he made a grab for the spoon. 'But I thought you'd want to spend it with me.'

'Normally I would. But this isn't a normal situation. You must understand that.'

They stared at each other for what felt like a long time but he didn't waver. At last Fran conceded defeat. 'Okay, Mick, have it your way. But don't make a habit of it. I know she's your long-lost mother but I'm your wife, remember.'

He sighed with relief and gave her a quick hug. 'Look, I'll make it up to you, I promise.'

She looked unconvinced and shrugged his arm away. 'I won't hold my breath.'

The address had seemed familiar on the phone. 'This isn't the house where you were born, is it?' he asked as she showed him into the narrow hallway of the flat.

'No, the Millers lived here before it was converted into flats. Our house was a few doors down. It's set in offices now. Come on, I'll show you around.' She beamed at him like a child demonstrating a new toy. 'This is the living room. It used to be the dentist's waiting room. When I think of the times I sat quaking in here. Of course, you wouldn't recognise it now; it used to be such a cold, formal room. I'm glad, though, that they kept the high ceiling, that plasterwork is beautiful and – '

'Yes, those mouldings are all coming back in. But Margaret, I don't understand – '

'Not another word till you've seen the rest of the flat. The kitchen and the bathroom are small but the main bedroom's not bad.'

'You're right.' He glanced around the bright, attractive room with its king-size bed and built-in wardrobes. 'Wish ours was half as nice.' Through the window, which had been left open at the top, came the sound of another tenant's radio playing loudly. 'But I just can't take it all in, the idea of you living in flatland.' He gave her a baffled look. 'It's just not you.'

Without responding to the question in his voice she crossed over to the window and drowned the radio out. She laughed as she drew the curtains. 'Can you imagine; this used to be the surgery? When I lie in bed at night I'll be haunted by the ghosts of all those poor souls shivering in terror.'

'Can't have been that bad,' he objected. 'Hadn't anaesthetics been invented then?'

'Back in the "olden days"?' She pulled a quizzical face.

'Come on, I didn't mean it like that.'

'No? Caroline always talks as if I grew up in the last century. Although, come to think of it, Mr Miller was a bit like something out of the Ark.'

'Like most of the people you told me about.' He grinned at her. 'But what's it all about? What are you doing here?'

Her face grew serious suddenly. 'I needed to get away for a few days, to give myself time to think. Susan and Tom asked me to keep an eye on the place while they're away on tour. It seemed the perfect opportunity, so I took it.'

'To think? About us, do you mean?'

'Yes.' She looked at him frankly. 'And about my marriage.'

'Oh, Margaret!' He felt a pang of guilt. 'If your marriage is in trouble because of me –'

'No,' she said quickly. 'You're not to blame. My marriage was in trouble long before I met you. But let's not talk about that now.' Her eyes gleamed. 'Come back into the living room.

I have something for you.'

'Happy birthday, darling.' She handed him a large parcel and watched anxiously as he tore at the bright wrappings. 'I hope I got the size right.'

'A jacket!' He fingered the soft wool and glanced at the label. 'Must have cost a fortune.'

'Not really. I got shirts to go with it. Save you trying to match the colour.'

'I don't know what to say.' He shook his head in wonder. 'I never expected anything like this.'

'Try them on,' she urged. 'There's a mirror in the bedroom.'

The clothes fitted perfectly. As he studied his reflection, admiring the cut of the jacket, he noticed a change in himself that he found difficult to define. Was there a new confidence in the way he held himself, a look of happy expectancy that hadn't been there before? He stared at himself with puzzled delight. Could something as simple as some new clothes do that for you? Or was it all in his imagination?

But Margaret had noticed it too. 'You look wonderful,' she said softly. 'You should always wear good clothes. You have the height, you have the build. You're a very handsome man, Michael.'

'Me, handsome?' To hide his embarrassment, he began to clown, remembering an old Danny Kaye film he'd seen on television. 'A swan? Me a swan? Ah, go on!'

Her lips twitched. 'You can joke if you like but it's true.'

'Maybe you're right.' That jacket definitely did more for him than the chain-store sweater Fran had given him for his birthday. 'I think I'll keep it on.' He glanced at her black, low-cut dress, the single string of pearls nestling around her smooth throat. 'You look pretty nice yourself.'

'Thank you. We'll be just right for where we're going. Do you like Italian food?'

'Luigi's chipper after the pub on a Saturday night,' he joked.

'I think we can do a little better than that,' Margaret said.

A small, intimate restaurant, dimly lit, the tables separated by screens so that the presence of other diners was hinted at rather than experienced. The service discreet yet attentive. He had never seen a menu so extensive. As for the wine list –

'I'm glad I let you choose,' he said when their meal came. 'I wouldn't have known where to start.' He felt no pretence with her. No embarrassment. 'I've a lot to learn.'

'I look forward to educating you.' Her bright hair glinted in the candlelight as she raised her glass to toast him. 'You know, I can't quite believe this. It's your birthday, darling, and here we both are.'

'I can't believe it either. Does *he* know?'

'That we're out together?' Her smile faded. 'I've no idea.'

He was puzzled. 'But how did he take it when you told him you were going away for a few days? Did he mind?'

'I – left a note.'

'You mean you didn't tell him? Did you think he'd try and stop you?'

'I don't know whether I'd have had the courage to face him. I just upped and ran.'

'You're afraid of him, aren't you?'

She bit her lip. 'I – Susan asked me that too but – he has

never been violent, Michael.'

'You're still afraid of him, though.'

'Yes.' She looked at him helplessly. 'I suppose I am.'

'He's not worthy of you,' Mick raged. 'He doesn't deserve you. When you meet a woman like you, a precious jewel, you appreciate her, you cherish her.'

'Is that the way you feel about your wife?' Her face was wistful.

He was taken aback. 'Well – I love Fran, of course, but – this isn't about me. It's about you and Vincent. The man isn't good enough for you. What on earth made you marry him in the first place? What did you see in him?'

'It seems hard to believe now.' She took a thoughtful sip of her wine. 'But there was a time when I found him quite attractive.'

'If you like the type.' Mick shrugged. 'But *marriage*? I just don't get it.'

'I was very unsettled after I came back from France,' Margaret said. 'I was still young, barely twenty, but somehow I felt too old to go back to college. Anyway, I had no interest in studying. I felt I had put all that behind me. I just drifted for a while. While I was deciding what I wanted to do with the rest of my life, I took a succession of waitressing jobs, mostly in places where students hung out – coffee shops, wine bars, that kind of thing. I had an allowance from my father so I didn't really need the money but it helped to pass the time.

'It was in one of those places that I met Vincent. Or, strictly speaking, it was at a party that he first saw me and he asked somebody about me. Anyway, he kept coming into the coffee bar where I worked and eventually he asked me out on a date. He was eight years older than me, with a lot of drive and ambition. I found this attractive. The boys of my own age seemed to me to be very immature and, after my experience with Martin, I was wary of trusting any of them. Vincent seemed to know where he was going, which was more than I did. I suppose, in a way, I just drifted into marriage with him.

'My parents made no real objections. It was obvious that Mummy thought I was marrying beneath me. She made the odd snide remark about his family but I suspect she felt that, under the circumstances, I was lucky to have got someone to marry me. I don't know what Daddy thought about Vincent; he was not a man to show his feelings but I remember him asking me just before the wedding if I was happy that I was doing the right thing. When I said I was he nodded and said something about Vincent being a good provider, and let it go at that. But even if he had objected it wouldn't have made any difference. I realise now that I was so bitter against my parents that I would have married him just to spite them.'

'And were you happy?' Mick asked.

'For the first few years I suppose we were. Vincent was very caught up in his work, of course. Caroline was born a year after we were married and she kept me pretty occupied. We had quite a good social life. Vincent was keen to have a son, though, but I wanted to wait a bit before having another child, so that caused a few arguments. The truth was, I didn't want to go through childbirth again. When I was expecting Caroline I had hoped that having a second baby would somehow make up to me for having had to give up the first one but it didn't work out like that.' Margaret's face was sad in the candlelight. 'Caroline was a difficult baby and for some reason we never bonded. In many ways she was closer to Vincent than she was to me. I was afraid that if I had another child the same thing would happen again – that, maybe, I just wasn't cut out for motherhood. But Vincent wouldn't take no for an answer and eventually, when Caroline was three and a half, I became pregnant again. I was just coming to terms with the idea and almost beginning to look forward to it when disaster struck. I had a miscarriage at five months. A little boy.

'Vincent was disappointed but not devastated. It was a setback, he said; we could always try again. But I couldn't cope with the loss. I felt so guilty because I hadn't wanted to be pregnant in the first place. I felt I was being punished for that and for having given my first baby away. I had a breakdown and was depressed for a long time. People get counselling now but in those days all they gave you was tranquillisers, anti-depressants, what Vincent calls "happy pills". Bad cases were given ECT. Luckily it didn't come to that. But I lived in a twilight world for a while.

'I recovered eventually, although I still have trouble sleeping. Things were never the same after that between Vincent and myself. He still wanted another child but I just wasn't prepared to risk it. It was only when the doctors told him that I would be in danger of another breakdown that he reluctantly abandoned the idea. Then, one night, in an attempt to make him understand why I felt the way I did, I very foolishly told him about you, Michael. How I had had to give you away when you were born. I stupidly thought it would bring us closer together; instead he became angry and accused me of having deceived him. I thought he was going to leave me but when he calmed down he said we must put it behind us and pretend it had never happened. I suppose I took the easy way out. But I just didn't have the energy to do anything else. I'd been through so much I couldn't face the thought of breaking up with him. So I did what he said. And buried the whole thing once again.'

He watched her eagerly. 'And you never thought that some day I'd come looking for you?'

'No.' He saw her eyes fill up suddenly. 'I never, never dreamed – ' She smiled at him through her tears. ' – that I would be given a second chance.'

'What will you do about Vincent?' Mick asked as they reached the front steps of the house. It was a cold night yet he still felt the warmth of the restaurant, the sense of well-being engendered by good food and wine and the company of someone you like. Across the street, the hedges surrounding the Square gardens were shrouded in shadow. Although he had never set foot in the neighbourhood till tonight, he felt a sense of familiarity with it because of all she had told him. 'Are you going to leave him?'

'I don't know. I have to think about it.' She inserted her key in the lock and the heavy door swung open. They stepped into the dimly lit hallway. 'Have you time for a nightcap?'

'Yes.' He followed her across the hall and waited while she opened the flat door. Although he knew he should be getting back to Fran he was reluctant to end the evening. Besides, he wasn't going to let Margaret go back alone to an empty flat.

Fran put down the magazine she had been leafing through, turned down the sound on the television and cocked a listening ear. Was that a key in the front door? A heavy footfall down below in the hallway, the sound of someone cursing as they stumbled into something. The man in the bedsitter, home from the pub, falling over Mick's motorbike? You could set your watch by him every Friday night. A door slammed downstairs at the front of the house in confirmation. She picked up the magazine again but found it hard to concentrate on the page.

If it was that time, Mick should be home soon. Before the buses went off for the night. She wondered what was keeping him till that hour. How long did it take to eat your dinner, for God's sake? We have a lot to talk about, he had said. We have a lot of catching up to do. Fran could understand it at first. It was only natural to want to know where you came from and all that. But three months had gone by and they were still at it. Was it her life story or his they were catching up on? His was nothing to write home about, so it must have been hers.

Margaret must have had a colourful past or else she was one of those women that are impossible to get away from, like the oul' bag downstairs. No, Fran grinned to herself, nobody could be as bad as Mrs McGrath; they broke the mould when they made her. But she might be like some of the customers who came into the bread shop, women who thought nothing of telling you the intimate details of their lives. As if you wanted to hear all about their husbands or their children while you were slicing up a pan for them. Most of them were cheerful enough but a few would be sorry for themselves, moaning about the hard time they had, how other people were always better off.

If she was that sort, Mick wouldn't be able for her. He was too soft-hearted. Much too kind for his own good, at times. But Fran couldn't complain. After all, his kindness was one of the things she had always loved about him. He'd a gentleness, a sensitivity that she'd never found in any other boy she'd gone out with. She smiled to herself as she remembered the very first time she'd laid eyes on him, before she'd even left school, that time in the sweetshop when she'd sold him the toy fire engine. There had been something about him she'd never forgotten. She'd often thought about him afterwards even though she'd despaired of ever meeting him again. But, as Mammy always said, if it's for you, it won't pass you by. And what a piece of luck to have spotted him in the pub that night. And, even better, to discover that, although he had got taller and even more gorgeous-looking, he was just as nice, not a bit full of himself like other good-looking fellas. It might have been *his* birthday but she had felt that night as if all her Christmases and birthdays had arrived together at the same time.

And now it was another birthday. And they hadn't been able to celebrate it together because of *her*. On an impulse, because she was feeling a bit low, Fran had done something she'd never done before. Even though it was past his bedtime she had packed Sean into his buggy and walked up with him to Clearys. It was too far to go and see her own parents at that hour. And anyway, Mick had made her promise faithfully that she wouldn't say a word to them about Margaret. But his parents knew, didn't they? So she thought it would be all right. Although, funnily enough, they had seemed a bit taken aback when she'd told them that he'd gone out with her tonight. Not that you could blame them, really, when you thought about it. After all, as Mick's father had said, 'What fella in his right mind would want to go out with his mother when he has a lovely girl like you at home?'

His Ma hadn't been so open about it. You wouldn't catch her saying a word against Mick to anyone. And especially not to her daughter-in-law. Which was no surprise to Fran, who had always suspected from the moment they had first met that her mother-in-law didn't particularly like her. Although she shut his Da up with, 'Mick knows his own business best, Maurice', Mrs Cleary had pursed her lips and you wouldn't need a crystal ball to tell that those bright little eyes of hers were trying to figure out what the score was. But whatever she came up with, she wasn't letting on to anybody. She had made tea and plied Fran with fruitcake, acting as if she were genuinely pleased to see her. As for the attention she lavished on Sean, cooing and chuckling over him until Fran was afraid that he'd make strange with all the attention he was getting, you'd think that never before had there been a baby like him.

And when it was time for them to go she'd insisted on sending Mick's father to walk back with them to make sure that she and Sean got home safely. 'Don't be a stranger, now,' she had said, patting Fran's arm. Her face had shown real warmth. Maybe I was wrong about her, after all, the younger woman thought. Even though she suspected that Mick wouldn't be pleased to hear that she had visited his parents without him, looking back now, she felt glad that she had gone.

No need to tell him about it just yet, though. She had other plans for him tonight. Although the birthday so far hadn't gone according to expectations, it wasn't over yet. She thought of the extra purchase she had made when she was buying his present the other day and grinned as she switched off the television. As she headed for the bedroom she smiled to herself again. Maybe this new mother of his could afford to bring him out for expensive meals but she, Fran, could do things for him that nobody else could.

She undressed in front of the mirror, smiling provocatively at herself as each garment slid off and fell unheeded to the floor. Then stood naked, admiring her creamy, rounded body and the way her bright curls cascaded to her smooth shoulders. Ran her hands over her curving breasts, then down to caress the mound of red gold fuzz at the base of her stomach. Excitement rose up in her as she turned away and opened the drawer of the dressing table.

Not tonight her usual bedtime garb of faded cotton T-shirt and leggings. Her excitement grew as she lifted out the short, black nightdress and shook out its satiny folds. This is your second present, birthday boy, she whispered. Tonight, Mick, you're going to have a birthday you'll never forget.

There was a lightness about it, a gaiety, a sweetness. Like nothing he had ever known before. And there was an urgency to it, a momentum building up to a crescendo. He went with it. It caught him and took him where it wanted to go. To a dizzying climax.

And then.

When it was over it was over.

He was the first to break the companionable silence that followed.

'That was beautiful. What's it called?'

'It's a nocturne by Chopin.'

He shook his head in wonder. 'I never knew a piano could sound like that.'

She looked at him eagerly. 'You don't know what it does for me to be able to introduce you to these things.'

Her throat was like warm alabaster in the firelight. Below it he saw the curve of her breast above the low neckline of her black dress. 'You don't know what it does for me just to be here with you,' he said.

'It does a lot for me too.' She sighed suddenly and looked at the clock on the mantelpiece. 'What about your bus?'

He grinned at her. 'I've missed it by now.' He felt no sense of urgency. Felt so comfortable he could sit there forever. 'The night's young yet. Why don't you turn over that tape while I fix us another brandy?'

'But your wife – ?' She paused with the tape in her hand and looked at him enquiringly. 'Won't she – ?'

'Fran'll be sound by now,' he said as he poured fresh drinks. 'She's a real early bird. Don't worry. She knows where I am.' He gave a quick grin. 'It's not like I'm out with another woman or anything.'

'That's true.' Margaret grinned back. As the first silvery notes began to fill the room, she said, 'This is a selection of waltzes. I think you'll like them.'

He felt the heat of the brandy spreading through his body. 'If you like them, I will.' Without thinking, he moved his chair nearer to hers so that he could watch her profile while she listened to the music.

Fran half-woke and lifted her head from the pillow. 'Mick?' But it was only the wind creaking through the apple trees in the back garden. The nightdress had worked its way up around her neck. She could feel her bare breasts digging into the mattress; her buttocks felt naked, exposed under the bedclothes. *Feck this!* She groped under her pillow to pull out the despised T-shirt. '*I think I'll* – Still clutching it she fell back asleep in mid-thought.

'Wake up, Mick.'

'What – ?' Startled, he sprang up, glanced around in confusion. The tape had come to an end. 'Sorry, I must have – '

'Only for a few minutes.' Her hand on his shoulder was reassuring. 'Look, there's a bed in the spare room. You'll be more comfortable there.'

'But I should go home. Fran will be – '

'I think it would be better if you waited till morning. You're not really in a condition to – '

'Maybe you're right,' he mumbled. His eyelids seemed weighted with lead. He felt an overwhelming desire to lie down again. 'Just for a few hours.'

'It's this way.' He felt a gentle grip on his arm leading him towards the door, out into the narrow hall. Had a confused impression of a small, cluttered room, a narrow bed, a musty smell. 'Sit down on the bed and we'll take off your shoes.' He felt her hair brushing his face as she bent over him to help him out of his jacket. 'That's right, now! Easy does it.' As his feet left the ground the pillow rose to meet him with astonishing speed. He buried his face in it and felt coarse fibres tickle the back of his neck as her hands arranged a blanket around him. 'You'll be fine now.'

'You have lovely hands, do you know that?' he murmured into the pillow as the room went black and the door clicked shut behind her.

In ways he was like Martin. Same colour eyes. Same eager way of looking at her. But he had something that Martin had never possessed. He had a solidity about him, a straightness, that reminded Margaret of her father. He had Daddy's hands too. Big, well-shaped hands, with capable, dextrous fingers. If things had been different Michael might have followed in his footsteps. If –

But it wasn't too late, was it? Maybe not to be a surgeon. He mightn't be interested, anyway. But he was young and intelligent, and so eager to learn. Given the opportunity, he could do anything he put his mind to. And what a pleasure it would be to give him that opportunity. There was so much she wanted to do for him.

She recalled his face earlier when he had dropped off to sleep listening to the music. He had looked so young, so vulnerable lying back in his chair. A wave of tenderness swept over her. And a sense of awe. He was her son. That beautiful young man was her son.

As she lay sleepless in the darkness of the unfamiliar room, Margaret was filled with joy. Never in her wildest dreams had she thought that things would turn out like this.

He was jolted into wakefulness. Remembered instantly where he was. Lay staring into the blackness while he steadied his thoughts. Although he figured that he couldn't have slept more than a couple of hours, his mind was alert. Snatches of Chopin hovered at the back of it, fragments of sentences, images. He could hear her voice. That lovely way she had of saying *Michael.*

Margaret. He said her name in the darkness. What a wonderful woman. She was everything he had thought she would be. No, that wasn't quite true. She was so much more than he had ever imagined.

And then it hit him.

She was in bed in the next room. Only a wall separated them. All at once he saw the purity of her face in profile, her smooth throat in the firelight, smelled her perfume. Pictured her body as she lay sleeping, her hair spread out across the pillow. Felt his own body spring to life at the thought.

'You couldn't sleep either?' Margaret was sitting at the tiny kitchen table, smoking a cigarette. Her face wiped clean of make-up and her hair tied loosely back, she looked younger and somehow vulnerable in her black silk dressing gown. 'Want a coffee?'

'Just water.' He eased past her to reach the sink. '*Lots* of water.'

Her lips twitched as she watched him drink greedily. 'Brandy can do that to you.'

'I'm learning.' He gave a rueful grin. 'Are you up long?'

'Since about five. I'm a poor sleeper at the best of times.'

'It's just after six now.' He yawned hugely. 'God, it's not

often you'll find me up at this hour on a Saturday. What time did we get to bed at?'

'Don't you remember?' she asked, half-teasingly. 'Must have been two.'

'Oh God!' He ran his hand across his forehead and felt the beginnings of a headache. 'Think I'll have that coffee, after all. Stay where you are. I'll get it myself.'

'No, let me. I know where everything is.' As she stood up she tightened the belt of the dressing gown, which had worked itself loose. He could see the shape of her breasts under the clinging silk. The skin of her throat looked very white against the black. 'Instant coffee okay?'

'Is there any other kind?' he joked. 'Don't forget you're talking to one of the plebs.' He sat down at the table and watched her as she busied herself with the kettle. Without thinking, he said, 'You've a tiny waist.' Felt his face flame up, wished he could take the words back.

'Thanks.' She didn't look at him but spooned in the coffee and poured the boiling water. 'Milk? Sugar?' When their eyes finally met, her expression was unreadable.

'Just milk, thanks.' As he took the cup from her he felt a sudden longing to put his arms around her, to pull her body close to his. He stopped himself just in time. To hide his confusion he asked, 'Do you mind if I have one of your cigarettes?'

Her face showed her surprise but she handed him one without comment and lit it for him with her lighter, then lit another one for herself. She looked thoughtfully into the distance. 'I'm going to have to ring Vincent today,' she said at last.

He had a sudden vision of her husband's stubby fingers pushing aside the black silk of the dressing gown, caressing the white skin underneath. Exhaling sharply, he spluttered over his cigarette. 'You can't go back to him.' He stared at her wildly. 'You mustn't even think of it.'

Fran was still asleep when he got home. She slept silently like a child, her face sculpted in innocence. It put him in mind of their honeymoon, when he would wake first and study her sleeping face, tracing its curves with a gentle finger, until she would open her eyes and smile sleepily up at him. As he stood watching, he saw her stir. But this time there was no smile for him.

'You're back.'

'Yes, I – '

'It's a wonder you bothered to come home.'

'How did you – ?'

'Did you think I wouldn't notice?' She gave a short laugh. 'Sean woke about six. I got up to give him a bottle. I couldn't believe my eyes when I realised – ' she sat up suddenly and glared at him. 'Where *were* you?'

He was taken aback by her vehemence. 'You know where I was. With Margaret.'

She looked sceptical. 'All night?'

'We got talking. We didn't notice the – ' Even as he said it he knew how lame it sounded. 'Too late to come home. Didn't want to disturb you,' he mumbled.

'Didn't want to disturb me? *Didn't want to disturb me!*'

He winced. 'You don't have to shout.'

'You were drinking, weren't you?' She grabbed his arm

and pulled him towards her. 'I can smell it off your breath. God, you've been drinking all night. You and that mother of yours. You were drinking all night. What kind of a – ?'

'No, we weren't.' He pulled his arm away. 'Margaret isn't like that. I had a few drinks, I admit that. I'm not used to brandy. She gave me a bed for the night. That's all there is to it. It was too late to phone. You wouldn't have thanked me for waking Mrs McGrath up at that hour, would you?'

'That's true,' Fran conceded. 'She's the last person in the world, but Mick, did you not realise I'd worry? Anything could have happened to you.'

'I'm sorry. I didn't think. It won't happen again.'

'It bloody well better not.' But her attitude had softened. 'Oh, Mick. I missed you last night. It was your birthday and I –'

'I missed you too.' As he bent to kiss her he felt a pang of guilt. 'I'll make it up to you.'

'Come back to bed, Mick,' she whispered, pulling him down with her. 'I don't have to get up yet.'

'No, I don't think I will.' He extricated himself from her arms and stood up. 'I'd never be able to sleep now. I'll have an early night to make up for it.'

'Ah, Mick.' There was surprise and disappointment on her face.

'But you stay on,' he said hastily. 'Tell you what, I'll bring you some breakfast and I'll see to Sean. How about that?'

'Oh well, in that case.' Her disappointment vanished. She snuggled down into the bedclothes again. 'It can wait till tonight. It'll be better then.' She smiled into her pillow. 'I have something I want to show you.'

'Great.' As he left the room he found himself wondering

if Margaret had gone back to bed after he left. Wondered, too, about how she would be spending her day.

Maybe she was reading far too much into it, Margaret told herself as she made her third cup of coffee of the day. She thought back to the scene in the kitchen just before dawn. It was not as if anything had happened, after all. She, herself, had been so aware of her own body under the thin dressing gown that maybe she had read too much into his gaze. It was ridiculous, when you came to think of it. Michael wasn't interested in her in that way. Apart from their relationship, she was eighteen years older than he was. And he was a happily married man.

Of course he had this romantic picture of her. She had realised that quite early on. But that was only natural. Wasn't she the long-lost mother of his dreams! Why wouldn't he want to spend time with her and make up for all the years they had missed? There was nothing surprising about that, considering she felt the same way about him. And there was no harm in a son admiring his mother, enjoying her company. It happened all the time. To think that there might be anything more to it than that was foolishness.

Yes, she had been reading too much into a chance look, an unguarded compliment. It was all quite harmless. Let him have his romantic picture of her. Life would teach him reality soon enough. And it was lovely for her to be at the receiving end of such devotion. Enjoy it while it lasts, she told herself. It made such a change from Vincent's attitude over the years. And she had great plans for Michael. There was so much she would be able to do for him.

But as her mind began to daydream of the possibilities, the thought of Vincent kept breaking in and spoiling things. She sighed to herself. There was something about him that seemed to rob her of all energy, making it difficult to think straight. If only the problem of Vincent would go away. But that wasn't very sensible of her. Pull yourself together, Margaret, she thought. Try to concentrate. There were arrangements to work out, phone calls to be made.

'Of course you can.' The voice on the line was as clear and immediate as if Susan was in the same room as her. 'Stay as long as you like. We're glad to have someone to keep an eye on things. It'll give you a chance to think things out.'

'I knew I could depend on you. Oh Susan, I wish you were here.'

'I wish *you* could be here, Margaret.' Her friend's voice soared with excitement. 'It's nine o'clock in the morning and I'm having my breakfast looking out over Central Park. The skyline of Manhattan is just like in the films. And it's magical at night. You should see the lights. The only thing is, it's freezing outside. It's bright, though. A bright, cold day – '

'It's cold here too.' But the sky was overcast, the air dank. The grey afternoon light that struggled through the long, narrow windows cast an unforgiving eye on the empty glasses sitting on the hearth and the ashes of last night's fire in the grate. 'It will probably rain.'

Lucky Susan, with her view of Central Park and the whole of America ahead of her. Her biggest worries making sure that their luggage kept up with them and that there would be a piano to practise on. Her biggest decisions what to wear, where to eat and how much to tip for room service. But, most important of all, she had her career and a husband who loved her.

Margaret's heart sank as she put down the phone. She was not looking forward to the next call she had to make.

'You took your time about ringing.' His voice was flat, unwelcoming. 'We could be dead for all you care.'

As always with him she felt wrong-footed, at a loss for words. 'I told you I needed a few days to think things over.'

'About w*hat* for God's sake? Look, Margaret, for the past three days we've been fending for ourselves – '

'Did Mrs Canvey not – ?'

'Bloody woman never stops talking. Anyway, if I wanted a housekeeper I'd have employed one. You're supposed to be my wife. Your place is at home here looking after us, not gallivanting off to God knows where.'

'I'm not gallivanting. I'm in Susan's flat.'

'Is he with you?' His voice was sharp.

'Who?'

'Don't play the innocent. You know very well who. That young pup.'

'If you mean Michael he's not here. Why should he be? He has a wife and child of his own.'

'You could have fooled me,' Vincent sneered. 'Maybe he should start paying a bit more attention to them. Not that it matters to me. What I want to know is: when are you coming home?'

'That's just it, I – '

'You've had a few days to think over whatever it is you

wanted to think over. Look, if you needed a holiday you should have told me.'

'It's not about a holiday. It's – it's about us.'

'*Us?* What about us?' His voice was bewildered suddenly. 'I thought it was about that young – about that fella you call your son.'

'He *is* my son.'

'Well, I've only *your* word for that. It could be a pack of lies, for all *I* know.'

Margaret sighed wearily. She could never get used to the twists and turns of a conversation with Vincent, the accusations, the red herrings. She always ended up feeling exhausted and outmanoeuvred. The thought of Michael gave her the courage to cut through his bullying tactics. 'It's partly about your attitude towards my son, but it's also about our relationship.'

'What about our relationship?'

The hostility in his voice caused her heart to begin thudding against her ribs. But at least she had got his attention. She held on to her courage. 'I'm not very happy about it – '

'*You're* not happy about it? What about *my* – ?'

If her heart had thumped any louder he would have heard it on the other end of the line. If it didn't stop thumping she was going to have a coronary right there in the cramped, chilly hallway of the flat. 'Look, Vincent, I can't talk any more at the moment. I'll have to ring you some other time.'

'Don't you dare hang up on – '

She slammed the receiver down, cutting off his furious voice. Then, with trembling knees and a thudding heart, she made her way shakily to the kitchen, where she poured herself a stiff vodka.

He rang her from the phone box on the corner.

'I had a brilliant night last night. The best birthday I ever had.'

'It was wonderful for me too. When will I see you again?'

'If this was *Star Trek* I'd be in the transporter straight away. "Beam me up, Scotty." Unfortunately – '

She laughed. 'I didn't mean that soon.'

'Well, I did. But Fran is insisting on cooking a special meal tonight. Because of my birthday – '

'Well, of course. You have to be there. I mustn't be greedy, darling. She needs you too. It's just that there are all those years I've missed out on.'

'I know. I feel the same way. Look, I'm coming over to see you tomorrow. I'll have to fix it with Fran. I'll ring you in the morning, let you know the time. But I *will* come.'

'Well, if you're sure – '

'Of course I'm sure. I want to come.' His voice was joyous. 'Try keeping me away.'

'You look like a dog with two tails, Mick.'

'Just happy, Fran. It's a grand evening out and – you're cooking me another birthday meal. What more could a man ask for?'

She showed her surprise. 'It looks like rain.'

'Does it? I didn't notice.'

'As for the meal.' She frowned. 'This new recipe's taking a bit longer than I thought.'

'Look, there's no need to go to so much trouble. We can always get a pizza,' he said hastily.

'Thanks for the vote of confidence, Mick. It's not just the recipe; it's that oven. It's so slow. But don't worry.' Her chin lifted stubbornly. 'It will be okay. It just won't be ready for a while, that's all.'

'In that case' – he turned to go out again – 'I'll just slip up and see my Ma while I'm waiting.'

'Clearys?' She gave him a startled look.

'Where else? It's a while since I was there. I'm surprised she hasn't sent a search party out by now.'

'Is this a good time to go? You know how hard it is to get away once you start talking.'

'My Ma's not that bad, Fran. Anyway you said the meal wouldn't be ready for ages. What's the matter? Do you mind me going to see her?'

'Now when have I ever?' Her face went pink. 'It's just – '

'You're just jealous because you have a popular husband.' He grinned at her. 'Can I help it if I have all the women after me?'

'I suppose not.' She smiled reluctantly. But he saw her frown as she went over to check the oven.

'Smells okay,' he said. 'But don't forget, if you make a bags of it, we can always get that pizza.' Then he dodged quickly before she threw the oven gloves at him.

He was still laughing as he ran down the stairs.

'Your mother's gone out for a message.' Da lowered the sound on the television. 'She'll be back in a minute.'

'How are things?' As usual, he had to search his mind for

something to say. 'Back any winners lately?'

'Mug's game.' His father tapped his pipe out into an ashtray and began scraping industriously at the bowl.

'*You've* changed your tune. What happened? Did you lose all your money?'

He expected Da to laugh; instead he gave him a sour look and kept scraping away at the pipe. 'Your mother and I don't change.'

What's eating him? Was it something I did? Or forgot to do? He searched his conscience. Came up with nothing. 'Ma okay?'

'Ask her yourself.' They heard the key turn in the front door. 'That's her now.'

Ma bustled in, bringing an icy blast of air with her. 'Cold enough to freeze a brass monkey,' she complained as she took off her overcoat. She had layers of clothing underneath but her face looked pinched from the cold and her hands had a blue tinge to them.

'God, Ma, you're like an onion with all those woollies.' Impulsively, he took her hand and tried to rub warmth back into her thin fingers. To his dismay she looked at him without smiling, her expression as cold as her hands.

He had a premonition of disaster.

'I've a bone to pick with you,' she said.

'Look, I *did* tell you.' He appealed to Da. 'I told Ma about it. She knew we'd met.'

'Maybe so.' His father's stern expression didn't change. 'But you gave your mother the impression that it was only the once.'

'Yeh, well, at the time that's all it was.' He saw the scepticism on both their faces. 'Okay, so I've been seeing a bit of my – of Margaret lately. Why shouldn't I? It's only natural.'

Da wasn't amused by the accidental pun. 'You shoulda been straight with us.'

'We brought you up to be honest,' Ma said. 'I thought we done a good job. Has all that been swept aside now that you've met this woman? She can't be much if she encourages you to lie.'

'You leave her out of this. It's got nothing to do with her.'

The light of battle flashed in Ma's eyes. 'Seems to me it's got everything to do with her.'

'Look,' he said hastily, 'I know I should have told you but I didn't want to hurt you.'

She curled her lip in the way only she knew how. 'And what are you doing now only hurting us?'

He looked at her helplessly. 'Don't take it like that, Ma.'

'How else do you expect me to take it?' Her voice was bitter. 'And to think I had to hear it from my own daughter-in-law.'

'Fran had no right – '

'She had every right. That wife of yours has been patience itself. In her place, I wouldn't be as long-suffering.' She glanced at Da, who nodded in agreement.

Mick was stunned. 'I never thought you'd side with Fran against me.'

She gave him one of her quick, birdlike stares. 'I'm not against you, Mick. I mightn't have given birth to you but I've always loved you as if you were my own.'

As if I were your own? The words were like a kick in the gut.

He stared at her in horror. 'I can't believe you said that, Ma.'

She didn't seem to hear him but rushed on. 'We took you in and –'

'Took me in! Like a stray dog!' He gazed at her incredulously. 'Is that all I was to you? Some kid you took in and cared for, out of the goodness of your heart?'

'No! No!' A look of consternation crossed her face. 'God, Mick, I never meant it like that.' It was too late to undo her words but she tried anyway. 'You know I loved you since the minute I laid eyes on you. I couldn't have felt more for you if I had given birth to you myself.'

He ignored the plea in her voice. 'Why did you say it then? As if I were your own?' The pain in his gut had grown worse. 'I always felt I *was* your own.'

She stared at him for a moment, obviously at a loss for an answer. Then she countered with, 'Why did you go sneaking off behind my back with this woman? Why couldn't you tell me about her?' Her voice filled with reproach. 'You never used to have secrets from me, Mick.'

Why did she always try to make him feel guilty? 'Don't do this to me, Ma. I'm not a child any more.'

Her expression changed. She opened her mouth, closed it again and looked helplessly at Da, who laid his pipe down in an ashtray and cleared his throat ponderously.

Mick stiffened, expecting a lecture. To his amazement, Da said in a conciliatory tone, 'Hold your horses, Mick. Your mother was upset. She didn't know what she was saying. You know what she's like when she gets her rag out.'

'Yes,' Ma put in eagerly. 'I was that upset I was beside myself with worry. I kept wondering where did we go wrong? I kept thinking he's no time for us any more now that he's met her.'

'Don't be ridiculous, Ma!' He looked at her indignantly. 'And you're wrong about Margaret. She's – she's a wonderful person. I can't expect you to understand what meeting her has meant to me. It's like – it's like there was always something missing from my life and now it's all fallen into place.'

'Missing?' Hurt showed on Ma's face. 'Were *we* not enough for you, Mick?'

He sighed. 'I told you you wouldn't understand.' The pain in his gut had eased but he felt a terrible sense of loss. 'This is no use. If we talk about it till the cows come home we still won't see eye to eye.'

'Maybe you're right.' Her sigh matched his. 'All I know is I don't want you and me to fall out. Can we forget about it, son? Put it behind us?'

'We can try,' he said slowly. He knew he would never forget what she had said. Maybe in time things might be the same between them as they had been before. But not just yet. The hurt was too raw.

'Why did you do it, Fran?' He pushed his plate away, the meal half-eaten. 'You never go near my parents. Why last night?'

'I've told you, and I've told you.' Her face was set in stubborn lines. 'All I did was call up to see them. It's not my fault they took it the way they did. If anyone's to blame it's

[340]

you. Going out like that on your birthday.'

'We've been over this already. If it was your birthday I could understand you being annoyed. But it wasn't yours. It was *mine*. The first birthday I've ever spent with Margaret. Of course, you begrudged me that, didn't you? You never wanted me to meet her from the start. So you just had to make trouble. And, if that wasn't bad enough, you let me go up there and walk into an ambush without warning me.'

'I tried to stop you.' Her voice had lost its certainty. 'I – '

'But you didn't, did you? You let me walk into a trap. How could you do it, Fran!'

'Don't be like that, Mick.' Her eyes looked scared. 'I've never seen you angry like this before.'

'Can you blame me?' His voice was stiff as he got up from the table.

'Where are you going?'

'Out, Fran. I need to be by myself.'

'But your dinner. You barely touched it.'

'I'm sorry Fran but I couldn't eat it. I'm just not hungry any more.'

'After all the trouble I – ' Her face tightened suddenly. 'You're going to see her, aren't you?'

'No, I'm *not*.' He glared at her. 'I'm off to Foley's for a pint. Or do I need your permission for that too?'

She was in the bedroom when he got back from the pub. Her face lit up when he put his head around the door. 'You're early, Mick.'

''Foley's is a bit of a kip. Not my scene. Never was.' He had pretended not to see Da and his cronies in their usual corner, had kept his head down when Uncle Thomas had signalled to him with a couple of podgy fingers. 'Anyway, I wasn't in drinking form.' Although a couple of pints had helped to take the edge off his anger, he found it hard to put warmth into his voice. 'What did you do?' he asked without any great interest.

'Watched a film on telly.' Her voice was equally casual. She threw him a sidelong glance. 'Mick, I – '

'Leave it, Fran.' He wasn't in the mood for another row. He withdrew his head from the door. 'I'm going to make a cup of – '

'No, wait. Come back a minute. *Please.*'

He sighed and popped his head back in again. 'What is it, Fran?'

She bit her lip. 'I'm sorry, Mick. I didn't mean to make trouble for you with your parents last night. And then I was afraid to tell you. That's why I let you go on up there today without warning you.'

He was touched by her admission. He knew how difficult it was for her to admit it when she was wrong. 'It's okay.' He felt himself soften a bit towards her. 'I'm over it now. But, Fran – ' He made his voice firm. ' – One thing I have to make clear. I must be able to see my mother, Margaret, whenever I want. You've got to understand that.'

'Yes, yes, I know.' Relief showed on her face. 'As long as you're not angry any more.'

'I've told you, I'm not.' He turned away again.

'Don't bother making tea,' she called after him eagerly. 'Come to bed.'

He felt a sudden reluctance. 'I'll be along in a little while.'

'Well, don't take all night.' There was a note of excitement in her voice. 'There's something I want to show you.'

It was made of some shiny, black material that caught the light. Badly cut, it strained over her breasts and clung unflatteringly to her stomach. The black lace that edged the bodice had a hard, scratchy look to it.

'It's – it's very nice,' he said slowly. He had a sudden memory of smooth, black folds falling sinuously to the ground. 'It's not silk, though, is it?'

Her smile faded. 'Silk? You must be joking.' Her eyes narrowed. 'What's the matter? Don't you like it?'

'Like it?' It looked cheap and tawdry, he thought with sudden revulsion. 'Well – '

'That's great!' Fran's eyes flashed. 'Just great.' She tugged at the straps of the nightdress and tried dragging it off but it clung stubbornly to the curves of her body.

Again a memory of black silk against white skin. 'Maybe it's a bit small for you,' he offered.

'Oh, so that's it?' she cried hotly. 'I'm too fat for it? Is that what's the matter?'

'No, no, of course not. That isn't what I – ' Oh God, how had he got himself into this? In confusion, he turned away and started to undress. He pulled his sweater over his head and disappeared into its depths. He re-emerged to see that she had changed into one of the long, baggy T-shirts she usually wore at night. She avoided his eye as she climbed into bed.

'You didn't have to change.' But he knew his voice lacked conviction. 'Look, I'm sorry, Fran.'

'That's okay, Mick.' Her lips tightened. 'Let's forget about it.' She lay on her side with her back to him. He stripped down to his shorts and got in beside her, touched her shoulder gently.

'Fran – '

She shook his hand away. 'Leave it, Mick. I'm tired.'

He felt a sense of relief. 'Okay, Fran. I'm tired too. It's been a long day.' He yawned and rolled away from her onto his back. 'Good night. Sweet dreams.'

Yes, he thought, it *had* been a long day. It seemed like centuries since they had sat together drinking coffee just before dawn. He heard her voice on the phone: 'All those years I missed out on.' Years we both missed out on, Margaret. But we're going to start making up for them now.

He felt a thrill of excitement as he stared into the darkness.

Roll on, tomorrow! He could hardly wait.

Two little girls sat at a table. One watched intently while the other built a house of cards. A cat slept peacefully under a chair. A cluttered mantelshelf took up most of the background. It was an old-fashioned setting: the girls' clothes, the furniture belonged to an earlier age. Yet the scene had a timeless quality to it.

'I always think it captures the essence of childhood.' There was a wistful note in Margaret's voice.

'I know what you mean,' Mick said. He took his eyes away from the picture and gazed around the large room, where people, singly or in groups, quietly studied the paintings hanging on the walls. Through an archway could be seen another room with more paintings. And, beyond that, another. 'I never realised it was such a big place.' He was dazzled by the colours and shapes around him. 'Difficult to take them all in.'

'Don't try to,' she advised. 'We'll just look at a few. It's your first time, after all. Then we'll go and get a drink and have something to eat.'

'Not yet, though.' There was something heady about the excitement he felt as they wandered from room to room. 'I think I want to keep coming back here for the rest of my life.'

'You will,' she said softly. 'You will.' She smiled into his eyes. 'Okay, we'll look at one more room and then we'll have that drink.'

She wouldn't hear of him treating her to a meal in a restaurant. He refused to let her pay for him two nights running. In the end they compromised and bought a takeaway which they ate by the fireside in the living room of the flat.

'Funny.' Margaret wiped her fingers on a napkin and sighed with pleasure. 'I was never that keen on Chinese food but that's the nicest I ever tasted.'

'What you ate of it.' He looked at her anxiously. 'You don't eat enough, Margaret.'

'I had plenty.' She laughed as she topped up his glass. 'And Chardonnay goes so well with it.'

'Mmm.' He savoured the smooth, buttery taste of the wine. 'I think I could get very used to the high life.'

'The high life?' She cocked an amused eyebrow. 'Chinese takeaways?'

He reddened. 'You know what I mean. Wine with meals, expensive jackets.'

Her face lit up. 'Your wife? Did she like the jacket?'

'She didn't see it.' He felt embarrassed and tried to hide it under a jumble of explanations. 'I would have, only – Fran went up to her mother's for tea. Her brother, Tony, picked her and Sean up before I left.'

'It looks well on you.' She didn't seem to notice his embarrassment. 'Darling, I've so much to make up to you.'

'It wasn't your fault. You don't have to feel that way.' But he was glad she did. 'It's not like you abandoned me on a doorstep. Ma and Da did the best they could.'

'But it's wrong you had to leave school so early.' She looked distressed. 'You should have gone to college, done a degree.'

'Yeh, well – water under the bridge.' Still a sore point. Dwelling on it would only make it worse. 'Let's forget about it, will we.'

She glanced at him thoughtfully. 'It's not too late, you know.'

'Go back to school, do the Leaving? You must be joking. Have you forgotten that I've a wife and child to support?'

'No, darling, I haven't forgotten. But it doesn't rule it out. Just makes it a little more difficult. Of course it would have been simpler if you were free.'

Free? To his surprise he felt a pang of regret. He banished it guiltily. 'I wanted to get married.'

'And the baby?' Her voice was gentle. 'Was it – ?'

'Planned?' He shook his head and grinned ruefully. 'We'd agreed to wait a few years. But Fran forgot to take her pill. I don't know how it happened. It's not like her to make a mistake. She wasn't too upset, took it in her stride. I was devastated until I got used to the idea. Once Sean was born, it was okay. It was a bit of a miracle to me to have someone of my own flesh and blood. Sometimes I worry, though, that I won't be able to give him all the things I didn't get. Still, if I stick at the job, do a few nixers in my spare time, we'll get by okay.'

She sighed. 'You're very young to have taken on so much responsibility.'

'Yeh, well.' He was anxious to get off the subject. 'I'm more worried about you at the moment.' He gave her a quick look. 'What's the latest on Vincent?'

'I rang him yesterday.'

'And?' He felt tension grip him. 'What did you decide?'

'Well, nothing, really. All I know is I don't want to go back to him.'

He sighed with relief. 'That's good to hear.'

She looked at him anxiously. 'I don't think he's going to like it.'

'Well, of course he's not going to like it. But what can he do?' Mick grinned at her. 'If he gives you any hassle just tell me about it and I'll show him the door.'

'More tea, Daddy?'

'What?' He threw her a preoccupied look. 'No, no. I've enough.'

'You didn't finish your salad.' Caroline frowned. 'Was it okay?'

'It was fine, sugarbush. I just wasn't hungry.' He gave a light laugh. 'You're a great little cook.'

She knew him too well to be taken in by his tone. 'You're a rotten liar, Daddy. Something's happened, hasn't it? You've been in bad form since yesterday. It's not Mum, is it?' Her heart missed a beat. 'She's not sick, is she?'

'No, she's not sick. Nothing like that. She's decided to stay on another couple of days.'

'Well, that's okay, isn't it?' Caroline was relieved. 'All right, I know you miss her but we're managing fine, aren't we? The world doesn't have to collapse because Mum takes a holiday.'

'You're right,' Vincent said. 'Let her cool her heels for a bit.'

Cool her heels? What a funny way to put it. She patted the teapot. 'It's still hot. Are you sure you don't want another one?'

'Maybe I will.' He smiled at her as he held out his cup. 'With you looking after me, what more could a man need?'

'Oh, Daddy, you don't mean that.' She was delighted. 'Don't you miss Mum, even a little bit?'

'No,' her father said firmly. 'I've told you. It's just fine with you and me.'

'Yes.' Caroline grinned at him. 'It is, isn't it?'

But, deep down, she knew that neither of them really meant it.

'Is that you, Caroline? What's all this about your mother being away?' The high voice sounded aggrieved. 'Of course, she never tells me anything.'

'We were surprised too,' the girl said unguardedly. 'It was a spur-of-the-moment thing, She just took off.'

'Took off? You mean Vincent isn't with her?'

'No, Gran, he's here. Do you want to – ?

'Abroad?' Her grandmother probed. 'Lanzarote? Tenerife? With friends?'

'I don't know, but Daddy will explain. Oh, by the way, there's something I've been meaning to ask you. It's about Michael – '

'Michael? Who's Michael?'

'You know. This cousin of yours, or is it Granda's. Where exactly – ?'

'Caroline!' Maeve St Clair's voice was bewildered. 'I haven't the faintest idea who you're talking about.'

'But you must.' Caroline was baffled too. 'He's been visiting us and Mum says – '

'A cousin, did you say?' her grandmother mused. 'Someone around my age?'

'No, Gran,' the girl said impatiently. 'He's *young*. About twenty-two.'

'Twenty-two?' The phone went quiet suddenly.

'Gran? Are you still – ?'

'What name did you – ? Michael?' Her grandmother's voice seemed to come from a long way off. 'Michael?' Then, 'Oh, *Michael!* I know who you mean now.' She gave a tinkling laugh. 'Dear me, I'm getting very forgetful.'

Gran forgetful? Daddy always said she had a mind like a razor.

Another laugh. 'Darling, he'd be *very* far out. No one important.'

Caroline's mind cleared suddenly. Of course. Why hadn't she seen it? Gran was such a snob. 'He's not that bad. Actually, he's quite handsome – '

'Caroline,' the voice at the other end of the line cut in sharply. 'You'd better let me talk to your father.'

About time too. 'Okay, Gran.' She found Vincent in his study, frowning over some papers.

'Shit!' His frown deepened. 'What did you tell her?'

'Just that Mum was away.' She stared at him in surprise.

'The less you tell that woman the better.' He sighed. 'Okay, I'll talk to her.' He picked up the phone and motioned for her to leave. 'Haven't you studying to do?'

Caroline smiled to herself as she went upstairs. Dad would be no match for Gran. He wouldn't be able to get off the phone before he had told her everything.

Not that there was anything to tell.

'Can I come in?' There seemed something vaguely familiar about the casually dressed, middle-aged man who gazed enquiringly at her from the doorstep. Behind him an early evening mist was settling over the Square gardens.

'I was on my way out.' She looked at him blankly. 'Who did you – ?'

He gave a boyish grin, a ghost from the past. 'Don't you remember me, Margaret?'

'Father Tim?' She stared at him in astonishment. The last time she'd seen the priest was when he'd officiated at her father's funeral thirteen years before. 'Have you come to see Susan? She's – '

'It's you I've come to see, actually.' Again that boyish grin. He stepped forward. 'Are you going to keep me out here in the cold till we both catch pneumonia?'

'You'd better come in.' Her thoughts in a whirl, she led

the way back to the flat door, unlocked it and ushered him into the living room, covering her confusion under a show of hospitality. 'You'll have a drop of whiskey, Father?'

'It's early yet,' he demurred. 'But – just to keep the cold out. Brandy, if you have it.'

She examined Susan's diminishing supply of alcohol. There were a couple of glasses left in the brandy bottle. She fixed a vodka for herself, noting that she needed to stock up. As she brought the drinks over she studied him in wonderment.

'I just don't believe it. After all this time.' He was still attractive in a rakish kind of way but the years had left their mark. His once handsome face was scored with lines. No longer the hopeful young man who loses to the hero in the last reel, more the heroine's world-weary uncle.

He smiled ruefully. 'You don't feel the years passing. But *you* don't look a day older.' His glass was raised in salute to her. 'And still as beautiful as ever.'

Still the same courtier. Same old, easy charm. That much hadn't changed, anyway. 'What are you doing with yourself these days?'

'This and that.' He shrugged. 'I do a bit of teaching, write the odd article.'

And as hard to pin down as ever. Although maybe he had finally found his niche: the greying hair in need of a trim, the sweater under the tweed jacket and the crumpled cords certainly bore out the academic image. 'Cigarette?'

He shook his head. 'Gave them up a few years ago.' He had lost his plumpness too. Gone was that sleek, well-fed look he'd had in his thirties. He must miss Mummy's afternoon teas, Mrs Roberts's cream cakes.

As she lit her own cigarette she wondered when he would get around to telling her the purpose of his visit.

'You mean you knew all about it at the time?' Margaret was stunned.

'Who do you think arranged the adoption? Managed to keep things quiet?' He spoke gently: the teacher explaining to a dull student. 'I had some good friends who were nuns. They were very discreet. It was the least I could do for Maeve. She deserved nothing less.'

For Mummy? What about me? 'But you never said anything.'

'Would you have thanked me if I had?' The priest gave a knowing smile. 'Somehow I don't think so.'

'I could have done with a friend.'

He looked at her blankly. 'Hadn't you your mother?'

'My *mother*? Oh, of course, I forgot.' She couldn't keep the contempt from her voice. 'You were always her creature.'

He ignored the jibe and said blandly, 'In matters like these I've always found "the less said the better". And I have to say, we carried it off very well, very well indeed.' He smiled faintly. 'It must have been one of the best-kept secrets in Dublin. Of course a lot of that was Maeve's doing. She's an extraordinary woman! Anyone else would have broken under the strain but not your mother. You should be down on your knees thanking God for what she did for you instead of bringing more worry to her like this. If any woman deserves to be canonised, it's her.'

'Canonised?' She looked at him in disbelief. 'How can you say that? She made me give my child away.'

His face hardened suddenly. 'You seem to be missing the point, Margaret. The whole thing was done for your benefit. So that you could put the experience behind you, start off with a clean slate. And it worked, didn't it? You made a good marriage, became an exemplary wife and mother. Until now, that is. Look...' His voice became gentle again, reasonable, persuasive. 'It's understandable that you'd want to know what happened to your son, nobody's blaming you for that – '

'Aren't they?' She couldn't keep the bitterness out of her voice.

' – but you can't turn back the clock, can't change the past. Now that you've seen him, why not leave it at that? Maybe meet once a year at Christmas, that kind of thing. He has his life. You have yours.'

'Meet once a year? You can't be serious – '

'That's where you're wrong, Margaret. You're the one who doesn't seem to realise the seriousness of it. Why do you think I'm here?' His face looked haggard suddenly in the fading light. 'I'm here because an old friend of mine rang me in deep distress. And why did she ring me?' For a moment his voice took on the cadences of the pulpit. 'Because she's convinced you're about to make another terrible mistake and she wants to do everything in her power to stop you before it's too late. And remember, Margaret, this time it won't be so easy to keep things quiet.' He looked at her earnestly. 'Believe you me, your mother has your best interests at heart.'

'No, she doesn't. She just doesn't want anyone to know about Michael. You said it yourself. "Keeping things quiet" is all she cares about.'

'There's nothing wrong with wanting to keep your name

from being dragged through the mud. But that's not something you've ever worried about, is it?' The priest's voice sharpened as if his patience had suddenly worn thin. 'You were always a headstrong girl. And you don't seem to have learned anything.' He looked coldly at her. 'Your family have always had a certain standing in the community. They have their good name to think about. They're entitled to that. And what about Vincent? You don't seem to have given him a thought.' He finished the last of his brandy and put down the empty glass. 'Take my advice. Forget about this young man. You don't owe him anything. Your place is with your husband. I know this is the 1980s and it's getting very popular "to do your own thing" and "let it all hang out". But church teaching hasn't changed, I can assure you of that.' There was no sign of the boyish smile now. No trace of the priest's former affability as he stood up to take his leave. 'Go back to your husband,' he said crisply. 'Forget all this nonsense before it's too late.'

'Nonsense?' Mick raged. 'Who does he think he is, interfering like that?'

'He said Mummy asked him.'

'But why? Why couldn't she have come to see you herself?'

'She'd never do that.' Margaret smiled faintly. 'That way she'd have to talk about it, about you. And that's something she's never, ever done over the years. She's always behaved as if nothing had ever happened.

'But don't you want to talk to her about it?'

'No, I don't. What would be the point?' She sighed heavily. 'I've never been able to talk to my mother about anything. It would just be a waste of time.'

'Particularly if she went on at you like that priest.' He nodded in sympathy. 'He had a nerve talking to you like that.' He looked at her anxiously. 'You're not still upset, are you?'

'Not as much as I was at the time. It was the contemptuous way he spoke to me. It was as if I had no rights. Utterly humiliating.' She gave a shaky laugh. 'It took a stiff drink to get things into perspective.' He noticed her hands shaking as she took out her cigarettes.

'Oh, Margaret. I wish I had been here. I wouldn't have let him away with it.' Impulsively, he grasped her hand. 'You need someone to stand up for you.'

Her fingers tightened briefly around his. 'You're so good for me, Michael. If only I had met someone like you instead of Vincent.' Her face was wistful as she took her hand away. 'Things might have been so different.'

'*I* wish I could have met someone like you.' He bent eagerly to light her cigarette. 'Don't get me wrong; I love Fran; I wouldn't say a word against her but sometimes I feel there's a lot about me she doesn't understand.'

'You've had your nose stuck in that book all evening, Mick. What's this one called: *Son of War and Peace*?'

'Very funny.' He put the book down reluctantly. 'It's *Ulysses*. By James Joyce.'

'Oh, yeh? That teacher you had in fifth year?'

'Ah, *Fran!*'

'Only joking, Mick.' Her eyes gleamed. 'I know who he was. I went to school too. That reminds me, what's a box of your old school books doing in the bedroom? If your Da was clearing out the attic he should have got rid of them himself, not go dumping them on us. What does he think this is, a rubbish tip?'

'He didn't dump them.' He avoided her eye and picked up his book again. 'I asked him for them.'

'I don't believe it. Leaving Cert Poetry? *The Mayor of Casterbridge*? That's one book I'd never want to look at again. What do you want stuff like that for?'

'There's things I want to read again.'

'Ah, come on, Mick. The Leaving? Who wants to go back over that again?'

'You forget I never got a chance to do mine.' His voice was stiff.

'I wouldn't lose any sleep over it.' Fran shrugged. 'I passed my Leaving. And much good it did *me*.'

He was stung by her attitude. 'I'd a feeling you wouldn't understand.'

Her eyes narrowed. 'But *she* does, huh?'

He found himself getting irritated. 'Look, you don't have to be jealous of Margaret, she's my *mother*, for God's sake.'

Her face went pink. 'I'm not jealous. I just don't understand why you need to spend so much time with her.'

'And I don't understand why you keep trying to make me feel guilty. There's no mystery about it. She's an interesting woman. She knows a lot about music and literature. It's opened up a whole new world for me. You wouldn't grudge me that, would you?'

'Of course not, Mick. But – '

'We're going to the Abbey theatre next week.'

'Oh – '

He looked at her face and added quickly, 'Why don't you

come with us?' As soon as the words were out he found himself half-regretting them. 'That is, if we can get another ticket.'

'I wouldn't want to interfere with your plans.' She shook her head. 'Forget it, Mick. Another time.'

'Maybe you're right.'

But the idea, once planted, took root. Maybe it wasn't such a bad idea for the two of them to meet. After all, it was about time they got to know each other. He mentioned it tentatively to Fran.

'I don't know about that.' She looked at him doubtfully. 'Maybe some time, Mick. But not just yet. Why don't we get Christmas out of the way first?'

'But that won't be for another three weeks.' Once he had made up his mind he was impatient to act on the idea. 'I was thinking about something a bit sooner.'

'I don't know,' she said again. 'Give me a chance to think about it.'

He found Margaret equally unenthusiastic. 'I don't know whether I'm up to meeting new people at the moment.'

'Why?' He was immediately concerned. 'You're not sick, are you?' He studied her face. 'I thought you were looking a bit pale.'

'No, no, I'm fine.' She gave a wan smile. 'Tired, that's all. Look, let's not talk about it at the moment. Let's just enjoy the time we have together.'

'You're not having second thoughts, are you?' He felt a stab of anxiety. 'You're not sorry you left?'

'No, of course not. I should have left Vincent years ago. I

don't know why I put up with him for so long. But it's not just Vincent, is it.' Her face grew sad. 'It's Caroline too.'

Caroline? He felt a spasm of guilt. 'I forgot about Caroline.' He forced himself to suggest, 'Maybe, for her sake –'

'I don't think so.' She shook her head. 'She'll just have to understand.'

'You're doing the right thing,' he said urgently. 'You weren't happy with him. He didn't value you.'

'I think maybe I didn't value myself.' Her face was bleak.

'Don't be like that, Margaret. What's done is done. Things will be different from now on, you'll see. But you're going to have to make plans for the future, get out, meet people. I worry about you being so much on your own.'

'There's no need to worry, Michael. I'm fine. I need this time on my own to sort things out. Besides, I do get out, I do meet people. I had a life before I left Vincent. I'm still living it.'

'Are you?' He looked at her doubtfully. 'Like what?'

'Oh, this and that.' Her eyes slid away from his. 'You know. Committees and things. Coffee mornings.' She smiled brightly. 'I meet lots of people, believe me. I'm fine, darling, don't fuss.'

'Well, if you're sure.' He put his doubts to one side. 'You would tell me if there was a problem?'

'Of course I would. But I don't need to tell you that my chief problem at the moment is ending my marriage with Vincent. Trying to work out what to do for the best. But don't worry, darling.' She smiled reassuringly. 'I'm getting there.'

So many decisions to make, Margaret told herself. You must pull yourself together, work on it, concentrate.

But she wasn't working on it, was she? She wasn't getting there.

She was drifting.

She was adrift on a sea of uncertainty.

Sleepless nights in the room that had once housed a dentist's surgery. Ghosts of her childhood peopled the walls.

Tossing and turning in the impenetrable blackness of a midwinter night.

A rudderless boat. Drifting.

Sometimes the shore was very far away.

Sometimes it seemed as if morning would never come.

'Margaret? I was trying to get you earlier. Did you go out?'

'No, I slept in. I mustn't have heard the phone.'

'Oh, to be one of the idle rich,' he joked. 'Wish I could have stayed in bed. There's a wind out that would skin you alive.'

'Are you coming over this evening?' He heard the eagerness in her voice.

'No, I wish I could. Fran's going out. I promised to mind Sean. But I'll definitely see you tomorrow.'

'I suppose it's stupid of me to be disappointed.' She gave a quick laugh. 'But I was really looking forward to seeing you.'

'I don't think you're stupid,' he said. 'I feel the same way.'

'What exactly is going on, Daddy?' Caroline scowled. 'Why won't you tell me?'

Vincent's expression was grim. Was it her imagination or had his face got thinner? He stared at her for what seemed ages before he spoke.

'I'm not exactly sure myself. But there's one thing I do know. Your mother seems to have taken leave of her senses.'

'I didn't really buy the holiday story,' she said slowly. 'It's been going on too long. What's the real truth, Dad? Where is she?'

He said reluctantly, 'She's staying in Susan and Tom's flat while they're away. She says she has things to think over.'

Caroline was baffled. 'Things? What kind of things?'

He looked uncomfortable. 'We-ell – '

Comprehension dawned. 'Are you and she splitting up? Oh, *Daddy!*'

'It hasn't come to that,' he said quickly. 'She's just – considering her position.'

'Considering her position?' Despite her concern, she couldn't help laughing. 'You make it sound like a company takeover.'

To her surprise he said grimly, 'Maybe that's not such a bad word for it. Maybe you've hit the nail on the head.'

Her eyes flew open. 'You're not saying there's someone else? There couldn't be.' She laughed in disbelief. 'Not Mum. She wouldn't have it in her.'

'Still waters run deep.' Vincent gave a significant nod. 'But he's the one I really blame. Since that fella came along – '

'That fella?' She looked at him incredulously. 'You can't mean Michael? I don't – '

Her father's face took on a closed look. 'I've said enough. Too much, probably. Look, we'll let the hare sit for a while.

Give her time to come to her senses.'

'But this is awful,' the girl raged. 'I don't understand how you can sit there and take it so calmly. If it was me, I'd – '

'What else can I do?' Vincent made a helpless gesture with his hands. 'When your mother gets in one of her moods – '

'She *has* been acting very strange lately,' the girl said thoughtfully.

'You don't know the half of it,' Vincent muttered. 'And not just lately.'

'Oh, Daddy!' She felt a rush of sympathy. 'I never realised – '

He sighed. 'Enough said, Caroline. But it hasn't always been easy, you know.'

'I didn't.' She shook her head. 'Poor Daddy. How awful for you.'

His face softened. He patted her hand affectionately. 'Look, sugarbush, this is my worry, not yours. Your mother and I are adults.' He smiled thinly. 'Well, I am, anyway. Between us we'll sort things out.'

'I hope so.' Caroline was not reassured. This concerned her too. She couldn't just stand by and watch her parents' marriage break up.

As she stared at her father an idea began to form in her mind.

'Anyone home?' Mick's heart lifted with anticipation as he stepped into the narrow hallway. Although it was a dank, cheerless evening with darkness falling outside, nothing could dampen the heady feeling of excitement he always felt just before he met Margaret. 'It's me.'

No answer. A quick check of the rooms showed the flat

to be empty. It had a deserted, unlived-in air which roused his suspicions. His excitement died. All of a sudden, he felt frantic. He went back and checked the rooms again.

It was okay. Her black dressing gown hung behind the bedroom door, her silver-backed brushes were still on the dressing table. A fire was laid in the living room grate. He breathed a sigh of relief. He was just being stupid. She would never have gone without telling him. She was probably out shopping. And he was earlier than usual. It was a slack time of the year and jobs were thin on the ground at the moment. Which was handy because it meant he could spend more time with her without Fran kicking up. The drawback was that there'd be less money in his wage packet at the end of the week. But he didn't want to think about that now. Better put a match to the fire. Although there was some background heating, the flat was chilly and she'd be cold when she came in. A cup of tea would be a good idea too. As he rummaged in the tiny kitchen it struck him how neat it was, nothing out of place, very little food on the shelves, just a few tins and packets. Margaret probably ate out mostly. He would if he were on his own. Where did she keep the teapot, though?

As he was pondering this, there was a loud buzzing sound. Someone at the street door wanted to come in. Puzzled, he went to investigate.

'It's *you*. I might have known.' The fair-haired girl on the doorstep viewed him with distaste. 'I came to see my mother.'

'She's not here at the moment.' He ignored the hostility in her voice, held the door open wide and smiled at her. 'Why don't you come in and wait.'

Without answering she walked past him across the hallway in through the flat door, headed straight for the living room and glanced around it suspiciously.

'I told you she wasn't here,' Mick said. He smiled again at her but she didn't respond. 'Look, why don't you sit down. I'm just making a cup of tea.'

To his relief, he spotted a teapot on a shelf near the cooker and grabbed it hastily.

'No biscuits, I'm afraid.' He kept his voice cheerful as he brought the tray into the living room and grinned at Caroline, who was still standing in the middle of the room. 'Looks like Margaret's on one of those twenty-four hour fasts.'

She didn't smile. Her face showed anger, then bewilderment. 'How could she do it? You're young enough to be – '

'Her son?' Mick asked.

'I don't know how you have the nerve to face me,' Caroline fumed. 'It's the most disgusting – '

'How many times do I have to tell you! You've got it all wrong.'

'No, I haven't,' she said fiercely. 'I know about these things.' Her face coloured suddenly. 'I've read about men like you.'

It was his turn to redden. He looked at her helplessly. 'It's not what you're thinking.' He saw her glance sceptically at the tea tray. 'Look, I don't live here. I'm just visiting, like yourself.'

She looked unconvinced. 'How did you get in, then?'

'I have keys.'

She gave a scornful laugh and looked triumphant. 'So I was right?'

'No, no, you couldn't be more wrong.'

Her face hardened. She made to brush past him. 'I think I'd better go.'

'No, you won't.' He felt his temper rising and caught hold of her arm. 'You're going to sit down, have some tea and listen to what I have to say.'

She tried to twist away. 'You're hurting me.'

He glared down at her. Their eyes locked. She was much shorter than he was but she wouldn't look away, refusing to be intimidated. She had courage, he thought. All of a sudden he became aware of his own strength. He loosened his grip and said more gently, 'I'll let go of your arm if you promise to sit down and listen.'

'Okay.' She capitulated reluctantly. 'But my father's going to hear about this.'

'Tell him what you want.' Watching her settle herself at the table, he came to a decision. As he searched for the right words he found himself praying that Margaret would forgive him for what he was about to say.

'She's not your mother!' Caroline shouted when Mick had finished speaking. 'I don't believe you!' For a moment he thought she was going to lunge forward in fury to attack him physically. To his relief, she remained in her seat. 'How dare you say that about her?' Her face was filled with disgust. 'Is that how you get your kicks, making allegations like that about people? You're sick, do you know that? *Sick, sick, sick.*'

He recoiled. Her reaction was like a punch in the face. The relief he had felt at having finally brought things out into the open vanished swiftly. Disappointment, hurt and resentment struggled for mastery inside him. Resentment won. When will you ever learn, Cleary? 'Ask Margaret, if you don't believe me,' he said stiffly.

'Don't you worry, I will.' She picked up her cup and began to sip her tea, her head held high, a spot of colour burning in each cheek. There was a short silence as he watched her trying to figure things out, arriving at an answer she didn't like. When she spoke her voice was subdued. 'Does my father know?'

'Oh, yes.' Mick didn't hide the bitterness he felt. 'It was his idea not to tell you.'

'I see.' She glanced at him uncertainly, clearly taken aback. She looked very vulnerable, he thought, and much younger than her years. He began to be sorry for her and felt his resentment soften.

'Look, I know this will take a bit of getting used to,' he said tentatively. 'But isn't it better than thinking I was Margaret's fancy man.'

'I don't know about that.' She tossed her head, rejecting the implied sympathy. Her lip curled and he was reminded suddenly of Vincent. 'At least that way it wouldn't have to be a permanent arrangement.'

'Thanks very much.' He gave a rueful laugh.

'Of course – ' she looked at him thoughtfully. 'Daddy called you a "passing fancy".' Another curl of the lip. A scornful smile. 'My father's a good judge of people.'

Smug little bitch! Any hopes he had had about Caroline were withering one by one. 'You've nothing to worry about then, have you?' He couldn't resist adding, 'If he's that great, why has his wife left him?'

Her eyes flashed. 'Don't talk about my father like that!'

'And don't you call me "a passing fancy",' he snapped back at her.

They stared at each other for a moment. Caroline was the first to look away. She bit her lip and said wistfully, 'I always wanted a brother.'

His spirits rose. He glanced at her hopefully.

'Me too,' he said. 'Me too.'

'I had a baby brother but he died before he was born. I only found out recently.' They had made fresh tea and were sitting by the fire, which was now blazing brightly. She looked thoughtfully into the flames. 'I wish he hadn't died. It was lonely growing up in that house. Daddy was always so busy and Mum never seemed to be there for me. Don't get me wrong, she was there physically – she didn't abandon me or anything – but I just couldn't seem to get through to her. She can be a bit remote at times. You must have noticed that?'

'Well, maybe sometimes.' He had a sudden picture of his first meeting with Margaret in the restaurant. 'But not since we've got to know each other.'

'It's obvious she finds you more interesting than me.' The girl's voice was bitter.

'Don't be ridiculous.' He looked at her uncomfortably. 'Of course she finds you interesting – a lovely girl like you. I mean –'

She shrugged. 'Don't bother to deny it. I've seen you together. I'll say this for Daddy. He might be a bit of a workaholic but when he's there he listens to me. Of course, he really cares for me. Not like her.'

'You're wrong. Of course she cares for you. I know she

does. But, look, let's talk about us for a moment. We're sister and brother.' He stared in wonderment at the young girl with Margaret's blonde hair and clear skin in the armchair opposite. 'I can't believe I'm sitting here talking to my sister.' His voice was gruff with emotion. 'You've no idea how much this means to me'

'*Half*-sister,' Caroline corrected him. She gave him Vincent's catlike stare. 'I suppose it should mean more to me. But there's no use in pretending. If things were different, maybe. As it is, all I can think about at the moment is my mother. Where is she? What have you done with her?' Before he could answer, she rushed on. 'Why are you *doing* this to us? Is one mother not enough for you? Why do you want two?'

He felt bewildered by the attack and put on the defensive. 'It's not as simple as that. I don't just see her as my mother. She's a friend too.'

'But you've a wife? And a little boy?'

'Sean?' He was surprised she knew so much about him. 'Your nephew,' he reminded her.

He saw a flicker of interest cross her face but she hurried on. 'Are they not enough for you? Why do you have to have *my* mother as well? It's not fair.' Her voice rose to a wail. 'You have so much and I have so little.'

He felt wrong-footed, guilty, resentful.

'That's not the way I see it,' he said.

She left soon afterwards. There was still no sign of Margaret. But: 'Daddy will worry if I'm not there when he gets home.' She looked at him coldly. It was obvious that the truce between them had been a temporary one. 'There's just him and me now.'

He didn't know how to answer this and fell back on formality. 'I'll tell Margaret you were here. I'm sure she'll – '

'Yes.' She hesitated in the doorway. He saw a struggle going on in her face. She said tentatively, 'If you get a chance, maybe you'd – ?'

He gave an apologetic shrug. 'I can't promise anything.'

'Oh, forget it.' She glared at him suddenly. 'Don't bother your head. I'll ask her myself.'

'You nearly missed me.' He met Margaret as he was about to go out the front door. 'I couldn't wait any longer. What kept you?' Behind her he could see sleety rain slanting down under the street lamps. It glistened on her hair and light raincoat. 'Come in out of the cold.' He hurried her into the flat and helped her off with her coat. 'Look at you, you're soaked through. How did you get so wet?'

Her face looked white and strained. 'Don't fuss, darling. I went shopping.'

'But you haven't bought anything.' He was puzzled. 'Unless you – '

'No, I didn't,' she admitted. 'I just walked instead.'

'In this weather? Are you mad? Look at you, you're shivering with the cold.'

'I went through the Green. It's funny how little it's changed over the years. I remember winters when the keepers had to break the ice to free the ducks. Poor things, they didn't know what was happening to them.'

'At least they have feathers to keep out the rain.' Without

thinking he took her chilly hand in his and drew her towards him. 'What you need is to get rid of those wet clothes and get into a hot bath.'

'A hot bath sounds wonderful.' She rested her head against his shoulder and sighed like a tired child. 'You're much too good to me.'

He liked the trusting way she leaned against him. 'No, I'm not. I'd say the same to Fran if she got a drenching like that.' As he put a protective arm around her shoulders it struck him with a kind of wonder that she was only a couple of inches shorter than him. And so slender for such a tall woman. 'You need feeding up, Margaret, do you know that? But first – ' His arm still around her, he urged her towards the door. 'I'm going to run that bath.'

He found clean towels in an airing cupboard and picked out two of the softest ones he could find. He handed them around the bathroom door. 'Will there be anything else, Madam?'

He heard a muffled laugh. 'Since you ask, Jeeves, coffee, black and strong. Will you put the kettle on?'

'I'll do better than that. If you like I'll bring you in a cup.' All of a sudden, realising what he had said, he felt his face flame up. 'Maybe that's not such a good idea. I'm sorry.' As his embarrassment grew he stumbled over the words: 'I didn't mean – I just didn't think – '

'It's okay, darling, I know what you meant. It was sweet of you. But I'm nearly finished anyway. Just put that kettle on. And Michael – I'm out of cigarettes, would you be an angel and – '

'Of course.' He seized the excuse gratefully. 'I'll buy bread and stuff while I'm at it. Your kitchen is beginning to look like Mother Hubbard's on a bad day.'

'What, not even a bone?' The bathroom door opened and she stood there in a white towelling robe with another towel wrapped turban-like around her head. The room behind her was clouded with steam. 'Poor doggie.'

It was silly. It was childish. But he couldn't help himself. 'Woof. Woof.'

Her delighted laugh made it okay.

'I wish I'd known you when you were growing up.' She had changed into cords and a sweater and was drying her hair by the living-room fire. 'Christmases, birthdays, First Communion. I feel I've missed so much.'

'Yes, but you know me now and that's what matters.' He placed the tray he was carrying down on the table. 'I hope you're going to have some of this soup.'

'I'm not very hungry.' She looked at him apologetically. 'I don't seem to have the energy.'

'That's because you're not eating enough. You can't expect to keep going on a diet of black coffee and cigarettes.' His voice was stern. 'You're thin enough as it is.'

She raised a quizzical eyebrow. 'Too thin?'

'Well, no.' He felt his face redden. 'It looks well on you. But – '

'But?' Her voice was playful as she took the steaming bowl from him. 'You like women to be – heavier, maybe?'

'Heavier! God, no!' he burst out. 'No, I didn't mean that.'

She smiled, said nothing and toyed with her soup.

He felt his face get hotter and avoided her eyes. Then, in a low voice, he said, 'I think your figure's perfect, Margaret. You know that.'

'Perfect?' She laughed ruefully. 'I wish it was. Oh darling, I'm sorry for teasing you. When you're embarrassed it makes you look about ten.' Her face changed. 'How I wish I'd known you at that age.' He heard the longing in her voice. 'I really envy your mother. I wonder does she know how lucky she is?'

'It hasn't been all joy for her either.' He thought of the last time he had met Ma. 'She does her best but sometimes she finds it hard to understand me. As for Da – '

'I don't think you're that difficult to understand.'

'That's the wonderful thing,' Mick said eagerly. 'I never have to explain myself to you, you always seem to know. That's one of the things I love about you.'

'Do you know what I love about you?' Margaret's voice was soft. 'You're so considerate, so kind. You really seem to care for me.'

'Of course I care for you. Why wouldn't I? You're my mother.'

'Yes. I'm your mother.' A look of sadness crossed her face. 'This might sound strange but – sometimes I have to remind myself that I am.'

Their eyes met in the firelight.

Yes, Margaret. Sometimes, like now, when I see you sitting there in that sweater that matches your eyes, and your bright hair drying in tendrils around your face, sometimes I have to remind myself too.

He was stuck at a red light when he remembered that he had forgotten to tell her about Caroline's visit. Oh well, he'd be seeing her again soon. Tell her then. As the lights changed and he gunned the bike away ahead of the leading car he felt his heart lift with delighted wonder. What a woman! He'd only just left her and already he was looking forward to seeing her again. When he had gone looking for his mother, who could have predicted that she would turn out to be such a fantastic human being?

He left the river behind without a backward glance and manoeuvred his bike through the narrow streets. The rain had stopped and he found himself admiring the way the lights from the street lamps glistened on the roadway, blending with the coloured lights thrown out by the cars. On both sides, Christmas decorations sparkled in shop windows. The city had a festive air, he thought, in keeping with his own mood. Suddenly he felt ravenously hungry. The soup he'd had with Margaret hadn't been that filling. But Fran was bound to have kept something hot for him in the oven. As he zoomed up the hill towards home his elation grew. What a lucky man he was! Two beautiful women in his life and they both loved him. The words of an old poem from childhood came into his mind. He grinned to himself. God was in his heaven. And all was right with Mick's world.

His euphoria was not destined to last long. Fran met him at the door with an agitated face.

'Sean has a temperature. I had to get the doctor.'

'Oh no!'

The baby lay quietly in his cot, a bright spot of red on

each cheek. His hair was plastered damply to his head. Mick listened to the quick, light breathing and touched his forehead gently.

'He's burning up, Fran.'

'I know, Mick.' She wrung out a face towel in a basin of water and placed it against one red, little cheek, then the other. 'The doctor said it'll be a few hours before we see the good of the antibiotic.'

'But it *will* work?' He couldn't keep the anxiety from his voice. 'It'll bring the temperature down?'

'I hope so.' She threw him a sombre look and went on sponging the baby's hot little body. 'This should help too.'

He envied her self-control. 'Fran! I should have been here. The one night I would have to be late.'

'It wasn't your fault.' Intent on her task, she only gave him half her attention. 'If the boss asked you to do a message, you had to do a message.'

Ashamed of the ready lie that had sprung to his lips, he was relieved not to have to meet her eye. 'Yeh, well,' he muttered. 'I should have known.'

'How could you? It came on so fast.' Fran's lips trembled. 'He was okay this morning.' She turned and looked at him. 'I wish you *had* been here, Mick. I was so frightened at first, I didn't know what to do. After the doctor went I kept thinking you'd be home any minute but you weren't. You should have rung me if you were going to be late.'

'I'm sorry, Fran. I should have been here.' She and Sean needed him. And he had let them down. But Margaret had needed him too. He thought of her white, strained face when she had arrived back at the flat soaking wet. And of the trusting way she had rested her head against his shoulder. She had needed him too. How could he be in two places at once? He felt helpless as he watched Fran sponging the baby's body.

'Can I do that? Give you a break. You've been looking after him all day.'

'No, it's okay.' She tried to smile but he saw the worry in her eyes. 'I feel better if I'm doing something for him. If you really want to help why don't you make us a cup of tea? I can't remember when I had anything to eat last.'

'Of course.' It was a relief to have something to do. For the second time that day he found himself rooting through kitchen cupboards. At least this time he should know where most things were kept. Not everything, though. Fran was untidy and never seemed to put things back in the same place. Despite his concern for Sean he found himself getting irritated at having to extricate plates and saucers from a crammed cupboard. He found himself comparing the dingy kitchen units with the more expensive oak ones in Susan's flat. And from there his thoughts touched on the gleaming pine kitchen in Margaret's own home. The best of everything had gone into that house. He pictured the mahogany staircase in the hall, the impressive stained-glass window, the paintings on the walls. The deceptive simplicity of comfort and good taste that only money could buy.

Did she miss it? he wondered. Of course she must. Stands to reason she must. Was that why she was so dejected when she had come in this evening? Was that why she had wandered the streets without buying anything? As he hastily threw a few sandwiches together he pondered the implications of this.

'Mick?' Fran's voice broke into his reverie. He started and threw her a guilty look as if she could somehow read his thoughts. He studied her exhausted face. 'How is he?'

'He's asleep.' She threw herself down on the couch with a sigh. 'I don't think he's as hot as he was.'

'Thank God for that!'

She nodded. 'I don't think I've ever prayed so much in my whole life.'

'I'm sorry, Fran.'

She yawned hugely, only half listening. 'For what, Mick?'

For everything, Fran. For not loving you enough. For taking you for granted. And what about the lies? Especially for the lies. Although I can't promise you they'll stop.

'For not being with,' he mumbled. 'I should have been here.'

If he had hoped for some kind of absolution, he was to be disappointed.

Fran's eyes were closed, her head thrown back against the sofa cushions, her breasts moving almost imperceptibly in time to her quiet breathing.

He traced her snub little nose with a gentle finger and touched the freckles that stood out like golden dots against the creamy skin. She looked so young lying there. Sleep had wiped away the exhaustion from her face, leaving it as smooth as a child's. He was reminded of the little girl in her First Communion photo which he had seen hanging in Hennessy's sitting room. Much too young to be anybody's wife or mother. He thought back to the first time they had met in the pub and that cheeky robin air that had so attracted him.

Supposing he hadn't taken up the challenge that night and had gone for one of Donie's sure things? Given himself time to grow up, to discover what he really wanted from life? Would it not have been better for both of them?

He felt guilty at even asking himself the question. If Fran knew what he was thinking – . But how could she? What she didn't know wouldn't harm her. But maybe it had, already. His guilt grew as he watched her sleeping face. She deserved someone better. Someone contented with his lot, not always looking around her and beyond her for something else. Or someone else?

But he'd found that someone else, hadn't he? His mother. That long-lost mother of his dreams. Earlier that evening he'd felt that his cup was running over with happiness, that he'd everything he could possibly want in life. His wife. His birth mother. His child.

And now? Now he was not so sure.

The hours passed. He had lifted Fran's legs onto the sofa, put a rug over her and left her to sleep undisturbed. Then he kept vigil by the baby's cot, sponging him occasionally with tepid water as he had seen her do, watching anxiously when he stirred restlessly in his sleep. Around midnight he noticed a change. Sean gave a sad little sigh, a sigh that wrenched at Mick's heart, causing him to lean forward in alarm. He saw the tension go out of the plump little body. The baby's face grew peaceful, his breathing more gentle. He still felt hot to the touch but the burning fever had gone.

Thank God! Mick felt his own limbs trembling with relief. He sat back shakily in his chair. His anxiety loosened its hold.

A wave of tenderness washed over him as he watched his sleeping son. How beautiful he was! And how much he loved him. Whatever his earlier doubts he knew that he could never regret bringing him into the world.

'I wish I'd known you as a child.' He remembered the wistful look on Margaret's face when she said that earlier. An idea struck him. There was nothing to stop her knowing Sean, was there? He pictured himself placing the baby in her arms. 'Here's my son. Your grandson.' Another link that went back to her father and *his* father before him. He wished he could have known his grandparents. But his grandfather was dead and his grandmother didn't want to know him. As for his father? Better forget about him.

He fought down a pang of regret. You can't have everything you want in this life, Mick. But there was still plenty he could have. He came to a sudden decision. If Margaret couldn't make him part of *her* family he would make her part of *his*. Somehow, he would make them accept her. He didn't know how he was going to do it. But do it, he would.

PART SIX

'Mrs Cleary!' Fran was astonished to see her mother-in-law standing on the doorstep. 'Mick isn't home yet. He's still at work.'

'I came to see you.' Ma's bright eyes regarded her unblinkingly. 'Are you going to leave me out here all day? It's cold enough to freeze a brass monkey.'

As Fran stepped aside to let her in she heard a movement behind her and Mrs McGrath's gap-toothed smile materialised out of the darkness at the back of the hallway. The smile widened at the sight of the visitor.

'Is that you, Nan Cleary? I thought I recognised the cough. When are you goin' to give up the oul' fags?'

'When *you* stop poking your nose into other people's business, Kitty.'

Ha, ha, that was one in the eye for the oul' biddy. Fran looked at her mother-in-law with new respect. As they headed for the stairs she shot a triumphant glance at Mrs McGrath. The old woman looked unperturbed.

'She was always a great one for the repartee,' she said good-humouredly. 'Still and all – ' No one was going to rob the landlady of the last word. Her voice followed them up the stairs. 'Them fags'll kill you, Nan. Don't say I didn't warn ya.'

'That oul' one's a pain in the hole.' Fran said automatically.

'She wants to know everything you've had for your breakfast.' She had said this so often she had stopped listening to herself. As she led the way into the living room of the flat she wondered what had got into Mick's mother. It would take a herd of wild horses to bring her around here on her own. Could something have happened?

'I heard you had to get the doctor for Sean.' There was what sounded like a note of reproach in Ma's voice, which immediately put Fran on the defensive.

'It was some kind of infection. But he's over the worst,' she said stiffly. 'I'd have told you if it was anything really serious. How'd you hear, anyway? Did Mick – ?'

'I haven't seen him.' Mrs Cleary shook her head. 'I met Kitty at Mass this morning.'

'The oul' biddy?' Fran frowned. 'I didn't know you and her were – ?'

'We're not,' Ma said hastily. 'God knows when I was talking to the woman last. But I do go to the ten o'clock Mass in St Peter's when I get the chance. She's a regular there. *She* came over to me,' she added pointedly. 'I didn't seek her out.'

'That's okay.' Fran allowed herself to be mollified. But the idea that her mother-in-law might have been checking up on her was not a pleasant one. 'That oul' one's a real spy in the camp,' she warned.

'I don't go in for gossip,' Ma said primly. 'Ask anyone. And Kitty's harmless, anyway. There's no real bad in her. But when I heard the little one was sick I said to myself I'll just drop in and – where is he, anyway?' Her eyes searched the room. 'Gone down for a nap?'

'Yes,' Fran sighed. 'He needs his rest. It's taken a lot out of him. I don't mind telling you, Mrs Cleary, he had us worried for a bit.'

'I know, Fran, I know. If it was my Mick, when he was a little fella, I'd have been up the walls. '

She found herself warming to the older woman's obvious sympathy. 'Have you time for a cup of tea, Mrs Cleary?'

'I'd murder a cup, Fran.' Ma reluctantly divested herself of her overcoat but kept on the jacket underneath. 'Hard to keep warm this weather,' she explained.

'What you need is a bit of weight on you,' the girl laughed, looking at the other woman's skinny frame without envy. She patted her own rounded bottom complacently. 'Besides, men like women with a bit of meat on them. Mick always says – '

'Does he?' Ma's lips tightened. She didn't return the laugh. 'I'm glad the baby's on the mend, Fran. You're a good little mother. I've no worries on that score.' She paused and looked uneasily at the younger woman as if not sure how to continue. Then she came to a decision. 'I – well – I was meaning to come around to see you, anyway.'

She was puzzled. 'So it's not about Sean, Mrs C?' That was a relief, anyway. Fran didn't want any mother-in-law telling her how to look after her child.

'No, it's not.' Ma's face was grave. 'It's about Mick.'

'Mick?' She felt a stab of alarm. Her mind ranged through all sorts of frightening possibilities. 'What about Mick?' Her voice sharpened with anxiety. 'There's nothing wrong, is there?'

To her surprise, the other woman said, 'That's what I want

you to tell *me*. I've been trying to keep out of it. But it's been on my mind ever since that night you came to see us.'

It took a moment for it to sink in. 'Oh, I see.' Fran's brow cleared. 'This is about *her*, isn't it?' She lifted her chin and said firmly, 'Look, Mrs Cleary, no offence, but this is between Mick and myself.'

'No, it isn't,' Ma said with equal determination. 'I'm his mother. This concerns me too.'

Their eyes locked. Fran wavered. 'Mick'll have my life, Mrs Cleary – '

'You leave him to me.' The light of battle burned in the older woman's eyes. 'Just tell me what's going on.'

'It's like no one else exists at the moment.' She clasped her hands around the mug of tea, drawing comfort from its warmth. 'Like he was caught up in a kind of spell.'

'But what kind of woman is she?' Her mother-in-law frowned. 'Does he talk about her?'

'Well, he does and he doesn't. It's hard to get a clear picture of her. One thing I do know: she's loaded. You should see the clothes she's given him.'

Ma's frown grew deeper. 'She gives him clothes?'

'Oh, yes.' Fran warmed to her theme. Despite her initial misgivings, it was a relief to be able to tell someone. 'A beautiful jacket. Must have cost a fortune. Shirts. A cashmere sweater, CDs, books. I wouldn't mind – ' she said indignantly, ' – but we hadn't got a CD player. So he went out and bought one on the never-never. Had to be a good one.' She gave an incredulous laugh. 'An ordinary Walkman wouldn't do him. Oh, no. Said you couldn't get a decent "clarity of tone".'

'Clarity of tone?' Ma laughed reluctantly. 'Mick always had a way with words.'

'It isn't funny.' Fran glared at her through the tears that were beginning to well up. 'I might have known you'd stand up for him.'

'I'm not standing up for him, Fran, love. And I don't think it's one little bit funny.' Mrs Cleary placed a soothing hand on her arm. 'I just don't know what to make of it, that's all. Mick was always a good lad, never gave us a moment's worry. But he'd get notions sometimes.' She looked thoughtful. 'I suppose it's in the blood. I always felt we should have let him go to university that time. But Maurice wouldn't hear of it. The Clearys are like that. Set in their ways. What was good enough for him and his brother should be good enough for Mick.'

'What's that got to do with me?' Fran wailed. 'All I know is that he's spending all his time with that woman. He's full of excuses and I never see him any more.' Tears spurted out of her eyes and down her cheeks. 'I'm losing him, Mrs Cleary. And I don't know what to do about it.'

'Losing him?' Nan Cleary looked perturbed. 'Ah, no, Fran, you're wrong.' She shook her head decisively. 'I'm telling you, Mick gets notions sometimes but they don't last. There was that English teacher at school, and his wife. It was nothing but "Suzie this" and "Jimmy that". He practically *lived* there at one time. You never hear any mention of them now.'

'But that was *years* ago. He was just a kid then. This is different. This isn't just going to blow over.'

'No, no, you're wrong.' There was a pleading note in Ma's voice. 'It's just a nine days wonder with Mick. Stands to reason he's all taken up with her at the moment. You can't blame him; she's his own flesh and blood, after all. But it won't last. He told me himself she comes from a different world. Once the novelty wears off – '

'Oh, yeh?' Fran wiped the tears from her eyes with impatient fingers. 'If you believe that, you'll believe anything. A different *world?* Do you not see what this is all about?' She looked earnestly at her mother-in-law. 'Mick's changed, Mrs Cleary. Sometimes when I look at him I think I'm living with a stranger. It's not just the clothes; it's everything. You said he gets notions. Did he tell you he was thinking about going back to school?'

'I don't believe you!' Nan Cleary was stunned. 'What's got into him?'

'It's that woman. With her money and her fancy education, she's driving a wedge between Mick and me. Between *all* of us. I'm telling you, if we're not careful we're going to lose him.'

'Lose him?' She saw dismay in the older woman's eyes. At last she was beginning to get through to her.

'Yes, lose him,' she said firmly. 'We just won't be good enough for him any more.'

'If that's the case – ' Nan Cleary's lips straightened to a thin line, ' – you're going to have to put your foot down. Tell him to stop seeing her.'

She raised her eyebrows. '*Tell* him?'

'*Ask* him, then.'

'I've tried that.'

'Well, there's only one thing left,' her mother-in-law said reluctantly. 'You're going to have to get to know this woman. Make friends with her.'

'Make friends with her?' Fran was affronted. 'Have you gone mad, or what?'

Mrs Cleary sighed. 'I don't like the idea of it, any more than you do. But you know what they say? You'll catch more flies with a spoonful of honey than with a jam jar of vinegar.'

'They can say anything they like.' The younger woman shrugged. She got up from the table. 'I think it's a crazy idea and I don't want to hear any more about it.'

But, as she headed towards the baby's room to lift him up from his nap, Fran's mind began sorting through the possibilities.

'Why didn't you tell me, Daddy? About Michael?' Caroline's voice was aggrieved. 'I had a right to know.'

Vincent's eyes narrowed. 'Did your mother – ?'

'No. *He* did. She wasn't there.' She searched his face. 'Why didn't you?'

He gave her a helpless look. 'I didn't want to upset you.'

'*Upset* me? How do you think I feel now?'

'Well – I – '

'I've had a half-brother all these years and you never told me. He turns up one day and you pretend he's a distant cousin. How could you, Daddy? You of all people? How could you lie to me?' Her voice rose to a wail. 'How can I ever trust you again?'

'Oh, honeybunch!' Her father looked stricken. 'Don't blame me. I only went along with it to protect you.'

'Went along with it?' She was surprised. 'So it wasn't your idea, then?'

'Oh, no,' Vincent said earnestly. 'It was your mother's.

You know how secretive she is. If it was up to me I'd have told you. But she *insisted*.'

The girl looked at him doubtfully. 'Mum insisted? And you let her have her way?'

'Looks like I did.' He gave another helpless shrug. 'The truth is I didn't know what to do for the best. I was afraid it would be too much of a shock for you.'

'It was even more of a shock hearing it from *him*,' Caroline said bitterly.

'That should never have happened,' Vincent frowned. 'The least she might do was tell her yourself. Where was she, anyway? Did he say?'

'No, I don't think he knew. But he was swanning around as if he owned the place.' A sore point ever since her visit to the flat. 'He even made tea for us.'

'Very cosy.' He grunted. 'Don't tell me he's moved in too?'

'No, he said he wasn't living there. But, at this stage, I just don't know what to believe. And there's something I don't understand.' Her brows knitted. She looked closely at her father. 'You said you'd sort things out. But you don't seem to be doing anything about it. And Christmas is only a few weeks away.'

'We won't be stuck. If the worst comes to the worst we can go to your uncle Peter's. But I'll think of something.'

'That's not what I'm talking about, Dad. I meant about Mum.'

'What do you expect me to do?' Vincent's voice was harsh.

'Biting the nose off me won't solve anything.' Caroline refused to be put off. 'You could go and see her. Ask her to come back.'

'Go crawling on my hands and knees? You must be joking. It didn't do you much good, did it?'

'Well, we don't know that. Maybe when she hears I was looking for her, she'll get in touch.'

'Oh, yeh?' He gave a cynical laugh. 'Don't hold your breath.'

'But I'm her daughter.' Caroline was distressed. 'What kind of woman doesn't care about her own daughter?'

He shrugged. 'The kind of woman who would give away her own son, I suppose.'

'Oh, Dad!' She looked at him, aghast. 'I never thought of it like that.'

'Don't upset yourself, sugarbush.' He put his arm around her shoulders. 'But you might as well face up to it: some people are born with ice water in their veins. And your mother happens to be one of them.'

'You don't seem to have enjoyed the film, Margaret.' Mick eyed her anxiously as they emerged from the darkness into the cinema foyer. 'Woody Allen is usually good for a laugh. What's wrong? Has something happened?'

'Today, you mean?' She gave him a startled look. 'No, nothing's happened today. Or yesterday, for that matter. Why do you think something might have – ?'

'Well, it's just that you seem so down, like you're worried about something,' he said hesitantly. 'Is it anything I've done?'

'No, of course not.' She smiled quickly. 'Look, I'm sorry for being such poor company. But I've a lot on my mind. Regrets about things – '

Regrets? He shot her a worried glance. 'Margaret – ?'

' – decisions to make.'

'Oh, decisions?' He seized on the word gladly. 'Well, of course you have. Stands to reason. But you don't have to make them on your own. That's where I come in.' He looked at her eagerly. 'Why don't we discuss it over a drink? You said yourself I'm a good listener. And two heads are better than one.'

'Not always.' She smiled wryly. 'And if you see a light at the end of the tunnel it's probably an oncoming train.'

'That's pure Woody Allen.' He grinned at her. 'Come on.' He took her arm and urged her across the foyer towards the steps. 'You'll feel better after a drink.'

'Maybe.' She shook her head. 'But I think I'll go straight back to the flat. I'm just not good enough company tonight.'

'Well, okay,' he was beginning reluctantly, when suddenly he had to jump out of the way to avoid colliding with another couple who were coming rapidly up the steps towards them. He had a quick glimpse of Sandra's startled eyes set amid spiky black lashes before his sister-in-law hurried past him. But it was the sight of the man whose hand she was holding that caused Mick's own eyes to widen with surprise. Mick stood staring after the couple and didn't turn away until he saw them go by the ticket checker at the entrance to one of the cinemas.

'Anything wrong, Michael?' There was a puzzled look on Margaret's face.

'Nothing. Come on, I'll take you home.' But, as they left the building, he gave a laugh of disbelief. 'That's the last couple on earth I'd have expected to see together. Somebody will have a bit of explaining to do in the morning.'

'Donie! Are you out of your mind? *Sandra*, of all people! If the Hennessys find out, you're dead meat.'

'Yerra, boy, you're a great one to talk.' His friend smiled cynically. 'That wasn't Fran I saw you with, was it.'

'Ah, for God's sake, Donie,' Mick said impatiently. 'It's not what you think.'

'No?' The black eyes gleamed.

'*No*. Will you be serious for a minute.' He returned to the attack. 'How long has this been going on? Since my *wedding*? But that was over two years ago.'

'Too long for *you*, obviously.' Donie looked sardonic. 'Rest easy, boy. It's been a kind of an on-and-off thing with me and Sandra. More off than on. But then she's that kind of woman.' He rolled his eyes dramatically. 'When she takes 'em off, she keeps 'em off. But I don't need to tell you anything about that.' His smile broadened. 'Looks like you got lucky too. That blonde! Fair play to you, Mick.' His voice was envious. 'I never shared your taste for older women. But you really hit the jackpot this time.' He began making appreciative noises. 'Mama mia! I wouldn't throw *her* out of the bed.'

'Donie! What are you *saying*?' Mick was scandalised. 'Would you ever shut up! That's my mother you're talking about.'

'Your *mother*?' Donie's eyes were startled. 'Ah, come on, Mick. Pull the other leg. Your *mother*?'

'Well, boy, if you say so, I believe you.' The Kerryman eventually allowed himself to be convinced. 'It's so ludicrous, it's probably true. After all, the Virgin Mary was only fourteen years older than her son.' His black eyes twinkled irrepressibly. 'Mind you, no one ever saw them coming out of the pictures together on a rainy Saturday night. Although, give him nothing but his due, by all accounts he did go drinking with her in Cana.'

'For God's sake, Donie.' Mick looked uncomfortable. 'Is nothing sacred with you?'

'Not much, Mick, not much.' The black eyes regarded him solemnly. 'But I do have a great regard for mothers. I think they're the salt of the earth. And that goes for all mothers. Yours, mine and Jesus Christ's. And if I said anything disrespectful about yours just now, I apologise. I meant no harm.'

'That's okay,' Mick said awkwardly. 'You weren't to know. Forget it, you crazy Kerryman.'

'Right, boy. Enough said. And about that other thing.' It was Donie's turn to look embarrassed. 'No need to mention it to Fran. Not that I'm worried about it getting back to her folks. Old man Hennessy doesn't bother me –

'Of course not.' Mick grinned.

' – but we wouldn't want them getting the wrong impression. Sandra and I – well – we're just friends – '

'Sounds like a bit more than that, Donie. The way you were talking.'

'Talk, that's all it was, Mick. Just talk.' The other man picked up his paintbrush decisively to signal an end to their conversation. 'There's nothing serious going on between us. Just a bit of harmless fun. But I wouldn't want Fran to get the wrong impression. So not a word to her. Right, Mick?'

'You don't have to worry about that, Donie. Fran and I have more important matters to discuss, believe you me.

Much more important.' Although his tone was buoyant, Mick found himself mentally crossing his fingers as his mind leaped ahead to the conversation he planned to have with Fran that night. Just don't let her put up too much of an argument, he prayed.

'Christmas Day, Mick? You want her to spend it with us? But I don't even know her.'

'It's about time you did, Fran. We'll have her over for a meal first. What about next Saturday?'

'We can't. It's Mammy's birthday. I promised – '

'Thursday or Friday then?' He refused to be put off. 'What do you think?'

To his delight, she nodded resignedly. 'Thursday, Mick. Maybe it's time I met her.'

It took a moment for it to sink in. 'Do you really mean that, Fran.'

She sighed. 'For a meal, anyway. We can talk about Christmas later.'

He gave a whoop of triumph. 'You're wonderful, Fran.' He pulled her into his arms and smiled down at her. 'Have I ever told you how wonderful you are?'

She gave a wry laugh. 'Not lately.'

'Don't be like that, love.' He refused to let her dim his joy. 'I know it's been difficult for you but you've been great about it. And all that's going to change now.'

'That's what I'm afraid of,' she said in a small voice. She buried her face against his chest. 'Nothing's been the same since you met her.'

'You can say that again!' He laughed as he tightened his

arms around her. 'Just wait till you meet her yourself. Margaret's a fantastic woman. You'll love her.'

Fran lifted her head and looked at him doubtfully. 'If you say so, Mick.'

To his dismay, Margaret was equally unenthusiastic.

'You don't think it's a bit soon?'

'*Soon?* Come on, Margaret, do you want to wait till Sean is old enough to come and collect you himself?'

She laughed, her hands admitting defeat. 'Maybe I'm just being a coward.'

'You a coward? You're the bravest woman I know.' He took one of her hands in his and smiled reassuringly into her eyes. 'It's going to be okay. In fact, it's going to be more than okay. Trust me.'

'I don't know where you got your optimism from.' Her voice was rueful. 'It wasn't from me.'

'I have enough for both of us. And if it's any consolation to you,' he added gently. 'Fran's as nervous as you are.'

'Wine, Mick?' She wrinkled her forehead. 'What do we want wine for?'

'Fran.' He hid his impatience. 'Any time I had a meal in her house we always had wine. Look, I want to do this properly.'

'But I don't know anything about wine.'

'It's okay. I'll look after that.'

She gave him a cheeky grin. 'Since when were you an expert?'

'I'm not. But I'm learning. Margaret knows a lot about wine.'

Her grin faded. 'I suppose she's a marvellous cook as well?'

'She is, as a matter of fact. Not that she eats much herself.'

'Oh my God!' She gave him a look of exaggerated awe. 'Don't tell me she's thin too?'

He was nettled by her tone. 'Ah, come on, Fran. Give her a chance. You haven't even met her yet.'

'No,' she said with dour amusement. 'I can hardly wait.'

What on earth should she buy for them? Racked with indecision, Margaret stared unseeingly into a gaily decorated shop window. The baby had been easy enough. A confident young saleswoman in Brown Thomas had steered her in the right direction. 'A nine-month-old-boy? No problem.' The salesman had skilfully nudged her into making a choice between a bewildering array of tiny garments, and then had sent her on her way, clutching her purchases, still in a fog of uncertainty. What kind of present did you give a daughter-in-law you were meeting for the first time? Clothes were out, obviously. Although – maybe a silk scarf? No, still too personal. Why give anything at all? Surely it wouldn't be expected? But then Christmas was less than a week away and she didn't want to go empty-handed.

Chocolates would be a safe bet. But suppose the girl was on a diet? What then? This was ridiculous. She would simply have to make up her mind and be done with it. Behind her Grafton Street was loud with the sound of carol singing, the laughter and conversation of shoppers. So many people looking forward to Christmas. Whereas all she could feel was dread. And, as if Christmas wasn't bad enough, there was tonight to get through first. Why had she ever agreed to it? She realised now what a mistake it had been. As she moved reluctantly away from the shop window she felt close to despair. When, oh when, would she ever learn?

'Have you put the meat in yet, Fran?'

'In a minute.' She looked at him distractedly. 'You said not to put it in too early.'

'So I did. Beef shouldn't be overdone.'

'Yeh, yeh. I *have* cooked a roast before. It's no big deal.' She dabbed vigorously at a stain on the back of the sofa. 'Will you look at the cut of the place. Since Sean started crawling he's putting his sticky hands everywhere.'

'Leave that.' He was exasperated. 'You're only making it worse. Look, the room isn't that bad. It looks a lot brighter since we put up the decorations. The crib looks well.' He had set it up himself, using the nativity figures that Ma had given them their first Christmas in the flat. 'Anyway, Margaret isn't expecting Buckingham Palace. It's you and Sean she's coming to meet. She doesn't care what the place looks like.'

'But I do.' Fran frowned. 'How do you think I feel having to live in a dump like this. And no amount of scrubbing or polishing will ever make any difference.'

'Okay, it's a dump,' he said shortly. 'But it's the best we can afford at the moment. Listen, I'll have to go. I don't know how long it will take me to get a bus. But we'll be back as soon as we can.'

'I don't see why you have to go and collect her.' This was another source of grievance with Fran. 'Why can't she make her own way over? I thought you said she'd a car?'

'Yes, she *has* a car. And, yes, she'll be driving it. But it'll be easier for her to find the place if I'm with her. Anyway, she needs a bit of moral support.' He regretted the words as soon as they were out.

'Moral support!' she spluttered. 'I could have done with a bit of support today. And I don't mean moral. It wasn't easy trying to get the meal ready, clean the place *and* keep an eye on Sean. I could have done with an extra hand.'

'Which you'd have got,' Mick pointed out as he took down his anorak from the hook on the back of the living-room door, 'if you'd agreed to have her over on a Saturday night like I wanted.'

'I've already told you, Saturday is Mammy's birthday and I promised.' Her tone grew self-righteous. 'You're not the only one with a mother, you know.'

'Yes, I know, but you could have given it a miss just this once. You know how important it is to me. She'd have understood.'

'How could she? Seeing as how she doesn't know anything about your precious Margaret,' Fran snapped.

Thank God for that! He stared at her irresolutely for a moment. 'I haven't time to argue about it.' He pulled the zipper on his jacket and turned to go. 'Margaret will be wondering what's keeping me.'

'God, we mustn't keep her waiting,' Fran said. 'That would never do.'

'I thought you'd be ready.' He was dismayed to find her sitting by the fire, still in her dressing gown. There was a half-filled glass on the hearth beside her. 'Aren't you going to get dressed?'

'Won't take me a minute.' But she made no move to get up. 'Have a beer while you're waiting.' She picked up her own glass. 'I had to take something to give me courage.' She drank, looking away from him into the fire.

Watching her, he tried to keep the anxiety from his voice. 'Not getting second thoughts?'

When she didn't answer, he squatted down beside her chair, put his arm around her shoulders and gently stroked her arm. 'Margaret, listen to me. You're not the only one to be nervous. Fran's been going through recipes all week, changing her mind every ten minutes. At one stage she was talking about redecorating the flat.' He laughed. 'Did you ever hear anything so foolish?' As he talked, he was aware of the tension in her shoulders. He felt the warmth of her arm through the thin silk of the dressing gown and caught a whiff of that subtle, expensive scent she always wore. He went on stroking her arm and said earnestly, 'I'm a bit nervous myself. But it's going to be okay, I promise you.'

'Oh, Michael!' He felt the tension leave her body suddenly, felt her relax back against his arm. 'You're right. I am nervous. I'm so afraid she won't like me.'

'Won't like you? How could she not like you?' She was so close he could smell the clean, flowery scent of her hair and feel its softness brush his cheek. For a moment he began to regret the plans they had made for the evening. The picture of the two of them sitting by the fireside drinking wine and listening to music was suddenly a very attractive one. He banished the thought firmly. There would be other times. But right now Fran and Sean were waiting for them back at the flat.

As if she had read his mind, Margaret sighed. She pulled away from him, stood up, reached for her glass and drained it. 'We'll go.' He heard the resolution in her voice. I know how much you have your heart set on it. Give me ten minutes and I'll be ready.' As she was going out the door she smiled at him and indicated across the room. 'That's one of the things I got for the baby. Do you think he'll like it?'

He followed the direction of her hand and saw something he hadn't noticed before: a large, fluffy, white teddy bear sitting on the lid of the baby grand.

'That's for Sean?' His heart lifted at the sight of the child's toy. It was going to be okay. Everything was going to work out fine.

'It's a beautiful car, Margaret.' The engine was so quiet he could hear the sound of the car tyres swishing over the wet streets. 'I've never driven anything like it. Never driven anything, actually, except the old van at work.'

'You can drive it any time you want.' She turned to smile at him from the passenger seat. 'I don't need it much at the moment. Susan's flat is so central. And when I get a place of my own – '

'I've been meaning to talk to you about that.' He changed gears smoothly and eased the car into its lane at the traffic lights. 'Maybe you could get somewhere a bit nearer?'

'Nearer *you*? On this side of the city, do you mean?' He heard the surprise in her voice. 'Well, I – don't know. I hadn't thought – '

'Just an idea,' he said hastily. 'We'll talk about it later. Don't look now but around this corner is the ancestral home of the Clearys.'

'Oh?' Her head shot up with interest. 'This is where you – ?'

'The very place.' He gave a self-conscious laugh as the powerful car swished into the narrow street. 'Number forty-six.'

The row of small, redbrick houses lay dreaming in the glare of the sodium lights. The street was empty; most people were indoors at this time of the evening. He saw the gleam of brass on the red painted doorway as they passed, the glow of television behind the closed curtains.

'Your parents still live there?'

'Yeh, probably stuck in front of the box at this stage.' He pictured their startled faces if he were to walk in the door with Margaret beside him. Some day, maybe. But not just yet. There was one big hurdle to get over first.

'Mick hasn't stopped talking about you since he met you.' Her smile didn't quite meet her eyes, he thought. She didn't offer to shake Margaret's hand.

Oh Fran! he pleaded silently. Can't you do better than that? In an attempt to lighten the atmosphere, he turned towards the baby, who sat in his high chair in his best pair of dungarees, his hair brushed into a shining coif above an unnaturally clean face. 'Well, Sean, what do you think of your new granny? Isn't she a smasher?'

'Go easy,' Fran warned from behind them. 'He'll make strange.'

'No, he won't,' Mick said. He urged Margaret forward. 'I want you two to get to know each other.'

'Hello, Sean.' Margaret smiled at him. But the baby looked at her doubtfully, glancing at Mick for reassurance. His bottom lip began to quiver.

'It's okay,' Mick said soothingly. He saw Sean hesitate, half-reassured. But just then Fran rushed over to throw a protective arm around his shoulders.

'It's all right, love,' she crooned. 'No one's going to hurt you.' A response that seemed to confirm the baby's fears. He turned bright red, tears spilled from his eyes and he began to protest loudly. Mick saw Margaret look stricken for a moment. She took a step backwards before looking irresolutely around her for somewhere to sit.

'It's nothing personal,' he whispered as he guided her towards the sofa. 'Just a stage he's going through.'

At the same time, Fran cried, 'I don't know what's got into him. He never makes strange with the other – . I mean with anyone.' She floundered suddenly and began making a big production of wiping away Sean's tears, crooning over him as she loosened the straps of the chair.

Nice one, Fran. He looked daggers at her. 'I think we could all do with a drink. Vodka for you, Margaret?'

'Thank you.' She had recovered her composure. She examined Sean cautiously from a distance. 'He's a beautiful baby. Reminds me a bit of my father.'

'He looks like you.' Fran's voice was grudging. 'I often wondered who he took after.' There was something truculent about the laugh she gave as she gathered the baby into her arms. 'Now I know.'

'Do you really think so?' Margaret's face lit up. But Mick glared at Fran. He picked up the baby bag and thrust it at her. 'Not in here,' he hissed. 'Change him in the bedroom.'

'It's quite all right,' Margaret said politely. 'I've changed nappies in my time. Don't mind me.'

'In that case – ' Fran was beginning. She tried to avoid Mick's eye but he looked at her firmly.

'Excuse us for a moment.' He plonked Margaret's drink down on the pock-marked coffee table near her. 'Come on, Fran. I'll give you a hand with Sean.'

'You could be a bit nicer to her,' he hissed. 'You never even thanked her for the flowers and the chocolate. And all the stuff she brought Sean.'

'Give me a chance.' Bright colour burned in Fran's cheeks as she crammed the baby's chubby feet into the legs of his sleeping suit. 'Anyway, she brought far too much. Who does she think she is? The Vincent de Paul?'

'What do you think of the wine?' he asked eagerly.

'It's just right.' She gave an appreciative nod. 'I couldn't have chosen better myself. You're a quick learner, Michael.'

He grinned back at her and found himself beginning to relax. 'I had a good teacher.'

The meal was going quite well, he told himself. Fran had really taken trouble with it. Although it was a good thing he had managed to persuade her to take out the meat before she cremated it. The vegetables were okay too. And the trifle looked great. But where she had really scored was in the laying of the table. He glanced appreciatively at the bright pottery, the gleaming glassware and cutlery they'd been given as wedding presents. The white table cloth and red napkins conjured up thoughts of Christmas. As did the long red candles which they'd lit once Sean was safely in bed.

The shadowy room outside the circle of the candles

seemed vague and mysterious. Inside the circle, the light glanced off Margaret's cheekbones and slender throat. It was true what they said about women looking even more beautiful by candlelight, he thought. Watching her, he was caught up in a spell of pure happiness.

'I don't know why people make such a fuss over wine.' He saw Fran wrinkle her nose over the long-stemmed glass. 'Give me a nice glass of Coke any day.'

Like a bubble bursting in mid-air, the spell was broken.

'It's an acquired taste,' he said shortly.

Fran looked unimpressed. 'An expensive taste, if you ask me.'

There was an awkward pause. He rushed to fill it.

'Margaret, is the horseradish okay?' When he picked up the jar, he wished that one of them had thought of transferring its contents to a sauce boat. 'I wasn't sure which brand to – '

'It's fine, darling.' She gave him a reassuring smile. 'It really brings out the flavour of the beef.' She turned to Fran. 'Don't you agree?'

'Oh, definitely,' the younger woman said. She plastered a piece of meat with the creamy sauce and bit into it defiantly. 'We have it all the time.' Her eyes challenged Mick's. 'Isn't that right, *darling*?'

His heart sank. They weren't out of the woods yet. As he poured more wine into the tall glasses he wondered what other pitfalls lay ahead.

'Say what you like about Sandra but she's a great mother to that little boy.' He knew Fran seldom discussed her sister in company but tonight she couldn't seem to keep off the subject. Margaret had heard all about Jason: what a lovable child he was, how his grandparents doted on him, what his teacher said about him at school. 'Of course, it's very hard for him without a father. Poor little fella. Your heart would bleed for him sometimes.'

What had got into her? Was she doing it on purpose to embarrass him? Or had the wine gone to her head? He noticed that she had accepted a second glass despite her declared preference for Coke. He tried to signal to her with his eyes but when she ignored him he said quickly, 'Margaret doesn't want to hear all this.'

'But then again, maybe he's better off the way things are,' Fran continued as if he hadn't spoken. 'That fella of Sandra's was no good, anyway. She's doing a grand job on her own.'

Was there no way of shutting her up? If they'd had a separate kitchen he might have been able to lure her out on some pretext but the layout of the living room defeated him. To retreat behind the kitchen counter and have a whispered conversation smacked of too many television sitcoms and would only compound the embarrassment. He glanced helplessly at Margaret, who had been sitting quietly listening. She took one look at his face and cut in smoothly.

'I agree, Fran. It's terribly important to give your children a good start in life. Michael and I were talking about that the other day.'

'Oh?' Fran glanced at her suspiciously.

'Yes.' Margaret's voice was eager. 'Has he said anything to you about going to university?'

'*University?*' Fran's jaw dropped. She threw a disbelieving look at Mick.

'There's nothing definite, Fran.'

'He'd have to get his Leaving first, of course. But that wouldn't be too difficult for him. There are places you can go to. It wouldn't take him long to catch up.'

'I could do it, Fran. I could get the points.'

'And, once he has his degree – '

'A *degree?*' Fran found her voice at last. 'What in the name of God does Mick want with a degree?'

The other woman looked taken aback. 'Well, he – '

'He already has a trade.' Her voice spelled it out definitively. 'He's a painter. He's getting on great in the job. Next in line for foreman.' Her tawny eyes locked briefly with Margaret's blue ones in the candlelight. 'He doesn't need a degree.'

'Maybe I don't want to spend the rest of my life as a painter,' Mick burst in. 'Has that ever occurred to you? Listen, Fran, if I had a degree I could get a better job.'

'Like what?' Her eyes challenged him.

'I don't know.' The possibilities were endless. Until tonight he hadn't dared seriously consider them. 'Teach, maybe. Work in an office. *Anything!*'

'Anything,' Margaret echoed. 'He could do anything.'

'And would you mind telling me – ' Fran's lips tightened. 'Just what are we going to live on while you're doing all this?' The challenge in her eyes grew. 'I suppose you have all that worked out as well?'

'Well, no.' His face fell. 'We haven't had time to look into it. There are grants,' he said lamely.

'Fat lot you know about it.' Her voice was scathing. 'From what I've heard, one person couldn't manage on the miserable pittance they give you, never mind support a wife and child. And nobody gives you a grant to do the Leaving,' she added with what sounded like triumph. 'You can be looking into it till the cows come home but that's not going to change.'

'I might be able to help there,' Margaret put in quietly. 'I have money of my own.'

Fran didn't give any sign that she had heard. Noticing that they had finished eating, she got up and began collecting the dishes from the table. Her face was set grimly while she scraped food from the plates, piling them on top of each other in a kind of frenzy, as if working against the clock. Watching her, Mick felt an old, familiar sense of despair.

He might have known she'd never agree to it. 'Calm down, Fran. Nothing's been decided yet. Sit down. Have another glass of wine.'

No answer. Just the clatter of cutlery. And the set of Fran's shoulders, more eloquent than words, as she brought the stuff over to the sink.

'Fran – '

'I think it's time I went.' Margaret patted his hand and stood up. 'I've had a lovely time but it's getting late.' She smiled at him reassuringly. 'I'll find my own way home.'

A lovely time indeed! It would have been if Fran hadn't gone and ruined it. He jumped to his feet. 'I'll come with you, make sure you get back safely.'

He saw Fran's head snap around. She gazed at him open-mouthed. But he didn't care what she thought. All he knew was that he had to get out of the flat and away from her.

He saw Margaret hesitate and glance doubtfully at Fran. 'Well, as long as you're sure?'

He met her gaze firmly.

'I'm sure.'

In their absence the fire had burned low in the grate but it only took him a few minutes to coax it back to life. As he watched the flames darting up the chimney, he heard the chink of glasses, and got to his feet.

'Brandy?' He smiled as he took it from her. 'I'll have to watch this. Do you remember the night I drank too much and fell asleep on you?'

The corners of her mouth twitched. 'How could I forget?' She raised her own glass, drank a generous mouthful and gave a sigh of relief. 'I needed that!'

He looked at her anxiously. 'Was it awful for you?' He felt immediately contrite. 'God, I'm sorry – but I wanted to – . Look, I should never have put you through tonight.'

'No, it was my fault,' Margaret said. 'I should never have mentioned the possibility of your going to university. Not the first time I met her. I should have waited.'

'Wouldn't have made any difference.' He felt bitter suddenly. 'Fran has never understood my dreams. Not like you.'

'Still – I can't help feeling responsible.'

'Why should you blame yourself?' He looked at her eagerly. 'You've done nothing wrong. The way I see it, you're the only one who has ever understood. There was a teacher once – but that was a few years ago. And he didn't really care, not the way you do.'

'Yes. I care,' Margaret said quietly. 'Probably more than you'll ever know. But I'm sure Fran does too.'

He shook his head and laughed shortly. 'Fran doesn't care about anything except getting her own way. That's all she's ever wanted.' He took a swallow of brandy and felt it warm its way down to his stomach. 'You saw how she was tonight.'

'Yes.' Her face was troubled. 'Look, Michael, you have to see it from her point of view. She probably feels a bit threatened. It would be a big change for her as well as for you. But once she realises what a great opportunity –'

'There's no point in talking about it,' he said wearily. 'I've told you, Fran isn't interested in opportunities for me, never has been.'

'But Michael –'

'No, it's true. I suppose I always knew this, deep down. Tonight just brought it home to me.' He sighed to himself and gazed unseeingly into the fire. 'She's never understood me. Not the way you do.'

'She's young.' Margaret's voice was gentle. 'In time, she'll –'

'I don't think time has anything to do with it.'

'But I think it has. After all, if she loves you–'

'But does she?' His bitterness grew. 'And do I love her? I just don't know any more. Oh, Margaret! It's all such a mess.' His voice caught suddenly. 'I don't think I ever should have married her. I realised that tonight when I saw you together.' He felt his eyes fill with tears and stared at her in anguish. 'Why couldn't I have met someone like you?'

Margaret gave a rueful smile. 'We've neither of us had much luck with our partners, have we? But it's too late now to –'

'No, it's not!' He left his seat, knelt down beside her chair and took her hand between his. 'It doesn't have to be.' He gazed at her earnestly. 'Not for us.'

'For *us*?' He saw the shock in her eyes, the dawning realisation. She shook her head and looked down at the floor. But she didn't take her hand away.

Emboldened by this, he plunged on. 'You're the most beautiful, the most wonderful woman I've ever met. All my life I've wanted to meet someone like you – '

'No, Michael, don't. Don't say any more. *Please.*'

Something about the way she said it sent a tremor through his body. He stared at her in growing excitement. 'You feel the same way? Oh, Margaret!'

'No.' She whispered it so quietly he could barely hear it. 'No.'

'You do. I know you do.'

He saw her shake her head dumbly. 'Why won't you look at me, then?' he demanded. 'Go on, tell me. Say it to my face. I'll go away and never bother you again if you can look me in the eye and tell me you don't feel the way I do.'

He held his breath and waited, her hand still clasped between his, his eyes searching her averted profile. Just as he was about to despair he heard her give a little sigh and saw her shoulders slump in defeat. His heart gave a leap of triumph.

'You can't say it, can you?'

'No.' Again he saw that little shudder of defeat. 'God help me but I can't.'

'Oh, Margaret!' His arms reached out for her. 'Margaret, my love.'

'No, Michael.' She tried to push him away. 'This is wrong. We can't! We mustn't!' He saw the distress on her face. 'I should never have said – '

'Don't be upset.' He stroked her face with a gentle finger. 'It's okay. I promise you; it's going to be okay.'

'But how can it?' She stared at him, distraught. 'We have no right to feel this way about each other.'

'I don't care what's right or wrong. I only know how I feel. But – ' An idea began forming in his mind. 'But – I don't think it *is* wrong.'

'Oh, *Michael!*' Her voice was despairing. 'Of course it is.'

'No, hear me out,' he said quickly as the idea began to take root. 'You only say that because you think we're related. But supposing we're not? Supposing it was all a mistake?'

'A mistake?' Her face showed her bewilderment. 'But how – ?'

'Look at it this way,' Mick said earnestly. 'I was never formally adopted. And there are no proper records. We only have the word of this old nun who remembers my Ma working in the convent kitchen.'

'Only her word for it?' Margaret looked puzzled. 'But they had my address. They got a social worker to contact me. They must have had some records.'

'Well, yes,' he conceded. 'I'm not saying they hadn't. But they weren't proper ones, that's what the social worker said. It was before they passed the Adoption Act and the whole thing operated under a cloak of secrecy. The right hand didn't know what the left hand was doing, was the way she put it. Who knows but there could have been several babies born around the same time and given to the convent to dispose of. Maybe your child went to someone else and the names got mixed up, either accidentally or on purpose. People wanted to cover their tracks, hide identities. That priest your mother knew; he'd have done anything to protect her name. Could you believe anything he said? And the nuns were probably just as bad.'

'But what makes you think it happened in your case?'

'Because it all adds up. It makes sense. Look,' he said urgently, 'do you really think if you were my mother I'd feel this way about you? Do you really think I'd want to – ? That you'd want to – ?'

'Well, no – '

'Come on, Margaret, you know we wouldn't.'

'Maybe not.' Although she was wavering she didn't seem wholly convinced. 'But – you have my father's hands. Fran said that Sean looks like me.'

'Because you both have blue eyes and blonde hair?' He gave a sceptical smile. 'And how long has your father been dead? Twelve, thirteen years, is it? How can you even remember what his hands looked like? Come on, Margaret, you see these things because you want to see them. They're in your imagination. They're not real. Not the way our feelings for each other are real.' He watched her anxiously. 'It makes sense to you too, doesn't it.'

'In a way it does,' she admitted. 'But when we first met we did acknowledge each other as mother and son.'

'Again, only because we wanted to believe it. But you have to admit there was never that kind of bond between us, not like the one I have with my Ma.' He looked at her candidly. 'There's a huge difference in the way we feel about each other.'

'Yes.' The look she gave him was equally direct. 'A huge difference.'

'Oh, Margaret!' He felt a sense of mounting excitement. 'Darling!'

'Wait.' She pushed his eager hands away. 'Even if you are right about the adoption, and we don't know that you are, there are other things to consider.'

'It's the most important thing, as far as I'm concerned. Look, I know there's Fran and there's Vincent. And it's all a mess. But I don't want to think about that now.'

'No,' she agreed. 'I don't either. But it's not just them. It's – ' She bit her lip and looked down. 'Well it's the age difference – '

'What about it?'

'A man your age wouldn't want – '

'Who told you that? Oh, Margaret, is that all that's bothering you?' He laughed with relief. 'As if age could make any difference. Not that you even look it. Have you any idea how beautiful you are? Have you any idea how much I want you?' His voice grew fervent. 'I've never wanted anyone so much in my whole life.'

Their eyes met. He saw her smile. This time when his hands sought her she didn't push him away.

He undressed her tenderly in the firelight, urging her gently to the floor to lie on a fleecy rug while he swiftly shed his own clothes. Then, naked, he knelt beside her and examined her body with awe.

'You're even more beautiful than I imagined.' He felt his own body tremble as he caressed her small, firm breasts, explored the soft terrain of her stomach, his hands passing lightly over the pale gold fuzz at its base and down the length of her slender limbs. 'Oh God!' He kissed her eyelids, her mouth, her throat, felt her passion mounting along with his. Heard her moan as her nipples sprang to life under his lips, felt her writhe beneath him as he moved downward, his tongue seeking out and probing her most secret places. She was the loveliest, the most –

'No! Stop!' Her body suddenly went still. He felt her pull away from him. 'No, Michael, we mustn't go any further!'

'But why not?' he gasped. 'Oh, God, Margaret – !'

'It's too dangerous. I stopped taking the pill when I left Vincent. I'm sorry, darling.' She looked at him questioningly. 'Unless you – ?'

'No, I never dreamed – I never expected I'd be – oh, God!' He collapsed against her, his disappointment intense.

'I'm really sorry.' She held him until he had got his breath back, then pushed him away gently, reluctantly. 'Put your clothes on, darling, and go home. Fran will be wondering what's keeping you.'

'But I want to stay the night with you. Please, Margaret. I won't do anything, I promise. I just want to lie beside you and hold you. Please let me stay.'

'No, I can't. Be sensible, dearest. The last thing we want is for your wife to suspect anything. You must go home and behave as if nothing had happened.'

'I don't know if I can.'

'You must. For both our sakes.' She turned away and began reaching for her clothes.

'Wait!' he pleaded. 'Let me look at you one more time.'

'No.' She shook her head firmly. 'The way you are at the moment it wouldn't be wise. Oh, darling,' her voice grew gentle, 'I'm sorry we couldn't have – but maybe it's for the best. Maybe we need to give ourselves time. Not do anything we might later regret.'

'Regret?' He looked at her anxiously. 'You're not sorry, are you? That we – ?'

'No, of course not.' Her smile reassured him. 'But this has all happened so quickly. Tomorrow we might feel differently.'

'No.' Mick shook his head. His voice was full of conviction. 'If it was a million tomorrows I'd never feel differently about you.'

He knew by the sound of her breathing that Fran was asleep when he tiptoed into the darkened bedroom. He slid in beside her, careful not to disturb her, and lay staring into the darkness, too excited to sleep. His mind teemed with images of Margaret and himself in the firelight, his body burned and tingled with the memory of what they had done together. He felt no guilt as he thought about it, only a great sense of wonder and a longing to be back at her side.

Tomorrow, he told himself. He would see her tomorrow.

Margaret woke at seven, while it was still dark, with the sour taste of last night's brandy in her mouth. After he had left she'd had another drink to help her face the reproaches of the night but, as it turned out, she had fallen asleep the moment her head had hit the pillow. She smiled to herself at the irony of it. Six hours of dreamless sleep. The best night she'd had in years. After what had happened she should have been tossing and turning all night blaming herself over and over in an orgy of self-recrimination.

Her smile vanished as she recalled the events of the night before. Had they really done those things together? Had she really let Michael make love to her? Maybe it had all been a dream? If she closed her eyes, it might go away. But that only made things worse. Lying there in the darkness, her body began remembering his caresses, felt again the touch of his lips, his body against hers. And, remembering, began to shudder with guilty delight.

This was madness, she told herself under the shower, soaping herself furiously as if she could wash away the memory of his hands. Nothing could come of their relationship. A young man, half her age? A young married man, at that? With a child? A young man who could be her –

No, no, they had sorted that out, hadn't they.

But had they?

Her mind shied away from the implications.

But it was still madness. How could she have done it? How could she have been so foolish? Look, nothing happened. Not much, anyway. Thank God, she had been able to stop him just in time. As the hot water sprayed over her body she comforted herself with that thought. There was still time to draw back. Tonight when he came to see her she would tell him. She would have to be strong for both their sakes.

As she was drying herself she heard a noise. Her heart missed a beat. There was someone in the flat. She pulled on a robe and went out to investigate.

'It's only me.' He was hanging his jacket in the tiny hallway, raindrops glistening in his hair. 'I hope I didn't startle you.'

'A bit.' Was it fright or excitement that made her heart race faster? 'There's nothing wrong, is there?'

'I couldn't wait till tonight. I rang in sick.'

'But Fran? Does she – ?'

'She thinks I'm at work.' He smiled at her like a guilty child. 'You don't mind.'

Mind? Something melted inside her at the sight of his smile. She touched his face, felt the iciness of the winter morning against her hand. 'I'm glad you came.'

'I am too.' His arms went around her. 'You smell wonderful.'

She sighed. Deep down she knew that the decision had already been made. Knew that she had always known it. But she had to ask something first.

'That nun you told me about, the one who remembered? Was she really that old?'

'In her dotage,' he murmured, his words half-muffled by her hair. 'I'd be surprised if she remembered what happened last week, never mind twenty-two years ago.'

Her sense of inevitability grew. 'In that case,' she said as she took his hand and led him towards the bedroom, 'don't you think we should finish what we started last night?'

'Was it as good for you?' he whispered.

'It was wonderful.' Her limbs were drowsy, lethargic. She felt sated with pleasure. 'How did someone so young learn to be such a great lover?'

'I had some good teachers.' In the light that was beginning to seep around the edges of the heavy curtains she saw him smile. 'You're pretty wonderful yourself.'

'This is time out,' he said. 'Just you and me together.' He grinned at her as he took the steaming coffee mug. 'We have the whole day.'

Time out? Borrowed time? It was bliss sitting there beside him, feeling the warmth of his body against hers, She buried her nose in the fragrance of her own cup and sipped gratefully. But doubt tugged at her. 'Your wife, won't she – ?'

'Fran never rings me at work. It's too much trouble. I could be anywhere. And anyway, she wouldn't please the old biddy downstairs by asking to use the phone. We're quite safe.'

She envied him his youthful confidence and longed to share it. 'Did she say anything about last night?'

'Not really. It was a bit of a rush this morning. I was awake half the night thinking about you. When I finally got to sleep I didn't hear the alarm. Fran had to wake me. There wasn't time to talk about anything but I got the impression the whole business of university is still bugging her.'

'She'll come round.' She tried to put conviction into her voice.

'Maybe. Maybe not. But frankly, at this moment, I couldn't care less.'

'But we're going to have to talk about it sometime,' Margaret said as she finished her coffee.

'Sometime, but not now. We'll talk later, sort things out. Right now – ' he put his own mug down on the bedside locker and turned to her, ' – all I'm interested in is making love to you again.' He stroked her naked shoulder. 'Would you like that?'

'Yes, oh yes!' She felt her body yielding to his. 'My darling, I never want you to stop.'

It was madness. Yes, it was wonderful; it was awe-inspiring, the passion they had for each other. But still madness. How could they hope to have a future together? Touching his sleeping features with gentle fingers, she noticed that he slept with the unconscious grace of a young animal, noiseless and utterly relaxed. What a beautiful body he had! Although she marvelled at the sight, it evoked deep wells of sadness in her. How could she expect him to stay with her always? To love her for ever? Even though he had promised this, over and over, before drifting off to sleep, she was filled with a premonition of loss.

'Hello.' He opened his eyes and smiled up at her. 'What time is it?'

'Must be about four. It's getting dark again.' She smiled back but her heart was heavy. 'You'll have to go soon.'

'Afraid so. I've to meet a mate from work. He'll have my wages for me.'

Anxiety clutched at her. 'You didn't tell him?'

'About us? Of course not. But Donie's a decent skin. We can trust him.'

'All the same – '

'Don't worry.' He sat up, gathered her close to him and nuzzled her ear. 'Wish I didn't have to go. Wish I could stay with you always.'

'It's not possible.' Her despair grew.

'Maybe it is. Maybe we can sort something out.'

'But – how?'

'I could leave Fran.'

A wild hope flared up, only to die instantly. 'Break up your marriage? No, Michael. Don't even think of it.'

'Why not? I don't love her any more. I love you.'

'You make it sound so simple. But it's not. Have you thought of all the people we'd be hurting. Not just Fran. Your parents – '

'I don't care about them,' he cried. 'You're the one I – '

'And your child? Have you forgotten him?'

She felt his body grow still.

'You could never leave Sean,' she said. When he didn't answer she touched his face and found that he was weeping silently. She drew him to her gently, stroking the back of his head, murmuring words of comfort.

'Margaret!' His face was wet against her breast. 'What are we going to do?

'Hush, my darling.' She kissed away his tears. 'Listen to me and I'll tell you.'

PART SEVEN

'The woman wants her sitting room done before Christmas, Fran.' Although he was telling the truth Mick couldn't help feeling guilty. Yet, at the same time, he was elated. His mind was still teeming with images of yesterday. He struggled not to let his feelings show in his voice. 'I have to do it today.'

'But today's Mammy's birthday. You've known for ages that it was the Saturday before Christmas.' Fran's voice was aggrieved. 'If you'd done the job when you said you would you could have come with us today.'

He hid his relief at escaping a Hennessy gathering. 'Sorry, love.' Although he didn't want to do it, guilt made him offer, 'I can pick you up afterwards if you like. Margaret lent me her car.'

He was surprised to see her shake her head. 'Don't bother. Denis is calling for me and Sean. He'll run us back afterwards.'

'Well, if you're sure?' An idea occurred to him. If he didn't have to collect them he might have time to call over to the Square after he'd finished the job.

To his dismay, Fran said, 'We won't be late. They have people coming for drinks after the meal but I said I wouldn't stay. Sean gets cranky if it gets past his bedtime.' As if she knew what was going through his mind, she gave him an accusing look. 'You will be here when we get home?'

He thought of what Margaret had said to him. *Act*

normally, Michael. Don't give her any reason to suspect. His eyes slid away from Fran's. 'Where else would I – ?'

'Ah, come on, Mick.' Her tone was acerbic. 'You know the answer to that one.'

He ignored the comment and turned away. As he was going out the door she called him back.

'About Christmas Day, Mick – ?'

God! He'd forgotten all about Christmas! 'What about it?' he asked gruffly.

'You're not still thinking of having her here, are you?' He saw the light of battle in her eyes. Again he remembered what Margaret had said.

'Look,' he sighed, 'why don't we talk about this tonight?'

'Just make sure you're here.' Fran's voice was abrupt.

'I will, I will.' Although his gaze was bland when he met her eye, the guilt hadn't gone away.

Just how long would it be, he wondered, before she found out the truth?

We must behave as if nothing had happened. No one must ever know. Had she really said that? Were they back to secrecy again? Lies? Deception?

It was the story of her life, Margaret told herself despairingly. For years she had carried her secret, denying it even to herself. And now she had another one. She felt bitter suddenly. What malign fairy had presided at her birth? Who had decreed that she should live a life of subterfuge, terrified of discovery? Would she ever live a normal life again?

What am I doing here? She gazed around the tiny kitchen and a wave of homesickness washed over her. Suddenly she was overwhelmed by a longing for her house and all her familiar possessions. Why didn't she just go back, say it was all a mistake and take up the threads of her life again? But the idea died as swiftly as it had been born. Go back to Vincent? How could she even contemplate such a thing? True, she had tolerated the wasteland of their marriage for years, had even become resigned to it, but that was before she had met Michael and discovered another mind and heart that beat in time to hers.

And now it was no longer just a question of heart and mind. Now their bodies were involved too. She looked back on the events of yesterday with a kind of wonder, running her fingers over her own body with remembered delight. *He touched me there. And there.* Now that she had discovered the joy of being with Michael, of sharing herself with him, of knowing his love, she could never go back to Vincent, to his impatient ways, his greedy caresses. Of that she was certain. But what wasn't so certain was the way ahead.

Could she face a life of deception, of stolen meetings, their relationship unacknowledged? Yesterday when she had held him weeping in her arms she had assured him she could. She had felt the stronger of the two, dried his tears, made plans for the future. She would get an apartment of her own, find a job, wait for him to come to her whenever he could. Had sent him away comforted, convinced that she had the solution to their problems. Had even managed to convince herself. But that had been yesterday. Today she was not so sure.

But what was the alternative? Come clean about their love for each other? Which was what he had wanted at the start.

I'm not ashamed, he had said. Why should you be? But he was young, idealistic, had no idea of the ways of the world. Seemed to have no concept of the scandal it would cause if the truth were known, the hurt to their families, the tongue-wagging, the innuendo. She shuddered to think of what people would say about her, the judgements that would be made.

But if it meant that they could be together, wouldn't it be worth it? What did it matter what people thought? Why let other people's opinions rule your behaviour? Wasn't that what had caused all the trouble in her life up to now? Surely it was time to break away from all that and be brave? Yes, people would talk. But it would be a nine days' wonder. Marriage breakdown was getting so common nowadays they would soon have someone else to talk about. And think of the relief of having everything out in the open at last. No more deception.

No more deception? What about self-deception?

The problem which her mind had been avoiding ever since the night Michael had told her his feelings refused to be denied any longer. Unclouded by the nearness of his body, the demands of her own desire, it presented itself now with merciless clarity.

No excuses. No confusing the issue with talk of forgetful old nuns, slipshod records, elaborate cover ups.

The truth, Margaret? What was the truth?

In her mind she remembered the certainty in the voice on the phone that day in early summer and heard the words that had hammered into her head. *Does the twentieth of November mean anything to you?*

Oh God! She was suddenly convulsed with horror. Oh God! What have I done?

'Tim isn't here,' a woman's voice said.

His housekeeper? She didn't sound like one. Did priests have housekeepers nowadays? 'He's at a seminar; he'll be away all day. Do you want to leave a message?'

Yes, Margaret did. Could he please ring back? It didn't matter how late.

As she got off the phone, she tried to talk down her fears. She was probably panicking over nothing. Michael was right. They would never have been attracted to each other in the first place if the relationship had been what they originally thought it was. It just wouldn't have happened. But it was better to make sure. She wasn't looking forward to talking to Father Tim again but he was the obvious person to ask. If anyone could set her mind at rest, he was the one. But supposing he couldn't? No, her mind shied away from the unthinkable. Father Tim will sort it out, she told herself.

And if he couldn't?

Why hadn't she waited? Her thoughts reproached her savagely. Why hadn't she made sure before she had gone to bed with him? They could have waited. Why? Oh, why hadn't they waited? She felt breathless suddenly. Her heart began to speed faster as if she had been running. Panic jostled her so that she couldn't keep still, pacing the room in an agony of uncertainty, fingers twisting and tearing at each other, her frightened thoughts threatening to break loose and gallop down the slope to – .

No! No! Stop! This is madness!

With a terrible effort of will she wrenched her thoughts back from the abyss. Pressing her hand against her chest to quieten its agitation, she forced herself to sit down, to light a cigarette with trembling fingers. It would be evening before the priest rang back. Maybe she should go out, go for a walk, look at the shops? As she was pondering this she heard her doorbell ring. Michael? Her heart leaped. No, he had his own key. Who then? The bell gave another peal. Eager to escape her thoughts, she went to the street door. And immediately repented of her action. Vincent, dressed in casual weekend gear, stood on the doorstep, his finger still on the bell push.

'You took long enough to answer the door,' he grumbled. 'It's freezing out here!'

Wishing she had the courage to slam the door in his face, she invited him in with a sinking heart.

'All set, Fran?' Her brother Denis grinned cheerfully at her. 'I've put the buggy in the boot. Give us the chiseller.' Taking Sean from her, he led the way to the car with his short-legged, confident swagger, every inch the salesman in his double-breasted suit. As he spun the four-year-old Fiesta swiftly out of its parking place he darted an envious glance at the silver BMW parked in front of it. 'Whoever owns that isn't short of a bob or two. I always said you married the wrong fella, Fran.'

'You're just jealous of Mick because he's taller than you.' They were back in childhood again. She was the younger of the two, endlessly on the defensive.

'You must be joking,' Denis chortled. But his sharp features had tightened. He gave her a quick, sideways grin. 'Mick still riding that clapped-out old Honda?'

'You think you're awful smart, don't you?' She hated the way he always managed to get under her skin. 'Well, you don't know everything.'

'No?' His grin widened as he took up the challenge. 'Go on, then, tell us. Surprise me.'

Fran hesitated. This wasn't just a childhood game, there was more at stake than that. But she just *had* to do something to wipe that superior smile off his face. She shifted Sean to a more comfortable position in her lap and said loftily, 'What would you say if I told you that Mick left that car there?'

'I'd say, "Sean, my boy, you're going to be visiting your Daddy in Mountjoy for the next coupla years." But that fella hasn't it in him to nick a bicycle, let alone a car.' He chuckled complacently. 'Go on, Fran, pull the other one.'

Fran's face went red. She turned to glare at her tormentor. 'He didn't steal it, ya eejit. It belongs to his mother.'

'His *mother*?' Denis was laughing openly now. 'Jaysus, now I've heard everything. Come on, willya! You don't expect me to believe *that*?'

Fran's heart sank. Who was the eejit now? Why hadn't she the wit to keep her mouth shut?

'Mick adopted?' Maisie Hennessy frowned as she painted her toenails, one foot propped up against the kitchen table, little pieces of cotton wool separating each toe. 'I don't believe it!'

'Yep.' Denis had a broad grin on his face. 'I always knew he was a bit of a bastard. Jaysus, Ma, I hope you don't expect us to eat our tea offa this.' He straightened a bottle of nail varnish which was threatening to topple over the table edge and flicked his finger at a stray tuft of cotton wool. 'Do you want us to get foot-and-mouth disease?'

'Cheeky devil.' Maisie was unperturbed. 'You'll be lucky to get anything.' She turned to glance accusingly at Fran. 'Why did you never tell us about Mick?'

'Because I didn't want people like Denis making jokes about it, that's why.'

'You've got very secretive.' Her mother's voice was aggrieved as she aimed a blob of silver at her little toe. 'You never used to be like that.'

'I'm not secretive,' Fran protested hotly. She looked with dislike at her brother, who was smiling to himself, obviously delighted at the effect his news was having. 'I know who the bastard is,' she muttered. 'And it isn't Mick.'

'Watch out for skin and hair,' Denis chuckled. 'Well, I'll leave you girls to fight it out.' He swaggered towards the kitchen door. 'Enjoy your birthday, Ma. I'll be back later with the ball and chain.'

'Can't wait to get home and tell that gabby wife of his,' Fran said bitterly. 'It'll be all over the country by tomorrow.'

'You're worse to pay any attention to him.' Maisie gingerly slid her varnished toes into a pair of embroidered mules and began working on her fingernails. 'There's no harm in that fella. He's like myself. His bark is worse than his bite.'

'Why is he always having a go at me?'

'He's just jealous. He's never forgiven you for taking his place as baby of the family.' She grinned wickedly at her daughter. 'Poor fella. I don't think he'll ever get over the shock of it.'

In spite of the anxiety that had been gnawing at her since she had got out of bed that morning, Fran couldn't help laughing. Trust Mammy to see the funny side of it. She knew that Mick often found her mother's sense of humour very hard to take and sometimes she went a bit over the top in poking fun at other people but there were times, like now, when it had a comforting effect. Nothing could be too wrong with the world as long as you were still able to laugh at it.

'Tell us, Fran, what's this woman like? What's-her-name, Margaret?' Maisie seemed occupied with waving her fingernails around in the air to dry them but her slightly prominent, blue eyes showed a shrewd interest. 'Is it true she's loaded, like Denis said? Fancy car? The works?'

'Yes.' It came out as a kind of strangled yelp. To her dismay, Fran felt her lips tremble, her eyes fill with tears. 'Oh, Mammy,' she wailed. 'He wants her to have Christmas with us.'

'With you?' Her mother stiffened, stopped waving her hand around and looked sharply at Fran. 'But you're coming to us this year. It's *our* turn to have you. You went to the other crowd last year.' She glanced over at Sean, who was sitting, tugging impatiently at the harness of the baby buggy to which he had been confined since they had first arrived in the house. 'And what about this little fella?' He started to whimper and she patted him soothingly. 'I can't wait to see his face when he sees the presents we've got him. *Of course* you're coming to *us*. Has Mick lost the run of himself, or what?' She stared in amazement at her daughter. 'Fran, love, are you cryin'?'

'No.' When she saw Sean look at her in alarm she tried to hold back the tears but, despite her efforts, they began to spurt from her eyes and down her cheeks. 'Oh, Mammy, I don't know what to do,' she sobbed.

Just then the kitchen door opened and Sandra, wearing an orange-coloured fake-fur jacket, erupted into the room, bringing a blast of wintry air with her. 'I had to go to three places to get the profiteroles,' she grumbled, slamming a couple of bulging carrier bags down on the table. 'And I'm – what's the matter with her?' she demanded, staring at Fran in amazement.

'God only knows.' Maisie looked distractedly from the weeping Fran to the whimpering baby in the buggy and then back to Sandra. 'I haven't the God's honest clue.' Her eyes narrowed as they rested on her elder daughter. 'Tell us, did *you* know Mick was adopted?'

'Adopted?' Sandra raised her eyebrows. 'Well, well, well! No I didn't, actually.' She gave a knowing smile. 'But I can tell you something else he's been up to.'

'Now, don't *you* start,' her mother said warningly. 'You're too fond of stirring things up.'

'I'm not the one stirring things up.' Sandra's smile grew more knowing. 'It doesn't matter to me if you don't want to hear.'

At the sight of that smile, a pain began to circle Fran's heart. She stopped crying and looked at her sister. 'Listen, you. If you have something to say, say it.'

'Okay then.' With maddening slowness Sandra removed her garish jacket, patted the pile lovingly before slinging it over the back of a chair, smoothed her leather mini with a defiant wriggle of her narrow hips and stood, surveying her audience with that same knowing smile. They stared back at her in silence. Even Sean, as if he realised the importance of the occasion, had stopped whimpering and was watching her with big, solemn eyes. Satisfied that she had their full attention, Sandra dropped her voice conspiratorially.

'Just listen to *this*.'

It was his *mother*, I keep telling you.' Fran's voice was despairing. Although the tears had dried on her cheeks, the pain still clutched her heart. 'There's nothing more to it than that.'

'That's what *you* think.' Her sister's eyes were bright with malice. 'Look, I'm only telling you what I saw. Like lovers they were.'

'Maybe it was some other woman.' Maisie's voice was unusually diffident. She rocked Sean on her knee as if drawing comfort from the baby's sturdy body. 'Some girl he met – ?'

'Maybe,' Sandra shrugged. 'How many tall, good-looking blondes does he know, for fuck's sake? This one had money written all over her.'

'I don't believe it!' Her mother groaned, burying her face in the baby's tousled curls and pulling him close to her chest. 'I don't want to listen to this.'

'And I don't either,' Fran cried furiously. 'You're only trying to cause trouble. You were always jealous of Mick and me.'

'Jealous? Huh!' Sandra's lip curled. 'I don't *need* to be jealous. I've got a – ' She stopped abruptly. 'Oh, forget it.'

'Got what?' Fran shot back at her. 'A nasty, vicious tongue, that's what you've got. You couldn't get a husband so you're making up stories about mine.'

'You poor little fucker.' An odd look crossed Sandra's face.

'I know you and me never got on. But you're my little sister. And I wouldn't wish this on my worst enemy. God! Men are such bastards! *I* ought to know. But I never thought it would happen to you.'

Fran stared at her in consternation. The sympathy in Sandra's voice was much more alarming than her malice had been. The pain around her heart was so tight now she was finding it difficult to breathe. 'Mick isn't like that,' she whispered. But even to her own ears the words lacked conviction.

'He's a man, isn't he?' Sandra said wryly.

Behind them Maisie found her voice. 'The little scut! His own mother! What kinda pervert is he?'

'They hardly know each other,' Sandra pointed out. 'It's not as if she ever changed his nappies for him.' She gave a cynical laugh. 'Not that *that* would put off some fellas I've known. Listen, Fran, you're going to have to take this seriously.'

Seriously? Was there any other way of taking it? Alongside her pain she began to feel a sense of mounting rage. How could Mick do this to her?

'That little scut!' Her mother's voice was savage. 'When Jim Hennessy hears what that fella's been up to, he's going to kick the shit out of him.'

'No!' Despite her growing anger, Fran knew a sense of alarm. 'Don't tell him. And the rest of you are to keep out of it.' She looked fixedly at the two other women. 'I'm going to sort this out with Mick myself.'

In the living room neither of them sat down; they watched each other warily like two opponents circling before a fight. Margaret saw Vincent's quick glance take in the drawn curtains, yesterday's ashes in the grate, the empty wine bottle on the hearth. She saw his lip curl. As she went over to the curtains to let in some light she braced herself for the inevitable barbed comment but, to her surprise, he stayed silent. When she turned around she saw he'd unzipped his windcheater and was sitting in a casual way on the arm of one of the fireside chairs, examining the room with interest.

'So this is the love nest?' he said at last with a scornful laugh.

'What?' she stammered, her heart beginning to thud uncomfortably.

'Susan and Tom.' His voice was impatient. 'You might remember; it's the first time I've laid eyes on the place.'

'Of course.' Relief flooded through her. She gave a flustered laugh. 'I forgot it's the first time you've – '

'That's because I was never invited, was I?' He looked at her narrowly. 'What's the matter with you? You're as jumpy as – ' His voice sharpened. 'Have you someone here?'

'No, no, of course not.' She tried to avoid his eye. But her heart had started thumping again.

'It's him, isn't it?'

'There's no one here, Vincent.' She spoke as calmly as she could. 'I'm surprised to see you, that's all.'

'Not as surprised as I am to be here.' His voice grew aggrieved. 'If it wasn't for Caroline – Look, Mags, I'm not going to beat around the bush. When are you going to forget all this nonsense and come home?'

'Nonsense?' She looked at him incredulously. 'Is that all it is to you? Nonsense?'

Vincent gave a thin smile. 'What else would you call it?' he asked with an air of unassailable logic. 'Look at it from my point of view. You leave behind my back. No warning, no explanations. Just a scribbled note. Is that rational behaviour? Ah, Mags!' He looked at her reproachfully. 'Surely to God you could have waited and told me to my face?'

Suddenly she found it hard to meet his eye. 'I couldn't wait,' she stammered. 'I was afraid you'd try to stop me.'

'Stop you? Why would I want to stop you?' A look of incomprehension crossed his face. 'If you needed a few days' break – not that it was the most convenient of times, I must point out, what with the new factory and all the other pressures I was under, which obviously didn't matter a damn to you – but, as I say, if you needed a break, who was I to stand in your way? When did I ever prevent you doing what you wanted to do? If you had to have a couple of days pampering yourself in the Strand in Rosslare or even a week in Lanzarote, working up a suntan, well, I'm a reasonable man.'

'This isn't about needing a few days in the sun,' she said slowly. 'I wanted time to think. About us. About our marriage.'

'What about our marriage?' He looked at her blankly. 'We had a good marriage until that young pup came along.'

Margaret's heart started thumping again. Anxious to steer the conversation onto safer ground, she forced herself to go on the attack. 'Good for you, maybe,' she shot back at him. 'You spoke just now of looking at it from your point of view. What about my point of view? Doesn't that count for anything?'

'Yes, yes,' he said impatiently. 'Don't make me out to be

some kind of tyrant. I've never trampled on your opinions, such as they were. And you can't say I haven't given you a free hand with the house. I've let you pick any colour scheme, lash out money on antiques, shrubs for the garden – '

'That's not what I – ' She ran out of steam suddenly. Her shoulders slumped. 'You don't understand – '

'Understand?' His voice grew bitter. 'The man who could understand you deserves a medal. I'd pin it on him myself. Tell me something. Did I treat you badly? Come home drunk every night? Beat you?'

She thought of what Susan had once said about there being more than one kind of battering, and summoned up her courage. 'Look, Vincent – '

'No, you look.' His voice rose, his face reddened dangerously. 'I said – did I beat you?'

Despite her resolve she felt intimidated by his anger. 'No,' she whispered.

'Leave you short of money? Go with other women?'

Again she shook her head.

'Well, then.' He glared at her. 'What in God's name had you to complain about?'

This was pointless, she thought. Like trying to discuss a rainbow with a colour-blind person. Without much hope she said, 'There's more to a relationship than that.'

'A *relationship!* Spare me the psychobabble,' he sneered. 'There was nothing wrong with our marriage till that so-called son of yours came along. He's the one to blame.'

They were back on dangerous ground. Although she knew it was unwise, she couldn't prevent herself from asking, 'What do you mean "so-called"?'

Vincent shrugged, his smile tinged with malice. 'You tell *me*. He turns up out of the blue. You're all over each other. What would any man think?'

Too late she saw the trap she had prepared for herself and evaded it frantically. 'How dare you suggest such a thing?' As she saw his eyes flash she took refuge in moral indignation and gazed at him accusingly. 'What a filthy mind you have! You've really gone too far this time.'

'Nothing would surprise me,' he blustered. But he looked uncertain, embarrassed even. 'Listen, Mags, in all honesty,' a little shrug and a smile as he prepared to recover lost ground, ' – I never believed there was anything going on. I mean, let's face it, what would a young fella like that see in a woman your age? I mean, no offence, don't get me wrong, you're a good-looking woman but you're no spring chicken. God!' Shaking his head in a kind of disbelief, he began to chuckle quietly to himself. 'I don't know what put the idea into my head in the first place.'

'Thanks a lot!' Although the danger was averted his words still had the power to sting. 'You were always gallant.'

'You're too touchy, Mags.' Vincent grinned, obviously delighted at having found a weak spot. 'I'm just being realistic. Anyway,' he said dismissively, 'it would be illegal.'

Margaret felt the colour drain from her cheeks. 'How – how do you mean?'

'There are laws against that sort of thing. God!' He grimaced suddenly. 'A woman having it off with a young fella half her age is disgusting, whichever way you look at it. But if he's her son as well, it's not just disgusting, it's also a crime. You could go to prison for it.' He gave her his catlike grin. 'Surely you knew that?'

Although her heart was beating wildly she forced herself to shrug, to sound unconcerned. 'I never gave it much thought.'

'Well, now you know,' he said half-jocosely. 'In case you're ever tempted. Look, Mags, I didn't come here to fight with you.' His tone softened and grew persuasive. 'Thursday is Christmas Day. I've booked the three of us into that little hotel in Wicklow, the one we stayed in a few years ago. I couldn't get anywhere else at such short notice. As it was, I had to twist a few arms – call in favours.'

Typical of him! Bitterness overcame her nagging sense of guilt as she stared at him. He would do anything to get his own way, she told herself. But not this time. With distaste she pictured the enforced intimacy of a hotel Christmas, the false bonhomie, the keeping up of appearances in front of strangers, Caroline complaining constantly about being cooped up for days without friends. As she conjured up her daughter's sullen face her feeling of guilt returned.

'How is Caro?' she asked hurriedly.

His lips tightened. 'How do you think she is? She doesn't say much but I know she misses you.' His expression softened. 'The girl has guts. A real little trooper. Look, Mags, you haven't answered my question. If you don't want to go to a hotel we can stay at home. It's not too late to get food in. What do you say? Come back for Christmas. We can talk about the other stuff later.'

'The other stuff?'

'Our *relationship!*' He made a dismissive gesture with his hands. 'All that jazz. Come on, Mags, what do you say?' He jumped up suddenly and came towards her. 'Caroline's not the only one who's missed you. I have too.' As his arms went around her he said, with that self-assured, hustling manner she'd often seen him use with clients. 'Come on, admit it. You've missed me too. okay, so there's been faults on both sides. But come back with me now and there'll be no recriminations, I promise you. We'll put it behind us, start off with a clean slate.' His lips sought hers confidently. 'What do you say, Mags? Is it a deal?'

'No!' Filled with revulsion, she twisted her mouth from his and tried to push his arms away. 'No, Vincent, I can't.'

'Of course you can.' Undeterred, he tightened his hold. 'God! It's great to feel you in my arms again.' His hands moved down her back, pressing her body close to his. 'I've missed making love to you, Mags.' He gave an excited laugh as he began forcing her backwards into an armchair. 'I don't think I can wait till we get home. It's been a month, for God's sake.' She felt his hand on her breast. 'You must be missing it too.'

'No, Vincent, don't!' She tried to push him away but he was too strong for her. She felt herself being pressed against the chair cushions. 'Let me go! Please!'

'Don't pretend you don't want it.' With a smile of triumph he cupped her face between his two hands and gazed down at her. 'You're as mad for it as I – '

'No!' Pinned by the weight of his body and the strength of his hands she stared back at him helplessly. 'No, Vincent!'

'No?' His smile faded. But he didn't loosen his hold. 'Listen, Margaret. I'm still your husband. I have rights, you know. You can't treat me like this. What's got into you, anyway?' He frowned suddenly, his eyes searching her face.

'Something's happened. Don't bother to lie. I know it has.'

Unable to avoid his eye, she felt like a trapped animal. She said nothing.

'Oh, my God!' She saw his dawning comprehension. 'So it's true? There is something going on between you?'

'No, there isn't!' Margaret found her voice at last, but even to her own ears her protests sounded feeble and unconvincing. 'Nothing happened.'

'You little bitch!' She felt his body recoil from hers and saw the revulsion in his eyes as he tore himself away from her. 'You filthy little bitch!'

'It's not true,' she said frantically. 'How can you think such a thing?'

'Don't bother playing games with me,' Vincent snarled. 'I can see through your lies.' He towered over her suddenly and she cowered back against the chair cushions, convinced he was about strike her. But, instead of raising his hand to her, he leaned forward and spat straight into her face. As Margaret recoiled in disgust, spittle running down her chin. she heard him say softly, 'You unnatural bitch! By rights you should be fucked on all fours like the animal that you are. It's only what you deserve.' His eyes raked over her, stripping her of all dignity.

'Oh, God!' Fumbling for a handkerchief, she rubbed frantically at her face. 'You wouldn't dare – '

'Don't worry,' he sneered. 'You're quite safe from me. *He* can do it to you. *I* wouldn't touch you with a bargepole. There's one thing I can guarantee, though.' His voice was venomous. 'You no longer have a daughter. I'll make sure Caroline will have nothing more to do with you.'

The threat was like a knife-thrust to her heart. She stared at him, shocked. 'You can't mean that!'

'Oh, yes I can. And I do.' He bared his teeth in a travesty of a smile. 'There has to be some justice in the world.'

'But it's not what you think,' she said brokenly. 'You're making a mistake – '

'A mistake?' Vincent's voice was savage. 'That would be too kind a word for what you've done.' He turned on his heel. 'I'll see myself out. And I won't be back. Hell will freeze over first.'

As the door banged behind him another one closed in her mind. It was over. After nearly nineteen years her marriage was over. Over and finished with. But there was no time to think about that now. No time to ponder the implications. Instead of the relief she had expected to experience, she felt defiled, contaminated by his venom. Nausea engulfed her suddenly. She rushed to the bathroom, retching violently. But even after the paroxysms had spent themselves and she had splashed water on her face until it was raw and stinging, she still felt unclean and could not wipe away the viscous feel of his spit against her skin, the memory of the contempt she had seen in his eyes.

'Oh, God!' Panic rose up in her as she stared at her distraught face in the mirror. 'What am I going to do if it turns out he's right?'

'It's no good trying to do the innocent with me, Mick Cleary!' Fran's features were contorted with rage. 'I know all about you and Lady Muck.'

'Lady Muck?' His heart gave a frightened lurch but he

forced himself to stay calm, to feign ignorance. 'Just because she was generous buying all those presents is no reason to call her names – '

'You must think I'm an awful eejit!' She gave an incredulous laugh. 'You must think I came down in the last shower. I'm telling you, I know about you and her.'

'About me and her?' He could hear himself stammering over the words. 'What are you getting at, Fran?'

'For God's sake!' There was cold fury in her voice. 'Do you want me to spell it out for you?'

He felt his face redden but he forced himself to meet her eye. 'If you mean what I think you mean – it's the filthiest, the most disgusting – ' His voice rose angrily. 'You little bitch! You have a filthy, warped, twisted mind. How could you even think of such a thing? My own mother!'

He saw her face turn white but she stood her ground. 'This isn't your Ma we're talking about. This is a woman you only met a couple of months ago. And calling me names won't change anything. Look, Mick, I've seen you together. Seen the way you look at her. The way she looks at you.'

A rush of guilty elation took him by surprise. He fought to hide his feelings and managed to laugh. 'She's my mother, for God's sake!'

'You wouldn't think it, to see the pair of you.' Fran looked unimpressed. 'If you could have seen yourself the other night. You were pathetic, like a trained monkey dancing to her tune. And she was lapping it up.' She gave a little sneer. 'Although she's probably well used to fellas making fools of themselves over her. I know her sort.'

All at once he hated her. He felt his fists clench and the

blood rush to his face. 'Shut up! For God's sake will you shut up!' Shaking with anger, he turned away from her, struggling to gain mastery over his feelings. As if aware that she had gone too far, Fran was silent behind him. When he was able to trust himself he turned to find her watching him. She no longer seemed angry. Just tired, her face white and strained.

'Okay, have it your way.' She gave a weary shrug. 'Maybe you are telling the truth. I just don't know any more. But there's one thing I'm certain of.' Their eyes met and he realised that her anger hadn't left her, she had drawn it into herself and made it part of her. 'If you bring that woman here for Christmas, me and Sean will go out that door together. And, I'm warning you, we won't come back.'

Suddenly he had the sense that events were moving too fast for him. His own anger faded, to be replaced by a feeling of apprehension. 'Look, why don't we talk about this in the morning?'

He saw her lips tighten. 'I've said all I want to say on the matter.' He saw the stubborn line of her jaw as she glanced over at the living-room sofa. 'You'd better sleep in here tonight. The way I feel about you right now, I don't want you anywhere near me.'

'Suits me,' Mick snapped back at her. He hid his misgivings under a show of bravado. 'The way I feel about *you* at this moment – after what you've accused me of – do you think I'd want to?' He saw a flicker of uncertainty cross her face but she turned away and left the room without saying anything.

God! That was close! The danger had been averted. But only just. With trembling hands he reached for the bottle of vodka left over from Margaret's visit and poured himself a generous slug. As the sharp liquid hit the back of his throat he felt an overwhelming sense of relief. Despite what he had said to Margaret the previous day about wanting things to be out in the open, he knew he was glad that Fran had not found out the truth.

She would have to know some time, he told himself. But not just yet.

Margaret was dreaming. *Winding corridors, passages that led nowhere, doors that opened onto other corridors. The way out ? Where was the way out?* Abruptly she awoke in the dark, her heart thudding in her ears.

The kitchen had a hard, unyielding look to it in the glare of the overhead light. Walls, worktop, sink gleamed icily to the touch. Night still glittered blackly behind window-panes which rattled uneasily as if someone were fumbling at the catch. Images from the dream resonated through her head. With a shudder she tried to banish them and concentrated on filling the kettle at the sink.

As she stood waiting for it to boil she imagined eyes peering in at her from outside and fought the urge to rush over and pull across the skimpy curtains. It would do no good. Their purpose was decorative, not practical. Anyway, she told herself, no one was outside looking in. No one was prowling the backyard. The danger was within, lying in wait at the back of her mind, ready to pounce. Panic gnawed at her as she made a cup of tea and escaped with it into the living room.

At least it was warmer here. The curtains were drawn across the tall windows; a few dying embers in the fireplace gave out a faint glow. Curled up in an armchair, she sipped the hot tea and began to relax, to let the images come back. *As she opened each door, her hope grew that she would find the exit, a hope that was dashed repeatedly. Until it gradually began to dawn on her that there was no way out.*

It was only a dream. Forget it. Drink your tea. Concentrate on thoughts of tomorrow. She would try ringing the priest again first thing. There was probably some perfectly good reason why he hadn't rung back. Maybe he had arrived home too late to contact her? That would explain why she had kept getting the answering machine the evening before. But once he got her message he would ring back. And then they would sort things out. Things would still be difficult, she wasn't going to deceive herself about that. But at least she would be free of this terrible nagging doubt. And once Michael came to see her again, they would talk, make plans for the future. A comfortable drowsiness stole over her. Her head began to nod.

Suddenly she was jerked into wakefulness by the slamming of a door nearby. Hasty footsteps on concrete. Then a car started up outside and drove off. She recalled her father's long legs hurrying down the front steps when she was a child: 'Back soon, Maeve. Off to do my rounds.' But there were no doctors living there any more, no hospital. It was all flats and offices now.

Some impulse drew her to one of the windows, to pull back a curtain and look out at the damp pavements glistening peacefully in the light from the street lamps. Strange to be back in the Square after all these years. To be back in Millers' instead of her own house. Who could have predicted such a thing? As she stood there she heard the rattle of milk crates further down the street and saw the sky grow pale above the dark mass of hedge surrounding the Square gardens. The first streaks of pink began to appear behind the rooftops. Pink with touches of gold.

At the sight of the new day, her spirits began to lift. Hope, unreasonable and unlooked-for, put out a few tentative shoots.

Mick switched on the light, blinking as the shabby outlines of the living room came into view. Seven o'clock. He stretched himself painfully and glanced in disbelief at the dishevelled nest of bedclothes from which he had just emerged. This wasn't happening. It was some kind of bad dream. He still felt shocked over the way Fran had banished him from their bed. In two years of marriage such a thing had never happened before. Up to yesterday the idea of his having to spend the night on the living-room sofa would have been unthinkable. But even more unthinkable, he reminded himself, would have been the idea of his making love to another woman. Yet it had happened. Oh, yes, it had happened! At the thought of Margaret his mind filled with warm exciting images. What a woman! Last Friday had been the best day of his life. He knew he should feel guilty about it. A part of him did feel guilty. But the rest of him exulted at the memory. How could he ever regret it?

Despite the fact that Fran had banished him from their bed? And that she would do an awful lot worse if she were to find out the truth? Well, that wasn't going to happen, was it? During the night, while he had tossed and turned on the sofa, he had made his mind up about that. Fran was not going to hear the truth from him until he was ready to tell her. In the meantime, all she had to go on were suspicions. And it was up to him to allay those suspicions.

As he was pondering on the best way to go about this, he heard the door open and she came in, bundled into an old dressing gown, yawning sleepily. From behind her he heard Sean's voice raised in hungry protest.

'Okay, Okay,' she grumbled. 'Keep your hair on.'

'I was just going to bring you in a cup of tea,' Mick said. His heart sank when she pushed past him without answering. As he watched her take a bottle of formula from the fridge and put it on to warm he tried again. 'Fran, I – '

'You look terrible.' Her gaze flitted from his face to the empty vodka bottle on the table. Although her voice sounded more critical than concerned, he could detect no trace of last night's fury in it. 'I bet you didn't get much sleep.'

'Not much.' Encouraged by her manner, he kept his own voice casual. 'How about yourself?'

'I didn't sleep either.' She threw him an oblique glance and busied herself with the bottle-warmer. 'Look, I've been doing a lot of thinking – '

'I've been thinking too – '

'No, let me finish, Mick. I think, maybe – well, maybe I went a bit over the top last night. I was angry. I said things.'

Relief flooded through him. 'I said things too – '

'But the things I said.' He saw embarrassment in her face. 'I've had time to think. It's just too – '

'Yes,' he said eagerly. It was going to be easier than he had thought. 'They were just off the wall. I mean how could you possibly – ?'

'Hold on a minute, Mick.' Her eyes narrowed. 'I had reason. I mean, as Sandra says, there's no smoke without – '

'*Sandra?*' He looked at her in astonishment. 'What does she want to stick her oar in for? What business is it of hers?'

She gave him a mulish look. 'You were seen.'

'Seen?' He felt himself stiffen. 'What do you mean "seen"?'

'At the cinema. Sandra saw the pair of you together.'

'At the *cinema*?' In his relief he exploded with laughter. 'The cinema, Fran?'

Her face went pink. 'It's not funny – '

'No, of course, it's not. I'm sorry, I didn't mean to laugh.' In his relief, he could afford to be magnanimous. 'It's just too – Listen, love – ' He gave her a quick look. ' – If that's all it was about?'

'No, there were other things.' But her voice had grown unsure.

'Other things? Like what?'

'I – it doesn't matter.' She bit her lip. 'Maybe I got it wrong.'

'Maybe you did.' Sensing his advantage, he went on the attack. 'You should have more cop-on than to be listening to your sister, Sandra. You know how she loves to stir things up.' Watching her face closely, he read her uncertainty, her readiness to be convinced. 'Come on, Fran.' He put on an air of injured innocence. 'You know me better than that.' He felt a petty sense of triumph when he saw her expression falter.

'Maybe I was wrong, Mick. I'm sorry.'

As he looked at her penitent face he knew he should have been ashamed of his own duplicity. Should have felt guilty for what he had done. But all he could think of was Margaret. The way her body had looked that night in the firelight, and the silky feel of her skin against his.

'Is this a bad time for you?' she asked tentatively. 'Would you like me to ring back?'

'Not at all, not at all.' To Margaret's relief there was no trace in Father Tim's voice of the acrimonious note on which they had last parted. 'I'll be saying the ten o'clock Mass but we have a few minutes to spare. What can I do for you?'

She hesitated. Now that she had finally got through on the phone it was difficult to know where to begin. And there was obviously no time to lead gently up to the subject. She would just have to plunge in straight away. Well, here goes. There was silence at the other end of the line while she blurted out her request. A silence that, to her apprehensive ears, sounded ominous. But the priest's voice, when he spoke, was more puzzled than accusing.

'A mistake? But why would you think that? Have you some reason for believing that this young man is not your son?'

Margaret found herself babbling about insufficient records, mistaken identities, faulty recollections. 'Just want to be sure everything is in order,' she said.

'There were no proper regulations at the time,' the priest agreed. 'And no doubt mistakes *were* made. Bound to be. People are only human, after all – '

'Yes, yes, they are,' she said eagerly. 'Do you think – ?'

'But I doubt very much if it happened in your case. Great care was taken – '

'But you can't be sure,' she pleaded. 'It was a long time ago – '

'Not that long ago, Margaret,' Father Tim said crisply. 'I

have a very clear recollection of it. But then I was directly involved.'

Her heart sank at his tone. 'But how can you be certain?'

'If you would just listen to me, like a good girl. I'm telling you, there was no possibility of a mix-up. We didn't go through the usual channels. The nun who handled it was an old friend of mine, who happened to know of a couple desperate to have a child. It was all done very discreetly, of course. And very few people were involved. I'm telling you, Margaret,' the priest said with a note of asperity, 'there couldn't have been a mix-up. That adoption was a once-off. No other children were involved. There was only one baby. And that was your son.'

She felt suddenly as if all the blood had drained from her body. She tried to speak but no words came.

'Margaret?' the priest asked sharply. 'Is there some problem you're not telling me about?' When she didn't answer he made a self-satisfied sound. 'Ah, I thought as much. I was wondering how long it would be before you discovered you had made a mistake. In my experience these things seldom work out. You'd have been better to have let sleeping dogs lie. Still, no use crying over spilt milk. Look,' he went on, in a more kindly way, 'I know you gave birth to him but you're under no moral obligation, not at this stage of his life. Even he must see that.' His voice grew brisk. 'You must distance yourself from him at once. The best way to do that is go back to Vincent. You've fences to mend there, I'm afraid, but I'm sure if you throw yourself on his mercy – '

'No, Father.' With a great effort of will Margaret found her voice. 'You're the one who's mistaken. There's no problem, no problem at all.' As her stomach began to cramp over she made an even greater effort to sound calm, unconcerned even. 'Just wanted to clarify something. Thank you for your time.'

'Margaret, wait a minute – '

But Margaret wasn't listening. She had dropped the telephone, leaving it dangling from its cord, and dashed to the flat's tiny bathroom, where, for the second time in twenty four hours, her body tried to purge itself of her fear and her guilt.

You're supposed to feel better once you've got sick. If anything, she felt worse. And this time it wasn't just a matter of trying to wash her face. This time her whole body felt unclean. No matter how long she spent under the shower, no matter how hard she scrubbed herself, over and over, she couldn't wash away her sense of self-loathing. Couldn't wash the voices from her head.

'You've disgraced us all.' Mummy's high voice cut into her savagely. 'Foolish, headstrong girl.'

'Jeopardised your future.' That was Daddy, more in sorrow than in anger. 'Ruined your good name. Broken your mother's heart.'

'Are you aware of the gravity of what you have done?' The priest's voice in Confession. A deep, sonorous voice that relished every syllable. 'The sins of impurity are the worst.'

The church had been empty and echoing, the last of the penitents departed. As she knelt to say her penance before the statue of the Virgin, its pale bulbous eyes had reproached her, their message loud and clear. 'You're a disgrace to

Catholic womanhood. No amount of rosaries will take away your shame.'

And now she had disgraced herself again.

The water ran cold in the shower. She got out, dressed herself hastily, rubbing her hair distractedly with a towel, combing it carelessly, indifferent to her appearance. She hurried into the living room but the voices pursued her, taunting her.

The woman tempted me.

Cherchez la femme!

It's always the woman's fault. It's up to her to set the standard.

They grew strident, vicious, battering her with Vincent's harsh tones.

Unnatural bitch!

You did it with your own son?

You whore! You animal!

Once again she saw the contempt in his eyes, felt herself recoil as his spittle hit her cheek. *'God! You've really surpassed yourself this time.'*

'No!' she moaned. 'No! I won't listen.' She went to the sideboard. With trembling hands she poured herself a vodka, then downed it at a gulp. Poured herself another. As its comforting warmth spread through her body she stumbled over to sit by the fireplace, to stare unseeingly into the empty grate. When the tumult in her head had quietened one thought floated to the surface, nagging her with its intensity. Oh, God! How was she going to tell Michael about this?

With a mixture of longing and dread she sat there waiting to hear his key in the lock.

'Are you sure you won't change your mind, Mick?' Fran asked when he dropped her and Sean off at her parents' house. 'After all, you're going to have to face them sometime.'

'Yes, but not today.' Although he didn't want to destroy the fragile peace between them, he had no intention of giving in to her demands. As he lifted the baby buggy from the boot of the BMW he allowed a note of indignation to colour his voice. 'After what that sister of yours said – '

'Maybe you're right,' Fran said quickly. 'Look, I'll talk to Sandra and Mammy. Tell them it's been sorted out. By the time you see them on Thursday – '

'Thursday?' He felt a jolt of surprise. 'But I thought now that we *have* sorted things – '

'You thought wrong.' As she bent to strap Sean into his buggy Mick saw her expression harden. 'Okay, maybe I was wrong about you and her. But that doesn't mean I've changed my mind about Christmas. As far as I'm concerned, it's all settled.' Straightening up, she looked him firmly in the eye. 'We spend the day with *my* folks. And your precious Margaret can spend it with *hers*.'

'You don't mean that,' he said uneasily.

'Don't I just!' There was the light of battle in Fran's eyes.

'Look, we'll talk about this tonight. I have to go now – '

'That's right,' she sneered. 'Better not be late for Margaret. You just can't wait to see her, can you?'

'It's not like that.' He glanced irresolutely from her to Sean, who sat in his buggy chewing on the thumb of his woollen mitten, and back to her scornful face. 'You don't have to be jealous,' he said lamely.

'Don't I? You could have fooled me.' Fran's voice was scathing.

'This is no good.' He gave a helpless shrug and turned away.

'Why don't you tell her that,' she called after him. 'And while you're at it you can give Lady Muck back that car.'

He slid behind the steering wheel, breathed in the car's expensive atmosphere and sighed with pleasure to hear the powerful engine purr into life. Like everything else about Margaret it had style, he told himself. Maybe someday he'd have a car like that.

But all thoughts of the BMW were banished from Mick's mind when he arrived at the flat in the Square and found her sitting dejectedly in an armchair, staring into the distance, a half-empty glass at her elbow. The room had a neglected air to it, he thought, not untidy exactly, more as if dust had been allowed to settle undisturbed. His gaze fell on the cheerless grate.

'Want me to light a fire?' He looked at her uneasily. 'That heating isn't enough. You need a fire at this time of year.

'Please yourself. Although I don't think there are any briquettes.'

He was alarmed by the indifference in her voice. 'What's wrong?'

She shook her head wordlessly.

His alarm grew. 'Margaret! Look at me. Tell me what's wrong.'

When she turned her head towards him he was shocked at her pallor.

'My God! You look like you haven't slept in weeks.' He examined her face anxiously. 'Are you sick?'

'I suppose that's as good a way of describing it as any.' There was a toneless quality to her voice that frightened him. He wanted to put his arms around her but something in her manner kept him at bay. He stared at her anxiously.

'Please tell me what's wrong.' When she said nothing a suspicion occurred to him. 'It's Vincent, isn't it? Has he been here causing trouble?' He felt sudden anger. 'If that bastard has laid a hand on you – !'

'Vincent was here yesterday. But that's not it.'

He looked at her, bewildered. 'What, then?'

She was silent for a moment, gazing away into the middle distance as if what she saw there was more interesting than their conversation. Watching her, he felt that she had gone away into herself and had forgotten him.

'For God's sake, Margaret!'

Her eyes were sombre as she turned to look at him. 'Michael, I don't think we should see each other again.'

'Not see each other – ?' He was stunned. 'But why? What's happened? Look,' he pleaded, 'you've got to tell me.'

She sighed, then said in the same unemotional voice as before, 'Do you remember Father Tim?'

He frowned. 'Father – ? Yes, yes, I know who you mean.' He felt his body tense up. 'Don't tell me he's still bothering you?'

'I rang him. Today.'

'But why would you want to do that?' He fought down his growing panic. 'I thought we'd agreed – ?'

'Michael.' This time she looked him full in the face. 'I *had* to know. I had to find out.'

'And did you?'

But as he gazed into her pain-filled eyes the truth had begun to dawn on him.

'He's a liar!' He paced the floor in an agony of denial. 'Surely to God you're not going to take the word of that priest?'

'What reason would he have to lie? It makes no difference to him.'

'He wants to split us up,' he raged. 'Doesn't want us to be happy.'

'He doesn't know about us. In fact, he got the wrong end of the stick, thought we had fallen out. If he had had any idea – but he hadn't, thank God.' He saw her shudder slightly. 'No, I believe he was telling the truth as he knew it.'

'As he knew it?' He clutched eagerly at the straw. 'But he could be wrong.'

'Michael, it's no use,' she said sadly. 'Stop trying to deceive yourself. That's been the whole trouble up to this.'

He was stung by her words. 'Are you saying it's my fault?'

'No. I'm not blaming you. If it was anyone's fault it was mine. I should have known better. Oh, God!' She gave him an agonised look. 'What a fool I've been! How could I have let myself do such a wicked, wicked thing?'

'It wasn't wicked,' he protested. 'It was beautiful. Everything we did together was beautiful. Look, I still can't believe it. Are you sure the priest isn't making a mistake?'

Margaret shook her head and said in a low voice, 'I'll never be able to forgive myself for what's happened.'

'It wasn't your fault. I was the one – '

'My own son!' She began to rock backwards and forwards in her distress. 'What kind of a woman would – ?'

'Don't be like that. Even if it's true, and I'm still not convinced it is, it doesn't make any difference to the way I feel about you. '

'How can you say that?' He saw the horror in her eyes. 'We're mother and son.'

'Maybe. They're just words, as far as I'm concerned. Nothing has changed since Friday. We're still the same people we were then.'

'Everything has changed.' He heard the despair in her voice. 'I just can't seem to get it through to you.'

'I've never really felt you were my mother,' he said doggedly. 'Not deep down. As I said, it's just a word. We've no history together. It was just an accident of birth.'

'An accident of birth? You can't mean that?'

'Why not? If we had met some other way. If we hadn't known – '

'But we do know,' Margaret said slowly. 'I think we knew all along.'

'No! Don't say that!'

'I think we were just pretending to ourselves – I think I was, anyway. And that's why I can't forgive myself. I should have known – '

'Look, we made a mistake. But that doesn't mean we're evil – '

'What we did was.' A shadow crossed her face. 'It's no good, Michael. We've got to stop seeing each other.'

'No!'

'It's our only hope. Nobody knows about us yet. Vincent

suspects. But he has no proof. And if we keep away from each other maybe he'll leave you alone.'

'It's too much to ask. Knowing you were only a few miles away – '

'Well, then I'll go away. There's nothing here for me, anyway. But we must stop seeing each other. If the truth got out it would ruin your life.'

'What about your life?'

She gave a little shrug. 'That's not important. Not now. But you have a wife, a son. You have everything to lose – '

'No!' In his distress he was no longer listening. 'You can't go away.' An idea occurred to him. 'I'll come with you. We'll go to a place where no one knows anything about us.' His voice broke suddenly. 'I love you, Margaret. I want to be with you always.'

'You don't understand.' He saw her eyes fill with tears. 'We've no future together.'

'And you don't understand,' he said urgently. 'It's not just the sex. I love you. I want to be with you. Look, if I promise never to lay a finger on you – '

'And how long do you think that would last?'

'But I mean it. You can trust me. I promise you.'

'But can I trust myself?' Her voice was sad. 'It's no use, Michael. It's hard enough for me to live with what I've done. But if it were to happen again – '

'I've told you it won't. Please, Margaret, I'll do anything.' He looked at her in desperation. 'Just don't ask me to stop seeing you.'

'It's no use.' She shook her head. 'It just wouldn't work.'

He stared at her in frustration. Suddenly he resented her

and the hold she had over him. Anger rose up in him. 'That's just typical of you and your family, isn't it? Run away. Pretend it never happened. That's you all over.' He saw her eyes widen with shock but his fury drove him on. 'You don't love me. You never have. After all, it isn't the first time you've done this to me, is it? When we met first you just didn't want to know, did you? If I hadn't come after you, if I hadn't insisted –'

'Michael, please listen to me –'

'Why should I listen to you? What have you ever done for *me*? Maybe the priest was right, after all.' He saw her flinch but his voice drove on relentlessly. 'Maybe you *were* the woman who gave me away, the woman who turned her back on me. And now you're doing it to me all over again.'

They stared at each other for an appalled moment. His anger died as swiftly as it had arisen. He was filled with remorse.

'Oh, God, I'm sorry! I should never have –'

Margaret was the first to recover her composure. Although her face was ashen she met his eyes squarely. 'You have every right to hate me –'

'I don't hate you. I love you.' He felt himself close to tears. 'I didn't mean what I said. I was angry. I wanted to hurt you –'

'But I'd like you to go now.'

'Margaret, please –'

'Just go, Michael. Although her voice sounded weary there was no doubting its determination. 'Please don't come back.'

Numb all over. No feelings yet. Margaret walked to the kitchen, holding herself carefully as if her body was made of glass. It was cold in the kitchen. But not as cold as she was.

Someone had taken away her heart and replaced it with a block of ice.

Numb. Frozen. If they were to cut off her arm she probably wouldn't feel it.

She wished it had been an arm. Or a leg. Anything but this.

The kettle came rattling to the boil, steam spurting from its lid. She couldn't remember having switched it on. Placing a hand on the hot metal she noted its heat against her skin in a detached kind of way as if the hand belonged to someone else. Maybe it did. There was a deadness to her that made all her actions seem like those of a robot viewed from a distance. Spoon in the coffee. Pour the boiling water. Pick up the cup. Don't drop it. Go into the living room. Put the cup down on a table while you open a new packet of cigarettes. Find your lighter.

He's gone, she thought, and he's never coming back.

Another door had closed. Slammed this time. Slammed so hard that echoes of it went reverberating along the corridors of her mind. Her thoughts ran frightened down those corridors. Up and down. Hunting possibilities. Looking for a way out. It was the dream all over again. Desperate to escape. But coming up against those closed doors every time.

Trapped. Nowhere to turn.

As she fumbled with the cigarette carton her hands began to shake violently. All at once, with alarming suddenness, cigarettes sprayed out over the table, some falling to the floor. Trying to subdue her treacherous hands, she bent to gather them up. But as she did so, her whole body was abruptly racked by shivering. An uncontrollable shivering that caused her teeth to chatter and her legs to tremble. To tremble so violently that they wouldn't support her. She fell to the ground, lay there gasping, her breathing harsh in her ears.

With an effort of will, Margaret dragged herself painfully into an upright position, crouched with her back against the side of a chair, her knees close to her body, hugging them tightly to control the spasms that convulsed her.

Oh God! How was she going to get through the rest of her life without him?

Time ceased to matter. Rain tapped against the window. The clock ticked away on the mantelpiece. Footsteps sounded on the pavement outside. An occasional car passed by. The room sang around her, distancing itself from her. Terror gripped her.

Help me! I'm in pain!

Not physical pain. But something much worse.

She tried reaching out mentally for something to sustain her. Some certainty. Some belief. But there was nothing. A terrible nothingness. Wave after wave of nothingness. Wave after wave battered against her until a silent crescendo was achieved. And she was left shaken and terrified, staring into the void.

I never meant this to happen, Mick told himself as he paced the empty, windswept beach. I never meant to fall in love with her. I just wanted to meet my mother, find out where I came from. I never meant to hurt anyone. He stared blindly at the shoreline, where waves the colour of pewter sucked and churned over the shingle while overhead gulls swooped under a sullen sky, their mournful cries intensifying his mood of despair. How could he have known this would happen? How could anyone?

But it had happened. And what joy it had brought. He thought back over their relationship. Their time together had been so short. A few months of getting to know each other, some brief hours of ecstasy. And now it was over. His loss hit him suddenly. Never to see her again, never to hold her in his arms. He just couldn't believe it. As he thought back to the scene with Margaret, he still felt stunned by what had happened, still couldn't seem to take it in. It was over, finished. Don't come back, she had said. Surely she hadn't meant it?

Not that he could blame her if she had when you thought of the cruel way he had spoken to her. Despite the cold wind he felt his cheeks burn at the memory, saw once again her white strained face, read the pain in her eyes. How could he have hurt her in that way? How could he have been so cruel? Right now he would have given anything, done anything to call those words back.

But there was no point in deceiving himself about it. Even if he had never said what he had said she still would have ended things between them. The phone call to the priest had made sure of that. He felt a sudden upsurge of bitterness towards the man who had sent his whole world crashing down on him. But why blame Father Tim? That was just shooting the messenger. Who to blame then? Chance? Some malicious fate which had caused their paths to cross?

Curse it! It wasn't fair! It just wasn't fair!

In a sudden rage he kicked savagely at the stony beach,

scattering chunks of wet sand everywhere. Then began hurling pebbles and small rocks, one after another into the wind, bouncing them off the waves without skill or direction, in a vain attempt to relieve the anguish that gripped him.

Oh, God! Why did she have to be his mother? Why couldn't they have met some other way? But even as he asked himself this the realisation came to him. If she hadn't been his mother they would never have met, would never have fallen in love. If he hadn't been her son she would never have given him a second glance.

'Oh, Christ!' The truth was like a punch in the gut. The pebble in his hand plopped aimlessly into the water as he roared out his pain across the empty beach. 'She's my mother, God dammit! My *mother!*' Suddenly he was bent double, racked with sobs, beating his fist against his forehead. A man shouldn't feel that way about his mother.

It was wrong! It was unnatural! It was wrong, wrong, wrong!

He lost count of time. Long after the paroxysm of sobbing ceased he stayed in the same position, squatting on his heels on the pebbly beach, his head buried in his hands. At length he became aware of the cold biting through his anorak and raised his head. The sea had lost its metallic glint. A dull grey was spreading over the waves. He could no longer make out the gulls. Pinpoints of light were beginning to appear all along the coast. He stood up, easing his cramped limbs, pulling up the hood of his jacket to keep out the wind. His rage and self-disgust had died down, leaving behind them an enormous sense of regret. As he headed back towards the darkening dunes beyond which lay the road where he had parked Margaret's car, one thought was uppermost in his mind.

Even if it was over and they could have nothing more to do with each other, he couldn't let it end the way it had. He would have to see her one more time and make things right with her. Ask her to forgive him. Once the decision was made he felt a bit happier and began searching his pockets for coins to make the call.

The short winter day was coming to an end. The shortest day of the year. Margaret stood at one of the long narrow windows, remembering how, just eight hours before in that same spot, she had watched the dawn come up over the Square.

Daybreak to sunset. Birth to death.

She shivered suddenly. It had begun to rain outside, a slow, sleety rain, pencil strokes slanting through the grey air. If there was ever a day that needed the cheerful blaze of a fire, this was it. But she had run out of fuel. Although an electric heater took the chill from the room, the dead hearth gave it a soulless, uninhabited look. Not that it mattered any more, she told herself. Nothing mattered now. Her earlier panic had subsided, to be replaced by a sense of fatalistic calm. She knew now what needed to be done; she had found a solution to the dream. Had found the best way out for everyone. And as soon as she had made the necessary arrangements she would take it. As she looked out over the darkening street she felt as if a great burden had been lifted from her heart.

Suddenly the shrill sound of a telephone bell intruded on her thoughts. She listened to it in a detached kind of way, still gazing out at the street, waiting until the ringing had stopped. When it started up again a few moments later she walked purposively to the flat's tiny hallway and broke the connection. Then she left the receiver off the hook.

'Did you give back that car?' Fran asked.

'What?' Mick looked at her blankly.

She felt herself getting impatient. 'Are you on another planet or something?' What was the matter with him? There hadn't been a word out of him since he came home. And he'd a face on him like someone belonging to him had died. 'That's the second time I – '

'Oh, the car?' His face cleared. 'No, no I haven't. I'll drop it back to her tomorrow night.'

'No, you won't,' Fran said sharply. 'It's Monday night, remember. My Christmas night out with Freda and the girls.'

'Can't you get a babysitter?'

'All booked up. And I'm not getting the oul' biddy downstairs. Don't even think of it. You'll just have to leave the car somewhere she can pick it up.'

'I can't do that.' He shook his head. 'Look, I'll think of something.'

'You'd better,' she said grimly. 'But tomorrow night is out.' She remembered what her mother had said earlier. Put the boot in, Fran. Don't let him away with anything. 'What about Christmas?' she demanded. 'Have you told her she can't come here?'

She saw a shadow cross his face. 'You don't have to

worry about that. She's made other plans.'

Fran was nonplussed. It had been easier than she had thought. She looked at him suspiciously. 'Just for the day? Or for the whole of Christmas?'

'The whole of Christmas.' He met her gaze, his eyes dark pools of misery. 'Look, I admit I've been spending too much time with her, and it's not fair to you. So I've decided – we've decided not to see so much of each other in future.'

'Well, that's more like it,' Fran said slowly. She knew she should have been jubilant. Instead she felt a nagging sense of doubt. It had been all too easy. It just didn't add up. 'There's something you're not telling me, Mick. What's happened?' Her voice sharpened suddenly. 'Has she given you the push?'

'No,' he said. But she saw his mouth tremble, saw the look of pain in his eyes. 'No, it's nothing like that.' His eyes slid away from hers. 'Look, you've got what you wanted,' he muttered. 'Leave it alone, will you.'

As she watched him, the truth struck Fran with sudden clarity. He's in love with her. He's not staying because he loves me. It's because she's his mother. If it was anyone else but his mother he'd have been gone like a shot. She felt the sharp pain of betrayal. He doesn't love me. He loves *her*. She looked down, tried to blink back the tears. But when she looked up again she saw that he had turned away and was heading for the door. Jealousy twisted inside her like a knife.

'That's right. Can't keep away from her, can you.'

'I'm just going to make a phone call.' He turned, gave her a helpless look. 'You don't object to that, surely?'

She hardened her heart against the appeal in his voice.

His own mother, she thought. His own mother! She stared at him in sudden fury.

'Make all the phone calls you like, Mick Cleary. But if you ever set eyes on that woman again, it's all over between us.'

PART EIGHT

Only four days to go till Christmas, Caroline told herself as she turned the corner of the Square. And, if Dad was right in what he'd said, it looked as if this was going to be the worst Christmas of her life. But Dad couldn't be right, could he? All wasn't lost. Not yet. She lifted her chin determinedly. She wouldn't let it be lost.

She'd been saying this to herself for the past fortnight ever since that awful day she'd gone to Susan and Tom's flat looking for Mum and finding Michael there instead. It was only after her conversation with him that the suspicion had occurred to her that Christmas might be in jeopardy. But she had refused to take it seriously. Mum would come back in time. Of course she would. Even up to last week when she and Dad had put up the decorations and decked out the tree she had still clung on to this hope. Wish Mum were here to see the lights, she'd said. 'Don't worry, she'll be back soon, sugarbush. I'll get her to see sense.' He had sounded so confident. And she'd believed him. Dad always kept his promises.

But not any more. On Saturday when he'd come home with a face like thunder, her faith in him had been shattered. 'It's all your fault,' she'd stormed at him. 'You didn't ask her properly. It's all your fault.'

She'd been sorry afterwards for saying it. She and Dad

had always got on so well. And it wasn't all his fault. It was Mum's. She was the one who had gone away without a word of explanation. Four whole weeks and she'd never been in touch. A fortnight ago when she'd left Susan's flat without seeing her mother, Caroline had sworn to herself that she'd never go back there again, that Mum was the one who'd have to make the first move. But after yesterday she'd been afraid to wait any longer. So here she was, once again mounting the steps to the front door, once again ringing the doorbell with a mixture of trepidation and hope.

And anger too.

How could Mum do this to them? To her own daughter? Caroline couldn't wait to tell her what she thought of *that*.

After the third ring, with the street door remaining solidly closed in her face, her resolution began to waver. Where could she be? Gone out shopping? Still in bed? Surely no one could stay sleeping through that racket?

It was cold on the doorstep, she could feel it pinching through the legs of her jeans and around the shoulder blades of a jacket that had seemed warm enough when she had left her own house earlier. Maybe she should come back again later. But still she hung about, reluctant to leave. She was making another onslaught on the bell push when a small, sharp-faced woman, all muffled up against the weather, came up behind her and inserted a key in the lock. She gave Caroline an enquiring glance as the heavy door swung open.

'My mother,' the girl said quickly. 'She's staying in Susan Miller's flat.'

'Oh, is that who you are?' The woman gave her an unfriendly look. 'Well, you've just missed her. I passed her in the street not five minutes ago.'

'Will she back soon, do you think? Maybe I should wait in the hall?'

'I'm afraid I can't help you there,' the woman said crushingly. 'I'm not a party to your mother's comings and goings.'

'Well, no, but – '

'I wouldn't mind but I was talking to her only last week and she was as nice as pie. Then today she sails by me with her nose in the air. Didn't give me a *reck*.' A note of grievance sounded in her voice. 'Not a *reck*! That's some people for you. All over you one day, don't want to know you the next.'

'That's not like Mum.' Caroline looked at her uneasily. Her mother might be a bit distant at times but she was always polite. 'Maybe she had something on her mind?'

'Well, it must have been something big then,' the woman said, partly mollified. She looked speculatively at Caroline. 'You're her daughter? And that young man who visits – ?'

'My brother,' the girl said curtly. 'Look, I'll come back later – '

'You could always come in and wait. She mightn't be that long. Of course, you know how busy the shops are at the moment. Still, I'm sure you could do with a cup of tea – '

'Thanks, but I don't drink tea.' Fighting her unease, she turned away from the older woman's inquisitive gaze. 'I'll come back this evening. She's bound to be in then.'

Don't worry, she told herself as she headed down the street. She won't want to spend Christmas in that dump. She'll come back. You'll see, Mum will come back.

But even though she repeated the words over and over in

her head like a mantra all the way home on the bus, nothing she told herself could rid her of that growing feeling of unease.

The Green was so much more peaceful than Grafton Street, Margaret thought. With just three days to go to Christmas, the brightly decorated shops had been hives of activity; Santa and his elves moving with smiling precision in Brown Thomas's window, children's rapt faces pressed against the glass; the smell of coffee wafting over the crowds outside Bewley's; carol singers blocking the pavements, their collection boxes rattling like magpies competing with songbirds. Hands had thrust out at her, voices cajoling her, passers-by jostling her, but, intent on her mission, she had ignored them all.

The bank had been crowded too but she had reached the counter eventually. 'A lot of cash to be carrying around with you,' the cashier had commented disapprovingly before counting out the notes, his nimble fingers bundling them up with much flashing of cuffs and snapping of elastic bands. But Margaret had not been interested in his opinion. With a brief nod of thanks she had gathered the money into the large handbag she'd brought for the purpose, and then had hurried past the waiting lines of people to get to the door, a blast of freezing air greeting her as she emerged onto the street.

It was easy to forget the passage of time once you had passed through the high archway of the Green. So little had changed. The old paths were still the same. The dark one near the hedges where people took shortcuts. The main thoroughfare past the fountains where the crowds went: even on a winter's day there was a fair sprinkling of people. The path beside the duck pond. There was always someone standing there with pieces of stale bread in a paper bag. And the seagulls were still trying to get to the bread before the ducks.

Look! There was the seat – or a modern successor to it – beside the hedge where you sat with Martin and told him about the baby. How long ago it seemed now. And yet, how swiftly the years had gone in between.

A young man sat on the seat under the hedge. A young man about the same age Martin had been. Same stocky build. Same dark hair. But, instead of a tweed jacket over a knitted pullover, he wore a dark overcoat, collar up to the throat, frayed denim jeans, dirty canvas runners on his feet. She smiled ruefully to herself. The Green might not have changed but people had. The young man's face was dark-bristled, unshaven. He stared incuriously at her as she went past, a bottle of cheap sherry clutched in his hand.

Everyone had their own way of coping, Margaret thought. But what happened when it was not enough to dull the pain? You could drink most of a bottle of vodka to get yourself off to sleep and still wake in the small hours knowing that nothing had changed, that tomorrow still had to be faced. And, after that, another tomorrow. And another.

The chemist's at the bottom of the street was a haven of warmth and light. Although it had changed hands several times since Margaret was a girl, the assistant had got to know her face in the few weeks she'd been coming into the shop.

'That prescription's run out,' she told her as she handed over the tablets. 'If you want a repeat you'll have to go back to your doctor for another one.'

'I'll have enough here.' And plenty more back at the flat. Doctors had been very accommodating over the years. You name them, she had them. Sleeping tablets, anti-depressants, tranquillisers. 'Enough to poison a regiment,' Vincent had said once. Although he had often encouraged her to take them he was proud of the fact that he had no need of such things himself. Margaret smiled faintly at the chemist's assistant. 'More than enough.'

A light, sleety rain began to fall as she crossed the street. Watch out for the cars, Delia's voice said. Little girls are made of sugar and spice. Little girls who went to St Celeste would grow up to be ladies just like Mummy. To sit on a cushion and sew a fine seam. Not like little boys who grew up to be doctors and dentists like their fathers.

But all that had changed. Just as the tall old houses around the Square had changed. Once upon a time there would have been a Christmas tree sparkling from every house, and holly and ivy wreaths on the front doors. Although the occasional door sported a garland, and one office window had a snow scene sprayed on the glass, today there were few concessions to the season. Once upon a time a young girl had walked along here with a young man. She was beginning to fall in love and the future was an exciting present waiting to be unwrapped.

'I love this time of year. It makes me feel lovely and warm inside. And safe.'

'Safe?' The young man looked puzzled.

'You know. Like being young again–'

He laughed, his face crinkling up with amusement. 'Listen to Granny.'

'No. I mean– ' she glanced up at her own front door with its garland of red-berried holly, ' – like being a small child again and something wonderful is going to happen.' Her eyes shining, she turned to him. 'Can't you feel it in the air?'

The front door needed a coat of paint, and the uncurtained windows were grimy. The house belonged to a firm of importers now, business obviously in the doldrums. The basement where Mrs Roberts had laboured so lovingly all those years ago was boarded up, the area steps littered with empty beer cans and scraps of paper. She shivered in the cold air and moved on, leaving the place to its ghosts.

God! How tired she was. Two sleepless nights in a row were taking their toll. The bag she was carrying seemed to get heavier and heavier with every step she took. Not much further now. And then she was climbing the steps of Miller's old house and turning her key in the lock. Almost there. Soon you can put your burden down. There were more ghosts here, she noted. But they were more recent ones. They still had the power to wound. When she entered the empty flat the events of the past few days crowded in around her. Snatches of conversation, angry faces, voices accusing her. Always accusing her.

As she sank into an armchair she felt a sense of relief at the thought that, very soon, the voices would accuse her no more.

'The phone, Mick? Of course you can.' Mrs McGrath was pleased to see him. 'Fran out on the town? I seen her go out all dickied up a while back.'

'Yes.' He dialled the number, wishing she would go away. Hard enough trying to find the right words without the added embarrassment of an audience. It was almost a relief to hear the engaged tone. 'I'll try again later.'

There was no sign of the old woman when he came down again. Thank God! He dialled the number. Still engaged. Strange. It was an old-fashioned phone, the kind you spun around with your finger, and it sometimes stuck on the turn. Easy enough to dial a wrong number. He tried again, taking more care. Still engaged. He swore quietly to himself in frustration. He just *had* to speak to Margaret, had to make things right between them. All day at work he had thought of nothing else. But what could he do if she kept leaving the receiver off the hook? Go and see her tomorrow?

No, he couldn't wait till tomorrow. He peered at his watch, barely making out the numerals in the dim hallway. An hour, maybe longer, before Fran came home. She had barely spoken to him since last night's ultimatum. And he knew it was important to patch things up with her, for Sean's sake, if for nothing else. There was no way she'd agree to him going out again that night. If he wanted to see Margaret he would have to go now. With any luck he could be across town and back before Fran arrived home. She need never know he'd been out.

Once he'd made up his mind he acted swiftly, tapping on the old woman's door with hasty fingers.

'Look, Mrs McGrath, I have to go out! Will you keep an eye on Sean for me?'

Despite his sense of urgency his heart leaped with excitement at the thought of seeing her again.

His first thought was that she had dozed off in the armchair listening to music, her feet tucked up under her, an empty glass at her elbow. The stereo was silent, its lights still blinking. Her face looked remote, yet peaceful in repose. Too peaceful. His horrified glance took in the pill bottles on the coffee table and, beside them, the bulky envelope, his name written on it in her neat, flowing hand. His blood ran cold.

'Oh, Margaret! What have you done?'

'But why?' Caroline's eyes were filled with pain and bewilderment. 'Why, why, why?'

'It was an accident.' Mick's voice was firm. If he kept saying it long enough he might begin to believe it.

Vincent was telling the hospital people much the same thing. 'My wife sleeps badly. She swallows these things like Smarties – not that they're much use. When one lot didn't work she just took some more. Nothing sinister about that.'

'I see.' The casualty officer was a thin, black-haired young woman with a tired face. It was hard to tell from her expression whether she believed him or not.

'She will be okay, won't she?' Caroline asked. 'Mum *is* going to be okay?'

The young doctor hesitated. 'The thing is – she's not responding. We think she might have taken something else, not just sleeping pills.'

'Oh, God!' Mick was aghast. 'But what?'

'We don't know, we're doing tests. I'm afraid I can't tell

you any more at the moment but I'll let you know as soon as there's any news.'

'Mum's going to die!' Caroline turned to her father after the doctor had left them. 'And I never got a chance to talk to her.'

'No, sugarbush. No.' Vincent put his arm around her, stroked her hair soothingly and urged her to sit down. 'She'll be fine, I promise. Look, you wait here and I'll get you a cup of tea.' As he passed Mick he threw him a glance of undisguised hatred. 'She leave a note?' he barked.

Mick stared at him dazedly, his mind still full of the frantic phone calls he had made, followed by the nightmare drive through the streets trying to keep up with the ambulance. 'I don't think so. There wasn't much time.'

'Just as well,' Vincent grunted. 'The less people know the better. Not that I care what they think of her. Not now. But I have a reputation to consider. As for you – !' His face contorted suddenly. 'You're the one to blame for all this. We were fine till you came along.'

'That's not true – '

'Listen, you!' Vincent snarled. 'If she doesn't pull through – if that poor child is left motherless, I warn you, I'll hold you personally responsible.' Without waiting for an answer he turned and headed down the corridor towards the coffee machine.

'Caroline – ' Mick went over to the girl who sat hunched in her seat, her long blonde hair half-hiding her face. She turned slowly towards him with frightened eyes.

'I knew there was something wrong,' she whispered. 'I went back again around teatime and I still couldn't get an answer. Even before you rang I knew something bad had happened. Oh, Mum – ' her voice rose into a wail. 'Don't die. Please God, don't let her die.'

'It won't come to that.'

'How do you know?' The girl shook her head despairingly. 'Poor Mum! She must have been so unhappy to do what she did.'

'Yes, I think she was.'

'I was so angry with her for leaving us but I've been thinking. She must have been unhappy for a long time. Dad wasn't very nice to her, I realise that now. And I wasn't much help either. But all that will change, I promise.' She looked earnestly at him. 'From now on I'm determined to make it up to her.' Her face crumpled suddenly. 'If only I get the chance.'

'You will,' he said fervently. 'You will.' He touched her arm diffidently. 'Look, Caroline, I – '

To his dismay she shook his hand away, her face full of reproach. 'Why did you have to take her away from us? I'll never forgive you for that.'

'I don't expect you to,' Mick said. 'I'll probably never forgive myself.'

But he saw that she was no longer listening to him, looking past him anxiously. He followed the direction of her gaze to see that Vincent had returned, accompanied by a nurse.

'They've moved her to Intensive Care,' he said grimly.

It was tucked away in a corridor to itself near the top of the building. They were the only people waiting outside the double doors across which someone had sprayed *Merry Christmas* in glittering letters under the sign marked *No*

Admittance. Please ring the bell for attention. At first, the peace of the place was welcome after the excitement of Accident and Emergency but, as time went by, the quiet corridor took on the air of a forgotten backwater. Occasionally a nurse would emerge from the unit, and all three heads would turn towards her, only to have their hopes dashed as she padded by quietly on rubber soles without looking at any of them.

At one stage a middle-aged man joined them. Casually dressed, with untidy greying hair straggling down over the collar of his polo-neck sweater, he had a slightly raffish air about him. Mick found it hard to hide his surprise when Vincent introduced him as 'Father O'Donnell'.

'An old friend of the family,' the priest added smoothly. 'Father Tim?'

'The very same. And you're Margaret's son, they tell me? Well, well.' He studied Mick with surprisingly shrewd blue eyes. 'It's a bad business,' he said sympathetically. 'Had you far to come?'

'Not far,' Mick said stiffly. But he found himself responding to the other man's attempts to put him at his ease, began chatting to him in a more relaxed manner. It made such a change from Vincent's hostility and helped to take his mind off things. After the priest had gone in search of the hospital chaplain he wondered if he should find a telephone and ring Fran but he was afraid to move in case news would come while he was away. So he stayed where he was while Vincent and Caroline sat huddled together nearby, pointedly ignoring him. Not that he wanted to talk to them, he was so taken up by his own thoughts.

It's stupid the way you try to make bargains with God.

Please don't let her die. I'll do anything –

Like what? Change what happened yesterday? Unsay the words?

I'd give anything. Do anything. Just give me a chance to make things up to her.

What was the use? God didn't make bargains.

And, even if He did, Mick had nothing left to bargain with.

Yet hope – obstinate, unreasoning hope – would raise itself.

Any minute now she was going to walk through those doors and tell him it was okay. It was all a mistake, she'd say. It never happened. Any minute now. And he'd get the chance to explain, to put his side of things. Any minute now. You'll see.

But, as the minutes turned into hours, hope began to die.

By the time the nurse in charge of Intensive Care came through the double doors, he had braced himself for the worst. So, when she drew near the little, waiting group, he was totally unprepared to see her face break into a smile.

'She's out of danger. It was touch-and-go for a while. But she made it.'

Mick listened to her in stunned disbelief, unable to take in her words. It was a couple of moments before the truth began to sink in.

She was alive! She wasn't going to die! Thank God, Margaret was alive!

But his joy was cut short when the nurse said to him, 'She doesn't want to see you.'

'But – ?' Mick stared at her in dismay.

She turned to Vincent and gave him a curious look. 'Nor you either, I'm afraid. The only one she's asking for is Caroline.'

'That's me,' the girl cried, coming forward eagerly. 'Can I see her now?'

'But only for a few minutes,' the nurse cautioned. 'She's still very weak. Come on, I'll take you to her.'

After they had disappeared through the double doors, Vincent turned to Mick and snarled, 'You heard the nurse. She doesn't want to see you. She's copped on to you at last. And about time too. Go on. Buzz off to whatever hole you crept out of. Just leave us alone. You've done enough damage already.'

He found the car, frost glinting on its roof and windows, where he'd parked it hastily, straddling two parking spots, in the now-deserted car park. As he rubbed at the windscreen, an ambulance pulling up outside the entrance caught his eye. Two attendants leaped out, expertly unloading a stretcher onto a trolley. Hard to believe that a few hours ago he had followed a similar trolley through lighted corridors, fear and hope in his heart. Hard to believe that it was all over. The unreality of the scene struck him suddenly. This wasn't happening. It was a nightmare! Oh, God! If only it was a nightmare! If only he could wake up!

But she's alive, he consoled himself. No matter what happened in the future, even if he never saw her again, he knew she was alive. Thank God she was alive!

But his heart was heavy as he slid behind the wheel of the

chilly car. Out of the corner of his eye he saw something lying on the passenger seat. A large envelope with his name on it? A lifetime ago he had tossed it there before his mad dash to the hospital. He opened it without curiosity. It was probably a book. Margaret was always buying him books. As if he could read at a time like this! To his surprise it was full of banknotes, done up neatly in bundles. He stared at them blankly.

Why money? Rummaging through the piles he discovered a piece of paper with a couple of sentences written on it in her neat handwriting. Switching on the overhead light he read, *I hope this will help you take the first steps towards realising your dream. Goodbye, my darling. Take care.*

Money? He struck out savagely at the bank notes, knocking some of the bundles to the floor. What good was money to him? All he had ever wanted was her!

Once nightmare has you in its grip it never lets up. He arrived home in the early hours of the morning to find the flat deserted, wardrobe doors hanging open, drawers half empty. Fran had packed hastily and had left, taking Sean with her.

Unlike Margaret, she hadn't bothered to leave a note.

'Someone to see you,' the nurse said. At least she assumed it was a nurse. She was in hospital. That much she knew. She seemed to be in a pool of light surrounded by darkness. Her body felt as if she had run the marathon. Uphill. Or had been stretched on a medieval torture rack. Or had been run over by a truck. Her mind moved painfully, trying to make sense of it all.

'Mum, can you hear me?'

Caroline's face, blotchy and red-eyed, loomed out of the darkness. 'Mum?'

She tried to speak but only a croak came out. Maybe it had been a truck, after all, crushing her larynx. She put a hand to her throat and was reassured by its familiar outlines.

'It's because of the stomach pump.' Caroline's voice was gentle. 'Would you like some water?'

The stomach pump? Memory came flooding painfully back.

'Caro, I'm sorry.' This time she managed to get the words out.

'Hush, Mum, it's okay. Don't try to talk yet.' She felt strands of Caroline's hair brush against her face and smelled their sweet soapy smell as the girl bent over her, holding a brimming glass of water to her lips with awkward but willing fingers. Margaret gulped eagerly at the cool liquid but she was too weak to sit up properly, and the water splashed over her chin and down in rivulets under the thin hospital gown.

'It's okay, Mum,' the girl's voice was soothing. 'Take your time. Everything's going to be fine.' As she spoke, Margaret had the strange sensation that, at that moment, Caroline was the mother and she was the child. But instead of feeling resentment at the role reversal she was filled with gratitude. And love.

I've found my daughter, she thought. I've finally found her. And she's found me.

As she reached up in wonder to touch Caroline's face, she felt a fleeting pang of pity for her own mother who had never known a moment like this.

Vincent came to see her the day before she left the hospital for the private clinic. Christmas had come and gone, washing over her and around her, without touching her, a vaguely festive presence in the corridors outside her room. She didn't ask him how he had fared over the holiday season, neither was he over-solicitous in his enquiries about her health. He came to the point of the visit in his usual peremptory manner.

'They say you'll be a couple of weeks in this clinic you're going to. I hear you're thinking of coming home after that?'

'For Caroline's sake.' Margaret nodded.

'You needn't worry, I won't trouble you. Our marriage is over, as far as I'm concerned. I haven't changed my mind about that.' He gave her a hard-eyed stare. 'I've already moved my stuff into the guestroom. I'll stay till the summer, till after Caro has done the Leaving Cert. Then I'll move out altogether.'

She said nothing. What was there to say, after all?

'Nineteen years of marriage down the drain.' She heard the bitterness in his voice. 'And what is there to show for it?'

'There's Caroline.'

'Yes, there's Caroline. But she's not mine any more, is she?' His bitterness grew. 'She wants to stay with you. She has some crazy idea you need her.'

'It's not crazy,' Margaret said. 'But you haven't lost her. She still needs you. She needs both of us. But we don't own her. You can't own your children. I've learned that. You have to let them go.'

'Maybe.' Vincent looked unimpressed. 'I hope that's not the only thing you've learned. If I agree to her living with you there mustn't be a repeat of your recent escapade – '

'Escapade?' Margaret was stung.

'I know, I know,' he sneered. 'What do they call it? "A cry for help"? Well, you're going to get help. You go into that clinic and get yourself sorted out, tackle your drink problem.'

'I haven't got a – '

'Don't give me that – there were enough empty vodka bottles under the sink in Susan's flat. Of course, I forgot, you had that son of yours to help you get through them. That's another thing.' He frowned. 'Has he been to see you since – ?'

'No,' she said dully. 'But then I didn't expect him to. Not after I sent him away – '

'Best thing you ever did,' Vincent grunted. 'If you take my advice – '

'I don't need your advice,' she interrupted, with as much spirit as she could muster. 'But I do need my rest. So I'd like you to go now. I want to take a nap.'

But she had hardly settled back against her pillows when there was a brief tap on the door and Father Tim came in, exuding affability, sure of his welcome.

'Just wanted a word, Margaret,' he said when the polite preliminaries were over. 'I called to see you before Christmas but you probably don't remember.'

She had a vague recollection of someone standing by her bedside praying. Banishing the memory, she gazed at him enquiringly. To her surprise, the priest seemed to be having difficulty in knowing where to begin. He seemed diffident suddenly, abashed almost.

'Do you remember that little matter we were talking about, the day you rang me, the day before your – accident?'

Escapade? Accident? Was there going to be another conspiracy of silence over this? 'The day before my suicide attempt, you mean?'

'It's not for me to attach labels,' the priest said smoothly. 'Anyway, if you remember, I told you that day there was no possibility there could have been a mix-up where your son was concerned –'

'Yes, I remember.' The words were branded indelibly on her memory.

'Listen, Margaret –' A look of embarrassment crossed his face. 'I spoke in good faith. You must believe this – but afterwards I got thinking – and then when I met the young man in question –'

'You mean Michael?'

' – I realised that there had to be a mistake, that he couldn't be –'

Margaret stared at the priest in disbelief. 'What are you trying to tell me, Father?' Her heart began to thump as the truth dawned on her. 'Are you saying now that you deceived me?' Her words came out in a gasp. 'That Michael is not, after all, my son?'

'Deceived, no. Not intentionally.'

'But is he – ?'

'No, he's not, Margaret.' The priest looked uncomfortably at her. 'He's not your son. He can't be. I've checked with the nuns.'

'It seems there were two babies born around the same time, that they know of,' the priest said. 'Both boys. One was your son. The other was born to a young woman, a kitchen maid in the old people's home attached to the convent. When your baby was a few days old he was handed over to an American couple who had come to Ireland especially to adopt a child. Their parish priest back in the States had some connection with one of the nuns in the order – a cousin, I think. A wealthy couple – fervent Catholics, I need hardly add, just the sort to give your child the kind of background he needed. They already had a little girl but the wife had been told she couldn't have any more children and they were anxious to complete their family. They travelled back to the States shortly afterwards and nothing more was heard of them but you can rest assured that your son went to a good home.'

'You sold my baby to America!' Margaret was stunned. Into her mind flashed an image. A red, little face. Milky blue eyes under a thatch of black hair. The memory faded as quickly as it had come. 'To some couple with money.' She stared reproachfully at the priest. 'How could you – ?'

'Not sold.' He looked shocked. 'It wasn't like that at all. I understand they were generous benefactors to the Church but there's nothing wrong with that, is there? And no money changed hands on that occasion, as far as I know.'

'As far as you know,' Margaret said bitterly. She stared at the priest, unable to take in everything he had said. A thought struck her. 'If my child was taken to America why was Michael told he was my son?'

'I'm getting to that.' Father Tim seized the change of subject gratefully. 'He was the other baby, you see. There was no mix-up at the time. I'm sure of that. Your son was safely out of the country before Michael was brought to the convent. He had been in a mother-and-baby home. His own mother, poor girl – a very sad story – but you don't want to hear about that. The mix-up happened last year when he went to see the nuns. The one he spoke to, Sister Eucharia, she must be getting on for eighty, she confused the names – an understandable mistake.'

She stared at him blankly. All that pain, she thought. All that misery. And for what? For nothing. 'I could have died,' she said slowly. 'How can it be understandable?'

The priest shrugged helplessly and said nothing.

At least some of the guilt was gone. After he had left she tried to cling on to that thought. Tried to console herself. At least she hadn't committed the unforgivable sin. What a relief that was. A relief too that she hadn't been the one who had abandoned Michael at birth. Not that she blamed whoever it was. Probably someone like herself who had been given no choice in the matter. But Margaret was glad she hadn't been the one. She had caused enough trouble in his life, as it was. Strange, all the same, the way things had turned out. To think that he had been right, after all, about the dotty old nun. She might have laughed at the irony of it if she didn't feel so very sad.

As the burden of guilt lifted, her sadness grew. She reached out for the memory of that little face, the little hands waving wildly in the air, the bewildered blue eyes, but the image eluded her grasp, hovering tantalisingly around the edges of her thoughts.

All the old feelings had come back. The pain, the longing, the appalling sense of loss. She was back in the nursing home with its distant view of the sea. Saw Susan holding the little blue matinee coat, and the look of sympathy on her friend's face. 'I'll never see him now,' she sobbed. 'Never.' The word was so final; it reverberated down through the decades ahead, spelling out her loss. But, as her sobbing spent itself, the thought struck her that maybe it was better that way. Maybe it was better to let go.

She dried her eyes with a feeling of relief. And a new sense of purpose. The future now wasn't as empty as it had seemed that day in the nursing home. She had a daughter now. Life had given them a second chance. She was determined that whatever happened she would not repeat the mistakes of the past.

'You've been through a hard time,' the counsellor said gently. 'What with the difficulties in your marriage. And then all the trauma of your relationship with Michael.'

'Yes,' Margaret shuddered. 'I'm only beginning to realise now what a terrible strain I was under. I can't tell you what a relief it is to have all that behind me.' As she gazed across at the sympathetic face of the woman in the easy chair opposite hers she marvelled at the way she had unburdened herself to someone who, up to a few weeks ago, had been a complete stranger. But it had been a lot easier than she would ever have thought possible. Ten minutes into the first of her daily sessions with the clinic counsellor she had realised that Christine was someone whose own life experiences had left her compassionate towards the weaknesses of others and that she would listen to what Margaret had to say without passing judgement on her. 'There are some things I can't regret, though.'

'Like what?'

'Meeting Michael, getting to know him. But – '

She hesitated. Looking down, she found herself studying the pale triangles of light cast on the carpet by a watery January sun, before glancing up to gaze out at the clinic garden, where shrubs huddled forlornly in bare flower beds and the leafless branches of trees were outlined against the wintry sky. 'But – '

'But – ?' Christine prompted gently.

'But I'm afraid I may have ruined his life.'

'You don't know that. Besides, he's an adult. He has to take responsibility for his own actions.'

'Maybe you're right.' Margaret sighed. 'But his marriage – '

'That's up to him. What about *your* life? *Your* marriage?'

'Well, that's over, thank God! I've had a letter from Vincent's solicitor about drawing up a separation agreement.' She stared at the other woman with sudden joy. 'The relief is indescribable. It's as if a burden has been lifted from me. It's one of the good things that has come out of all this.'

'And the other good thing?'

'My new relationship with Caroline. It's wonderful. She comes to see me every day. We're making plans for when I go home. The doctor said I can leave here at the end of the week'

Christine nodded. 'Yes, I wanted to talk to you about that. Now Margaret, there's something we've touched on several times already but I think we need to talk about it a bit more.'

'I know what you're going to say.' Margaret met her eyes squarely. 'It's about my drinking, isn't it?' She saw the other woman's look of assent. 'For the last few years of my marriage I was in despair. I knew things were very wrong between us but I just couldn't admit to myself that I no longer loved my husband. It was easier to take a drink than to face up to the implications. After I met Michael I got the courage to leave Vincent but it was done on the spur of the moment, not properly thought out. I was living on my own in a borrowed flat. I felt very lonely and isolated. When Michael wasn't there I had no one to talk to. No one else to confide in. I've always kept other people at arm's length, bottled up my feelings. Susan was the only close friend I had and she was in America. I began to feel anxious and depressed. Drinking was a way of coping with my feelings.'

'And do you feel like a drink now?' the counsellor asked. 'Have you missed it at all since you came in here?'

'No,' Margaret said. 'You know I told you that when I woke up in the hospital after my suicide attempt I was just so grateful to be alive, to have been given another chance. Well, I decided after that never to touch spirits again. I've had plenty of time to think about it since I came in here and I haven't changed my mind.'

'I think that's a very good idea, Margaret. Have you discussed this with your daughter, at all?'

She nodded. 'Caroline hadn't realised that it had become a problem but she's been very supportive since we talked about it. I've told her that I might have the occasional glass of wine in company but I won't ever again drink alone. She's happy with that. And I'm very happy about it too. I've a feeling that it will work out okay. I have no desire to drink vodka again.' She shook her head decisively. 'It reminds me of a time in my life I want to forget. A road I don't want to go down again. I've been given the chance to make a fresh start.

And I'm going to take it.'

'That's good,' Christine said. 'You're still a young woman, Margaret. You've the rest of your life ahead of you. It's good to see you so positive about the future.' She glanced at the clock to signal the end of the session. 'I'm so glad about you and your daughter.' She smiled at Margaret as she took her leave. 'I always think our children help to give such meaning to our lives.'

'Will you go looking for him?' Caroline asked.

'Who?'

'Your son – the boy who went to America.' She looked at her mother in surprise. 'Who else do you think I meant?'

'Nobody,' Margaret said hastily. 'I just wasn't thinking.'

'Well, will you?'

'No, I don't think so. I think maybe it would be better to leave things as they are. Trust that wherever he is he's well and happy. Father Tim said he went to a good home and would have got every advantage.' Unlike some, she added silently.

'Yes.' Caroline gave a satisfied nod. 'We don't really need him, do we?'

'No,' Margaret agreed.

'And once you come home, we'll be a family again. You and me and – '

'Caroline,' she said gently. 'You know that isn't possible. Your father and I – '

'I know, Mum, I know. But at least we'll all be under the same roof. For a while anyway. Maybe you can work something out,' she said hopefully. 'Now that it's just the two of you.' Her face darkened suddenly. 'Now that *he's* not around to come between you.'

'Darling, our marriage was in trouble long before Michael came into our lives. I realise that now. He just helped bring things to a head.'

'I don't think I'll ever forgive him for that.' Caroline scowled. At that moment she reminded Margaret very much of Vincent. 'A real cuckoo in the nest. But listen, Mum. I've just thought.' Her face cleared. 'If he's not your son, then there's no excuse for him to come around any more, is there?'

'No,' Margaret said slowly. 'No excuse.'

'Well, shouldn't someone tell him, in case he – ?'

'I don't think you need worry about that, Caro.'

'But if he doesn't know,' the girl persisted.

'But he will know. Father Tim said the nuns would tell him. Don't worry, darling, I doubt if we'll see him again. They'll probably put him in touch with his real mother.' Sadness pressed down on her suddenly but she kept her voice brisk. 'And don't forget he has a wife and son. I imagine he'll want to be spending a lot more time with them from now on.'

'Well, if you're sure – '

'I'm sure,' she said firmly. 'Let's not talk about it any more. That's all behind us now. Let's talk about the future.' She tried to inject her voice with a note of confidence. 'You'll be leaving school soon. You have a whole range of choices before you. Isn't it exciting?'

'Yes, it is. But it's a bit scary too.'

Margaret patted her hand. 'I know, darling.'

The two sat in silence for a moment. Then Caroline turned to her mother.

'But what about you, Mum? I'm not the only one with a future. You have choices too.'

'Yes, I have.' With the realisation came a quick surge of excitement. But despite the excitement her sadness remained.

Forget the past, she advised herself firmly. She smiled at her daughter and made a silent pledge to the future.

In time, she told herself, the sadness would ease.

Once he had looked forward to Saturday. Now it was an empty, meaningless day. Keep busy. Fill in the hours. Hoover the flat. Buy a few groceries. Change that plug top for the old woman as he had promised. As he worked, the rooms echoed emptily around him. His chores done, he stood in the bay window of the living room, drinking a mug of coffee. Glancing out at the bright morning, he wondered what Fran and Sean were doing. Out walking, probably. Sean loved a trip in his buggy. And now that the weather was sunny –

Oh, God! The realisation hit him again. Sean!

He had got used to not having Fran around. Had no longer missed her after the first couple of weeks. In a way her going had been a relief. But he would never get over losing Sean.

The reminder of one loss led to another.

He wondered what Margaret was doing right now. Wondered if she ever thought of him.

'Have you made any more plans about doing the Leaving?' Ma asked.

'I've been thinking of studying for it at night. I can't afford to give up the job and go full time. Jimmy Joyce says he'll help me with the English. And there's another teacher who'll give me a grind in Maths. Course I could wait a couple of years and apply to college as a mature student. But I don't want to wait.'

'That's you all over, Mick. You never do.' Her button-bright eyes studied him thoughtfully. 'Maybe you shouldn't have sent back that money. It would come in handy now.'

'I couldn't have kept it. She didn't know what she was doing.'

'She wanted you to have it.'

'Ma! She thought she was going to die. I couldn't profit from something like that. What kind of a man do you think I am?'

'Well, you're not much good at taking advice but your heart's in the right place.'

'Is that supposed to be a compliment?'

'I wouldn't want to give you a swelled head, Mick. Did she ever acknowledge the money?'

'No, but I'm sure she got it. I sent it by registered post.'

'Funny she never wrote back,' Ma probed delicately. 'You being such good friends, an' all, before it happened.' She gave him a quick look. 'It wasn't your fault, was it, that she tried to do away with herself?'

'I don't know, Ma. If you knew how many times I've asked myself that question.' Mick said miserably. 'But it's very complicated. Stuff happened that you don't want to know about. But all that's behind me now. Look, I've no regrets about sending the money back. But I have other regrets. Sometimes I wish I'd never gone looking for her. It caused so much heartache. It probably broke up Margaret's marriage and it certainly ended mine.'

'Marriages don't break up that easily, Mick. I never thought you and Fran were well suited.'

'You did tell me I was too young to get married,' he remembered ruefully.

'Too young to know your own mind. She wasn't the right girl for you. You were like chalk and cheese. Can't you see that now?'

'Yes, I can.' He smiled wryly. 'Much good it does me, though.'

'You'll meet someone else.' Ma's voice was gentle.

'Maybe. Although I hear Fran hasn't wasted any time. She's started seeing someone, Donie says.'

'Donie?' She looked surprised. 'How does he – ?'

'Didn't I tell you? He's been secretly going out with her sister, Sandra. After Fran went back to live with her parents, Sandra moved out with her little boy, Jason. She's shacked up with Donie now. They're talking of getting married.'

Ma pursed her lips. 'You'd think he'd have more sense than to get mixed up with that lot. How did the Hennessys take it?'

'Old man Hennessy wasn't too happy about it but Maisie was delighted. That woman has wedding bells in her ears. She'll find Donie a tougher nut than me, though.' He grew bitter suddenly. 'When I think of the way she railroaded me.'

'That's all behind you now, Mick.'

'You're right.' He nodded. 'Too late now for regrets.'

'Well, there's one thing I've never had any regrets about, Mick Cleary,' she said robustly. 'I'd do it all over again if I had to.'

'What's that, Ma?'

'Bringing you home from the convent that day, a week before Christmas. I'll never forget the excitement. Lizzie had to cook Christmas dinner that year – '

'Christmas, Ma? My birthday's in November.'

'I know, Mick. I'm not in my dotage. Not yet, anyway. You

were three weeks, going on four, by the time you came to us.'

'But?' He stared at her in puzzlement. 'Margaret said that I – that her baby was taken from her as soon as he was born.'

'Well, maybe he was.' She looked at him doubtfully. 'All I know is what I'm telling you – '

'Something doesn't add up.' He looked at her urgently. 'What was the name of that nun I went to see in the convent?'

'Ah, Mick, not that again?' A look of dismay passed over Ma's face. 'You're like a dog with a bone.'

'This is one bone that has to be picked clean,' he said decisively. 'Eucharia! I remember now – Sister Eucharia.'

'That one! Even when I knew her she was a silly old fool. If you have to go back there – ' Ma gave him a resigned look, ' – ask for Sister Ignatius. I hear she's in charge now. At least you'll get some sense out of her!'

'Yes, I'm afraid you were given the wrong information last time, Mick.' Reverend Mother was a neat-featured, efficient-looking woman in her fifties. 'Unfortunately I was away at the time and Sister's memory isn't what it used to be.' Her brisk glance went from Mick to the decrepit old nun who sat near him, fingering her rosary beads distractedly, and then back to Mick. 'But we're all fallible creatures, aren't we? Liable to make mistakes.'

'But what a mistake! You gave me the wrong mother.'

'I didn't think it would do any harm,' the old nun spoke up suddenly. Although her voice quavered it was surprisingly clear for such an ancient-looking creature. 'He was a lovely young man. It seemed such a shame.'

'You mean it wasn't a mistake?' He stared at her, astonished. 'You knew!'

Reverend Mother made a swift, quelling movement which the old nun ignored. 'I hadn't the heart to tell him about his own poor mother – '

'What about my own mother?'

'She died,' the younger nun interposed swiftly. 'From complications a few weeks after you were born. It seems she had received no care during her pregnancy, not that that can be laid at anyone's door, you understand. She hid her condition, you see, right up to the last minute. No one in the community had any idea – '

'The community?' Mick was bewildered.

'She worked in the kitchen here. Poor girl, they were different times then. And, of course, no one had any idea who the father was. So when she died – '

'So my mother's dead?' He shook his head in wonder as he tried to make sense of what he had been told. 'All those years I kept hoping to meet her. All those years. And all that time she was dead?' A thought occurred to him. 'But what about the baby clothes I was wearing?' The truth dawned on him. 'They weren't mine, were they?'

'Greta's child had nothing,' the old nun whispered. 'And the other child had so much.'

'But why did you lie to me?' He rounded on her suddenly. 'Why did you let me believe Margaret was my mother?'

'Strictly speaking, Sister didn't lie,' Reverend Mother put in smoothly before the old nun could answer. 'Your mother was also named Margaret. She was known as Greta to the staff here but her Christian name was Margaret. It's on all the certificates. So you can see how the confusion arose.'

As Mick was trying to take in this information he saw the

old nun turn towards him. 'You were looking for your mother,' she said. 'And the other woman's baby had gone to America. I thought it would make both of you happy.' Her face crumpled like a child's after a scolding. 'I meant no harm,' she whimpered.

He gave a helpless shrug and turned back to find the younger nun watching him carefully. 'I can show you the relevant certificates. We obtained copies once we realised that a mistake had been made.'

'Realised – ?' He gazed at her in dawning suspicion. 'How long have you known?'

Reverend Mother's eyes slid away from his. 'Some months now – since the other parties involved began making enquiries.'

'The other parties? You mean she knows? Margaret knows?'

'I presume so.'

'But why did nobody tell me? Why didn't you get in touch?'

'I suppose I've been a little remiss about that.' The nun looked at him blandly, the barest hint of apology in her voice. 'But I thought you already knew. I was full sure someone else would have told you.'

'So your own mother died.' Ma's face was full of sympathy. 'And they never found out who the father was?'

'Funny the way things turn out.' He smiled wryly. 'Remember when I was a kid and you said she was probably "an innocent young one up from the country, taken advantage of by some blackguard". Looks like you were right, after all.'

'Poor girl.' Her voice was sad.

'Yes, Ma. Did you know her?'

'No, I had changed jobs by then. I kept in touch with some of the nuns. I had them pestered making novenas for me but I never knew Greta. But, tell us, Mick. Did your heart nearly break when you heard that she was dead?'

'It came as a bit of a shock,' he admitted. 'But here's another funny thing. Once I got used to the idea I didn't feel too badly about it. Because suddenly I realised that all those years I was hankering after a mother I had a perfectly good one in you.' He gave her a baffled grin. 'A great one, in fact.'

'I done me best, Mick.' She smiled deprecatingly. 'But I'm just an ignorant woman. I never had much education – '

'Don't put yourself down, Ma. You're one of the wisest women I know.'

Her face went pink. 'Do you mean that, son? Really?'

'Yes, Ma. *Really*. I just wasn't bright enough to see it before,' he said haltingly. 'You've never made the mistake of trying to live my life for me. And you're not just wise. You're the best mother anyone could ever have. You stood by me when everyone else turned against me. No matter what I've done you've always believed in me.' He gazed at her, his voice thickening with emotion. 'It was lucky for me that it was *you* who brought me home that day from the convent. You and Da.'

Ma's eyes were bright. 'We were the lucky ones, Mick. I prayed and prayed for years that we would have a child. And then you came along.' She gave a little laugh. 'It just goes to show that you should never give up, that you'll get what you're looking for if you want something badly enough.'

He glanced at her quickly. 'Or someone?'

'Or someone.' She nodded. 'The thing to do is not to give up hope.'

The auctioneer's board outside the front gate had a Sold sticker across it.

'Another few weeks and you'd have missed us,' Caroline said. 'Dad's gone already, moved into his own apartment. Mum's new house in Stillorgan is smaller than this but it's really nice. I'm looking forward to living in it.' As she stared at Mick, he saw a new maturity about her mouth and chin, a strength that had only been hinted at previously. 'Look, my mother is happy now. She's put her life back together again. She's got herself a job in an antique shop and is talking of going back to do a degree. Give me one good reason why she would want to see you again.'

Feeling as if the age difference between them had shrunk, he met her level gaze squarely. 'I can't think of one,' he admitted. 'All I know is I want to see her.'

She studied him for a moment. Now that they were no longer related, the old antagonism had gone. 'Well, she's a grown-up person,' she said at last. 'She can make up her own mind. Wait here.'

As he stood in the pine-clad kitchen he felt the breeze from an open window blow gently against his face. Out in the garden a blackbird warbled insistently. Despite the beauty of its song he felt a knot of apprehension in his stomach.

Maybe this was a mistake, after all.

And then Margaret appeared in the doorway, with a smile that reached right up to her eyes.

'I was hoping you'd be back,' she said.